PRAISE FOR JAYNE ANN KRENTZ'S

THE GOLDEN CHANCE

"If you're in the market for irresistible romance and high-powered corporate intrigue, run, do not walk, to the nearest bookstore and pick up this splendid novel by the fabulous Jayne Ann Krentz."

—*Romantic Times*

"Philadelphia Fox is one of the feistiest, most memorable heroines in years. *The Golden Chance* is Jayne Ann Krentz at her very best. Pure entertainment."

—Susan Elizabeth Phillips, author of *Fancy Pants* and *Hot Shot*

". . . a breezy, funny tale of love conquering all."

—*Publishers Weekly*

SILVER LININGS

"Jayne Ann Krentz entertains to the hilt in *Silver Linings* . . . the excitement and adventure don't stop."

—Catherine Coulter

"The Krentz mark of excellence is more than evident in the snappy dialogue, steamy sensuality, and vivid characterization. Don't miss this outstanding romantic adventure."

—*Romantic Times*

"Wonderful characters, a great plot with lots of action, and a fine romance with lots of sparks—what more could you ask for?"

—*Rendezvous*

Books by Jayne Anne Krentz

The Golden Chance
Silver Linings
Sweet Fortune
Perfect Partners
Family Man
Wildest Hearts
Hidden Talents
Grand Passion
Trust Me
Absolutely, Positively

Published by POCKET BOOKS

JAYNE ANN KRENTZ

SWEET FORTUNE

POCKET BOOKS

New York   London   Toronto   Sydney   Tokyo   Singapore

This book is a work of fiction. Names, characters, places and incidents are products of the author's imagination or are used fictitiously. Any resemblance to actual events or locales or persons living or dead is entirely coincidental.

An *Original* Publication of POCKET BOOKS

POCKET BOOKS, a division of Simon & Schuster Inc.
1230 Avenue of the Americas, New York, NY 10020

Cover art by Tom Hallman
Cover lettering by Jim Lebbad

Printed in the U.S.A.

SWEET
FORTUNE

CHAPTER ONE

I can't see."

"It's all right, Mrs. Valentine. Your eyes are fine." Jessie Benedict leaned anxiously over the frail figure on the hospital bed and patted the hand that clenched the sheet. "You took a nasty fall and you've got a few cracked ribs and a concussion, but there was no harm done to your eyes. Open them and look at me."

Irene Valentine's faded blue eyes snapped open. "You don't understand, Jessie. I can't *see.*"

"But you're looking right at me. You can see it's me standing here, can't you?" Jessie was alarmed now. She raised her hand. "How many fingers am I holding up?"

"Two." Mrs. Valentine's gray head moved restlessly on the pillow. "For heaven's sake, Jessie, that's not the kind of seeing I'm talking about. Don't you understand? I can't *see.*"

Understanding dawned and Jessie's own eyes widened in shock. "Oh, no. Mrs. Valentine, are you sure? How can you tell?"

The elderly woman sighed and closed her eyes again. "I can't explain it." The words sounded thick and slurred now. "I just know it's gone. It's like losing your sense of smell or touch. Dear God, Jessie, it's like being *blind*. All my life it's been there, and now it's just gone."

"It's the blow on the head. It must be. As soon as you've recovered from the concussion, everything will be fine." Jessie looked down at her and thought how small and fragile Mrs. Valentine appeared when she was not wearing one of her colorful turbans or the flowing skirts and jangling necklaces she favored.

Mrs. Valentine said nothing for a minute. She lay motionless on the hospital bed, her hand still clenched around the sheet. Jessie wasn't sure if she had fallen asleep.

"Mrs. Valentine?" Jessie whispered. "Are you okay?"

"Didn't fall," Mrs. Valentine muttered heavily.

"What did you say?"

"Didn't fall down those stairs. I was pushed."

"Pushed." Jessie was horrified anew. "Are you sure? Did you tell anyone?"

"Tried to tell 'em. Wouldn't listen. They said I was all alone in the house. Jessie, what am I going to do? The office. Who's going to keep the office open?"

Jessie squared her shoulders. This was her big chance and she was not going to blow it. "I'll take care of everything, Mrs. Valentine. Don't worry about a thing. I'm your assistant, remember? Holding things together while the boss is out of the office is what assistants are for."

Irene Valentine opened her eyes again briefly and gazed at Jessie with a dubious expression. "Maybe it would be better if you just closed the office for a couple of weeks, dear. We don't have all that many clients, heaven knows."

"Nonsense," Jessie said briskly. "I'll manage just fine."

"Jessie, I'm not sure about this. You've been with me only a month. There's so much you don't know about the way I run the business."

A nurse bustled through the door at that moment and smiled pointedly at Jessie. "I think that's enough visiting for now, don't you? Mrs. Valentine needs her rest."

"I understand." Jessie patted the frail hand that clutched the sheet one last time. "I'll be back tomorrow, Mrs. V. Take care and try not to worry about the office. Everything's going to be just fine."

"Oh, dear." Mrs. Valentine sighed and closed her eyes again.

With one last concerned glance at the pale woman in the hospital bed, Jessie turned and walked out into the corridor. She cornered the first official-looking person she saw.

"Mrs. Valentine believes she was pushed down the stairs of her home," Jessie informed him bluntly. "Have the police been notified?"

The resident, an earnest-looking young man, smiled sympathetically. "Yes, as a matter of fact, they were. First thing this morning after she was found. I was told there was no sign of any intruder. It looks like she simply lost her balance on the top step and tumbled to the bottom. It happens, you know. A lot. Especially to older people. You can check with the cops, if you like. They'll have filed a report."

"But she seems to think there was someone in the house. Someone who deliberately pushed her."

"In cases such as this, where there's been a severe blow to the head, the patient often loses any memory of what really happened during the few minutes just before the accident."

"Is it a permanent memory loss?"

The doctor nodded. "Frequently. So even if there had been an intruder, she probably would have no real recollection of it."

"The thing is, Mrs. Valentine is a little different," Jessie began, and then decided the young man probably did not want to hear about her employer's psychic abilities. The medical establishment was notoriously unsympathetic to that sort of thing. "Never mind. Thanks, Doctor. I'll see you later."

Jessie swung around and hurried toward the elevators, her mind intent on the new responsibilities that awaited her back at the office. In a gesture that was unconscious and habitual, she reached up to push a strand of hair back behind her ears. The thick jet-black stuff was cut in a short, gleaming bob. It was angled from a wedge at her nape to a deep curve that fell in place just below her high cheekbones. Long bangs framed her faintly slanting green eyes and emphasized her delicate features, giving her an oddly exotic, almost catlike look.

The feline impression was further enhanced by her slender figure, which seemed to throb with quick energy when she was in motion, or appeared sensually relaxed when she sprawled in a chair. The black jeans, black boots, and billowing white poet's shirt that Jessie had on today suited the look.

She frowned in thought as she waited impatiently for the elevator to reach the hospital lobby. There was a lot to be done now that she was temporarily in charge of Valentine Consultations. And the first thing on the list was to cancel a previous engagement.

The thought brought both giddy relief and simultaneous disappointment. *She was off the hook for this evening.*

But she was not certain she really wanted to be off the hook.

This unpleasant and confusing mix of emotions was something she was having to deal with frequently of late, and matters were not getting better. Her intuition warned her that as long as Sam Hatchard was in her life, things were only going to get more complicated.

Jessie strode quickly down the street, her boot heels moving at a crisp pace along the sidewalk. It was a beautiful late-spring day, if one ignored the faint tinge of yellow that hung over Seattle. Smog was something nobody really wanted to talk about in what was considered the most beautiful and livable of cities. People tended to ignore it when it had the audacity to appear. They preferred to talk about the rare sunshine instead. And it was perfectly true that the smog would disappear soon, blown away with the next rain. Fortunately, in Seattle a rain shower was always on the way.

The trees planted in a row along the sidewalk formed a fresh green canopy overhead. The rapidly evolving Seattle skyline, with its growing number of high-rise buildings, was spread out against the sparkling backdrop of Elliott Bay. Ferries and tankers glided like toy boats on a deep blue pond. In the distance Jessie could barely make out the rugged Olympic Mountains through the haze.

Jessie narrowed her eyes against the glare. She reached into her black shoulder bag and whipped out a pair of dark glasses. Sunny days were always disconcerting in the Pacific Northwest.

It took Jessie about twenty minutes to cover the distance to the quiet side street where Valentine Consultations had its offices. The tiny firm was housed in a small two-story brick building located several blocks from the First Hill Hospital, where Mrs. Valentine had been taken that morning.

The outer door of the aging structure bore the legend of Irene Valentine's business and the stylized picture of a robin, the logo of a small, struggling computer-software-design firm which shared the premises. Jessie opened the door and stepped into the dim hall.

The opaque glass door on the right opened. A thin, rumpled-looking young man in his early twenties stuck his head out. He looked as if he had slept in his clothes, which he probably had. He was wearing jeans, running shoes, and a white short-sleeved shirt with a plastic pocket protector full of pens and assorted computer implements. He peered at her through a pair of horn-rimmed glasses, blinking against the light. Behind him machinery hummed softly and a computer screen glowed eerily. Jessie smiled.

"Hi, Alex."

"Oh, it's you, Jessie," Alex Robin said. "I was hoping it might be a client. How's Mrs. V?"

"She's going to be okay. Bruised ribs and a concussion. The doctors want to keep her in the hospital for a couple of days, and then she's going to stay with her sister for a while. But she should be fine."

Alex scratched his head absently. His sandy hair stuck up in patches. "Poor old lady. Lucky she wasn't killed. What about her business?"

Jessie smiled confidently. "I'll be in charge while she's away."

"Is that right?" Alex blinked again. "Well, uh, good luck. Let me know if you need anything."

Jessie wrinkled her nose. "All we really need are a few new clients."

"Same here. Hey, maybe we should try advertising our combined services." Alex grinned. "Robin and Valentine: Psychic Computer Consultants."

"You know," said Jessie as she started up the stairs, "that is not a bad idea. Not bad at all. I'm going to give that some thought."

"Hold on, Jessie, I wasn't serious," Alex called after her. "I was just joking."

"Still, it has distinct possibilities," Jessie yelled back from the second level. She shoved her key into the door marked VALENTINE CONSULTATIONS. "I've already got a slogan for us. 'Intuition and Intelligence Working for You.'"

"Forget it. We'd have every weirdo in town knocking on our door."

"Who cares, as long as they pay their bills?"

"Good point."

Jessie stepped into the comfortably shabby office and tossed her shoulder bag and sunglasses down onto the faded chintz sofa. Then she crossed the room to the mammoth old-fashioned rolltop desk and grabbed the phone. Best to get this over with before she lost her nerve, she told herself.

She threw herself down into the large wooden swivel chair and propped her booted feet on the desktop. The chair squeaked in loud protest as she leaned forward to punch out the number of her father's private line at Benedict Fasteners.

"Mr. Benedict's office." The voice sounded disembodied, it was so composed and exquisitely professional.

"Hi, Grace, this is Jessie. Is Dad in?"

"Oh, hello, Jessie." Some of the professionalism leaked out of the voice and was promptly replaced by the comfortable familiarity of a longtime acquaintance. "He's here. Busy as usual and doesn't want to be disturbed. Do you need to talk to him?"

"Please. Tell him it's important."

"Just a second. I'll see what I can do." Grace put the phone on hold.

A moment later her father's graveled voice came on the line. He sounded typically impatient at the interruption.

"Jessie? I'm right in the middle of a new contract. What's up?"

"Hi, Dad." She resisted the automatic impulse to apologize for bothering him at work. Vincent Benedict was always *at work,* so any phone call was, by definition, an unwelcome interruption.

Jessie had concluded at an early age that unless she took pains to avoid it, she would end up apologizing every time she talked to her father.

"Just wanted to let you know something's come up here at the office," she said, "and I won't be able to go to dinner with Hatch and the Galloways this evening. Got a real management crisis here, Dad."

"The hell you do." Benedict's voice thundered over the phone. "You gave me your word you'd help Hatch entertain the Galloways tonight. You know damn well it's crucial for

you to be there. I explained that earlier this week. Galloway needs to see a united front. This is business, goddammit."

"Then you go to dinner with them." Jessie held the phone away from her ear. Nothing, literally nothing, came before business in her father's world. She had learned that the hard way as a child.

"It won't look right," Vincent roared. "Two men entertaining Ethel and George will make the whole thing look too much like a goddamned business meeting."

"For all intents and purposes, that's what it is. Be honest, Dad. If it weren't a disguised meeting of some kind, you and Hatch wouldn't be so concerned about it, would you?"

"That's not the point, Jessie. This is supposed to be casual. A social thing. You know damn well what I'm talking about. We're concluding a major deal here. Hatch needs a dinner companion and Galloway needs to see that I'm backing Hatch one hundred percent."

"But, Dad, listen . . ." Jessie was afraid she was starting to whine and stopped speaking abruptly.

It was impossible to explain to her father how much she resented being ordered out on a business date with Sam Hatchard. Vincent would not understand the objection, and neither would Hatch. Two birds were obviously being killed with one efficient stone here, after all. Hatch could pursue company business and the courtship of the president's daughter at the same time.

"Sending you along is the perfect solution," Vincent continued brusquely. "The Galloways have known you for ages. When they see my daughter with the new CEO of Benedict Fasteners, they'll be reassured that the shift in management has my full support and that nothing is going to change within the firm. This is important, Jessie. Galloway is from the old school. He likes a sense of continuity in his business relationships."

"Dad, I can't go. Mrs. Valentine was injured today. She's in the hospital."

"The hospital? What the hell happened?"

"She fell down a flight of stairs. I'm not sure yet just what happened. She's got a concussion and some broken ribs. She'll be out of the office for a few weeks. I'm in charge."

"Who's going to notice? You told me yourself she doesn't have a lot of clients."

"As her new assistant, I'm aiming to fix that. I'm going to develop a marketing plan to improve business."

"Jesus. I can't believe my daughter is working on a marketing plan for a fortune-teller."

"Dad, I don't want to hear any more nasty comments about my new job. I mean it."

"All right, all right. Look, Jessie, I'm sorry about Mrs. Valentine, but I don't see how that changes anything concerning tonight."

"But I'm in charge here now, Dad. Mrs. Valentine is depending on me to hold things together, and there's a ton of stuff that has to be done around here."

"Tonight?" Vincent demanded skeptically.

Jessie glanced desperately around the empty office, her eye finally falling on the blank pages of the appointment book. She tried to sound firm. "Well, yes, as a matter of fact. I'm going to be very busy getting the files in order and working up my new plan. You should understand. You've never worked anything less than a twelve-hour day in your life. Usually fourteen."

"Give me a break, Jessie. Running Benedict Fasteners is hardly the same thing as running a fortune-teller's operation."

"Don't call her a fortune-teller. She's a psychic. A genuine one. Look, Dad. This is a business I'm running here. Just like any other business." Jessie lowered her voice to an urgent, coaxing level. "So, would you do me a favor and tell Hatch I'm sort of tied up and won't be able to go with him tonight?"

"Hell, no. Tell him yourself."

9

"Dad, please, the guy makes me nervous. I've told you that."

"You make yourself nervous, Jessie. And for no good reason, far as I can tell. You want to stand him up tonight when he's counting on you, go ahead and stand him up. But don't expect me to do your dirty work."

"Come on, Dad. As a favor to me? I'm really swamped, and I don't have time to track him down."

"No problem tracking him down. He just walked into my office. Standing right in front of me, in fact. You can explain exactly why you want to leave him stranded without a dinner date two hours before he's set to finalize a major contract."

Jessie cringed. "Dad, no, wait, please . . ."

It was too late. Jessie closed her eyes in dismay as she heard her father put his palm over the receiver and speak to someone else in his office.

"It's Jessie," Vincent snorted. "Trying to wriggle out of dinner with the Galloways tonight. You handle it. You're the CEO around here now."

Jessie groaned as she sensed the phone being handed into other hands. She summoned up an image of those hands. They were elegant, beautifully masculine. The hands of an artist or a swordsman.

Another voice came on the line, this one as dark and quiet and infinitely deep as the still waters of a midnight sea. It sent a faint sensual chill down Jessie's spine.

"What seems to be the problem, Jessie?" Sam Hatchard asked with a frightening calmness.

Everything Hatch did or said was done calmly, coldly, and with what Jesse thought was a ruthless efficiency. On the surface it appeared the man had ice in his veins, that he was incapable of real emotion. But from the first moment she had met him, Jessie's intuition had warned her otherwise.

"Hello, Hatch." Jessie took her feet down off the desk and unconsciously began twisting the telephone cord between her fingers. She swallowed and fought to keep her tone crisp and unhurried. "Sorry to spring this on you, but something unforeseen has come up here at the office."

"How could something unforeseen come up at a psychic's office?"

Jessie blinked. If it had been anyone else besides Hatch, she would have suspected a joke. But she had decided weeks ago that the man had no sense of humor. She glowered at the wall. "I won't be able to help you entertain the Galloways tonight. My boss is in the hospital and I'm in charge around here. I've got an awful lot to do and I've really got to get going. I'll probably have to work most of the evening."

"It's a little late for me to make other plans, Jessie."

Jessie coughed to clear her throat. Her fingers clenched around the phone cord. "I apologize for that, but Mrs. Valentine is depending on me."

"There's a lot of money riding on the Galloway deal."

"Yes, I know, but—"

"George and Ethel Galloway are looking forward to seeing you again. George made a point of it. I'm not certain how they'll interpret the situation if you fail to show up tonight. They might think there's a buyout in the works or dissension between your father and me if I turn up alone."

Each word was an invisible blow, nailing shut the escape route she had hoped to use. "Look, Hatch . . ."

"If Galloway gets the idea that Benedict Fasteners is about to change hands or is in trouble, he might not want to go through with the deal. I would be extremely disappointed to lose this contract."

Jessie began to feel cornered. This was something Hatch did very, very well. She gazed around the office with a hunted sensation. "Maybe Dad could go with you?"

"That would be a little awkward, don't you think?"

The cold reasonableness of the words heightened Jessie's nervousness. Nobody on earth could make her as nervous as Sam Hatchard did. She twitched the phone cord and began swinging the swivel chair from side to side in a restless movement. "Hatch, I realize this is awfully short notice."

11

"And not entirely necessary, I think." Hatch's voice was very quiet now. "I'm sure Mrs. Valentine doesn't expect you to work nights."

"Well, not usually, but this is kind of an emergency."

"Is there really anything there that can't wait until tomorrow?"

Jessie stared helplessly at the pristine work surface of her desk. She had a problem with honesty. When pushed into a corner, she tended to tell the truth. "This isn't the kind of business where you can schedule things, you know."

"Jessie?"

She swallowed again. She hated it when Hatch gave her the full force of his attention. She was far too vulnerable. "Yes?"

"I was looking forward to seeing you this evening."

"What?" Jessie straightened as if she had just touched a live electrical wire. The abrupt motion snapped the phone cord taut. The instrument toppled off the desk and landed on the floor with a resounding crash. "Oh, hell."

"Sounded like you dropped the phone, Jessie," Hatch observed as he waited patiently for her to come back on the line. "Everything all right?"

"Yes. Yes, everything's fine," she gasped as she straightened the twisted cord and replaced the telephone on the desk with trembling fingers. She was furious with herself. "Look, Hatch . . ."

"I'll pick you up at seven," Hatch told her, sounding preoccupied again, which he probably was.

He frequently did two things at once, both of which were usually business-related. The present situation was a perfect example. Jessie knew that courting her definitely came under the heading of business.

"Hatch, I really can't—"

"Seven o'clock, Jessie. Now, I'm afraid you'll have to excuse me. I've got to go over some final figures on the Galloway deal with your father. Good-bye." He hung up the phone with a gentle click.

Jessie perched on the edge of the chair and stared numbly at the receiver in her hand as she listened to the whine of the dial tone. Defeated, she dumped the instrument back into its cradle and lowered her forehead onto her folded arms. She should have known there would be no easy way out of the Galloway dinner. The invitation had not been a casual one. Hatch was pursuing her. Nothing had been said yet, but it was no secret that Hatch had marriage in mind.

She was fascinated by Hatch. She might as well admit it. But she knew she dared not give in to his plans to marry her. For Hatch, the wedding would be no more than the consummation of yet another business deal. This particular contract would guarantee him a lifetime chunk of Benedict Fasteners, which was something he wanted very badly.

At the moment, courting Jessie was near the top of Hatch's list of priorities. She knew she was at least temporarily as important to him as any business maneuver in which he was presently involved. That meant she was in a very treacherous position. There was no denying her own interest in him, and on those occasions when he made her the sole focus of his attention, she was in serious danger of succumbing entirely.

A moth dancing around a flame.

Jessie closed her eyes and conjured up a picture of the man who had become her nemesis during the past two months. His personality was strongly reflected in his physical characteristics. He was built along lean, powerful, curiously graceful lines. His long-figured swordsman's hands went well with his austere, ascetic features.

She had tried to tell herself in the beginning that there was no fire beneath the cold, polite surface of the man, but she had known she was fooling herself right from the start. The problem was that, just as with warriors and saints, the fire in Hatch would never burn for any woman. It burned for an empire—the kingdom he planned to build on the cornerstone of Benedict Fasteners.

Hatch had the full support of Vincent Benedict and the

entire Benedict family for his ambitions. He had dangled an irresistible lure in front of all the Benedicts: in exchange for a chunk of the small, thriving regional business that was now Benedict Fasteners, he would take the company into the big time. Benedict Fasteners was a company based quite literally on nuts and bolts. It designed and manufactured a wide variety of products used in construction and manufacturing to hold things together. It had the potential to grow into a giant in the industry, a conglomerate that could dominate a huge market share. All it needed was a man of vision and enterprise at the helm.

Everyone in the family was convinced that Sam Hatchard was that man.

Of course, the only one who had really needed to be convinced was Vincent Benedict, the founder of the firm. And he had taken to Hatch immediately. The relationship that had developed between the two men was as profound as it was inevitable. Jessie had sensed it from the first moment she had seen her father and Hatch together in the same room. Hatch was the son her father had never had. Which might make him an excellent choice to take Benedict Fasteners into the big time but definitely made him lousy husband material, Jessie thought grimly.

Sam Hatchard was thirty-seven. Jessie had concluded that it would probably be another thirty years, if ever, before he mellowed. She was not about to give him that long. She was surely not that big a fool.

But the terrible truth, the heavy burden that weighed her down these days, was the knowledge that although she was running from Hatch, she was not running fast enough, and she knew it. The moth in her was strongly tempted to play with fire. Hatch had sensed the weakness and he was deliberately using it. It was no big secret. Everyone in the family was using it.

In one of the saner corners of her mind, Jessie was well aware that if she allowed herself to fall into Sam Hatchard's clutches she would be condemning herself to a marriage of unbearable frustration and unhappiness. She would be repeating the same mistake her mother had made in marrying Vincent Benedict. She would be tying herself to a driven man, a man who would never find room in his life for a wife and a family.

The end result of all her wallowing about in such a morass of conflicting emotions was, naturally, chaos for Jessie. For the last month, as Hatch's subtle pursuit gradually intensified, she had found herself dancing closer and closer to the flame, unable to resist, yet unable to surrender to what she knew would be disaster. It was ridiculous. She had to put a stop to the bizarre situation.

She had to learn to just say no.

The phone rang in her ear. Jessie started and jerked back in the chair. She automatically stretched a hand out toward the receiver and then hesitated, letting the answering machine take the call. There was a click, a recorded message of her own voice saying that the office was closed but that all calls would be returned as soon as possible, and then her friend Alison Kent came on the line.

Ever since Alison had become a stockbroker, her voice had taken on the upbeat cadences of a professional cheerleader. Jessie could almost see her old friend wearing a short skirt and waving a pom-pom as she made her cold calls.

"Jessie, this is Alison at Caine, Carter, and Peat. Give me a call as soon as possible. I've just found out about an incredible opportunity in a new fat-free cooking-oil product but we're going to have to move fast on this one."

Jessie sighed as the machine clicked off. For Alison, still new on the job, every deal was the opportunity of a lifetime, and Jessie always had a hard time keeping her distance. She had to admit that her initial enthusiasm had been high when she had agreed to become Alison's first real account at Caine, Carter, and Peat. Visions of making a killing had danced through her head and she had even wondered if she might have an aptitude for playing the market full-time. But a series of recent losses had given Jessie a more realistic view of Wall Street.

She dreaded returning Alison's phone call because when she did she would very likely end up buying a lot of shares in some company that wanted to market fat-free cooking oil.

The phone rang again and this time Jessie heard Lilian Benedict's voice on the answering machine. Her mother's warm, cultured tones poured over Jessie's frayed nerves like rich cream.

"Jessie? This is Lilian. Just checking to see if you'd had a chance to talk to Vincent about the loan for ExCellent Designs yet. Oh, and by the way, enjoy yourself this evening, dear. Wear the little black dress with the V in the back. It's wonderful on you. Give my best to Hatch and the Galloways. Talk to you later."

There was another click followed by a pregnant silence as Jessie contemplated the fact that even her own mother was trying to push her into the arms of Sam Hatchard.

The situation was getting out of hand. Jessie got to her feet and began to pace the office. Nobody had actually used the word "marriage" yet in her presence, but it did not require Mrs. Valentine's psychic abilities to know what everyone was thinking, including Hatch.

A month ago when Jessie had first begun to realize what was happening, she had actually laughed. She had been so certain she could handle the pressure of the crazy situation. But now she was getting scared. There was no doubt but that she was being gently, steadily, inexorably maneuvered toward an alliance that a hundred years ago would have been baldly labeled exactly what it was, a marriage of convenience.

If she was not very careful, she was going to find herself in very big trouble. People who played with fire frequently wound up in the emergency room with singed fingers.

Jessie glanced at the clock and saw with dismay that it was nearly six. She would have to hurry if she was going to get back to her apartment and get dressed before Hatch showed up on her doorstep.

Hatch was never late.

Hatch pushed the folder of computer printouts across the desk toward Vincent Benedict. "Take a look. I think you'll like what you see."

Vincent scowled impatiently at the folder. "Of course I will. You're a magician with this kind of deal. Nobody puts a contract together better than you do."

"Thanks," Hatch murmured. It was true, he was very good at putting together projects such as the one he had recently completed between Benedict Fasteners and Galloway Engineering, but it was nice to be appreciated. Especially by Vincent Benedict.

Benedict continued to frown thoughtfully across the wide expanse of desk. It occurred to Hatch that Jessie had gotten her eyes from her father. They were a curious feline green, very clear and very intelligent. But there was a vulnerable quality in Jessie's gaze that was definitely not present in her father's eyes.

Vincent was nearing sixty, a vigorous, ruggedly built man whose heavy shoulders were a legacy of his early years in the construction business. His hair was white and thinning slightly. His face had no doubt softened somewhat over the years, but the hawklike nose and square, strong jaw still reflected the image of a man who had come up in the world the hard way. This was a man who had made most of his own rules in life, but he had played by those rules. If you were honest with Vincent Benedict, he was honest with you. If you crossed him, you paid. Dearly.

Hatch understood that kind of code because he lived by it himself. He had learned it long before he'd entered the corporate world, learned it in the hardworking, hard-playing world of his youth and young manhood, a world where real labor meant working with your hands. It meant ranching, construction, driving trucks.

The code had been drummed into him on the job, and after work it had been reinforced during nights spent in smoky taverns where a man learned to drink beer instead of white wine and where he picked up basic psychology by listening to the words of country-western music.

Hatch had liked Benedict right from the start. There had been an immediate rapport between them, probably because their origins were so similar. Vincent Benedict was one of the very few men Hatch had ever met whom he actually respected; he was also one of the even fewer number whose respect Hatch wanted in return.

"Are you worried about Galloway getting cold feet tonight?" Hatch asked after a minute during which it dawned on him that Vincent was not paying close attention to the figures on the printout.

"No." Vincent drummed his fingers on the desk in an uncharacteristically restless gesture and scowled.

"Did you have some questions?" Hatch prodded, wondering what the problem was. Benedict was usually nothing if not forthright.

"No. Everything looks fine."

Hatch shrugged and opened the second folder to scan the numbers inside. He had seen the potential in Benedict Fasteners immediately when Benedict had hired Hatchard Consulting briefly for advice on doing business with a Japanese company. The company had recently opened up a plant in Washington and had wanted to use local suppliers. Most were unable to meet the quality-control demands of the Japanese. Vincent Benedict had been wise enough to see the future could be even more profitable if he found a way to do so.

Hatch had shown him the way, and in the process concluded that Benedict Fasteners was precisely the ripe, cash-rich little business he had been looking for to use as a springboard to an empire. Vincent had refused to sell outright, but had hinted there was a possibility of a deal.

Benedict had given Hatch a one-year contract as chief executive officer, during which time both men agreed to size up the situation and each other as well as the future.

The ink had hardly dried on the CEO agreement before Benedict had started playing matchmaker.

It had quickly become clear that the price tag on a share of Benedict Fasteners was ensuring the firm stayed in the family. There was only one way to do that, but by then Hatch had met Jessie Benedict and had decided the price was not too high. In fact, the whole deal appeared very neat and satisfactory all the way around.

The Galloway contract was in the bag, of course. The dinner tonight was just a social touch. It would cement the relationship and emphasize to Galloway that from now on he would be dealing with Sam Hatchard, the new CEO of Benedict Fasteners. Jessie's presence would attest to the fact that the transfer of power had Vincent's blessing.

"She says you make her nervous," Vincent growled suddenly.

Hatch looked up, his mind still on the numbers in front of him. "I beg your pardon?"

"Jessie says you make her nervous."

"Yes." Hatch returned his attention to the printout.

"Dammit, man, doesn't that bother you?"

"She'll get over it."

"Why do you make her nervous, anyway?" Vincent demanded.

Hatch glanced up again, amused. "What is this? You're not worrying about your daughter at this late date, are you? She's twenty-seven years old. She can take care of herself."

"I'm not so sure about that," Vincent muttered. "Twenty-seven years old and she still hasn't found a steady job."

Hatch smiled briefly. "She's found plenty of jobs, from what I've heard. She just hasn't stuck with any of them very long."

"She's so damn smart." Vincent's scowl deepened. "She

was always smart. But she's changed jobs so often since she got out of college that I've lost count. No direction. No goals. I can't believe she's gone to work for a goddamned fortune-teller now. It's the last straw, I tell you."

Hatch shrugged again. "Take it easy. In a month or two she'll probably quit to go to work at the zoo."

"I should be so lucky. She seems real serious about this new job with the psychic. She's been there a month already and she sounds more enthusiastic than ever. She hasn't gotten herself fired yet, and that's a bad sign. People usually start thinking about firing Jessie within a couple weeks of hiring her. Hell, she didn't even last two weeks at that damned singing-telegram job. Guess it took 'em that long to figure out she couldn't sing."

"Give her time."

Vincent eyed him suspiciously. "It doesn't bother you that she's always bouncing around? Doesn't it make her seem kind of flighty or something?"

"She'll settle down after she's married."

"How do you know?" Vincent shot back. "What do you know about women and marriage, for crying out loud?"

"I was married once."

Vincent's mouth fell open. "You were? What happened? Divorced?"

"My wife died."

Vincent was obviously stunned that Hatch, whom he'd come to think of as a friend, if not the son he'd never had, had never mentioned his previous marriage before. "Oh, Jesus. I'm sorry, Hatch."

Sam met Vincent's eyes and said, "It was a long time ago."

"Yeah, well, like I said, I'm sorry."

"Thank you." Hatch went back to studying the printout. "Stop worrying about your daughter. I'll take care of her."

"That's what I'm trying to tell you. She doesn't seem to

want you to take care of her, Hatch. She's not exactly encouraging you, is she?"

"You're wrong," Hatch said gently. "She's been very encouraging in her own way."

Vincent gave him a dumbfounded look. "She has?"

"Yes." Hatch turned a page of the printout.

"Dammit, how can you say that? What has she done to encourage you?"

"She gets very nervous around me," Hatch explained patiently.

"I know, dammit, that's what I've been telling you. What in God's name . . . ?" Vincent broke off, incredulous. "You're saying that's a good sign?"

"A very good sign."

"Are you sure about that? I've got two ex-wives and neither Connie nor Lilian was ever nervous around me," Vincent said. "Nerves of steel, those two."

"Jessie's different."

"You can say that again. Never did understand that girl."

"That's an interesting comment, given the fact that you intend to leave Benedict Fasteners to her."

"Yeah, well, she's the only one in the family I can trust enough to leave it to." Vincent snorted again. "Whatever else happens, Jessie will do what's best for the firm and the family. That's the important thing."

"But she obviously has no interest in or talent for running Benedict Fasteners," Hatch pointed out.

"Hell, that's why I brought you on board. You're the perfect solution to the problem." Vincent pinned him with a sharp look. "Aren't you?"

"Yes."

At five minutes to seven Hatch carefully eased the new silver-gray Mercedes into a space on the street in front of Jessie's Capitol Hill apartment building.

He got out of the car and automatically looked down to

check the polish on his wing-tip shoes. Then he centered the knot on his discreetly striped tie and straightened his gray jacket. Satisfied, he started toward the lobby door.

Hatch was very conscious of the sober, restrained elegance of his attire. He was careful about such details as the width and color of the stripes on his ties and the roll of the collars on his custom-made shirts. He did not pay attention to these things because of any natural interest in fashion, but because he did not want to accidentally screw up on something so basic. In the business world a lot of judgments were made based on a man's clothes.

Hatch had grown up in boots and jeans and work shirts. Even though he had been functioning successfully in the corporate environment for some time now, he still did not fully trust his own instincts when it came to appropriate dress, so he erred on the side of caution.

His wife, Olivia, had taught Hatch most of what he knew about the conservative look favored by American corporate powermongers. For that advice some part of him would always be grateful to her. That was about all he could find to thank her for after all these years.

Hatch glanced at his steel-and-gold wristwatch as he rang the buzzer at the entrance of the aging brick building.

When he had first bought the watch he had worried that it was a bit too flashy. He'd had the same qualms about the Mercedes. But both had appealed to him, not only because they were beautifully made and superbly functional but also because they represented in a very tangible way the success Hatch had made of his life. It was a success his father, a bitter, whining failure of a man, had always predicted would elude his son.

When Hatch was in a philosophical mood, which was an extremely rare event, he sometimes wondered if he had fought his way to his present level of success primarily to prove his father's predictions wrong.

The gold hands on the watch face told Hatch he was right on time. Not that it would do him much good. Jessie was inclined to be late whenever Hatch was due to pick her up. He knew from previous experience that she would be rushing frantically around the apartment collecting her keys, checking to be certain the stove was turned off, and switching on her answering machine. Anything to delay the inevitable, Hatch thought wryly.

He took his finger off the intercom button as Jessie's breathless voice finally answered.

"Who is it?"

"Hatch."

"Oh."

"Were you expecting someone else?" he asked politely.

"No, of course not. Come on in."

The door made a hissing sound as it unlatched itself, and Hatch went into the interior lobby. He took the stairs to the second floor and walked down the hall to Jessie's apartment. He knocked softly and she opened the door, peering out with a vaguely accusing frown.

"You're right on time," she muttered.

Hatch ignored the reproach in her voice. He smiled with satisfaction at the sight of her, his gaze moving appreciatively over the close-fitting little black dinner dress that skimmed her waist and stopped just below her knees. "Hello, Jessie. You look very good tonight. As usual."

And she did. But then, Jessie always looked good to him. There was a vibrant, feminine, mysterious quality about her. She made him think of witches and cats and ancient Egyptian queens.

For all its exotic quality, Jessie's face mirrored both intelligence and a deep, womanly vulnerability. Both appealed to Hatch. His response to her intellect he understood immediately. He was a man who had always preferred intelligent women. The other kind irritated him.

But his reaction to Jessie's vulnerability still surprised him. It had been a long time since he had felt protective toward a woman, and he did not remember the compulsion being nearly as intense the last time, not even back in those

23

early days with his first wife, Olivia. He could not explain to his own satisfaction just why he reacted this way to Jessie. She was, after all, an entirely different kind of woman than Olivia had been, his dead wife's opposite in many ways.

Jessie was lively and volatile, whereas Olivia had always been serene and charming. Benedict's elder daughter was proving feisty and difficult. Olivia had always been well-mannered and refined. Jessie was the sort of female who put up roadblocks for a man, even though she wanted him. Olivia had known instinctively how to cater to the male ego.

Hatch knew Jessie was going to make him wait tonight because she was annoyed at being maneuvered into the date in the first place and even more annoyed with herself for being unable to escape the net.

Olivia might have made him wait, but only for a couple of minutes, and even then just so that she could make a proper entrance. Above all, she would have understood the importance of tonight's engagement and given Hatch her full support. She had always supported him in his career.

Jessie could not have cared less about Hatch's career.

Hatch sighed inwardly as he crossed the threshold. Jessie stepped back, holding the door open. She promptly stumbled over the large iron horse that served as a doorstop. Hatch reached out and caught her arm to steady her. Her skin felt like silk and he could smell the faint spicy fragrance she was wearing.

"Damn," she said, glancing down. "Now look what's happened. I've got a run in my hose. I'll have to change."

"No problem." Hatch pretended not to hear the irritation in her voice as he closed the door softly behind himself. "I've built a few extra minutes into our schedule. We're not due at the restaurant until seven-forty-five."

She glared at him over her shoulder as she headed toward the bedroom. "You told me seven-thirty."

"I lied."

The bedroom door slammed shut behind her, but not before Hatch had had a chance to notice the deep V cut into the back of the little black dinner dress. A great deal of smooth, cream-colored skin was showing in the cut-out portion.

Hatch smiled again and glanced around the small, cozy room. He had not had occasion to spend a great deal of time in Jessie's apartment, much to his regret, but whenever he found himself in it, he was oddly intrigued by the eclectic, colorful decor.

The place reflected Jessie's constantly shifting, often whimsical interests. The furniture was basically modern and consisted of a lot of glass, black metal, and high-tech designs. There were framed posters on the walls because Jessie changed her mind too often to risk investing in expensive paintings. One could always throw a poster away when one got tired of it, she had explained when Hatch had inquired about them. Near the front window there was a low glass table with a collection of miniature cacti arranged on it. The spiny plants looked vaguely bewildered here in the damp environs of the Pacific Northwest. The last time Hatch had been in the apartment there had been ferns on the table.

There was a wall of books behind the sofa. The titles ranged from works on magic and myth to self-help volumes on how to find a creative, fulfilling career. There were none of the trendy books one often saw in a woman's apartment about how to find and keep a man, Hatch noticed. The collection of fiction covered nearly every genre from romance and suspense to horror and science fiction.

The only thing that appeared to stay constant in Jessie's world was her unswerving loyalty to her family. Hatch had observed during the past two months that she was in many ways the heart and soul of the Benedict clan.

Loyalty was something that Hatch prized highly in a woman, probably because he'd experienced so little of it from them in the past. It had become clear to him that if he embedded himself deeply enough into the Benedict family, he would enjoy the same degree of loyalty the others got from Jessie. His entire courtship strategy was based on that observation.

The phone on the glass end table warbled just as Hatch started to leaf through a book entitled *Toward a New Philosophy of Ecology*. He noticed it was a birthday gift to Jessie from her cousin David.

"Get that for me, will you, Hatch?" Jessie called from the bedroom.

Hatch picked up the phone. "Yes?"

"Hi," said a bright, bubbling voice. "This is Alison from Caine, Carter, and Peat calling for Jessie Benedict."

"Just a minute." Hatch put down the phone and went down the hall to knock on the closed door of the bedroom.

"Who is it, Hatch?"

"Sounds like a broker."

"Oh, God. Alison. At this hour? I've been ducking her calls all day." Jessie opened the door and stared at Hatch with dismayed eyes. "I thought I could avoid her until tomorrow morning. She's trying to sell me stock in some company that's making fat-free cooking oil. Do you know anything about fat-free cooking oil?"

"Only that it's probably too good to be true."

"I was afraid of that. What am I going to tell her?"

"Why don't you just say no?" Hatch inhaled the subtle scent that was emanating from her bedroom. Through the crack in the doorway he could just make out the corner of a white-quilted bed. A pair of discarded panty hose lay in seductive disarray on the white carpet.

"You don't understand," Jessie hissed in exasperation. "I can't say no to Alison. She's a friend and she's new in the business and she's working very hard to build up a list of clients. I feel I should help her."

Hatch raised his brows, went back out into the living room, and picked up the phone.

"Jessie is not interested in any shares in fat-free cooking oil," he said. He paid no attention to the burst of chirpy, chattering protest on the other end of the line as he calmly hung up the phone.

Then he turned to see Jessie staring at him from the hallway. She had a shocked, annoyed expression on her face. He smiled blandly back at her.

"It's really very easy to say no, Jessie."

"So I see. I'll be sure to remember your technique," she snapped.

CHAPTER TWO

Of course it was no problem at all for people like Sam Hatchard to say no, Jessie thought, still seething as she opened her menu in the crowded downtown restaurant. The Sam Hatchards of this world did not worry about other people's feelings or fret overmuch about what might happen when one casually said no.

Hatch was not one to concern himself with the fact that poor Alison was new in the business of selling stocks and bonds, a woman struggling to make it in a ruthless, cold-blooded, male-dominated world. He would not care that Alison desperately needed to build up her commissions if she was to hold on to her job at Caine, Carter, and Peat. He would not be bothered by the fact that Alison was a personal friend of Jessie's.

Jessie looked up, feeling Hatch's cool, emotionless topaz eyes on her. He was sitting at the opposite side of the small table, politely responding to a question from a beaming George Galloway. But even as he said something very intelligent and shrewd to George about long-term interest rates, Jessie knew part of Hatch's mind was on the problem of how to handle Jessie Benedict. She was, after all, a top priority at the moment. Almost as important as interest rates.

Jessie shivered and knew that only part of the atavistic thrill that flashed down her spine was dread. The other part was pure feminine anticipation. She scowled, feeling like an idiot, and concentrated on her menu. George Galloway was an old-fashioned kind of man. Hatch had, therefore, selected one of the few restaurants downtown that still featured a wide variety of beef on the menu. Jessie preferred seafood.

"Tell me, Jessie, dear," Ethel Galloway said brightly, "how is your mother? I haven't seen Lilian in ages."

Jessie, searching through the short list of fish dishes at the end of the menu, looked up and smiled. Ethel was in her late fifties, a plump, pleasant-faced, grandmotherly woman. She was an excellent complement to her bluff, down-to-earth husband. Jessie had known them both for years.

"Mom's fine," Jessie said. "She and Connie are really excited about expanding their interior-design firm. Business is booming."

Ethel chuckled. "Oh, yes. The design business. What do they call their firm? ExCellent Designs or something like that, isn't it? In honor of the fact that they're both ex-wives of Vincent's?"

Jessie grinned ruefully. "That's right. They always claim they found a lot more in common with each other than they ever found with my father. Dad agrees."

"And your half-sister?" Ethel continued. "Little Elizabeth. She's still doing well in school?"

Jessie's smile widened enthusiastically. She felt a rush of pride, the way she always did when she talked about Elizabeth. "Definitely. She's determined to go into scientific research of some kind. She's just finished a fascinating project dealing with the chemical analysis of a toxic-waste dump for her school's science fair. Can you imagine? Toxic-waste chemistry and she's only twelve years old."

Ethel gave Hatch a meaningful glance. "Sounds more like the proud mother than a half-sister, doesn't she? You have to understand that Jessie has had a big hand in raising Elizabeth. Connie and Lilian have been very busy with their design business for the past few years and I do believe the child spends more time with Jessie than with her mother."

"I see." Hatch studied Jessie with an unreadable expression. "I imagine Jessie would make a very good mother."

Jessie felt herself turn an embarrassing shade of red, but the Galloways didn't seem to find the remark off-base in the least.

"Well, well, well," George said, chuckling heartily as he gave Jessie a knowing look. "Sounds like things are getting serious here. Your father implied as much last time I talked to him. Are congratulations in order yet?"

"No," Jessie managed in a croaked voice as she picked up her wineglass. She took a sip and nearly choked as it went down the wrong way. Eyes watering from the strain of trying not to cough, she shot a quick glance at Hatch. He was smiling his remote, mysterious smile. He was fully aware of his impact on her. She longed to reach across the table and throttle him.

"Jessie is feeling a little pressured these days," Hatch explained gently to his guests. "It's no secret that everyone in the family is matchmaking."

"Oh, ho." Ethel gave Hatch a droll look. "So that's the way of it, then, hmm?"

Jessie wished she could count to three and vanish.

"Pretty damn obvious why they'd all want you two to get together," George observed cheerfully. "Your marriage would certainly simplify things, wouldn't it? Keep Benedict Fasteners in the family and at the same time give Vincent the man he needs to take over and move the company into the big time."

"George, really." Ethel slanted her husband a chiding glance. "You're embarrassing poor Jessie."

"Nonsense." George turned a paternal smile on Jessie. "Known her since she was a toddler, haven't I, Jessie?"

"Yes," Jessie agreed with a sigh.

"And we know, of course, that Vincent intends to leave the company to her," George concluded.

"Unfortunately, I don't particularly want it," Jessie muttered.

"But you will take it," Hatch observed quietly, "because if you don't, Vincent will either sell it when he retires or continue to run it until he drops dead at his desk. Either way, the family will lose the future potential of Benedict Fasteners, which is enormous. It could easily be worth five times what it is today within five years."

"If you're running things, that is, eh?" George gave Hatch a shrewd glance.

Hatch shrugged. "I do have a few ideas for the firm."

"Ideas that he's done a wonderful job of selling to Dad and the rest of the family. Everyone's convinced that if Hatch remains CEO, we'll all get filthy rich," Jessie said a little too sweetly. Nobody seemed to notice the sarcasm except Hatch, who merely gave her one of his faint, polite smiles.

"Everyone's right," Hatch said.

A shark, Jessie thought nervously. The man was a cold-blooded shark. The fascination she felt for him was nothing more than the instinctual interest of a deer staring into a wolf's glowing eyes.

Ethel's brows lifted. "How did you and Hatch first meet, dear?"

Jessie managed a brittle smile. "I believe we first spoke the morning he fired me from my job in Benedict's personnel department. Isn't that right, Hatch?"

Ethel and George Galloway looked at her in shock.

"He fired you?" Ethel echoed in disbelief.

"Yes, it was all very traumatic, actually." Jessie saw the faint hint of irritation in Hatch's expression and she began to warm to her topic. Getting any kind of rise out of Hatch was a victory of sorts. It happened so rarely.

"Didn't know you'd gone to work for your father," George said. "Thought you'd always avoided working for Vincent."

"I had been working there only a few weeks. Dad had insisted I at least try a job at Benedict. He claimed I owed it to him and to the family. I was between jobs at the time . . ."

"As happens so frequently in Jessie's life," Hatch murmured.

Jessie glowered at him. "I finally agreed to give Benedict a shot. It wasn't too bad, to tell you the truth. I discovered I rather liked personnel and I think I was starting to get the hang of it. But two days after Hatch was installed in the management suite, he canned me."

"Good heavens." Ethel glanced at Hatch.

"I'm sure it wasn't all that traumatic for Jessie," Hatch said calmly. "After all, she's used to getting fired. Happens regularly, doesn't it, Jessie?"

She shrugged. "I've had my share of shortsighted, old-fashioned bosses," she informed the table loftily.

Hatch nodded. "Poor bastards."

Jessie glared at him, wondering if he was actually trying for a bit of humor or if he was serious in his sympathy for the long line of managers who had preceded him in her life. She concluded he was serious. Hatch was always serious. "As I said, I was getting along fairly well in personnel. Admit it, Hatch. Most of the people I recommended for employment have made excellent employees."

"Your hire recommendations were not the problem."

George turned directly to Hatch. "So why in hell did you toss her out of Benedict?"

Hatch put down his menu. "Let's just say that Jessie is not cut out for a happy life in a corporate environment."

"Translated, that means I tended to be on the side of the

32

employees, rather than management, when there was a dispute," Jessie explained. "The new CEO did not approve of my approach."

George Galloway gave a muffled snort of laughter. "What did Vincent say?"

"Vincent," Hatch said, "was profoundly grateful to me for terminating Jessie's employment with Benedict Fasteners. He'd been trying to figure out a way to get rid of her since the day after he'd hired her. It took him about twenty-four hours to realize he'd made a major mistake when he'd put Jessie to work in personnel."

"I must admit it all turned out for the best, however," Jessie assured the Galloways. "A month ago I landed a terrific new position with a wonderful firm called Valentine Consultations. I feel that I've finally found my true calling in life. Mrs. Valentine says that if things work out the way she believes they will, she'll make me a full partner in the firm."

"What sort of consulting work does Valentine do?" George turned to her with a businessman's natural interest.

"You don't want to know," Hatch warned softly.

"Nonsense. Of course we want to know, don't we, Ethel?"

"Certainly," Ethel confirmed. "We're always interested in what Jessie is doing. You do lead an adventurous sort of life, my dear."

"Mrs. Valentine is a psychic," Jessie explained with a broad smile.

"Oh, Lord." Ethel rolled her eyes.

"No wonder Benedict's praying you'll marry her," George said, leaning confidentially toward Hatch. "She's getting worse."

"I'm sure it's just a phase," Hatch said imperturbably as the waiter approached.

Two hours later Jessie breathed a sigh of relief as Hatch brought his gray Mercedes to a halt outside her apartment building. She reached for the door handle before he had finished switching off the engine.

"Well, there you go, Hatch," she said, infusing her tone with a false note of good cheer. "The Galloway deal is signed, sealed, and delivered. Tell Dad I did my duty. Now, if you don't mind, I've got to run. Big day tomorrow at the office. I'm sure you'll understand."

Without glancing to his side, Hatch touched the button that locked all the doors.

Jessie heard the solid *click* and sat back, resigned to the inevitable. "There was something else you wanted?"

Hatch turned slightly in the seat and draped his arm over the wheel, one long finger idly stroking its smooth surface. She found herself staring at that finger, hypnotized by the oddly erotic gesture.

"I think," Hatch said finally, "that we need to talk. Please invite me in for tea."

Jessie jerked her gaze away from his gliding finger and shot him a sharp glance. There was just enough light coming from the streetlamp to reveal the determination in his expression. The request for tea was more like a demand. Well, he had a point. Maybe it was time they talked. They had played cat-and-mouse long enough.

"All right," she said.

Hatch released the locks and Jessie opened her door before Hatch could get around to her side of the car.

Conversation had been sparse since Jessie and Hatch had left the restaurant. It was even sparser as they went down the hall to her apartment. When they reached her door, Hatch took the key from her hand and fitted it into the lock.

Jessie stepped inside, found the light switch, and flipped it on.

Hatch reached for Jessie's burnt-orange duster. He eased it from her shoulders slowly, letting her feel the weight of his hands. She was suddenly conscious of just how much material was missing from the back of her dress.

"Would it be so bad, Jessie?" he asked quietly.

She stepped briskly away from the lightweight coat, leaving it in his fingers. "Would what be so bad?"

"You and me." He tossed the duster over the back of a chair. His eyes held hers as he shrugged out of his suit jacket.

There was no point in pretending she didn't know what he meant. Jessie turned toward the shadowed kitchen. "Yes."

"Why?" He followed her, one hand loosening the knot of his tie.

"Don't you understand, Hatch?" Jessie opened a cupboard and took down two mugs. "It would be a disaster for both of us."

"You haven't given us much of a chance yet." He took a seat at the counter, one well-shod foot hooked on the bottom rung of the kitchen stool. "Every evening we've had together, all four or five of them, has followed the same pattern as this one."

"What do you mean?"

"First, I've had to corner you and cut off all the obvious exits. Then I've had to coax you or blackmail you or lay a guilt trip on you in order to keep you from backing out at the last minute. When I do get you out to a restaurant, you spend the time baiting me. Then I take you home and you say good night downstairs and dash out of the car as if you're running off to meet another man. You call that giving us a chance?"

"Certainly makes one wonder what you see in me, doesn't it? But I guess we both know the answer to that." She switched on the kettle with a savage little twist of her fingers. "I'm Vincent Benedict's daughter."

Hatch responded only with mild curiosity to that unsubtle taunt. He smiled quizzically. "You think I'm interested in you just because of the company?"

Jessie sighed. "I think that's a big part of it."

"The company is what brought us together. And I want it very badly. But I would not marry you to get it unless I also wanted you just as badly. And I do. Want you, that is."

Jessie gasped and her hand jerked so quickly that she

scattered a spoonful of tea leaves all over the kitchen counter. "Damn."

"Relax, Jessie."

"You always have this effect on me."

"I know," he said softly.

"How can you expect me to get serious about a man who makes me feel like a complete klutz?" She put another spoonful of tea in the pot and reached for the hissing kettle.

"Jessie, please. I know there's a mutual attraction here. And we both have the best interests of Benedict Fasteners at heart. So why won't you give me a chance?"

She leaned back against the counter and eyed the tea as it steeped. "Okay, okay. I'll give you an answer but you aren't going to like it."

"Try me."

"I'll admit I'm attracted to you, but I'm not going to get involved with you, Hatch. I am not going to get serious about you. I am definitely not going to marry you, even though everyone else thinks it would be a really nifty idea."

"Because?"

She drew a deep, steadying breath. "Because you are a carbon copy of my father."

He considered that in thoughtful silence. "No," he said at last. "I'm not."

"You're right. You're worse than my father in a lot of ways. Harder. More driven. More consumed by your work. If that's possible. There's a reason my father has two ex-wives, Hatch. And the reason is not that he's a womanizer or that he's the kind of man who has to trade in older wives on younger ones in order to feel powerful and successful. The truth is, he chose good women both times he married and he knew it. He would still be married if he had his way."

"I know."

"If you ask Connie and Lilian, they'll tell you that they each married him because when he made them a top priority he was irresistible. They each left him because once he had married, he went right back to Benedict Fasteners, his true mistress."

"That's a rather juvenile, self-centered view of things, isn't it? No woman should expect to be the only focus of attention in a man's life. Running a successful business like Benedict Fasteners takes a lot of time and energy, Jessie. You know that."

"Too much time and energy, as far as I'm concerned. Connie and Lilian will both tell you they got sick and tired of trying to compete with the company. *I don't intend to make the same mistake they did.* I won't commit myself to a man for whom business will always come first."

"Jessie . . ."

"My father is a workaholic. So are you. Workaholics don't make good family men, Hatch. I know. I'm the daughter of one, remember?"

"That's a pretty extreme view."

Jessie was incensed. The man was being deliberately dense. "Don't you understand? If I ever decide to get married, I'll want a husband who cares more about me than he does about building a corporation, a man who will think it's just as important to get to his children's school plays as he does to a meeting with a client. I want a man who knows that life is short and that people—and especially family—are far more important than business."

"Calm down, Jessie, you're getting worked up."

"You wanted this little chat." She was vaguely aware her voice was rising. She picked up one of the mugs. "You asked me a question and I'm answering it. What's more, I'm not finished. In addition to a man who is not totally addicted to his job, I want one with blood instead of ice water in his veins. I want one who's got some real, honest emotions and who isn't afraid to show them. You're always so damn cool and controlled. I want a man who can—"

"That's enough, Jessie."

She broke off quickly as Hatch got to his feet. When he stepped toward her, closing the distance between them in two strides, she panicked and dropped the mug she had been clutching.

Hatch reached her just as the mug crashed on the countertop and rolled into the sink. His artist's hands closed slowly, inevitably around her upper arms and he pulled her against him with unnerving gentleness.

"I think," Hatch said, his mouth inches from her own, "that it's the comment about having ice water instead of blood in my veins that I take exception to the most. Kiss me, Jessie."

Wide-eyed, Jessie stood very still, looking up at him. This was the first time he had ever taken her in his arms. If she kissed him, it would be the *first time*. The monumental importance of the occasion threatened to overwhelm her. She shuddered. "Hatch, I was just trying to make a point."

"Kiss me," he commanded again, his voice very soft even though his eyes were very brilliant. "Find out for yourself if it's blood or ice water that keeps me alive."

"Oh, Hatch . . ." Jessie threw caution to the winds. In that moment she knew she could not go to her grave without finding out what it was like to kiss Sam Hatchard just once. The tension she felt in his presence had been building for weeks and it had to be released.

With an anguished little cry she wrapped her arms around his neck and pulled his head down to hers. Standing on tiptoe, she crushed her mouth against his.

Her first impression was that she was peering over the rim of a volcano. Boiling lava simmered deep down in the heart of the mountain, just as her intuition had warned her. There was definitely heat here, but it was under awesome control, surrounded by layers of frozen stone. Images of banked fires and smoldering furnaces flickered in her mind.

Moth to the flame.

Hatch's mouth moved slowly on hers, taking complete control of the kiss with effortless ease. Jessie was not quite certain just when she was no longer doing the kissing but became, instead, the one being kissed.

Hatch's elegant, dangerous hands tightened on her arms as he held her against the length of him. She could feel the long, hard muscles of his upper thighs and was deeply aware of the strength in him. It compelled and fascinated everything that was feminine within her.

But overshadowing all the other impressions that were pouring in on her was a sense of Hatch's pure self-mastery.

Jessie did not know what she had been expecting, perhaps some proof that Hatch would be as cold physically as he was in every other aspect of his life. Perhaps she had hoped such a discovery would calm the storm of conflicting emotions she felt toward him.

What she found instead was infinitely more disturbing. It would have been reassuring to know that there really was no emotion buried in this man. To discover that the fire was there, just as she had suspected, but that he had complete control of it, was unsettling in the extreme.

Jessie began to tremble. Alarmed, she brought her hands up and pushed at Hatch's shoulders. He let her go at once, his gaze amused and all too knowing. The pace of his breathing was unchanged, slow and steady as ever.

Jessie stepped quickly away from him, aware that her mouth was quivering. She bit her lip in an effort to regain her self-control as she stalked to the cupboard and got down another mug.

"Well, Jessie?"

"I think you'd better go." She poured the tea with shaking fingers.

He waited a moment longer and then, without a word, he turned and walked out of the kitchen and out of the apartment.

When the door closed behind him, Jessie sagged heavily against the counter, shut her eyes, and gulped down the hot tea.

* * *

The dowdy, worried-looking woman was hovering in the hall outside the offices of Valentine Consultations the next morning when Jessie arrived for work. Jessie was so excited at the prospect of a real live client that she nearly dropped her key.

"I'm sorry," she apologized. "Have you been waiting long? I'm afraid Mrs. Valentine isn't here today, but perhaps I can help you?"

"I'm Martha Attwood," the woman said, glancing around uneasily. "I had an appointment."

"You did?" Jessie opened the door and led the way into the office. "I'm Mrs. Valentine's assistant. I don't recall setting up an appointment for you."

"I called her at home the night before last." The woman trailed slowly into the office, looking as though she expected to find crystal balls on the tables and dark, heavy drapes covering the windows. "I told her I wasn't sure if I really wanted to hire her. She said to come in this morning. Just to talk, you know."

"Certainly. Have a seat, Mrs. Attwood. Coffee?"

"No, thank you." Martha Attwood sat down on the edge of a chair, her handbag perched on her knees. She cast another anxious look around the office. "I don't really believe in this sort of thing. Bunch of silly mumbo jumbo, if you ask me. But I don't know where else to turn. I'm desperate and the police say there's nothing they can do. There's been no actual crime committed, and my daughter . . ." Her face started to crumple. "Excuse me."

Jessie sprang up from behind the desk and came around the corner to extend a box of tissues. "It's all right, Mrs. Attwood. Just take your time."

Martha Attwood sniffed several times, blew her nose, and then dropped the used tissue into her purse. "I'm so sorry. It's the stress, you know. I've been under so much of it lately."

"I understand."

"She was doing so well in college. I was so proud of her. She was studying computer science."

"Who was studying computer science?"

"My daughter. Susan. She was always so mature for her age. Even as a child. Quiet. Hardworking. Sensible. Never got into trouble. I never dreamed she'd do something like this. I feel as though she's run off and abandoned me. Just like Harry did."

"Where, exactly, has Susan gone, Mrs. Attwood?" Jessie sat down beside the woman.

"She's gone off and joined some sort of cult. It's operating here in the Northwest somewhere. At least, I think it is. Her last letter was postmarked from right here in Seattle. Dear God, I still can't believe it. How could Susan get caught up in something like that?" Mrs. Attwood reached for a fresh tissue.

"Let me get this straight, Mrs. Attwood. You know where your daughter is?"

"Not exactly. I just know she's dropped out of her studies at Butterfield College and joined DEL."

"DEL?"

"In her letter she said it stands for Dawn's Early Light. I gather it's some sort of cult that thinks the rest of us are going to poison the environment so badly that we'll all be destroyed. But the DEL people claim they can save the planet."

"I've never heard of this particular cult."

"In her last letter Susan said she wasn't free to tell me too much yet because the DEL Foundation is trying to maintain a low profile, whatever that means."

"What is she doing for the foundation?"

"I don't know," Mrs. Attwood wailed. "They're using her, somehow. I'm sure of it. God knows what they have her doing. I can't even bear to think about it. Dear heaven, she was going to get a degree in computer science. She would have had a good job, a bright future, not the sort of life I had. I just can't believe this is happening. I came to you because I didn't know where else to turn. I can't afford a private detective, which is what I really need."

Jessie frowned thoughtfully as she absently patted the woman's hand. "Why did you call Mrs. Valentine if you don't believe in her psychic abilities?"

Mrs. Attwood blew her nose again. "Because the leader of DEL, a man named Dr. Edwin Bright, is obviously some sort of charlatan. He must be. He's convinced innocent young people like my Susan that he has special powers to predict the future and that he can change it. I guess I had some vague notion that if Mrs. Valentine could find some way to expose the man, Susan might lose her faith in him."

"You're working on the theory that it takes one to know one?" Jessie asked dryly.

Mrs. Attwood nodded, looking more miserable than ever. "It occurred to me that a . . . well, a professional like Mrs. Valentine would know all the tricks a man like Bright would use to convince others he had special powers. I mean, she must have been using such tricks, herself, for years."

Jessie bristled. "I think you should understand, Mrs. Attwood, that Mrs. Valentine has a genuine talent. She is not a fraud."

"It doesn't matter to me, don't you see?" Mrs. Attwood said hastily. "Either way, she'll recognize an impostor, won't she? Be able to expose him? And I'm sure Edwin Bright is an impostor."

"I'm really not sure we can help you, Mrs. Attwood."

Mrs. Attwood clutched at Jessie's arm. "Please. I don't know where else to turn. I'll pay her to help me prove Bright is a fake. Will you tell her that? I don't have a lot of money, but I'll find some way of paying the fees. *Please.*"

Jessie felt her irritation dissolving swiftly in the face of the woman's obvious desperation. It was so hard to say no to someone who was clearly at the end of her rope. And besides, this was a potential client.

"Let me see if I understand," Jessie said carefully. "You

don't actually want to buy the services of a true psychic. You simply want Valentine Consultations to prove that this man who runs the Dawn's Early Light Foundation is a fake, right?"

"Yes. Exactly."

"Hmmm." This was something she could handle on her own, Jessie told herself with gathering excitement. The client was not even looking for a genuine psychic. A successfully completed case such as this one could open up whole new realms of possibilities for Valentine Consultations. It was the perfect place to start her new marketing program. *Valentine Consultations, Psychic Investigations.*

"Say you'll help me," Mrs. Attwood pleaded.

"You do realize that even when their leaders are exposed, people don't always lose faith in them, don't you?" Jessie felt obliged to point out. "People who need to follow a leader will make all sorts of excuses for that leader so that they can keep on following him. It's possible we could prove this Bright is a fraud but not be able to convince Susan of it. Do you understand, Mrs. Attwood?"

"Yes, yes, I understand. But I have to try. I have to get my Susan out of the clutches of DEL."

"All right," Jessie said, making her decision on a crest of rising enthusiasm. "Valentine Consultations will take the case."

Mrs. Attwood blinked in the face of Jessie's new gung-ho attitude. "Thank you." She opened her purse. "I've brought some things along. A picture of Susan. Her last letter. There isn't much. If you can think of anything else you might need, let me know."

Her first real case. Jessie picked up the photo of a shyly smiling young woman who appeared to be about twenty years old. She wore glasses and her hair was tied back in a ponytail. There was something rather innocent and naive about Susan Attwood's face. She looked as though she had grown up in a small farm town, not a city.

"I will certainly keep you informed, Mrs. Attwood. And

don't worry, I'll get started on this right away. In fact, I'm going to consult with Mrs. Valentine immediately."

"Where is Mrs. Valentine?" Martha Attwood peered through the open doorway of the inner office.

"She took a nasty fall the night before last and she's still recovering."

"Oh, dear. Will she be able to work on my, uh, case?"

"Don't you worry about a thing, Mrs. Attwood. I'm Mrs. Valentine's assistant and I'm in charge around here now."

Mrs. Attwood cleared her throat, looking vaguely alarmed. "You're sure?"

"Absolutely positive. Relax, Mrs. Attwood. I was born for this kind of thing. It's in my blood. I just know it."

Irene Valentine looked even more worried than Mrs. Attwood had appeared. She lay back on the white pillows and listened to the entire tale, shaking her head slowly back and forth.

"I don't know, Jessie. I don't like the feel of this."

Jessie stared at her in astonished delight. "The *feel* of it? You've got your psychic abilities back, then, Mrs. V?"

"No, no, I mean I just don't like the plain old ordinary human feel of it. It doesn't take any psychic ability to sense a little trouble on the horizon, my dear. Just common sense. And my common sense tells me this cult business is way out of our league."

"But, Mrs. V, just think what a case like this could do for the image of Valentine Consultations."

"This isn't the sort of thing we normally handle, Jessie, dear. You've been with me long enough to know that. We deal with people who are under a lot of stress. Or people who are confused about things. We soothe their fears of the future and give them self-confidence. We're therapists of a sort, not private detectives."

"But this is an ideal chance to expand our business," Jessie said, unwilling to give up. "Please, Mrs. V. I told the client we'd take the case. I can work on it while you're recovering. It's not like I'm going to try to fool the client. Mrs. Attwood herself said she really doesn't expect to hire someone with genuine psychic ability. She just wants someone who can prove this Bright character is a fraud. That should be easy enough to do."

"Don't count on it. Con men are extremely clever." Mrs. Valentine narrowed her eyes. "You really want to take on this case, don't you?"

"It's a great opportunity for me to prove myself to you, Mrs. V. Let me at least do a little research on the cult and this guy Bright. If it looks too big for us to handle, I'll tell Mrs. Attwood she'll have to go to someone else. What do you say?"

"If I had any sense, I'd say no."

"Mrs. V, *please*. I have a feeling about this case. I know I can handle it."

Mrs. Valentine sighed. "As it happens, I've just taken a nasty blow on the head and I'm obviously not thinking clearly at all. All right. Do a little research, dear. Find out what you can about DEL and this man named Bright." She fixed Jessie with a firm gaze. "But you are not to go any further than that on your own, understand? Keep me posted every step of the way, and please don't do anything foolish. We don't know what is involved here, and I do not want you taking any chances."

Jessie grinned, satisfied. "Don't worry, Mrs. V. I'll be careful."

"Why do I get this overwhelming sense of impending doom?"

"You must be psychic." But Jessie regretted the little joke instantly when she saw the tears in the corner of Mrs. Valentine's eyes. "Oh, God, I'm sorry, Mrs. V. I didn't mean to upset you. You *are* psychic and you will get your inner sight back when you've recovered from the fall. I know you will."

"I hope so, Jessie." Mrs. Valentine wiped away the tears and smiled mistily. "I feel as if some part of me has been amputated. It's a dreadful feeling."

"I can imagine. Do you still think you might have been pushed down those steps?"

"I don't know what to think. The doctor explained to me about how one loses one's memory after a head injury. And the police were very nice. An officer came around again this morning and assured me there was no sign of any intruder in the house. My sister says nothing was missing or out of place. I guess I just slipped and fell."

Jessie nodded. "Well, to tell you the truth, I'd rather believe it was an accident. The idea of someone deliberately pushing you gives me the creeps."

"I agree. Best change the subject. How did your date go last night?"

"It was a disaster, just as I predicted." Jessie forced a smile. "You see? I may have some psychic ability of my own, Mrs. V."

"Yes." Mrs. Valentine looked very serious suddenly. "Yes, you may, Jessie, dear. I have suspected for some time now that you have a natural, intuitive ability that you have never fully developed."

"Really?" Jessie asked, surprised.

"It's the reason I took you on as my assistant. The thing is, I can't quite figure out what sort of talent you have, dear. No offense, but there's something rather odd about the way your mind works."

"A lot of my previous employers have said something along those lines."

CHAPTER THREE

Jessie looked down at her half-sister who was standing with her in Vincent Benedict's reception area. "You ready, kid?"

Elizabeth Benedict, curly brown hair in a neat halo around her head, her serious green eyes shielded behind a set of thick-lensed glasses, grinned bashfully. She tugged on the strings in her hand. The strings were attached to several helium-filled balloons which bobbed merrily in the air above her head. "Ready."

Jessie glanced at the trim middle-aged woman sitting at the nearby desk. "His calendar's clear for lunch?"

"I cleared it, Jessie, just like I did last year for you. He doesn't have a clue."

"Thanks, Grace. We couldn't manage this without you. All right, Elizabeth, here we go." Jessie shifted the huge bouquet of cut flowers and knocked on the heavy paneled door.

"What the hell is it now, Grace?" Vincent called out irritably from the other side of the door. "I said I didn't want to be disturbed for a couple of hours."

Elizabeth's grin faded, and behind the lenses of her glasses, her young eyes took on an uncertain expression. She glanced up at her sister uneasily.

"Don't worry," Jessie advised. "You know his bark is worse than his bite. He's forgotten it's his birthday, as usual. When he realizes what's happening, he'll lighten up. Come on." Jessie pushed open the door and marched into the room.

Vincent Benedict looked up with a ferocious scowl. "What the hell? I said I didn't . . . Oh, it's you two. What are you doing here?"

"Happy Birthday, Dad." Jessie put the huge basket of flowers down squarely in the center of the desk in front of her father. "We're here to take you to lunch."

"Good God. Is it that time of the year already?" Vincent took off his glasses and gazed at the mass of balloons and flowers. His expression warmed ever so slightly as he swung his gaze back to his daughters. "Shouldn't you be in school, Elizabeth?"

"Sure," Elizabeth admitted. "But Jessie wrote a note saying I had an urgent appointment. The teachers always believe Jessie's notes."

"I have a talent for making excuses." Jessie untwisted the balloon strings from Elizabeth's fingers and reattached them to the nearest lamp. The balloons hovered over the massive desk, looking very much out of place in the solemn atmosphere of her father's office. "Nice touch, don't you think? The balloons were Elizabeth's idea."

"I figured no one else would give you balloons. Do you like 'em, Dad?" Elizabeth anxiously awaited the verdict.

Jessie caught her father's eye. It was automatic. She'd been doing it for years in this sort of situation, she reflected. She was always on the alert to make certain her father understood he was not to casually hurt Elizabeth's feelings the way he had frequently bruised her own when she was younger.

Vincent pretended to ignore the warning look as he

contemplated the balloons with a deliberate air. "Definitely a nice touch. And you're absolutely right. No one else is very likely to give me balloons for my birthday. Or flowers." He touched one of the petals. "Thank you, ladies. Now, what was this about lunch?"

"Pizza or hamburgers. Your choice." Jessie perched on the edge of the desk. "Elizabeth and I are treating."

Vincent frowned down at his desk calendar. "Better let me check my schedule. I thought I had something on for today."

Elizabeth grinned hugely. "Jessie made Grace keep your calendar clear for today, Dad."

"Is that right? A conspiracy again, eh?" Vincent raised his brows at Jessie.

"Whatever works," Jessie murmured, fingering one of the petals of a brilliant red lily.

"What the hell, it's my birthday." Vincent turned back to Elizabeth. "Pizza or hamburgers, huh? That's a tough choice. I think I'll go with the pizza."

Jessie relaxed. The battle was over. It had not been too bad this year. There had been far worse battles in the past. Maybe her father was finally mellowing. She looked at her sister. "Pizza it is. Witness a true executive decision, kid. Dad is definitely a man of action."

"Damn right," Vincent agreed as Elizabeth giggled again.

Jessie hopped off the desk. "Let's get going. We want to beat the crowd to the pizza parlor. It gets real cutthroat in there at lunchtime."

The office door swung open before Vincent could get to his feet. Everyone automatically turned around to gaze at the man filling the open doorway.

"Somebody die?" Hatch asked, his gaze resting on the bright bouquet of flowers.

"Not yet." Vincent stood up and reached for his jacket. "Just another birthday. My daughters are taking me out to lunch. Seems my calendar has been mysteriously cleared for an hour or so this afternoon."

"You can come with us, if you want," Elizabeth told Hatch shyly.

Jessie smiled loftily. "I'm sure Hatch is much too busy to join us. I'll bet he's got all sorts of megabuck deals that need his personal attention this afternoon. Isn't that right, Hatch?"

Hatch regarded her meditatively, idly tapping the folder in his hand against the door frame. "I think I could manage to get away for an hour or so. Unless Vincent would rather hog all the female company for himself?" He glanced at the older man.

"Hell, no. There's two of 'em. Enough to go around. You're welcome to join us. Jessie and Elizabeth are buying."

"In that case, how can I refuse?"

"It's pizza," Jessie warned quickly, her heart sinking. She could almost see the computer that served as Hatch's brain as it quickly reprioritized his afternoon. First things first. And item number one on his agenda was the courtship of Jessie Benedict, even if that meant taking an hour out of his precious schedule to eat pizza.

"I'll try very hard not to get any tomato sauce on my tie," Hatch said seriously.

Jessie narrowed her eyes and decided he was not joking.

"Jessie's going to tell us all about her new case," Elizabeth announced. "She's going to start work on it right away while Mrs. Valentine is in the hospital."

"Is that right?" Hatch cocked a faintly mocking brow. "Going to help some little old lady talk to the shade of the dear departed, are we? Or maybe banish a few evil spirits from a haunted health club?"

"No," said Jessie, stung by the cool sarcasm. "As a matter of fact, I'm going to help rescue a young girl who's been kidnapped by a bizarre cult."

That wiped the condescension off Hatch's face. "The hell you are!"

* * *

His first, albeit vain hope was that she had been teasing him again, deliberately baiting him the way she so often did. If that was the case, he was reluctantly willing to admit that this time she had managed to draw a reaction.

But as Hatch sat next to Elizabeth in the pizza-parlor booth and listened to Jessie talk about her new "case," he realized this was no joke. He glanced at Vincent, silently willing the older man to put his foot down. Unfortunately, although Benedict looked singularly annoyed, it was obvious he was unable to think of any barriers to put in Jessie's path other than overwhelming disapproval. Disapproval was not doing the trick.

Hatch glanced surreptitiously around. He felt out of place sitting in the garishly decorated pizza parlor. True, his and Benedict's were not the only two business suits in the restaurant, but they were definitely the two most expensive suits.

Hatch knew full well Vincent had planned to work through lunch. Benedict always had lunch sent in unless he was doing business over the meal, in which case he usually took his guests to his club. Hatch knew the basic schedule because he followed a similar one.

But today they were both sitting here eating pizza and listening to Jessie talk about a farfetched plan to rescue some idiot who'd gotten involved in a cult. As if Jessie knew anything about cults.

Jessie and Elizabeth appeared oblivious of the fact that they were not garnering any male support for the crazy scheme. Hatch watched both females down vast quantities of pizza while nattering on excitedly about just how Jessie should start her investigation.

"The library would be a good place to begin," Elizabeth said seriously. "You can check the newspaper indexes to see if there are any articles on Dawn's Early Light or its leader."

"Good idea," Jessie mumbled around a bite of pizza. She looked at her father. "I don't suppose you've ever heard anything about it, have you?"

"Hell, no," Vincent muttered. "Sounds like a bunch of damned tree-huggers. Stay out of this, Jessie. You've got absolutely no idea what you're doing."

"I'm just going to ask a few questions and see what I can turn up."

"You're supposed to be an assistant fortune-teller," Hatch pointed out coldly. "Not some sort of unlicensed private investigator. Stick to learning how to read tea leaves and crystal balls. You've got no business researching cults, much less trying to discredit their leaders. People who lead cults don't take kindly to other people trying to prove they're frauds. You could be opening up a real can of worms here."

Jessie traded a meaningful glance with her sister. "You get the feeling we're doing lunch with a couple of real corporate wet blankets, Elizabeth?"

Elizabeth grinned. "You said their main problem was that they didn't know how to have fun."

"How right I was." Jessie waved a slice of pizza at Hatch and her father. "You two better be careful or Elizabeth and I are going to walk off in a huff and stick you with the bill."

"We'll talk about this later," Hatch said evenly as he saw Vincent's mouth tighten.

"Sorry, didn't mean to bore you," Jessie drawled. "By all means, let's change the subject."

Vincent glanced at Hatch. "This is the wildest thing she's come up with yet."

"I think it sounds like fun," Elizabeth said loyally.

Hatch eyed Elizabeth thoughtfully. The girl was a little shy but certifiably brilliant. Hatch did not doubt that someday she was going to cure rare diseases or journey into remote tropical jungles in search of exotic plants. In the meantime it was obvious Jessie was struggling to make certain the younger girl built a relationship with her father.

Hatch had figured out weeks ago just what Jessie's role in the complex Benedict family was. She was the go-between who held everything together, the one who linked Vincent to the clan and the rest of the clan to Vincent. It was clear that her real job in life was holding the Benedict family together. Anything else that might come along in terms of employment was going to be strictly part-time. He wondered why none of the family, including her own father, realized that.

"Don't forget you're supposed to pick Elizabeth up at ten o'clock on Saturday to take her to the science fair," Jessie reminded Vincent.

"I won't forget. Got it on my calendar." Vincent gave his younger daughter a knowing look. "You going to win first prize again this year?"

"Maybe." Elizabeth spoke with shy confidence. Then she frowned. "Unless they give it to Eric Jerkface."

Hatch frowned curiously. "Who's Eric Jerkface?"

"The science teacher's favorite. He looks like he came right off of some television show featuring cute kids, and he knows how to kiss up to the teachers. You know what I mean?"

"Of course Hatch knows what you mean." Jessie smiled blandly at Hatch over her sister's head. "He's very familiar with that kind of corporate mentality, aren't you, Hatch?"

"Very." Hatch shot her a withering glance and turned back to Elizabeth. "What's Jerkface's project?"

"He's doing something on extraterrestrial life."

Jessie was incensed. "Nobody even knows if there is any extraterrestrial life. How can he do a project on the subject?"

"Eric Jerkface talked the teacher into it," Elizabeth explained.

"Well, the project's bound to bomb next to yours," Jessie declared. "You're going to knock the socks off the judges with your chemical analysis of a toxic-waste dump, isn't she, Dad?"

"Right," Vincent agreed readily. Then he scowled at Elizabeth. "I just hope you're not going to turn into one of those radical environmentalists."

"Ecologist, Dad, not environmentalist," Jessie said quickly. "And Elizabeth hasn't decided which scientific career she wants to pursue yet, have you, Elizabeth?"

"No. I'm still making up my mind." Elizabeth concentrated on her pizza.

"No rush, I guess. Just don't take as long to make up your mind about a career as Jessie's taking," Vincent muttered. "What's the difference between an ecologist and an environmentalist, anyway?"

Elizabeth assumed a serious, pontificating tone. "Ecology is the *science* of studying the environment. Environmentalism is the social and political movement that causes all the headlines."

"I wonder if Edwin Bright is a genuine ecologist turned con man," Jessie mused, "or just an opportunist."

"I don't see that it matters," Hatch said flatly. "Either way, you don't have any business getting involved."

"But that's just it." Jessie's smile was radiant. "This is business. I'm working for a living. I should think everyone would be pleased. Just think, I'm actually holding down a job for longer than one month."

"Save me," Vincent growled.

Jessie turned to Elizabeth. "I'll tell you something, kid, you definitely deserve first place, and if for some reason Eric Jerkface actually wins, we'll all know it was because he was the teacher's pet and got by on his looks and charm alone."

Hatch reached for the last slice of pizza. "You haven't even seen Jerkface's project."

"Doesn't matter. Elizabeth's is tons better."

Hatch smiled slightly. "I get the impression that once you choose a side, you stick to it, come hell or high water. Is that right, Jessie?"

"Jessie is nothing if not loyal." Vincent eyed his eldest daughter with a severe glare. "Sometimes to a fault."

"I don't see it as a fault," Hatch said. "I've always considered loyalty an extremely valuable commodity."

"Just another business commodity you can buy or sell, right, Hatch?" Jessie inquired coolly.

Hatch deliberately wrapped his fingers around his glass of water. It was better than wrapping them around Jessie's throat, he told himself philosophically.

Half an hour later Vincent stalked back into his office and threw himself down into the big leather chair behind the desk. He leveled a blunt finger at Hatch.

"This problem with Jessie," Vincent announced, "is all your fault."

"My fault?"

"Damn right. If you hadn't fired her when you first came on board, she'd still be working here at Benedict Fasteners instead of running around investigating weirdo cults."

"Come off it, Vincent. You were so grateful to me the day I fired her that you bought me a drink, remember? She was a loose cannon here at Benedict. Hell, she was wreaking havoc downstairs in personnel. If she'd stayed, your whole organization would have been in a shambles by now."

"It wasn't that bad."

"Oh, yes it was," Hatch shot back. "The department heads were up in arms. The word was out. Want a few extra days of sick leave? See Jessie in personnel and give her a good sob story. She'll arrange things. Want a long weekend? See Jessie in personnel and tell her your grandmother died again. Jessie will fix things up for you. Think you got overlooked for promotion because your boss secretly hates your guts? See Jessie in personnel. She'll be on your side."

Vincent winced. "Damn. It *was* getting out of hand, wasn't it?"

"Yeah. And nobody dared call her to heel because she was the boss's daughter. How long do you think that could have gone on before every last shred of corporate discipline disintegrated, Benedict?"

Vincent held up his hand. "You're right. She was a loose

cannon around here. But that doesn't change the fact that if she were still working here at Benedict she wouldn't be dealing with cults."

Hatch went to the window and stood thinking quietly for a few minutes. "Maybe you're panicking over nothing."

"I am not panicking. I am seriously concerned. And what's this 'me' business? You're just as panicked as I am. I saw the way your jaw dropped when she exploded her little bombshell about starting an investigation. First time I've ever seen you looking like you'd been caught off-guard, Hatch. I'd have gotten a good laugh out of it if we'd been talking about anything else except Jessie's damn-fool cult-busting project."

"All right, maybe you . . . maybe *we* are seriously concerned over nothing." Hatch swung around to face him. "Look, the worst that can happen is that Jessie manages to locate the headquarters of this DEL crowd and asks to see Susan Attwood. Or maybe she'll try to talk to the leader, the one they call Bright."

"So?"

"So, think about it logically, Vincent. How would you react? More than likely Jessie will be politely told to mind her own business and that will be the end of things. She's not a threat to anyone, and whoever's running the show at Dawn's Early Light will know that. They'll treat her like an annoying reporter and just stonewall her."

Vincent gave that some thought. "You're probably right. But, hell, I wish she'd stay out of it. Why can't she find a regular job like everybody else?"

"Jessie's not like everyone else." Hatch walked over to the desk and stood looking down at the huge basket of bright flowers. "Does she always bring you flowers on your birthday?"

Vincent's eyes softened as he followed Hatch's gaze. "Started a couple of years after Elizabeth was born. Connie and I were already having problems and she and Lilian were talking about going into the interior-design business together. They were spending a lot of time on the project and somehow Jessie wound up taking care of Elizabeth a lot. One day Jessie showed up here at the office with a bunch of flowers in one arm and her little sister in the other. Said she was taking me to lunch. Been the same every year since. I've sort of gotten used to it."

Hatch cautiously touched the petal of a flame-colored lily. It was as soft as gossamer silk, as brilliant as a sunrise. "Kind of strange. Giving a man flowers, I mean."

"Like I said, you get used to it."

"Nobody's ever brought me flowers."

"Don't whine about it," Vincent said with a grin. "Marry the woman and you'll probably get flowers for your birthday too. How did things go last night?"

"The Galloway deal is closed."

"Well, hell, I know that. I mean how did things go between you and my daughter?"

"I'm not going to tell you every detail of my personal life, Benedict. But I will tell you this: I found out I'm working under a serious handicap."

"What handicap?"

"She thinks I'm too much like you in some ways."

"Bullshit. That's just an excuse. Besides, she *likes* me."

Hatch remembered Jessie's quivering mouth crushed beneath his own and the feel of her arms wrapped around his neck. "She likes me too. But she doesn't think I'll make her a good husband. Says she doesn't want to marry a man who's more concerned about his work than his family."

"*Women.* They don't understand the demands of the business world. Always want to come first in a man's life. You'd think they'd figure out that companies like Benedict Fasteners don't just run themselves. I thought Jessie would have more common sense."

"Something tells me common sense is not one of Jessie's biggest virtues," Hatch said.

Vincent scowled. "Jessie's all right. Hell, what you said at lunch hit the nail on the head. She's real loyal. In the end she always does what's best for the family. You know what the real problem is here? You're still making her nervous. That's what the real problem is. You want some advice, Hatch? Stop making her nervous, goddammit."

"Advice? From a man with two ex-wives? Forget it. I'd rather muddle through this on my own." Hatch ceased stroking the scarlet lily and headed toward the door.

But on the way back down the hall to his office, Vincent's words rang in his ears. *She always does what's best for the family.* Hatch nodded in cool satisfaction. He was counting on it.

"So how did the big date go last night?" Elizabeth asked as Jessie drove her back toward her Bellevue school.

"I told you, it wasn't a date, it was a business dinner." Jessie guided her little red Toyota onto the bridge that crossed Lake Washington via Mercer Island. She kept her expression serious, trying to look as if she was having to concentrate very hard on the sparse afternoon traffic. Elizabeth knew better.

"Hey, Jessie, this is me, your very smart kid sister, remember?"

"You mean my smartass kid sister."

Elizabeth shrugged. "Everything I know, I learned from you."

"Don't blame your bad manners on me. Bad manners are usually the result of hanging out with a bad crowd. Remind me to check out your current peer group."

"You can spot them right away when we get to school. They're the ones wearing black leather jackets and safety pins in their ears. So how'd it go, Jess?"

"What do you care?"

"Are you kidding? Everybody in the family cares. Mom says the situation is very delicate." Elizabeth studied the expensive landscape of Mercer Island with a thoughtful expression. "She says the best thing that could happen for everyone is for you to marry Hatch."

"This may come as a shock, Elizabeth, but that's not really a good enough reason for me to marry him. Not that he's asked me."

Elizabeth shot her a shrewd glance. "The moms are going to want to know how last night went too."

"I'm aware of that," Jessie said through set teeth.

"What are you going to tell 'em?"

"As little as possible. It's none of their business."

Elizabeth frowned. "I don't think they see it that way. I heard Lilian talking to Glenna on the phone yesterday. She was saying they all had a 'vested interest' in this relationship. I think that was the phrase she used."

"You know what 'vested interest' means, Elizabeth?"

"There's money involved?" Elizabeth hazarded.

"You've got it." Jessie smiled without any humor. "If I marry Hatch, Benedict Fasteners stays in the family and has a good chance of going big-time. Which appears to be everyone's fondest dream." *Including Hatch's.*

"The moms say Hatch is a real corporate shark and that he'll know how to turn Benedict into a giant in the industry."

Jessie shrugged. "I wouldn't be surprised. But I can't see being married to a shark, can you? Too many teeth."

Elizabeth giggled. "Just don't let him bite you."

"I'll try to avoid it."

"Jessie?"

"Yeah?

"What happens if you don't marry him?"

Jessie hesitated and then decided to lay it on the line. "Dad might sell the company when he retires. But my guess is that he'll never retire. He'll just continue to run it the way he has been for the past thirty years."

"Would that be so bad?"

Jessie chewed on her lower lip. "I don't think so, but everyone else seems to."

"Including Dad. You know, I think it would be kind of sad for him if you don't marry Hatch. Dad really wants Benedict Fasteners to grow, doesn't he? He's real excited about the idea."

"What is this? Are you going to lay a guilt trip on me too? I don't need anyone else pushing me into this marriage, Elizabeth."

"Sorry." Elizabeth was silent for a moment. "Do you think Hatch likes you? I mean, just you?"

"You mean me without the business attached?" Jessie thought about the kiss that had taken place in her kitchen last night. She remembered the sensation of banked fires and relentless self-control. "Maybe, Elizabeth. But with Hatch, business will always come first."

"He's started asking you out a lot these days, hasn't he? And he didn't have to go to lunch with us today. I think it was because he really wanted to be with you."

"Right now I'm a priority for Hatch. That means I'm the focus of a great deal of his attention. It wouldn't last five minutes after the wedding. Heck, we'd probably spend our honeymoon with a fax machine and a modem hooked up beside the bed so he could stay in touch with the office. Hey, don't you have soccer practice this afternoon?"

"Yep."

"I thought so. Don't forget to wear your sun-block cream."

"Geez, Jessie. I'm not a kid any longer. I won't forget."

"Sorry. What are you doing after soccer practice?"

"Jennifer and I are going to the mall to hang out with some friends."

"Alone?" Jessie asked sharply.

"No," Elizabeth said with elaborate patience. "I just told you, we're going to hang out with some friends. Jennifer's mother is going to drop us off and pick us up later."

"I don't think it's a good idea for a kid your age to be hanging out at the mall at night without an adult," Jessie said firmly.

Elizabeth giggled. "Mom and Lilian say you're overprotective."

Jessie sighed. "Maybe I am."

There was a slight pause before Elizabeth said, "Hey, Jessie?"

"Uh-huh?"

"You think Dad'll be too disappointed on Saturday if Eric Jerkface gets first place at the science fair?"

"Nope. He might be mad at the judges, because he knows how smart you are and he'll probably figure you got ripped off if you don't get first place. But he would never be disappointed in you, Elizabeth. No matter what happened. You know that, don't you?"

"Yeah, I guess so." Elizabeth relaxed. "Kind of hard on Dad, I guess, having to go through all this dumb school stuff a second time around. You and me being so far apart in age and all."

"Don't worry about it, kid," Jessie said grimly. "This is the *first* time around for him."

At five o'clock that afternoon Jessie opened the office door labeled "Dr. Glenna Ringstead, Ph.D., Clinical Psychology," and went into the softly lit waiting room. It was empty. Her aunt's secretary, a sober-looking woman with short graying hair, looked up and smiled in recognition.

"Hello, Jessie. Dr. Ringstead's just finishing up with her last patient of the day. Have a seat."

"Thanks, Laura."

The inner door opened at that moment and a woman in her late thirties emerged. She was wiping her tear-reddened eyes with a tissue. Jessie discreetly studied a print on the wall. Her aunt's waiting room always made her uneasy. The people one found in it always appeared so terribly depressed.

The patient went over to Laura and mumbled something about an appointment for the following week, paid her bill, and then left. Glenna Ringstead stepped out of her office a moment later.

Jessie's Aunt Glenna was Lilian Benedict's sister, but it

61

was easy to forget that fact. The two women were as different as night and day. In many ways Lilian was a lot closer to Vincent Benedict's other ex-wife than she was to her own sister.

Glenna had been married once. Lloyd Ringstead had been an accountant at Benedict Fasteners who had walked out on his wife and son years ago and never contacted them again. Jessie barely recalled her Uncle Lloyd. Her aunt had never remarried.

Glenna was an attractive woman in a severe sort of way. She was in her early fifties and she wore her silvered blond hair pinned in a no-nonsense coil that gave her the regal look of an Amazon queen. Her large black-framed glasses were something of a trademark. She had worn them for years. They went well with her trim, tailored beige suits and her air of grave authority.

"Hello, Jessie." Glenna smiled her cool, remote, professional smile. "Come on in and sit down. I assume you're not here to consult me in my professional capacity. You haven't asked for advice from me since the day I told you not to try so hard to force a relationship with your father."

"Let's see, that was when I was about fifteen years old, wasn't it? Right after Elizabeth was born." Jessie grinned cheerfully. "Don't take it personally, Aunt Glenna. I haven't taken advice from anyone else since."

"The entire family is well aware of that."

"I appreciate your taking some time to see me today. I won't keep you long, I promise." Jessie trailed after her aunt into the inner office and flopped down in a chair next to a table that held a massive box of tissues. She stuck her jeaned legs out in front of her and shoved her hands into her front pockets. Something about Glenna's depressing office triggered all her irreverent impulses.

"Don't worry about the time, Jessie."

"Thanks." Jessie glanced at the tissues sitting on the table next to her. "I guess your patients must go through a lot of these."

"Therapy can bring a lot of deep emotions to the surface," Glenna pointed out.

"Yeah, I'll bet. Mrs. Valentine keeps a big box on hand too. Amazing how clients in both of our lines of work tend to cry a lot." But at least Mrs. V's clients rarely left the office crying, Jessie thought silently.

"Speaking of your new line of work, how are things going at Valentine Consultations?" Glenna sat down behind the desk and folded her hands in front of her as if preparing to discuss a particularly troublesome form of neurosis.

"Terrific. I know how someone in your profession must feel about Mrs. Valentine, but I assure you, we're not stealing any business."

"I'm not worried about it. People who are going to a psychic are obviously not yet ready to deal with their real problems. I can wait."

"Because sooner or later they'll wind up in your office?"

Glenna nodded. "If they're serious about resolving their inner conflicts, yes. How did the date go last night?"

Jessie made a face. "Not you too, Aunt Glenna."

"That bad, is it? I suppose Lilian and Constance have already grilled you?"

"I'm afraid so. I'm trying to let everyone down easy."

Glenna studied her intently. "Then you're really not interested in Hatch?"

"Oh, sure, I'm *interested*. But I could never marry the man, Aunt Glenna. He's too much like Dad. Beating one's head against a stone wall is damn hard work. It's taken me years just to put a few dents in Dad. I'm not about to start all over again with another workaholic."

"Is that how you see Sam Hatchard?" Glenna asked seriously. "As a man who is too much like your father?"

"When it comes to his attitude toward work, yes. But that's not what I wanted to talk to you about."

"What did you want to talk about?"

"I need to know something about the psychology of cults."

"Cults? Religious cults?"

"Any kind of cult, I guess." Jessie recalled Susan Attwood's long, rambling letter to her mother. It had contained very little hard information, just a lot of grand promises to save the world. "The particular cult I'm interested in appears to be telling its followers that there's an environmental catastrophe on the way and the members are the only ones who have a shot at finding the secret to survival."

"The principle behind most cults is a belief that only the chosen few will be saved," Glenna mused. "The members see themselves as the only ones who are on the one true path. Everyone else will be damned. Jessie, for heaven's sake, tell me you haven't gone off the deep end this time. You're not seriously interested in joining a cult, are you?"

Jessie grinned. "Gone off the deep end? Is that technical jargon?"

Glenna sighed ruefully. "Hardly."

"Don't fret. I'm not about to join a cult. We all know I don't take orders well."

"That's true enough. And the people who tend to join cults are people who like clear-cut rules to follow. Rules make them feel safe. They are not required to think for themselves or to make decisions. You would be surprised at how many people will cheerfully give up those rights in exchange for rules. So what is this all about?"

"Actually, I see this as a major career move for me." Jessie hunched forward in her chair and began to tell her aunt about the new case.

Ten minutes later Glenna Ringstead leaned back, looking resigned. "I suppose it won't do any good to advise you to drop this so-called 'case'?"

"I can't, Aunt Glenna. This is my big chance."

"That's what you said a year ago when you joined Exotic Catering," Glenna reminded her.

Jessie flushed. "How was I to know it was really an escort

service? I thought I was actually going to learn how to run a gourmet catering operation. It could have been the opportunity of a lifetime."

"Oh, Jessie." Glenna shook her head.

"Look, Aunt Glenna, I'm really serious about this job. I like working with Mrs. Valentine. She feels I might have genuine talent or at least a healthy dose of intuition, which she says works just as well. I'd like to prove myself useful to the firm by helping her develop a larger clientele and expand her operations."

"Jessie, this is ridiculous. You can't go on hopping from one job to another for the rest of your life. Furthermore, your choice of careers is getting more and more bizarre."

"I've found my niche this time, Aunt Glenna. I'm sure of it."

"You're much too smart to believe in this psychic nonsense."

"I think Mrs. V really does have some psychic ability."

"Jessie, really."

"Maybe it's just intuition combined with a lot of common sense. Who knows? Whatever it is, she does have a certain talent, I'm sure of it. Aunt Glenna, I love this job. I want to make a go of it. What do you say? Will you give me a few pointers on the cult mentality?"

"I can't believe I'm letting you drag me into this. This is definitely outside my field of expertise, you know."

"Hey. You're the only shrink in the family. I'll take what I can get. Oh, before I forget, how's David doing? Has he heard from any of the grad schools he applied to yet?"

Glenna picked up a gold fountain pen and examined it closely. "He's been accepted into the Department of Philosophy at Parkington College. He got the word yesterday."

"He made it into Parkington? His first choice? Aunt Glenna, that's *terrific.*"

"It's certainly what he seems to think he wants more than anything else in the world, isn't it?"

Jessie nodded with great certainty. "It's the right thing for him, Aunt Glenna. I can feel it in my bones. David was made for the academic world."

"I hope you're right." Glenna carefully put the pen down on her desk, aligning it neatly with her clipboard. "I had rather thought for a while that he would eventually join Benedict Fasteners."

"That was never a viable option for David, and you must know that as well as I do."

"Vincent did try to encourage him."

"We all know Dad was desperate for a son, and for a while he thought he could ram David into the mold. But I saw right off it would never work and I told him to stop trying to force the issue. It was hopeless."

"David was certainly very grateful to you for getting him off the hook with his uncle. He's always been somewhat in awe of Vincent. I think he might have tried to make the situation at Benedict work out if you hadn't stepped in."

"Hey, rescuing him from Dad's clutches was the least I could do."

"Yes, you're definitely the little Miss Fix-It of the Benedict clan, aren't you? Everyone in the family turns to you when someone is needed to intercede with Vincent."

Jessie's smile faded. She eyed her aunt thoughtfully. "You know as well as I do that David would have hated the corporate world. He would have been especially unhappy working for my father. David has spent enough of his life trying to please Dad and he feels he's never succeeded. He deserves a chance to pursue his own goals."

"Only time will tell if you're right, won't it?"

Jessie's intercom rang at seven-thirty the following evening. She paused on the verge of tossing an entire pound of cheese ravioli into a pot of boiling water. With a groan she wiped her hands on a dish towel and went to answer the summons.

"It's me," Hatch announced over the speaker. He sounded bone-tired.

Jessie froze in front of the speaker. "What do you want?"

"Let me in and I'll tell you."

She frowned. "Have you been drinking, Hatch?"

"No. Working."

"Figures. What are you doing here?"

"I just left Benedict for the day. Haven't had dinner yet. What about you?"

"I was just about to eat."

"Good," said Hatch. "I'll join you."

Jessie could not think of a reasonable excuse not to open the downstairs door. Then again, she chided herself, maybe she was just not trying hard enough. Something in Hatch's weary voice was sparking a decidedly dangerous flare of womanly sympathy. She tried to squelch the sensation. The last thing she could afford to risk was to go all nurturing and empathic toward a shark like Hatch.

She punched the lock release, wondering if she was doing the right thing.

Three minutes later Jessie heard footsteps out in the hall. The apartment doorbell chimed. She answered it with a sense of reluctant anticipation.

Outside in the corridor she found Hatch leaning negligently against the wall, expensive suit jacket slung over one shoulder. He looked exhausted. His dark hair was tousled as if he had been running his fingers through it and his subdued gray-and-maroon-striped tie had been loosened with a careless hand. His eyes gleamed as he looked down at her.

"Seriously, Hatch," Jessie said, holding the door open cautiously, "what do you want?"

"Seriously, Jessie," he retorted, not moving away from the wall, "what I want is to find out what it would take to get you to send me flowers."

She blinked and groped swiftly for a way to hide her startled confusion. "Well, for starters, you could make yourself useful to Valentine Consultations."

"Yeah? How?"

"Tell me how to go about investigating a cult. I've been reading like crazy for the past day and a half, but I'm getting nowhere fast."

"Hell. Are you still on that stupid Attwood case? I was afraid of that."

"If that's the best you can do, good night." She started to close the door in his face.

"Follow the money," Hatch said wearily.

"What?"

"Follow the money trail. It takes money to finance something like a cult, just like any other business. Find out how the cash comes into the organization and where it goes. Once you know that, you'll know everything."

Jessie stared at him, astounded. "Hatch, that's *brilliant*. Absolutely brilliant. Why didn't I think of that? Come on in, pour yourself a drink, sit down, and make yourself at home. We have got to have a meaningful discussion."

Ignoring the flare of surprise in Hatch's eyes, she grabbed hold of the end of his boring tie and hauled him forcibly into the apartment.

Hatch did not put up much resistance.

CHAPTER FOUR

A hissing noise from the kitchen made Jessie release her grip on Hatch's tie. "Oh, my God, the boiling water." She whirled and rushed back into the kitchen.

Hatch followed more slowly.

"There's a bottle of wine on the counter," Jessie said over her shoulder as she picked up the package of ravioli. "Go ahead and open it. And then start talking."

"About what?" Hatch tossed his jacket down and picked up the wine.

"About following the money, of course."

"Were you planning to eat that entire package of ravioli all by yourself?" He went to work on the cork, his hands working in a smooth and controlled fashion.

"Yeah, but now that you're here, I'm feeling generous. I'll let you have some." She dumped the cheese ravioli into the boiling water. "I've got some sourdough bread and enough salad to fill in the gaps. Now, what about following the money?"

"If you're not a little more subtle, I'll get the impression you only invited me to stay for dinner because you're planning to use me." The cork came out of the bottle with a small, polite pop. "Where do you keep the glasses?"

"To the right of the sink." Jessie concentrated on gently stirring the boiling ravioli. The kitchen was suddenly feeling very warm. Hatch seemed to be taking up all the available space. Predictably, she could feel a wave of klutziness coming on. She reminded herself to be careful. "And you're right. I am using you. Start talking."

"Always nice to feel wanted. Mind if I sit down first?" Hatch took one of the counter stools without waiting for permission. "Damn, I'm really beat tonight. Hell of a day." He loosened his tie a little more and took a swallow of his wine.

Jessie risked a sidelong glance and realized he was telling the truth. Hatch had definitely had a long, hard day. She firmly suppressed the little flicker of guilt that immediately assailed her. "Your own fault, Hatch. You shouldn't spend so much time at the office. You're as bad as my—"

He cut her off with an upraised palm. "Don't say it. I'm not in the mood for another comparison between me and your father. You know, this is the first time I've had a chance to see your domestic side."

"Don't blink or you'll miss it."

"I'll keep that in mind. Still, there's something appealing about seeing you standing there at the stove."

"Is that the way you like your women? Chained to the kitchen?"

"I think I'll avoid that question. Aren't you going to ask me about my hard day at the office?"

She shot him a suspicious glance, uncertain, as usual, whether or not he was trying to joke with her. He looked perfectly serious sitting there, leaning against the counter. She decided to humor him. "Did you have a hard day at the office, Hatch?"

"Yeah."

"Must have been a real pain having to stop by here and put in some additional overtime working on the big courtship, hmmm?"

"You're determined to make this as difficult as possible, aren't you?"

"I'm trying to stop it before it gets going," Jessie said bluntly. "There's no future in it." She picked up her own glass of wine and took a sip. "For either of us. We'd frustrate, irritate, and generally annoy each other to death."

"You're wrong, Jessie. I think we have got a future. And I think we can learn to coexist, provided you make some effort. Be careful with that glass. It's going to fall off the counter if you don't watch out. I don't have the energy to go over there and rescue it."

She glanced down to see that she had set the wineglass right on the edge of the white tile. Cautiously she moved it to safety. "Whew. Another disaster narrowly averted. Let's hope I don't accidentally set fire to the apartment or something equally dramatic while you're here."

"I told your father that the fact that I make you nervous is a good sign."

"Is that right? I consider it a sure indicator that we weren't meant for each other." She picked up the pot of boiling ravioli and started to dump it into a colander that was sitting in the sink. Steam gushed upward toward the ceiling. Jessie yelped as she suddenly realized just how warm the handles of the pot had gotten. *"Damn."*

"Here. Let me take that." Hatch was there beside her, moving with surprising speed for a man who claimed to be exhausted. He deftly removed the pot from her fingers. "Why didn't you use hot pads?" He set the empty pan on the stove.

"I was in a hurry." Jessie held her fingers under a stream of cold water. "I got a little careless, that's all." *Because you have a way of turning me into a nervous wreck,* she fumed silently.

"You sound as if you're blaming me. It's not my fault you forgot the pads. You ought to stop and think before you pick up a hot pan, Jessie."

She lifted her eyes heavenward. "Lord help us, he's an authority on kitchen management too. Is there no end to this man's talents? Tell me about following the money, Hatch."

"After dinner. I'm tired and I want some food before you start grilling me."

"You're just stalling," she accused as she turned off the tap and started ladling out the small salad she had made earlier.

"Right, I'm stalling." Hatch sat down at the counter again and picked up his wine. "What's that stuff?"

"Pesto sauce. I made it myself."

"I'm in luck. You can cook."

"Look, Hatch . . ."

"After dinner, okay?" He smiled his faint, unreadable smile. "I give you my word I'll tell you what I can after I've had a chance to relax."

She frowned. "Promise?"

"Word of honor."

Jessie decided she would have to be satisfied with that much. She went to the cupboard to pull down two octagonal black china plates. "All right," she continued, determined to be conciliatory now that she was going to get what she wanted. "Just how bad was your day at the office?"

Hatch narrowed his gaze in surprise. "Bad enough. We've got trouble on a construction project down in Portland. Your father and I spent the afternoon getting briefed by the engineers and the on-site manager. On top of that, your father has decided that we have to bid on a job in Spokane simply because a company called Yorland and Young is also bidding on it. I've told him the job is too small for us and not worth the effort of undercutting Y and Y's bid."

"Dad sees Yorland and Young as a competitor."

72

"Yeah, well, it's not. Not any longer, at any rate. We're starting to play in a different ballpark. Vincent shouldn't be fooling around with a small contract bid like that one anyway. Your father's problem is that he gets too involved in the details and doesn't pay enough attention to the big picture. That's the main reason Benedict Fasteners is still small."

"I know." Jessie shrugged. "Dad built that company from the ground up. He can't stand letting go of all the details."

"He's going to have to get used to the idea. No point hiring other people to handle things if you don't let them do their jobs." Hatch rubbed the back of his neck as he surveyed the plate being set in front of him.

Jessie sat down across from him and forked up a large ravioli. "Dad's old-fashioned when it comes to management techniques. Just like he is about wanting to keep the firm in the family."

"You don't think the company should stay in the family?"

"I don't mind the idea. I just wish he wasn't leaving it to me. I wish he'd give equal chunks of it to my cousin, David, Elizabeth, and me when he retires. But Dad won't even listen to that idea."

Hatch narrowed his eyes. "You've tried to get him to divide up Benedict Fasteners among the three of you?"

"Oh, sure. Lots of times. A lost cause. He thinks it would lead to the ultimate destruction of the company."

"He could be right," Hatch said slowly. "None of you three has the foggiest idea of how to handle the firm, which means that, inevitably, you'd have to hire someone from outside, someone who would then get his fingers into the pie. And that could spell the beginning of the end."

"I agree that none of the three of us knows how to run Benedict," Jessie snapped. "So why leave it to me?"

"Because you'll do what's best for the company and the family, won't you?" Hatch murmured. "And you won't have to hire an outsider. You'll have me to run it for you."

"You don't want to just *run* it, though, do you, Hatch? You want to own a chunk of it."

"You're right. But in turn, I'm willing to let you adopt me into the clan."

"Adopt you?" Jessie put down her fork with a clatter. *"Adopt you?"*

"Figure of speech." Hatch took another sip of wine. His long, elegant fingers slid along the tapering stem of the glass as he set it back down on the counter. "You don't have to be afraid of what will happen once your father allows me to buy into Benedict, Jessie. I'll take care of you and the company. You have my word on it."

Jessie stared at him, unable to tear her glance away from the intensity in his topaz eyes. She could almost feel his hand gliding down the length of her spine. She shivered and wondered if Mrs. Valentine was right about her having some faint smidgen of untrained psychic awareness. The very air around her seemed to be vibrating with an almost palpable aura.

The downstairs door buzzer broke the spell. Jessie jumped and her elbow struck the fork she had just put down. The implement bounced off the counter and clattered onto the floor.

"Now see what you did?" Jessie glowered at Hatch as she leapt off the stool and went to answer the summons.

Hatch ignored the fallen fork.

"Who is it?" Jessie asked into the speaker.

"Jessie, it's me. David. Got some good news."

Jessie smiled. "I think I already know what it is. But come on up and tell me anyway." She pushed the button to let him into the building and turned her head to speak to Hatch over her shoulder. "It's my cousin, David. Aunt Glenna told me he's been accepted into graduate school. Parkington College, no less."

Hatch's brows rose. "Ah, yes. David, the philosopher-wimp."

Jessie rounded on Hatch furiously. "Don't you dare call

David a wimp. That's what Dad calls him and I will not tolerate it from either of you."

"Take it easy, Jessie. I only meant—"

"It makes me sick the way you wheeling-and-dealing corporate types look down so condescendingly on the academic world. As if your way of making a living was somehow superior and more manly than teaching and studying. I swear, Hatch, if you say one insulting word to David under my roof, I'll kick you right out the door, in spite of what you may or may not know about investigating cult finances. Do you hear me?"

"I hear you. The neighbors probably do too. For the record, I don't have anything against the academic world. When I called David a wimp I was referring to his habit of asking you to go to your father for financial assistance. I'll bet graduate school is going to cost a bundle. Naturally he's come straight to you. That's what everyone else in the family does, isn't it?"

Jessie glared at him, her cheeks burning because he was hitting close to home. "I'll have you know David hasn't asked me to go to Dad for more money." Mentally she crossed her fingers and prayed that was not the reason David had decided to visit her.

"He will." Hatch forked up another ravioli just as the doorbell chimed.

Jessie swung around on her heel and marched to the door. She threw it open to reveal her cousin, an intense young man of twenty-two.

Even if one did not know about David's aspirations to pursue an academic career, one could have guessed his future from his attire. He favored jeans, slouchy tweed jackets, and black shirts. He wore round tortoiseshell frames that enhanced his look of earnest, insightful intelligence, and his unkempt blond hair gave him an air of ivory-tower innocence. Glenna had always stressed to everyone else in the family that David was a very sensitive individual.

"Come on in, David. You know Hatch, don't you?"

"We've met." David nodded tentatively at Hatch, who inclined his head coolly in return.

Neither man made an effort to shake hands. Hatch did not even get off the stool. He went back to eating ravioli, looking faintly bored.

"Glass of wine, David?" Jessie offered quickly. "To celebrate?"

"Thanks." David accepted the glass and glanced around rather diffidently for a place to sit. "Sorry to bother you, Jessie. Didn't know you had company."

"That's all right. Hatch wasn't invited either." Jessie smiled serenely, her eyes sliding away from Hatch's mock ing gaze. "We were just talking business, weren't we, Hatch?"

"In a way," Hatch agreed.

"We were definitely discussing business," Jessie said tartly. "What else would you and I have been talking about?"

"I can think of a wide variety of subjects. But they'll keep."

David glanced quickly from Hatch's face to Jessie's. "Well, this is certainly interesting. I take it the Big Plan is on track?" He sat down on the stool next to Jessie's.

"What's the Big Plan?" Jessie asked as she resumed her seat.

David raised one shoulder in an eloquent manner. "You and Hatch get married and Benedict Fasteners grows into a Giant in the Industry and the whole clan lives happily ever after. Come on, Jessie. Everyone knows the Big Plan. It's all your mother, my mother, and Elizabeth's mother talk about these days. So how's it going? Is romance in bloom?"

"To be perfectly honest, we were at each other's throats before you walked in the door, weren't we, Hatch?" Jessie tore off a slice of sourdough bread.

Hatch's gaze rested briefly on her throat. "Not quite, but

it's a tantalizing thought." He turned toward David. "I hear you're going on to graduate school in philosophy."

David nodded, looking distinctly wary. "Parkington has one of the most respected philosophy departments in the nation. It was one of the first to offer a doctorate in the philosophy of science and technology in Western civilization."

"That's your field of interest?

"Yes, as a matter of fact it is." There was a defiant note in David's tone now. "Modern science and technology is in the process of changing our world in fundamental ways. It could easily be destroying us. Just look at the depletion of the ozone layer and the effects of acid rain. Most of our thinking on the subject is straight out of the late eighteenth and early nineteenth centuries, the age of the machine. That kind of outmoded thinking has to change because we desperately need new perspectives on man and nature. That's the task of philosophy."

"And you think you can change our outmoded thinking?" Hatch asked.

"Well, maybe not yours," David admitted sarcastically. "But I have hopes for other people, like Jessie."

Sensing disaster, Jessie rushed in to divert the conversation. "David, I was absolutely thrilled when Aunt Glenna told me you'd been accepted at Parkington. I'm so pleased for you."

"Parkington's one of those fancy private colleges back East someplace, isn't it?" Hatch picked up a chunk of bread, took a bite that showed his strong white teeth, and leaned his elbows on the counter as he chewed. "Expensive."

"Well, yes, as a matter of fact." David shot an uncertain glance at Jessie, as if asking for guidance.

"David," she said firmly, "tell me something. Do you know anything about a group that calls itself DEL? It stands for Dawn's Early Light. Some sort of environmental extremist group, I think. They supposedly recruited some students from Butterfield College. Did you ever see any of them on campus?"

"DEL?" David looked thoughtful, an expression he did very well. "Yeah, I think I did hear something about it a few months ago. Led by a so-called climatologist, I think. I didn't pay too much attention. They held a couple of small group lectures and talked to some people, but they didn't hang around long. We get that kind of thing all the time around a college campus. Why?"

"I'm looking for a student at Butterfield who apparently joined DEL. Her name is Susan Attwood. Know her?"

"No. What year?"

"Sophomore, I believe."

David shook his head again. "Haven't run into her."

Jessie sighed. "I suppose it was too much to hope that you might have known her."

"There are a few thousand students at Butterfield," David pointed out. "Why are you looking for this Susan Attwood?"

"Jessie's pursuing a new career option," Hatch said. "Psychic cult-buster."

"What?" David wrinkled his intelligent brow. "Is this some sort of joke?"

"Got it first try," Hatch told him. "It's a joke. Unfortunately, Jessie's taking it seriously. No sense of humor, our Jessie."

Jessie shot Hatch an annoyed glance. "Ignore him, David. This is a serious matter. I'm trying to research DEL for a client of Mrs. Valentine's whose daughter ran off and joined the cult."

"What are you supposed to do? Get her back?"

"If possible. The client believes this Edwin Bright person has hypnotized her daughter and others somehow. She assumes he's claiming some psychic ability to forecast disaster. She wants Valentine Consultations to prove the guy is a phony."

"Sounds a little out of your line, Jessie," David remarked, helping himself to a chunk of the sourdough.

"Very observant of you," Hatch said approvingly. He was apparently surprised by such a show of intelligence. "It's way out of her line."

"Stop it, both of you," Jessie ordered. She leaned forward and folded her arms on the counter. "David, could you do me a favor and see what you can find out about DEL's activities on campus? What I'd really like is an address. There's nothing in the local-area phone books and I couldn't find anything at all in the newspaper indexes. Your mother gave me some books to read on cults in general, but I need specific information on this one."

"Well, I suppose I could ask around and see if anyone knows someone who talked to the DEL people when they were on campus. But I'm not so sure this is a good idea, Jessie."

"It's not," Hatch agreed.

"Sounds more like a job for a real private investigator," David said.

"It is," Hatch said.

"Pay no attention to him, David," Jessie instructed. "He and Dad are being extremely tiresome and depressingly downbeat about my new career. Only to be expected, I suppose. The corporate mentality, you know."

"Uh-huh. I know. Very narrow thinkers."

"How true." Jessie stifled a smile and ignored the impatient glance Hatch gave her. "Will you give me a hand, David?"

David smiled. "Sure. I'll see what I can do. But don't count on much, all right? Most of the people I know don't get involved with cults and related crap."

"Anything at all would be useful."

"All right." David glanced at his watch. "I'd better be on my way. I only stopped by to give you the good news, but since you already know it, I might as well leave you two alone." He got to his feet and flashed a quick glance at Hatch, who was finishing the last of his ravioli. "Uh, Jessie?"

"Yes?"

"Would you mind walking downstairs with me? I wanted to talk to you in private for a minute if that's okay."

"Sure." Jessie got down off the stool.

Hatch gave David a hard look. "Why don't you ask him yourself, instead of using Jessie as an intermediary?"

David flushed. "I don't understand." His glance flickered to Jessie.

"Ignore him, David. It's all one can do. I'll go downstairs with you." She hurried toward the door, chatting excitedly about Parkington in an effort to cover the awkward moment.

David was silent as they started down the stairs. "He's right, you know," he finally said on a long, drawn-out sigh.

"Who?"

"Hatchard. I did want to ask if you'd feel out the old man for me on the subject of a loan. Think he'll spring for another one? He's already made it pretty damn clear what he thinks about my going for a doctorate. Hell, he gave me a bad-enough time when he found out I'd changed my undergraduate major from business administration to philosophy."

Jessie nodded sympathetically. "I know. I'll talk to him, David. I can't promise anything."

"I realize that. But he listens to you more than he does to anyone else in the family. You're the only one who seems to be able to beard the lion in his den with any real success."

"Probably because I just keep pounding on him until his resistance is finally worn down. It's very wearing, you know. On me, I mean. I get so tired of it."

"Why bother to do it?" David asked reasonably.

"In the beginning, when I was much younger, I think I started doing it just to get some attention for myself. Later, in my teenage years, I was naive enough to think I could actually change him, make him *want* to pay more attention to his family."

"Mom says that kind of change is virtually impossible."

"She may be right. All I know is that after Elizabeth came along I got very angry at Dad. It infuriated me to see him ignoring her the same way he had always tried to ignore you and me. So I became even more aggressive about getting him to play the part of a father."

"You've had some success in terms of Elizabeth. You know, Uncle Vincent's a lot more aware of what's going on in her life than he ever was with either one of us."

"Only because I've learned a few tricks. I've formed a conspiracy with Grace, his secretary. She helps me get things onto his calendar. I nag him. I plead with him. I yell at him. And at best I've got maybe a fifty-fifty success rate. He still calls half the time at the last minute to tell me he can't make a school function because he's got a crisis at the office."

"I'll bet." David shoved his hands into his jacket pockets. "But at least he's always been around, hasn't he? He didn't just disappear the way my old man did."

"Oh, David, I know. I'm sorry for whining like this."

As always when the subject of David's father came up, Jessie was consumed with sympathy and guilt. Her cousin was right. At least Vincent Benedict had stuck around to be nagged and harangued by his elder daughter. Lloyd Ringstead had vanished, never to be seen or heard from again. David had been only four.

"Forget it. Nothing more boring than old family history."

"I suppose," Jessie agreed. "But I'll say this much for Dad. He does have some sense of what you might call patriarchal obligation. At least when it comes to money."

"Only because it's a means of controlling the rest of us," David said bitterly. "He likes being in control."

"I know that's part of it. Still, look on the bright side. I think he'll probably come through with another loan for you." Jessie smiled and stood on tiptoe to give David a quick hug. "Don't worry. I'll talk to him."

"Hatchard is right. I guess I shouldn't ask you to do it. You already did enough when you convinced Uncle Vincent I was never going to be the heir apparent to Benedict Fasteners." David gave her a rueful smile. "You know, without your help I'd probably still be there busting my ass trying to please the old man. Even Mom wanted me to try harder."

"You'd have been very unhappy spending the rest of your life running Benedict Fasteners. Anybody can see that."

"Not anybody. You were the one who realized it first. Thank God for Sam Hatchard. Without him Uncle Vincent would probably be trying to mold you or Elizabeth into a corporate shark."

"I'm not sure God is the one who deserves the credit for giving us Sam Hatchard."

David grinned as he opened the lobby door. "You may be right. He's not what you'd call real angelic, is he? Don't worry, Jessie, you can handle him. My money's definitely riding on you."

"Dammit, David, this isn't some kind of sporting event," Jessie called out after him as he went through the doorway and out into the night.

But it was too late. Her cousin was already halfway down the path to the sidewalk. He lifted a hand in farewell but did not look back.

Jessie stood on the other side of the heavy glass door and stared bleakly out into the darkness for a few minutes. Then she turned and walked slowly back upstairs. She wondered how difficult it was going to be to wheedle the information she wanted out of Hatch and then get him out of her apartment. Something told her it was not going to be an easy task.

She was right. She knew she was in trouble the minute she

opened the door and saw him sprawled on the couch, sound asleep. He had not even bothered to take off his beautifully polished wing tips.

Jessie slowly closed the door and leaned back against it. If she had any sense, she told herself, she would wake him up and hustle him out the door.

She definitely should not allow him to spend the night there on the couch. It would set a dreadfully bad precedent. A man like Hatch would use that sort of precedent to his own advantage, no doubt about it. One thing always led to another. Come tomorrow morning, she would have to give him breakfast.

Too dangerous by far. When all was said and done, there would be no way of getting around the fact that he had made himself very much at home in her apartment.

Jessie moved cautiously away from the door, considering the best method of awakening him. She came to a halt beside the couch and stood looking down at Hatch for a long while. The strength and willpower that were so much a part of him did not appear the least bit diminished by sleep. By rights he should have looked a little vulnerable, but he did not.

Jessie wondered if sharks actually slept.

There was no denying the fact that Hatch did appear exhausted. The man worked much too hard. Fourteen-hour days plus courtship time on the side.

She studied the strong, tapering fingers of one supple masculine hand as it lay on the black leather cushion. Everything that compelled her and repelled her about Hatch was embodied in his graceful, dangerous, powerful hands.

With a small sigh, Jessie turned away and went to the closet to get a blanket. She was going to regret letting him stay. She just knew it. But she could not bring herself to awaken him from his exhausted slumber.

She pried off the heavy wing tips and spread the blanket over Hatch's sleeping frame.

When she had finished, she went into the kitchen and put

the dishes into the sink. Then she placed the empty wine bottle in the recycling bin Elizabeth had given her and headed for the bedroom.

Several hours later Jessie came awake on a rush of adrenaline. She sat bolt upright in bed, confused by two powerful stimuli. The phone on the bedside table was warbling loudly and there was a half-naked man standing in the open doorway of her bedroom. She did not know which had awakened her.

For a handful of seconds she could not move. She could only sit there clutching the sheet.

The phone rang again.

"Better get that," Hatch advised, one hand braced against the door frame.

Jessie blinked and reached out for the phone.

"Jessie? It's Alex. Alex Robin. I'm calling from your office. Sorry to wake you, but you might want to come on over here. I went out to get something to eat a while ago and when I got back I came upstairs to use the rest room. I found the door to Valentine Consultations open. Did you leave it unlocked?"

"No." Jessie pushed hair out of her eyes and tried to think. "No, I'm certain I locked up when I left, Alex. I'm always very careful about that."

"I know. Listen, I think someone's been inside here, but I can't be certain. Maybe you'd better check to see if anything's missing. You may want to call the cops and report a break-in. If that's what's happened." Alex paused. "Nothing's broken or anything, as far as I can tell."

"I'll be right over, Alex. Thanks."

Jessie slowly replaced the phone, her eyes on Hatch's shadowed face. She realized he was wearing only a pair of briefs. Sometime during the night he had awakened and undressed. Talk about making himself at home, she thought. Give the man an inch and he took a mile.

"I have to go over to the office. Alex, the downstairs

tenant, thinks someone might have broken in to Valentine Consultations." Jessie pushed back the covers, belatedly realizing her nightgown was hiked up around her waist. Hastily she retreated back under the sheet. "Do you mind?" she asked acidly.

"No." Hatch yawned and ran his fingers through his tousled hair. "I'll go with you. I had no idea the life of an assistant fortune-teller was so exciting. You keep worse hours than I do, Jessie."

CHAPTER FIVE

It's damn near three o'clock in the morning," Hatch muttered as he slipped the Mercedes into a space in front of the building that housed Valentine Consultations.

He was not pleased about having his first night in Jessie's apartment interrupted in this fashion. Granted, he had not been in her bed, but when he had awakened earlier and discovered he had been allowed to stay, he had known progress was finally being made. "What the hell was this Alex guy doing at the office at this hour?"

"He's a computer jockey," Jessie explained as she yanked the door handle. "He works weird hours." She jumped out of the car and dashed toward the darkened entrance of the building, fishing for her keys.

"Hold it, Jessie." Hatch got out and slammed his own car door before following her up the walk. The lady was far too impulsive. He would have to work on curbing that tendency. "Not so fast."

"Oh, for heaven's sake, Hatch. I let you come along because you insisted, but don't get the idea you're in charge around here. Save the dynamic-leadership act for Benedict Fasteners." She started to shove the key into the lock and belatedly realized the door was already open.

Before she could turn the handle, Hatch shot out a hand and clamped it over hers. The small bones of her fingers and wrist felt astonishingly delicate. "I said, not so fast," he repeated very quietly.

She glanced down at where his hand covered hers. He knew she was silently debating whether or not to test his strength. Her eyes lifted briefly to meet his, and he saw the annoyance in them. She had obviously realized she did not stand a chance of shaking off his grip.

"For Pete's sake, Hatch. The door is already unlocked. Alex must have left it that way for us."

"Fine. I'll go in first." Without waiting for a response, Hatch calmly shouldered Jessie aside and shoved open the door. He stepped over the threshold into the darkened hall and stopped, groping along the wall. He found the switch and flicked it. Nothing happened.

"What is it? What's wrong?" Jessie was trying her best to peer around him.

"The hall light is out." *A bad sign.* His instinct warned him the smartest thing to do at this point was back out of the place.

"It's been out for ages." Jessie tried impatiently to shove past Hatch's unyielding form. He did not move.

"Alex," she called over Hatch's shoulder. "Alex, are you in there? Is everything all right?"

A low groan from off to the right inside the hall was the only answer.

"Alex." Jessie panicked now, shoving furiously at Hatch. "Get out of my way, Hatch. He's hurt."

"Damn." Hatch moved slowly into the darkened interior as his eyes adjusted to the deep gloom. "I should have gone back for the flashlight."

"There's a light switch just inside his office door. I'll get it."

Quick as a cat, she darted around him the instant he ceased blocking the doorway. "Jessie, come back here."

But she was already racing for the door of the office, which was just barely visible in the shadows. A flash of anger and alarm galvanized Hatch. Jessie was not just impulsive, she clearly lacked even an iota of common sense.

He moved forward to jerk her back, but he did not have to bother halting her mad dash for the dark office. Before he could grab her, she gasped, yelped, and promptly tripped over a man's prone form lying in the middle of the hall.

"Alex."

The man on the floor groaned again and struggled to sit up. "Jessie? Is that you?"

Hatch watched as Jessie crouched beside Alex. Then he frowned as he tried to discern the outlines of whatever was housed in the darkness of the office beyond the doorway. There was no sound from within the room, but the hair on the back of his neck was stirring.

"Dear heaven." Jessie was fussing over the figure on the floor. "What on earth happened? Alex, you mustn't move until we see how badly you're injured."

"I'm okay, I think. Just got banged on the head. Didn't completely lose consciousness. Hurts like hell, though. Who did you bring with you?"

"The name's Hatchard." The sense of uneasiness grew. Restlessly Hatch stepped around Alex's feet and moved into the doorway of the office.

"The light switch is on the right," Jessie said.

The rush of thudding footsteps, however, came from the left. A body hurtled forward toward the door. Hatch had a fleeting impression of a slight, wiry form covered from head to toe in black. Something metallic glinted in the upraised fist.

"Shit." It had been years since Hatch had last confronted a man who was wielding a knife. He still remembered the occasion with great clarity. The memorable event had taken place, as such events often do, in the alley behind a tavern that catered to truckers and cowboys.

He'd thought those days of barroom brawls and dirty alley fights were behind him. Hell, he was supposed to be white-collar now, he reminded himself. He had the silk ties and handmade shirts to prove it.

After all the years that had passed since his last brawl, Hatch was vaguely surprised to find that his reactions were automatic. He feinted to the side and lashed out with his foot, catching his assailant on the leg as he went past. The blow was off-center but it was powerful enough to destroy the man's balance.

The knife glinted evilly as the attacker whipped around, struggling to regain his feet.

"Outta my way, you fucking bastard." The voice was high-pitched and raw with desperation. It was also muffled by the black cloth of a stocking mask. "Get outta my way. *I'll cut your fucking throat for you.*"

"Oh, my God, *Hatch.*" Jessie's horrified shriek filled the darkness.

Hatch followed up on the small advantage he had created by getting his attacker off-balance. He snapped out another kick and slashed at the knife arm with the edge of his hand. The blade fell from numbed gloved fingers and clattered to the floor.

There was a sharp, shrill gasp and another vicious curse. Then the assailant turned and fled through the hall, nearly colliding with Jessie. The running man leapt over Alex's prone form and vanished out the door into the night.

"Hatch, are you all right?"

"I'm okay, Jessie." A primitive surge of anger flared in Hatch as he realized his quarry was escaping. He ran out into the hall and got as far as the outer door before he realized it was hopeless.

Frustrated, he stood on the front step of the building, restlessly searching the shadows of the dark street. There was no sign of anyone, no sound of running footsteps. Nothing.

The light in Alex's office snapped on behind Hatch. Reluctantly he turned to see that Jessie was on her feet, staring at him with eyes made huge by concern.

"Are you sure you're all right?"

"Yes."

"There's a knife in here."

"He didn't get a chance to use it. I'm okay, Jessie."

"You're sure?"

"Dammit, I'm *sure*." Hatch heard the frustrated fury in his own voice. He made a grab for his self-control and his temper. It was not an easy task. It occurred to him that he was dealing not only with the adrenaline of the short-lived battle but also with a fierce anger that was focused one hundred percent on Jessie.

Apparently the little idiot did not yet realize that if it had not been for Alex lying there on the floor, she would have dashed straight into the office and wound up being the one confronting the bastard with the knife in his hand. Hatch longed to point that out to her in an extremely blunt fashion, but told himself that now was not the time.

"What about you, Alex?" he said to the injured man.

"I'm okay too. I think. Like I said, I didn't completely lose consciousness. I've just been dazed for the past few minutes."

"I assume you're the one who called Jessie?"

"Yeah. Sorry about that." Alex found a pair of horn-rimmed glasses beside his leg and put them on. They sat somewhat crookedly on his nose. Then he gingerly touched his head. "Didn't realize anyone was still around or I would have called the cops first. I wasn't even sure there had been a break-in. Nothing seemed disturbed upstairs. Thought maybe Jessie had just left the door unlocked." He gave Hatch a questioning look. "Guess we'd better call the police now, though, huh?"

"Yes," said Hatch. "I think that would be a very logical

next step. Although I doubt there's much they'll be able to do."

Jessie swung around, clearly startled. "What do you mean? There's been a break-in and an act of violence."

Hatch gave her a pitying glance. "Jessie, get real. It happens all the time in the big city."

She frowned. "Yes, well, it's never happened to me."

"You just got lucky. Where's the phone?"

"Over on the desk near Alex's computer." She tipped her head slightly to the side. "Hatch, are you angry?"

"What the hell gave you that idea?"

Three hours later Hatch opened Jessie's refrigerator door and rummaged around inside until he found the skim milk. He closed the door and started opening cupboards until he located a box of cereal. Then he started searching for bowls and spoons.

He was putting breakfast together on his own because Jessie, who had recently emerged from the shower wearing a pair of snug-fitting black leggings and a voluminous orange sweater that fell below her hips, was not much help at the moment. She was still chattering away excitedly about the break-in. It was obvious she was viewing the whole thing as a grand adventure.

Hatch realized he was still seething. Every time he thought about what had nearly happened earlier, his gut went cold. As furious as he was, he was also vividly aware of the fact that he would have liked nothing better in that moment than to haul Jessie over to the couch and make concentrated, determined love to her.

He had wanted Jessie for some time, but never so intensely as he wanted her right now. It was the aftermath of the fight, he told himself. Rampaging hormones or something.

But deep down he knew it was because some primitive part of him actually thought that if he claimed her physically he might be able to control her in other ways. Control her so that next time she would follow orders in a crisis. Control her so that he could keep her safe.

Follow orders? Jessie Benedict? Who was he kidding?

She was sitting at the counter, blithely unaware of his precarious mood. She pushed a thick curve of witchy black hair back behind one ear and her jeweled eyes gleamed with excitement. "I suppose the cops were right," she allowed. "The guy broke into the building and started going through the upstairs offices first. When he didn't find anything valuable, he went back downstairs and discovered Alex's computer equipment." Jessie drummed her fingers on the countertop. "But I don't like it."

"Nobody *liked* it, Jessie."

"I mean, something doesn't feel right about it. I think I'll go visit Mrs. Valentine today and see what she thinks. She might have some insights into this thing."

"Jessie," Hatch said wearily, "you're not going to try to tie this break-in to your DEL case, or something equally stupid, are you?"

"Why not? I don't care what the cops said. The whole thing is very suspicious. The guy did go through the offices of Valentine Consultations first."

"The cops also said guys like that tend to go through a place in a methodical fashion. Makes sense to start upstairs and work down. Use some logic here, instead of drama, Jessie. What could he have been searching for in Valentine Consultations? You haven't discovered anything incriminating about DEL yet, and you're not likely to do so. The DEL crowd probably knows that better than anybody."

"Maybe."

He considered the stubborn, mutinous set of her mouth out of the corner of his eye as he poured milk over the cereal. "You're trying to overdramatize your Big Case, Jessie. Forget it. Waste of time."

"Oh, yeah?"

"Yes." He sat down across from her and reached for the

coffeepot. "Eat your breakfast like a good girl and then you can send me off to the office with a wifely little kiss."

Jessie scowled ferociously. "Don't get any ideas just because I let you spend the night on my couch."

"I'll keep that in mind." Hatch dug into his cereal. He was actually getting a lot of ideas, but he figured he could wait to tell her about them.

Negotiating with Jessie was a tricky business, and he had no intention of giving away too much information in advance. He waited for her to lecture him further, but when she spoke again, she surprised him with her question.

"What did you do to that jerk in Alex's office, Hatch?"

"Took out my frustrations on him."

"I mean, seriously, what did you use on him? Karate or something?"

"Nothing that fancy. Just some old-fashioned alley-fighting techniques."

"Where did you learn them?"

"In an old-fashioned alley. Look, could we change the subject? I had what is frequently referred to as a misspent youth. I'd prefer to forget it."

"Whatever you say. Still, I'm glad it was you who went into that office instead of me."

"Which brings up an interesting point," Hatch said, deciding to seize the opportunity. "The only reason you didn't go charging into that office first was that you conveniently happened to stumble over Alex. I warned you not to rush blindly into that place."

"We all know I don't take orders well, Hatch. Want some more coffee?"

"Quit trying to change the subject. You're walking on thin ice, lady. I am not in a good mood this morning."

"Oh, my. Are you going to yell at me?" She fixed him with an expression of great interest, as if waiting for a show to begin.

"I've resisted this long, I think I can manage to hold back

what would seem to be a very natural urge under the circumstances. But I wouldn't advise you to push me."

"Veiled threats. How exciting. I've never seen you quite like this, Hatch. It's a whole new you. I'll bet you're only holding back because you don't want to lose any of the territory you think you gained last night by conveniently falling asleep on my couch."

"Is that right?"

"I know exactly how your mind works, Hatch. You've weighed the pros and cons of losing your temper with me and decided that it's in your own best interests not to yell at this rather delicate stage of the game."

"You think you know me very well, don't you?"

"Well enough to know how you think." She took a swallow of coffee and wrinkled her nose. "But I'll admit I didn't realize you'd make coffee like this. It tastes like pure, refried, undiluted grounds." She tried another tentative sip. "With perhaps just a hint of old tires thrown in for body."

"I grew up on a cattle ranch. Nobody drinks weak coffee on a ranch."

A wary spark of interest lit her eyes. "You grew up on a ranch? Where was it?"

"Oregon."

"Do your folks still live there?"

"No." He wished he had kept his mouth shut, but one look at her expression told him it was too late to close the subject. She was curious. A curious Jessie Benedict was a dangerous Jessie Benedict.

On the other hand, it was gratifying to have her exhibit some real interest in him.

"Where are your parents living now?"

Hatch sighed. "When I was five my mother decided she couldn't take ranch life any longer. Or maybe it was my old man she couldn't take. Whatever, she filed for divorce and left. Went back East and married some guy who worked for an insurance firm."

Jessie's brows came together in a swift frown. "What about you?"

Hatch shrugged. "I stayed on the ranch with Dad until I was sixteen and then I left."

"You went off to college early?"

"No. I just left home early. Dad and I were not what you'd call a real father-and-son team. We didn't get along." Hatch shoved aside the memories of the weak, whining, bitterly angry man who had raised him. "Not that I was a model son, you understand. I was in trouble from the time I was nine years old. At any rate, when I left home, I lied about my age and found work on a ranch in California. Dad died in a car accident two years later."

"Then what happened?" She was riveted now.

"I went back to Oregon, sold the ranch, and used the money to pay off the bank. The place was buried in debt. My father was not much of a businessman. Hell, he wasn't much of anything. After he died I told myself I was going to prove him wrong."

"About what?"

Hatch studied his thick, dark coffee. "He had a habit of telling me I was never going to amount to anything."

"Well, he was certainly wrong about that, wasn't he?" Jessie's eyes flickered briefly to the gold-and-steel watch on his left wrist.

Hatch smiled grimly. "I guess you could say that everything I am today I owe to my old man."

"What about your mother? Is she still alive?

"Yes."

Jessie chewed thoughtfully on her lower lip. "Ever see her?"

"Not much." Hatch swallowed another bite of cereal. "I call her every Christmas."

"That's not very often, Hatch."

Her reproachful eyes refueled his irritation. "For God's sake, Jessie, let the subject drop, will you? It's none of your

95

business, but the fact is, she's no more interested in hearing from me than I am in hearing from her. She built a whole new life for herself back East. She's got two more sons, both lawyers, and a man who makes her a lot happier than Dad ever did."

"But what about you?"

"I haven't been real fond of her since she walked out and left me alone with that sonofabitch she married the first time around." Hatch shrugged.

"She should have taken you with her."

"Yeah, well, she didn't. I probably reminded her too much of my old man. Jessie, I do not want to discuss this any further. Is that clear?"

"Yes."

Hatch took a deep breath and made another grab for his self-control. His past was not one of his favorite topics. He glanced at his watch. "I'd better get moving. Got an early-morning meeting with the site manager on the Portland project." He stood up, automatically checking his pockets for keys and wallet. "See you this evening. I'll probably be home around seven-thirty or eight."

"Home? Are you talking about here?"

"Right."

"Now, wait just a minute, Hatch. I've got plans for today. Maybe for tonight too. You can't just move in on me."

"Sorry, Jessie. I'm in a rush. Haven't got time to argue." He took one stride that brought him around the end of the counter, kissed her lightly on the forehead before she could protest, and then headed for the door.

"Dammit, Hatch. Just because you spent last night here does not mean you're going to make a habit of it. Do you hear me?" She was on her feet, coming after him.

"We'll talk about it later, Jessie."

"Oh, yeah? Well, I've got news for you. I don't serve dinner after eight o'clock at night. If you come here that late, don't expect to get fed."

"I'll bear that in mind." He gently closed the door behind him, cutting her off in mid-tirade.

He paused a moment, smiling a little as he heard her slam the dead bolt home. Then he went down the stairs feeling reasonably satisfied. Small battles won here and there led to major victories.

At least he was now fairly certain he finally had her full attention.

Jessie might not want to admit it, but the fact that he had spent the night on her couch was a turning point in their relationship. It added a whole new layer of intimacy to things. The very fact that she had not awakened him and kicked him out last night said a lot. Probably a lot more than she wanted to acknowledge.

Sharing the adventure of the break-in at three o'clock this morning was another binding clause, however unplanned, in the contract he was forging.

All in all, Hatch decided as he walked outside and got into the Mercedes, the business of courting Jessie Benedict was finally starting to come on-line. He sensed success in the offing.

This was one merger he was definitely looking forward to consummating.

Jessie studied the notes she had made on the pad in front of her as she listened over the phone to David rattling off the information he had managed to dig up at Butterfield College.

"Good luck with that name I gave you. It's not much, but it's all I think I'll find," he said. "Frankly, most of the students here on campus weren't particularly interested in dedicating themselves to the cause of the DEL Foundation. The DEL people were basically viewed as loonies."

"Hardly surprising. Anything on Dr. Edwin Bright himself?"

"Just that the 'doctor' in front of his name is a little

suspect. Probably one of those mail-order degrees. No one seemed to know what field it was in."

"Hah. Definitely a con man. Thanks a million for the help, David." As she hung up the phone, Jessie stared at the name she'd written on the pad: Nadine Willard. She actually had a place to start. A clue. She was beginning to feel like a real live investigator.

Nadine Willard worked at an espresso café across the street from the front entrance of Butterfield College. She proved to be a thin, rather washed-out-looking young woman with pale, wary eyes, pale, lanky hair, and bad skin. But she was willing to talk if Jessie would wait until she took her break.

Jessie killed the time by ordering a cup of dark-roasted coffee and after the first sip, immediately wished she'd abstained. Her nerves promptly went into overdrive. One cup of Hatch's brew was apparently enough to last a person all day. No wonder the man was able to work fourteen-hour days.

Jessie sat fiddling with the unfinished coffee and idly studied the mix of campus types seated around her while she contemplated Mrs. Valentine's reaction to the news of the break-in. It had been, to be perfectly truthful, rather disappointing.

"Oh, dear," Mrs. V had said, looking alarmed. "I do hope that nice Alex Robin was not badly hurt."

"He's fine, Mrs. V. Back at work already," Jessie had assured her. She had realized then that Mrs. Valentine had had no enlightening psychic revelations regarding the incident and decided not to mention the remote possibility that it could have been related to the DEL case. No point upsetting the woman. A good assistant shielded one's boss from the petty little day-to-day annoyances of the job.

Jessie was getting bored enough to risk another sip of the dark-roasted coffee when she saw Nadine Willard finally coming toward her.

"Okay, I guess I can talk to you now." Nadine sat down

across from Jessie. "You wanted to know about Susan Attwood?"

"That's right. Her mother is very concerned about her going off to join DEL. Did you know Susan well?"

"No, not really. I don't think anyone did. Susan was not what you'd call real friendly. One of those computer nerds, you know? Kept to herself. She and I had a class together during the winter quarter. When DEL first showed up on campus, I went to one of the evening lectures and Susan was there. We talked a little about the whole thing afterward."

"Were you interested in joining DEL?"

Nadine shook her head. "Nah. Just curious for a while. You know. I mean, everyone knows the environment's in trouble and all, but what can you do? Susan was fascinated right from the start, though. She tried to talk me into going with her when she accepted the invitation."

"What invitation? To join the group?"

"No. It was like a tour of the DEL facilities, you know. She went out to the island and was so impressed she decided to stay and go to work for the foundation."

"Island? What island?" Jessie was getting excited now. She told herself to calm down. She had to take things step by step and make notes. Investigators always took notes. Hastily she whipped out her pad of paper and a pen.

"The DEL Foundation owns an island in the San Juans."

"A whole island?"

"Sure. It's not that big a deal, you know. There are other privately owned islands out there, I guess. At any rate, you have to have a special invitation to go ashore and see the facilities."

"Where does one get an invitation to take the tour?" Jessie asked, tapping the pen restlessly against the table.

"At a DEL lecture, I guess. But there hasn't been one around this campus for weeks now. Maybe they've been recruiting on one of the other campuses in the area." Nadine shrugged her thin, wiry shoulders.

"Damn. I don't suppose you have any brochures or

handouts left over from the lecture you attended, do you? Something with a phone number or an address on it?"

"I doubt it. I wasn't interested, so I didn't keep most of it."

"Damn," Jessie said again. "Sorry."

Nadine paused. "You can have my invitation if you want it. I'll never use it."

"What?" Jessie dropped her pen in astonishment. "You got one?"

"Sure. We all did. I kept it because Susan suggested I hang on to it, just in case I changed my mind, you know."

"Is the invitation transferable? Can anyone use it?" Jessie was having a hard time containing herself now.

Nadine frowned. "I don't see why not. There's nothing on it that identifies me. I think it just says something about the bearer and a friend being welcome to tour the facilities. There's a charge, though. A stiff one. Two hundred dollars apiece. You can write it off as a donation to the foundation, I think."

"Two hundred dollars? Apiece?" Jessie was shocked. "That's a lot of money for a tour."

"Yeah. It's one of the reasons I didn't go. Susan said they stipulate a high donation in order to discourage curiosity seekers."

Jessie made her decision. "Nadine, I will gladly pay you for the invitation." She reached for her purse and yanked it open. "How much do you want for it?"

Nadine thought about it. "I dunno. Maybe twenty bucks?"

"I'll give you fifty," Jessie said, feeling extremely magnanimous. She would put it on the expense account, she told herself. She was not so sure that account would run to the two hundred she would need to take the DEL tour. She would have to approve it with the client. But she was almost certain Mrs. Attwood would want her to go to the island.

* * * *

The invitation, which was inscribed "Admit bearer and one friend," was safely tucked into Jessie's purse an hour later when she returned to the office. She was feeling inordinately pleased with herself until she saw Constance Benedict, Elizabeth's mother, waiting for her just inside the hall.

One glance at Connie's face was enough to tell Jessie that this was no casual visit.

"Hello, Connie. What on earth are you doing here?"

"I'm working on a downtown condo residence. Thought I'd stop by and see you for a few minutes before I went back over to the Eastside."

"Something wrong?" Jessie's stomach clenched suddenly. "Elizabeth's okay?"

"Yes. But I want to talk to you about her." Connie sounded grim as she followed Jessie up the stairs and into the office.

"Have a seat." Jessie motioned her to the sofa.

Constance was a few years younger than Jessie's mother. She had not had Elizabeth until she was thirty-five, nine months to the day after marrying Vincent.

After the divorce Constance had admitted she had known Vincent was probably not going to make an ideal spouse, but she had been panicked by a ticking biological clock. She had apparently regretted the marriage within a few short months.

She had stuck it out, however, until Elizabeth was nearly two. By then she had become close friends with Lilian Benedict, the only other woman in the world who really understood what it was like to be the wife of the head of Benedict Fasteners.

Constance was a strikingly handsome woman. Dark-haired and dark-eyed, she had an instinct for making the most of her dramatic coloring, just as Jessie's mother did. She favored strong colors and vivid makeup. She had a lush, full figure that somehow always looked chic and sensual rather than dowdy. Today she was tightly sheathed in a short-skirted turquoise suit.

"All right, what's the problem, Connie?" Jessie sprawled in the swivel chair behind the rolltop desk and waited. She knew she would not have to sit in suspense for very long. Connie was very much like Lilian in that they both had a habit of coming straight to the point.

"Vincent called this afternoon. He left a message for me at the office."

Jessie's stomach tightened again. "And?"

"And he says to tell Elizabeth that he's very sorry but something has come up and he won't be able to take her to the school science fair."

Jessie's worst fears were confirmed. She closed her eyes as frustration and anger washed over her. *"Damn him.* Damn him, damn him, damn him. He knows how important this fair is to Elizabeth. He *promised* he'd be there."

"We all know what Vincent's promises are worth, Jessie. If you're a business associate and the promises have to do with a contract or a deal, they're solid gold. You can take them to the bank. If you're family, they're written in snow. They melt almost as soon as you have them in your hand."

"I know that. But sometimes . . ." Jessie slapped the surface of the desk with her open palm. *"Most* times, I can get him to come through. I thought that he understood this science fair was really important to Elizabeth."

"I think he does understand." Connie shrugged. "And I believe he genuinely regrets not being able to take her. It's just that with Vincent, business is always more important than anything else. Jessie, you should know that better than anyone."

Jessie winced at the accusation in Constance's words. "This is all my fault, isn't it? That's why you're here. To tell me that it's all my fault."

"Well, yes, to be perfectly blunt." Constance sighed. Her eyes held a hint of sympathy beneath the accusation. "I've warned you before that unless you can guarantee Vincent's actions, it's far kinder not to set Elizabeth up."

"I didn't set her up." But she had. Jessie knew she had done exactly that. She had set Elizabeth up for a bad fall. Guilt lanced through her, as sharp as any knife. "Oh, God, Connie. I'm so sorry."

"I realize that. But I'm beginning to think it would be better if you didn't try to create a relationship between Elizabeth and her father. Let the chips fall where they may. She'll survive it. You did."

"But it means so much to her when he takes her out for her birthday or to a school project. I don't want her growing up the way I did, with Dad as some distant, remote figure who occasionally pats her on the head and asks if she needs any money. You can't say all my efforts have been in vain, Connie. You know she has a much better relationship with him than I did at her age."

"I know. And I've been grateful for what you've managed to accomplish. But now that she's about to become a teenager, I don't know if it's wise to keep trying to arrange things between them. Teenagers take rejection and disappointment so seriously. They're so emotional at that age. She was really counting on him being at the science fair on Saturday. She's going to be badly hurt."

Jessie clenched her hand into a small fist. "Have you told Elizabeth yet?"

Constance shook her head. "No. I'll do it tonight." Her mouth twisted with brief bitterness. "By rights, I should make you do it, shouldn't I?"

"Yes." Jessie bit her lip. "Connie, this is Thursday. Give me until tomorrow to see if I can change his mind, all right?"

"It won't work. You'll just be delaying the inevitable. Vincent said this was *business*, remember?"

"Just give me a few hours."

Constance shook her head as she got to her feet and

collected her purse. "I suppose it won't make much difference if I tell Elizabeth tonight or tomorrow."

"Thanks. I'll try to make this work, Connie. I promise."

"I know you will, but . . . Oh, well. We'll see." Constance glanced around the shabby interior of Valentine Consultations. "So this is your latest career move, hmmm? When are you going to settle down and find a real job, Jessie?"

"This is a real job. Why won't anyone take it seriously?"

Constance went to the door. "Probably because of your track record. You're always getting yourself fired, remember?"

"Well, I'm not planning to get myself fired from this job. This one is going to work out. Connie?"

"Yes?"

"You promise you won't tell Elizabeth until I've had a chance to talk to Dad?"

"You're wasting your time, Jessie, but you have my word on it." Constance paused before going through the door. "By the way, how are things going with the heir to the throne?"

"Don't hold your breath. He's just like Dad. You wouldn't really want me to make the same mistake you made, would you?"

Constance frowned. "I thought matters were getting serious between you and Hatch."

"Sheer idle speculation, rumor, and gossip. Most of it started by Dad. I wouldn't marry that man if he were the last male on earth."

Constance's expression relaxed. "Good. Sounds like it's all going to work out for the best, then. I'm glad. I like Hatch, and Benedict Fasteners needs him desperately. We all do."

"Dammit, Connie, I said I wasn't going to . . ."

But further protest was useless. Constance had already closed the door behind herself.

CHAPTER SIX

At eight-thirty that evening Jessie was still sitting at the rolltop desk in the office. She finally forced herself to admit defeat. Her father had not returned any of her calls.

She had not even been able to get past Grace, Vincent's secretary, all afternoon. No, at eight-thirty it was obvious her father, who was probably still at his desk, was not answering his phone.

Jessie knew the pattern all too well. He would not get back to her now until after the weekend. Then he would apologize and explain that he had been called away on business. And everyone knew that business came first.

All the old anger and pain from her own childhood boiled within her anew. Most of the time she could keep it buried, but it had a bad habit of resurfacing whenever Elizabeth was threatened with the same rejection.

"Bastard." Jessie picked up a pen and hurled it across the room.

She listened to the pen clatter as it struck the wall and bounced on the floor. Outside the window a late-spring twilight was fading rapidly into night. It was starting to rain. At least the ugly yellow haze which had blanketed the city for the past few days had finally cleared.

Jessie got to her feet and went into the inner office. She yanked open the bottom drawer of Mrs. Valentine's small file cabinet and picked up the bottle of sherry her employer kept there for medicinal purposes.

Jessie poured a dollop of sherry into her coffee mug and replaced the bottle. She returned to the outer office, turned off the light, propped her feet on the desk, and sprawled back in the squeaky chair. She sipped the sherry slowly. For a long while she sat watching the gloom descend outside the window. It was like a black fog that seemed to be trying to seep into the office, filling every vacant corner.

"You bastard," Jessie whispered as she took another swallow of sherry.

When she heard the footsteps on the stairs, she paid no attention. It was Alex, no doubt, heading for the rest room. He would assume she had gone home for the day hours ago, as she usually did.

She waited for the footsteps to go on down the hall. But they halted, instead, on the other side of the pebbled glass. Belatedly Jessie realized she had not locked the door.

She glanced across the width of the room and saw the dark shadow of a man through the opaque glass. She held her breath, torn between getting up to lock the door and thereby betraying her presence inside the office and sitting tight and hoping he would leave.

She hesitated too long. The door opened and Hatch came into the room, his jacket hooked over his shoulder. His shirt was open at the throat and his tie hung loose around his neck.

"I take it you've changed your regular working hours?" he asked calmly.

"No."

"I see." He paused and glanced around the office. "This looks like a scene straight out of a hard-boiled-detective novel," Hatch said. "There sits our tough, alienated heroine guzzling booze from a bottle she keeps in the desk drawer. She is clearly lost in moody contemplation of the hard life of a private eye."

"I'm surprised you find time to read anything except the *Wall Street Journal*," Jessie muttered. "How did you know I was here?"

"I went to your apartment. Got there shortly before eight o'clock, I might add. Per your instructions. When you didn't show, I decided to try here."

"Very clever."

"You're in a hell of a mood, aren't you?"

"Yeah." Jessie took another swallow of sherry and did not bother to remove her feet from the desk. "I get that way sometimes."

"I see. Got any more of whatever it is you're drinking?"

"It's Mrs. Valentine's tonic. Bottom drawer of her file cabinet."

"Thanks. Don't bother getting up."

"I wasn't going to."

Hatch went into the inner office and returned with the bottle and another coffee mug. "Mrs. Valentine's tonic looks like good Spanish sherry. Is this the source of her psychic powers?"

"Bastard."

"Are we discussing me or your father?"

"Dad."

"Figured I had a fifty-fifty shot at guessing right." Hatch pulled up a chair and sat down. He put the bottle on the desk. "What's he done now?"

"He's found something more important to do than take Elizabeth to her school science fair."

"Yes. That's Saturday, isn't it?" Hatch took a long swallow of the sherry and contemplated the remainder.

Jessie snapped her head around sharply. "That's right. Saturday. What's Dad doing on Saturday that's so important he has to miss Elizabeth's big day?"

"He's going down to Portland," Hatch said. "I told you we're having some problems there."

"Damn him." She slammed the mug down onto the desk, her rage flaring high once more. "Dear God in heaven, I could strangle him for this. Elizabeth is going to be heart-broken. And he doesn't give a damn." Tears burned in her eyes. She blinked angrily.

"You're being a little hard on him, Jessie. You know he cares about Elizabeth. But this thing down in Portland is—"

"I know what it is, Hatch," she said through her teeth. "This is *business,* isn't it? *Business as usual.*"

"There's a lot of money involved in the Portland project. Jobs and the company reputation are on the line too. We have to keep to the schedule."

"That's right, go ahead and defend him. You're no better than he is, are you? You'd have done the same thing in his shoes."

Hatch's fingers tightened around the mug. "Don't drag me into this. It's between you and your father."

"Not your problem, is it? But the truth is, you're on his side because you think like him. You have the same set of values, don't you? The same priorities." She narrowed her eyes. "Business always comes first. What do a twelve-year-old kid's feelings matter when there are a few thousand bucks on the line?"

"Dammit, Jessie, I'm not the one who changed his plans for Saturday. Don't blame me for this mess. You set it up and you knew as well as anyone that Vincent might alter his plans if business got in the way at the last minute."

The fact that he was right only made things worse. "Are you telling me that you wouldn't have acted the same way in the same situation?"

"Christ, Jessie, take it easy, will you?"

"Just answer me, Hatch. No, don't bother. We both know what the answer is, don't we? You would have done exactly the same thing."

"That's enough."

Jessie stared at him, astounded by the flash of raw temper. She had never seen Hatch lose his self-control like this. Until now she had found baiting him a challenge, a way of protecting herself from the attraction he held for her. But having succeeded at last in drawing a reaction, she realized she had made a mistake.

"It's true and you know it," she muttered, unwilling to back down completely.

But Hatch was already on his feet, looming over her. His hands clamped around the wooden arms of the chair. "Shut up, Jessie. I don't want to hear another word about how much I resemble your father. *I am not your father, goddammit.*"

"I know that. But you certainly could have been his son. A real chip off the old block, aren't you? You'd have gone down to Portland on Saturday, wouldn't you? Given the same situation, you'd have done what he's doing. Admit it."

"No, I damn well would not have gone down to Portland," Hatch told her, his voice a dangerously soft snarl. His eyes glittered in the gloom. "Not if I'd promised a little girl I would take her to a science fair instead. I do not break my promises, Jessie. If I make a commitment, I keep it. Remember that."

"Let me up, Hatch." Her lower lip was trembling. She could feel it. Out of long habit she caught it between her teeth to still it.

"Why? Am I making you nervous?"

"Yes, dammit, you are."

"Tough."

"Hatch, stop it." Jessie drew her legs quickly up underneath her and stood in the chair. She teetered there for a few seconds and then she stepped over the arm of the chair and onto the desktop. She glared down at Hatch, feeling a little safer in this position.

Hatch straightened, reaching for her with his powerful, dangerous hands. "Come here."

"Hatch, no. Don't you dare touch me, do you hear me?" Jessie sidled backward until the backs of her knees came up against the rows of little cubbyholes that lined the top of the desk.

"I hear you. But I don't feel like listening to you just now." His hands closed around her waist and he lifted her effortlessly down off the desk.

"Hatch."

He lowered her feet to the floor, gripped her upper arms, and pulled her against his hard length. "I've had it with you lumping me into the same category as your father. From now on, Jessie, you're going to start seeing me as an individual. I'm me, Sam Hatchard, not a clone of Vincent Benedict. I make my own decisions and I do my own thinking and I make my own commitments. And I damn sure keep those commitments."

"Hatch, listen to me, I'm not confusing you with my father. Believe me, that is not the issue. I'm just saying you have the same list of priorities and I don't like the list."

He cut off her frantic defense in mid-sentence by covering her trembling mouth with his own. Jessie froze beneath the onslaught of his kiss. The argument she was composing went out of her head in an instant. She sagged against Hatch as her knees gave way.

Jessie could hardly breathe. She was ablaze already. The soul-searing sensuality of the kiss shook her to the core, calling forth a response that dazed her. A liquid heat was pooling in her lower body, intense and compelling.

"Say my name, Jessie." The command was rough against her soft mouth. "Say it, dammit."

"Hatch. Please, Hatch. Please." She wrapped her arms

around his neck, clinging to him as the desire swirled in her blood.

When her feet left the floor again she thought she had fallen over the edge of a volcano. But a moment later she felt the sofa cushions beneath her back and dimly realized that Hatch had carried her across the room. His wicked, beautiful hands were moving over her, yanking at the buttons of her shirt.

She felt his fingers glide over her breast and she cried out. The weight of him came down on top of her. Instinctively she raised one knee and discovered she was already cradling him between her thighs.

All the torment and uncertainty of the past few weeks coalesced into a driving need to find out what lay at the heart of this whirlpool in which she found herself.

Jessie heard her shoes hit the floor. She heard the zipper of her jeans sliding downward, felt the denim being pulled away along with her panties.

When Hatch's fingers found the hot core of her she would have screamed if she'd had the breath to do it. As it was, she had to content herself with wrapping herself even more tightly around him and lifting her hips in a way that pleaded for a more intimate union.

"You want me, don't you, Jessie? As much as I want you. Say it."

"I want you. I've wanted you from the beginning." She caught his earlobe between her teeth and bit. Hard. "And you knew it, damn you."

"I knew it. You were making me crazy." Hatch retaliated for what she had done to his ear by taking one taut nipple between his lips.

Another wave of shimmering excitement and need washed through Jessie. When Hatch pulled slightly away, she moaned in protest and tried to drag him back.

"Just give me a second." His voice was ragged with desire. He yanked open his shirt but did not bother to take it off.

Instead his hand went straight to the fastening of his pants, jerking at the belt and zipper. He pulled a small plastic packet out of one pocket, ripped it open with his teeth, and then reached down again.

Then he was on top of her once more, crushing her into the cushions.

"Put your legs around me, Jessie. Tight."

She did so, following his commands blindly. She felt him at the entrance of her body, poised and ready. Every muscle in his back was rigid with sexual tension. Jessie sucked in her breath as she sensed the size of him.

He started to push himself into her, and she dug her nails into his shoulders. She breathed deeply.

"Jessie. Jessie, look at me."

She opened her eyes warily and gazed up at him through her lashes. The lines of his face were starkly etched, his eyes brilliant as he entered her.

She knew she had driven him over some internal precipice and that she probably should have been afraid. But something that was wild and powerfully feminine deep within her gloried in the knowledge.

He pushed harder against her, easing himself into her. "So tight. Hot and tight. *Jessie."* He surged forward suddenly, thrusting deeply and completely into the moist, clinging heat of her.

Jessie gasped as he filled her. She shut her eyes as her body struggled to adjust itself to the glorious invasion. She did not dare move yet.

Hatch groaned heavily and went still. "Damn, you feel good. I knew it would be good but I . . . Jessie, did I hurt you?"

She licked her lips. "I'm all right." Her fingers bit deeper into the muscles of his shoulders as she moved her hips in a tentative fashion.

"Oh, Christ."

Whatever self-control Hatch still retained evaporated beneath the gentle, cautious movement of her thighs. His arms closed around her so tightly Jessie wondered if she would ever be free again. He began moving swiftly, each thrust more forceful than the last.

Then Jessie felt his wonderful fingers sliding down between their bodies, felt him search out the sweet spot between her legs, and suddenly she was no longer a moth dancing around a flame, but part of the fire itself.

"Oh, my God, Hatch. Hatch. *Please.*"

"Jessie."

Hatch surged forward one last time, his gritty shout of satisfaction muffled against her mouth. And then he collapsed against her, his body damp and heavy and satiated.

Hatch stirred and opened his eyes when he realized Jessie was starting to wriggle beneath him. "Can't you lie still?" he muttered.

"You're getting heavy."

She was probably right. She was so soft and delicate compared to him, and he was no doubt crushing her into the faded cushions. But, damn, it felt good just to lie here on top of her, breathing in the scents of her moist body and of their recent lovemaking. A deep awareness of the intimacy of the moment flowed through him, making him loath to move.

He looked down at her and thought he saw the same cautious awareness in her cat-green eyes. He also saw uncertainty and wariness mirrored there. From now on she would take him very seriously. Hatch smiled slightly.

"I didn't think we'd go nuclear quite so fast," he said, not without satisfaction.

"But you were prepared for any eventuality, weren't you?" Tears appeared at the edges of her beautiful eyes.

Hatch was startled. He reminded himself that Jessie was an emotional creature. He framed her face gently between his palms. "I've wanted you from the beginning. You knew it. The tension was always there between us. It was just a matter of time."

"I suppose you think this changes everything." She

blinked back the tears, clearly struggling for an air of cool challenge. She failed miserably.

"I suppose I do." He brushed his mouth across hers. "I'll take care of Saturday, Jessie."

She scowled. "What are you talking about?"

"Like I said, I'll take care of it. You can call Constance and tell her that Vincent will be escorting Elizabeth to the science fair."

Jessie's eyes widened. "Just how do you plan to make that happen?"

He shrugged. "I'm the CEO of Benedict Fasteners, remember?"

"Yes, but my father is president. And nobody gives my father orders."

"I can handle Vincent." Hatch sat up reluctantly, unable to tear his gaze away from the slender, naked length of her. He watched her blush beneath his scrutiny, and he smiled again. Her breasts shifted enticingly as she leaned over the edge of the sofa and groped for her clothing.

"Why?" she demanded in a small, tight little voice as she held her shirt up like a shield in front of her breasts.

"Why what?" Deprived of the sight of her breasts, he stared lingeringly at the moist hair between her legs.

"You know what I'm talking about." She waved a hand helplessly in the air.

He raised his eyes to meet hers. "That's a dumb question. We were bound to wind up in bed sooner or later. I was planning on later, but you couldn't resist pushing me, could you? And for some crazy reason, I let you push me right over the edge tonight. This wasn't the way I had planned things, honey. I wanted to do it right. Flowers and champagne. The whole works."

"I wasn't talking about . . . about what just happened. I meant why are you suddenly offering to get Dad to the science fair?"

"Oh, that." Hatch shrugged. "Maybe I want you to learn

something about me. Something more than what you seem to think you already know."

"I see." She clutched the shirt more tightly to her throat and stared up at him. Her catlike eyes were narrowed with ill-concealed anxiety. "It's not because I let you do what you just did, is it? Is this your notion of compensating me for a toss in the hay? Because if it is, you can just bloody well forget it."

"I think it's safe to say that you don't have one single shred of psychic ability, Jessie. If you did, you'd have known better than to make an asinine statement like that. Put your clothes on. We'll go out and get something to eat." Hatch knew that earlier, before she had emptied him of the sexual tension that had been gnawing at him for weeks, he probably would have been enraged by the accusation. Now, however, he was feeling too lazy and satisfied to take any real offense.

"I'm not hungry."

"I am. Starving, in fact." He grinned slowly down at her, aware of a happy, exuberant sensation that he had not felt in a long time. "Trust me. You'll feel much better after you've had something to eat and a chance to get back into fighting form. You're just temporarily dazed, that's all."

He was right, just as he had known he would be. By the time they had dressed and he had walked her down the street to a nearby café, Jessie was well on the road to recovery. She started to chat conversationally about a wide variety of subjects. They all had one thing in common. They did not touch on the subject of their relationship.

Later, as Hatch parked his car in front of her apartment, it dawned on him exactly what tactic she had decided to employ in order to deal with the new situation between them. He switched off the engine and sat back to study her in the shadows.

"I'll be damned," he said, amused. "You're just going to pretend it never happened, aren't you? You disappoint me, Jessie. I didn't think you'd take the coward's way out."

"What did you expect me to do?" she flared. "Throw myself all over you and beg you to marry me?"

He considered that. "No, probably not. But I didn't think you'd try to ignore the whole thing either. What are you going to do the next time we make love? Act like it's all a huge surprise?"

"Don't get the idea I intend to make a habit out of that sort of idiotic incident." She slung the strap of her bag over her shoulder and reached for the door handle. "It's not as if I don't have other, more important things going on in my life."

He reached out and flicked the door-lock button, trapping her. "Such as?"

She sat back in the seat and crossed her arms beneath her breasts. "Such as the investigation I'm conducting. I suppose you've forgotten about that, haven't you? You never did bother to tell me about following the money."

"Haven't had a chance," he pointed out. "We've been a little busy today, haven't we? What with getting up at three in the morning to investigate break-ins and making love on your office sofa."

She shot him a quick searching glance. "Tell me now."

"About the money? There's not a whole lot to tell until we know more about DEL. The first thing to find out is how they finance the operation."

"Donations, apparently." She chewed on her lower lip. "I might know more when I get back from visiting their headquarters."

She could not have jolted him more if she had dropped a live grenade into his lap. "Visiting their headquarters?" Hatch shot out a hand and caught her chin, turning her so that she had to meet his eyes. "What the hell are you talking about now?"

She shooed his hand away and smiled rather smugly. "I've been working today, Hatch. With David's help I tracked down someone who knew Susan Attwood, a young woman named Nadine Willard. She and Susan had both attended one of the lectures DEL gave to interested students at Butterfield College, and Nadine just happened to have an extra invitation to visit DEL headquarters. She said anyone who had one could probably go see the place. It's on an island in the San Juans."

"And you're going to go up there? By yourself?"

"Why not?"

"Are you crazy?"

"Probably, or I wouldn't have found myself flat on my back on Mrs. V's office sofa an hour ago."

Hatch was incensed all over again. He could not believe the effect this woman had on him. Deliberately he clamped down his ironclad self-control and forced himself to speak coldly and quietly.

"You are not going up there alone. I absolutely forbid it." He got a sinking sensation in his gut when Jessie's smile turned even more smug.

"Want to come with me and see if you can spot the money trail?" she inquired softly. "The invitation is for the bearer and a friend."

"Now, hold on just one damn minute," Hatch ordered, already reeling under the implications.

"You could always think of it as a mini-vacation, Hatch. I'll bet you haven't taken a vacation in ages, have you?"

"Dammit, Jessie." Hatch realized he desperately needed time. "Look, you're not to do anything at all until I get back from Portland, understand?"

"Portland? You're going down there?" she asked quickly.

"Somebody has to go, Jessie. I told you it was important. Since your father already has a previous commitment, that leaves me. In the meantime, I want your word of honor you won't traipse off to the San Juans alone while I'm out of town."

"Well . . ."

"Let me make that clearer," he said coolly. "You're not getting out of this car tonight until I have your promise not to leave Seattle without me."

"Since you feel that strongly about it, I suppose I can wait." She gave him a triumphant look. "As it happens, I'm going to the science fair too. I won't be going anywhere until Monday. One other thing. The tour requires a two-hundred-dollar donation to the foundation."

"Two hundred dollars? Dammit to hell, Jessie . . ."

"The price of doing business," she murmured blandly. "Even psychic investigators have expenses. Maybe you can put it on your gold card."

"Damn."

Hatch did not trust himself to say another word as he walked Jessie to her door and saw her safely inside her apartment. Still smoldering with pure masculine outrage, he went back outside to his car, got in, and drove to the offices of Benedict Fasteners.

If he was going to Portland on Saturday, he needed to review some files tonight. He would deal with Jessie when he returned.

He would have to deal with Vincent Benedict first thing in the morning, however.

Hatch did not look forward to either project.

Two hundred dollars? Just to keep an eye on Jessie?

"Damn."

"What the hell are you talking about, Hatch?" Benedict's bushy white brows met in a solid line above his glowering eyes.

"You heard me. I'm going down to Portland in your place." Hatch noticed that the birthday flowers on the desk were wilting quickly. They would not last much longer. He wondered why Benedict had not ordered them thrown into the garbage. "You've promised to take Elizabeth to the science fair, remember?"

"Jesus. Of course I remember. But this problem in Portland has gotten too big to handle over the phone. It has to be taken care of in person as soon as possible. You know that. We agreed on it. What the devil's gotten into you, Hatch?"

Hatch planted both hands flat on the surface of Benedict's desk and leaned forward. "I promised Jessie you would take Elizabeth to the science fair. It means a lot to her. Not to mention Elizabeth."

"So what? This is business. These things happen. Both my girls understand that."

"You still don't get it, do you, Benedict? I made Jessie a promise. She needs to learn that when I make a promise, I keep it. If I don't come through on this one, you can probably kiss off any possibility of a marriage between me and your daughter."

"Goddammit, you're serious, aren't you?" Benedict looked appalled.

"Real serious. Better sort out your priorities here, Vincent. You know damn well I can handle the problem in Portland."

"That's not the point. You're needed here. We've got that situation with the bid on the Spokane project to deal with, remember? Or have you forgotten Yorland and Young?"

"We can finesse that for a few days. For the record, I still don't think it's worth the effort anyway."

"Is that right? Well, I happen to want that contract."

"I'll get it for you if it means that much to you," Hatch said impatiently. "But in the meantime, let's get it clear that you are going to take your daughter to the science fair tomorrow."

Vincent snorted and sank back in his chair, brows still beetled. "You sure Jessie won't understand?"

"Oh, she'll understand, all right. She'll understand only too well." Hatch bit out each word. "What she'll understand is that if I don't keep this promise, I'm just what she thinks I am."

"Which is?"

"Too much like you."

119

"*Women.* What the hell's the matter with 'em anyway? Their priorities are all screwed up. They don't understand how the real world works."

"I've got news for you, Benedict. Women do not think the same way men do. Unfortunate, but true." Hatch straightened, removing his hands from the desk. He was satisfied he had made his point. "Have a good time watching Elizabeth win first place tomorrow."

Vincent sighed. "Hope you know what you're doing."

"I usually do. That's why you hired me in the first place, remember?"

"Should have known this would happen," Vincent said glumly.

"What would happen?"

"Should have known you'd be giving me orders by now," Vincent said. "Knew it wouldn't take you long to take over completely. You just make damn certain you marry that gal of mine. Hear me?"

"I hear you."

Hatch plucked a scarlet lily from the fading bouquet on the desk and carried it back to his own office. He sat down behind his desk and studied the delicate flower for a long while.

Benedict was right. They had just arrived at a subtle turning point in their relationship. Hatch had given the older man orders and Vincent Benedict had taken them. Hatch knew his hold on Benedict Fasteners was more secure than ever.

His hold on Jessie Benedict, however, was still far too tenuous.

He stared at the scarlet lily and remembered the expression on Jessie's face when she had climaxed in his arms.

CHAPTER SEVEN

Eric Jerkface did not win first place at the science fair. When the award was handed out it went to a grinning Elizabeth Benedict. Her father was standing proudly beside her when the film crew took the shots for the evening news. Jessie was so excited she could hardly contain herself. Constance, looking sophisticated in a white suit that clung to every full curve, smiled with delight.

"Are you going to tell me how you pulled off this little miracle?" Constance murmured in Jessie's ear under cover of a round of applause. "I can't believe you got Vincent here. He made that business down in Portland sound more important than the Second Coming."

"Don't thank me, Connie. We owe this one to Hatch."

"He did it for you, didn't he?" Constance slid her a speculative glance.

"Who? Hatch? Umm, yes. I believe he did."

"You don't sound overly thrilled. It was a lovely gesture, Jessie."

"The thing is, Connie, men like Hatch don't make lovely gestures unless there's a price tag attached."

"Such cynicism is unbecoming in a young woman, my dear. It's only us tough old broads who get to indulge in that kind of thing."

"What do I get to indulge in?" Jessie asked.

"Safe sex, if you're lucky. And if you would stop being so damn picky. Your mother's starting to worry about you, you know. Lilian says she did not raise you to go into a convent."

Jessie felt herself turning a vivid shade of red as memories of the previous night on Mrs. Valentine's sofa burned through her mind again. "For heaven's sake, Connie."

"Well, well, well." Constance gave her a warm, approving glance. "Congratulations. I assume we have Hatch to thank for that blush too?"

Jessie fought for composure. "As I said, Connie, when men like Hatch make lovely gestures, there's usually a price tag attached."

"Take some advice from a tough old broad. Pay the price. By the way, speaking of the cost of doing business these days, I know this isn't exactly the time or place to ask, but have you had a chance to talk to Vincent about another little loan for ExCellent Designs?"

Jessie groaned silently. "No, not really. I've been a little busy lately, Connie. I'll say something to him as soon as I get a chance."

"Thanks." Constance smiled at her in gratitude. "Lilian and I would approach him ourselves, but those kinds of conversations always turn into screaming matches between the three of us. You know your father when it comes to money. He won't give it out unless there are strings attached. He likes to control people that way. You're the only one who seems to be able to talk him into being reasonable on the subject."

"Only because I go on screaming longer than you or Lilian," Jessie pointed out morosely.

The film crew was hovering over Elizabeth as she did her best to explain her chemical analysis of a toxic-waste dump to a reporter who wanted it summed up in a thirty-second sound bite. Jessie rushed forward as soon as the reporter was finished and hugged her sister tightly.

"I knew you'd do it, kid. You were fabulous. Wasn't she, Dad?"

"Damn good job, Lizzie." Vincent gazed down on his younger daughter with genuine paternal pride. "I can't say I'm surprised, though. You are one smart little cookie, aren't you? I'll bet it comes from my side of the family."

Elizabeth turned pink and her grin grew wider. "I knew you'd be here today, Dad. Mom said you might not be able to make it at the last minute, but I knew you'd be here."

Constance Benedict gave her daughter a hug and then stood on tiptoe to brush her ex-husband's cheek with a quick, affectionate kiss. "Thanks for coming, Vince," she murmured.

Vincent caught Jessie's eye. "Wouldn't have missed it," he said heartily. Jessie gave him a cool smile in return and turned back to congratulate her sister again.

Fifteen minutes after the conclusion of the awards ceremony, Elizabeth scurried off to admire a friend's project and Constance stopped to chat with an acquaintance. Vincent came up beside Jessie, who was watching a small robot buzz around a tabletop.

"Still mad at me?" he asked, his eyes on the robot.

"Let's not talk about it, okay? You're here. That's the bottom line, as they say in the business world."

Vincent exhaled heavily. "I'm sorry, Jessie. I wanted to be here. I'd planned on it. You know that. It was just that we ran into problems down in Portland."

"I know, Dad. Forget it. Like I said, you're here."

"Only because you sicced Hatch on me."

"I didn't sic him on you. He took it upon himself to make you show today."

"Hell, you got what you wanted. I can understand why you're a little upset with me, but why don't you sound more thrilled with Hatch?"

Jessie watched the robot roll to the edge of the table and

halt as if by magic. "Probably because I know how his mind works. He'll figure I owe him for this."

"Maybe you do. There's a price tag attached to everything in this world." Vincent followed her gaze as she watched the robot make a hundred-and-eighty-degree turn and scoot to the other side of the table. "Tell me the truth, Jessie. How do you really feel about the man?"

"What have my feelings got to do with it? All you care about is marrying me off to him so you can keep the company in the family and watch Hatch take it big-time, right? Don't go all paternal and concerned on me now, Dad. We know each other too well for that kind of nonsense."

"Goddammit, you may not believe this, but I want you to be happy, Jessie. The thing is, I think you and Hatch can make a go of it. There's something about the two of you. When you're in the same room together I can almost see the sparks."

"That's probably just the two of us sharpening our knives for battle."

"Come on, Jessie. This is your old man, remember? I know you well enough to be sure you aren't exactly indifferent to Hatch. I'll never forget the day he fired you. You came out of that office looking shell-shocked, like you'd just done ten rounds with a lion."

"Shark," Jessie corrected. "And it wasn't that big a deal. I've been fired before, Dad."

"Hell, I know that. You've made a career out of getting fired. But somehow in the past you've always come out of it looking as if you were the one who had fired your boss, instead of vice versa. This was the first time I'd ever seen you look like you'd actually lost a battle. That's when I knew for sure it could work between you and Hatch."

Jessie gritted her teeth. "You're not exactly the world's leading authority on what it takes to create a successful long-term relationship, Dad."

"You don't have to spell it out. I know damn well I haven't

been a good role model in the husband-and-father department. Who knows how I would have turned out if Lilian or Connie had been more like you? They both gave up on me, you know. Lost patience somewhere along the line. But you, you're a fighter. You keep after what you want. And you've got Hatch while he's still young. You can work on him, can't you?"

"Young? The man's thirty-seven years old."

"Prime of life. I'll tell you something, Jessie. From where I stand these days, thirty-seven looks damn young. And he's got the guts and the brains it takes to make Benedict Fasteners very, very big."

"What makes you so sure he's got what it takes?"

Vincent grinned. "Partly my own instincts and partly his track record."

"I figure the instinct part is based on the fact that he's a lot like you."

"Now, Jessie, that's not true. Fact is, our management styles are damn different. Hatch has got all kinds of ideas for the company I'd never have approved if he hadn't talked me into them. He's got what they like to call *vision,* if you know what I mean."

"Vision?"

"Yeah, you know. He's aware of new management stuff like concurrent engineering and design. He knows how to deal with foreign markets. He thinks big. Me, I'm a more basic kind of guy. Hatch says I get bogged down in the details, and he's right. Takes vision to pull a company into the big time."

Jessie gave him a speculative glance. "So what makes his track record so impressive?"

"Well, for one thing, he's come up the hard way. No one ever gave him a handout. He's tough. A real fighter. The kind of guy you like to have at your back in a barroom brawl, if you know what I mean. Should have seen what he did to a company called Patterson-Finley a few years back."

Jessie got an odd sensation in the pit of her stomach, although she had never heard of Patterson-Finley. "What, exactly, did he do to it?"

"He was a consultant to one of its smaller rivals. Engineered a takeover bid for them designed to gain controlling interest in Patterson-Finley. It was brilliantly handled. Patterson-Finley never knew what hit 'em. Put up one hell of a fight, naturally, but Hatch sliced 'em into bloody ribbons. When it was all over, Patterson-Finley damned near ceased to exist. It was a wholly owned subsidiary of the smaller firm."

"I think I know why people call him a shark."

"Damn right," Benedict said proudly.

"Tell me, Dad. If you had it to do over again, would you have allowed some woman to work a few changes on you back when you were thirty-seven?"

"Who knows?" Vincent's eyes rested on Elizabeth's brown head and his expression softened slightly. "Sometimes I think maybe I missed some of the important stuff with you."

"Ah, well, I wouldn't waste too much time worrying about it, if I were you. After all, it couldn't be helped, could it?" Jessie smiled sweetly. "You had a business to run."

"Better watch it, Jessie," Vincent retorted. "Men don't take kindly to sharp-tongued females. You're liable to end up an old maid if you aren't careful."

"That's a thought." Jessie deliberately widened her eyes in innocent inquiry. "Think I can scare Hatch off with my sharp tongue?"

"No, but you might piss him off. And that, my darling daughter, you might seriously regret. Say, are you sure that all this interest in ecology isn't going to turn Elizabeth into one of those damn radical tree-huggers?"

"Dad, I've got news for you. We're relying on tree-huggers like Elizabeth to save the world."

* * *

When the downstairs door buzzer sounded at one o'clock that morning, Jessie came awake with a start. She sat blinking in the darkness for a moment, orienting herself. The buzzer screeched again and she pushed back the covers.

Barefoot, she padded out of the bedroom and into the living room. "Who is it?" she asked, pressing the intercom button.

"Jessie, it's after midnight. Who the hell do you think it is?"

"Hatch. What on earth are you doing here at this hour?"

"You know damn well what I'm doing here. Let me in. It's cold out here and I'm likely to get mugged any minute."

Jessie tried to think clearly, failed, and ended up pushing the release button. Then she rushed back into the bedroom to grab a robe.

She was running a brush through her short hair when the doorbell chimed. Aware of a dangerous sense of anticipation mingled with a curious dread, she went to answer it.

Hatch was standing in the hall, looking as if he'd had a long day followed by an even longer drive. He was in his shirtsleeves and he was carrying his jacket and a bulging briefcase. His eyes gleamed at the sight of her in her robe and slippers.

"So how did we do at the science fair?" he asked as Jessie stood staring up at him.

She forgot her trepidation entirely and gave him a glowing smile. "We won. Elizabeth was thrilled. Dad was thrilled. Connie was thrilled. I was thrilled. Everyone was thrilled. Reporters came and they even took film of Elizabeth and Dad for the evening news. I saw it at five-thirty. It was wonderful. Elizabeth looked so happy standing there with her father beside her as she accepted the award. You made her day."

"Good. Glad it all worked out okay."

"Okay? It was much better than *okay*. It was wonderful." Without stopping to think, Jessie threw herself impulsively

127

against Hatch, wrapped her arms around him, and brushed her mouth lightly over his. "Thank you. We owe it all to you."

"You're welcome." Hatch dropped the suitcase at his feet and clamped his hands around Jessie's waist. His palms slid warmly up her back, holding her tightly to him while he took advantage of the situation to deepen the kiss.

Jessie told herself she should probably struggle. She did not want Hatch getting the idea that he could show up on her doorstep at any time of the day or night and expect such a warm welcome. But somehow she could not bring herself to fight him off tonight. His mouth felt too good on hers, deliberate and sure, with a controlled eroticism that set her nerves tingling. He wanted her and, heaven help her, she wanted him.

It was Hatch who broke off the kiss. "I'd better get in out of the hall before one of your neighbors decides to see what's happening." He released her with obvious reluctance in order to pick up the briefcase and move on into the room.

Jessie stepped back, quashing the tide of sensual longing that he had elicited with his kiss. She searched frantically for something appropriate to say. She just knew he had read far too much into that greeting at the door. He was already making himself at home, hanging his jacket in the closet and stowing the briefcase on the floor beneath it. When he sat down on the couch and started to take off his shoes, she panicked.

Out of hand, she thought. Things were definitely getting out of hand. Give Hatch an inch and he clearly felt he could take a mile. And she had given him a great deal more than an inch, she reminded herself.

"How did things go in Portland?" she managed to ask politely while she clutched the lapels of her robe and wondered what to do next.

Hatch gave her a hooded glance as he unlaced his other shoe. "Under control again. We're back on schedule."

"Oh. Good." She glanced over her shoulder into the kitchen. "Uh, did you want a cup of coffee or anything?"

"Nope. All I want is bed. It's a four-hour drive down to Portland. I left at four this morning. Spent the whole day until nine o'clock this evening chewing on everyone involved in that project and then I got into my car and drove four hours to get back here." He stood up and started toward her, unbuttoning his shirt en route. "I'm beat."

"I see. Well, then, you'll probably want to go straight home to your place and get some sleep." She gave him a bright little smile.

"You're right about one thing, at least. I want to get some sleep."

He scooped her up in his arms, carried her into the bedroom, and tossed her lightly down onto the bed. He leaned over her as he tugged the robe free and dropped it on a chair.

Jessie lay back against the pillows and watched with a deep, disturbing hunger as he stripped off the rest of his clothing. She might as well face it, she told herself. She was not going to kick him out. Not tonight, at any rate.

"You can make the coffee in the morning," Hatch said as he got into bed wearing only a pair of briefs. "Just be sure you make it strong."

He turned on his side, facing her, and anchored her with a possessive arm around her waist. She could feel the sinewy muscles of his forearm pushing lightly against the soft weight of her breasts. In an agony of anticipation, Jessie waited for his wonderful, powerful hand to glide down her hip and over her thigh.

Nothing happened.

Jessie looked closer and noticed Hatch's astonishingly dark lashes lying against his high cheekbones. His breathing was slow and even. He was already asleep.

She touched his shoulder gently, knowing she was at least partially responsible for his exhaustion tonight. He had done it for her, she realized. She had to remind herself that his motives had certainly not been entirely altruistic. She was temporarily a high priority for Sam Hatchard. He was willing to indulge her to a certain extent while he courted her.

Still, he had come through in a way she had never expected. He had made a commitment and he had kept it. He had even taken on her father in order to make good on a promise to her. Jessie had to admit she did not know any other man on the face of the earth who could have pulled off the feat of getting Vincent Benedict to the school fair today.

"I hope," she whispered into the darkness, "that you don't think you can just show up like this and fall into my bed any night you happen to feel like it."

"Now, where would I get an idea like that?" Hatch asked without opening his eyes.

Hatch awoke the next morning, inhaled the womanly fragrance of the white sheets, and exhaled with satisfaction as he realized he was finally in Jessie's bed.

Another turning point, he decided, pleased. Another victory in the small, important war they were waging.

Hatch reached for Jessie and found the other side of the bed empty. He groaned and opened his eyes. A rain-drenched daylight was filtering through the slanted blinds and the aroma of coffee wafted in from the kitchen.

Some victory. A whole night in Jessie's bed and he had not even managed to make love to her while there.

Maybe he was working too hard lately.

Hatch shoved back the covers and sat up slowly. He glanced around with deep interest, enjoying the intimate sensation of being in Jessie's bedroom. Her robe still lay on the chair. The mirrored closet door was open, revealing a colorful array of clothing. A selection of loafers, running shoes, sandals, and high heels were scattered carelessly on the closet floor.

Jessie was obviously not a fanatic about neatness. Just as

well, Hatch told himself as he went into the bathroom. Neither was he.

The small tiled room was still steamy from Jessie's recent shower. Hatch opened the sliding glass door and stood gazing at the collection of items arranged on the ledge beside the shower handle. There were a variety of shampoo bottles and soaps, a woman's razor, and a long-handled back brush. The scent was fresh and flowery.

When he got into the shower, Hatch felt as if he were invading some very private, very female place. It made him acutely conscious of his maleness and of how alien that maleness was here in this female sanctuary.

The sense of possessiveness that rippled through him as he stood there in Jessie's shower made Hatch's mouth twist in a faint, wry smile. Everything felt right, somehow, as if he had been waiting a long time for this moment.

When he emerged from the bedroom twenty minutes later he found Jessie sitting at the kitchen counter with the morning paper. She glanced up quickly as he came into the room and he caught the flash of nervousness in her eyes just before her elbow struck the coffee cup that was sitting next to her.

The cup went spinning across the counter. Hatch watched with interest as it teetered precariously on the edge and then went over the side. As Jessie stared in dismay, he reached out and caught the empty cup before it hit the floor.

"Another cup of coffee?" Hatch asked calmly as he picked up the pot and poured one for himself.

"Yes, please." She carefully refolded the paper.

"Anything exciting in the headlines?" He sat down across from her and grimaced as he tasted the weak brew.

"There's another article about the damage being done to the earth's ozone layer by pollutants." Jessie frowned. "You know, I can see why people would be attracted to a cult that focused on saving the world from environmental disaster. The issue has the same awful sense of impending doom that the thought of global war has. Don't forget, there was a time when everyone wanted to build a bomb shelter in his backyard."

"Speaking of which, have you given up that damn-fool idea of using the invitation to visit DEL headquarters?" Hatch asked without much real hope.

"Of course not. I'm going to phone and make the arrangements first thing tomorrow morning." She eyed him warily. "Are you still going to insist on going up there with me?"

"I don't see that I have much option."

"Sure you do. You can decide to let me go alone."

"No way, Jessie. We don't know what you're getting into. You're not going up there alone, and that's final."

"It'll probably take a couple of days," she pointed out. "That's a heck of a long time to stay away from Benedict Fasteners. The company might fall apart without you."

"Don't you think I know that? Stop trying to talk me out of going with you. You aren't going alone."

"What about the company?"

"I'll leave your father in charge. He's run it for the past thirty years. No reason he can't handle it for a couple more days."

"I suppose you've got a point." She frowned. "Are you going into the office? It's Sunday."

"There are some things I have to clear up if I'm going to be out of town for a couple of days."

"I see. Are you really sure you can afford to take the time off?"

He raised his brows. "Don't bother trying to get rid of me, honey. I'm here to stay."

She bit her lip. "Hatch, we have to talk about this."

"The trip to the San Juans?"

"No, *this*. You. Here. In my kitchen at eight o'clock in the morning." She drew a deep breath. "If we're going to have an affair or something, we need to set a few ground rules."

"We're not having an affair." Hatch got to his feet and carried his cup over to the sink.

"What do you call this business of showing up on my

doorstep at one in the morning and spending the night?" she demanded.

"I call it being engaged to be married." He caught her chin on the heel of his hand and gave her a quick, hard kiss. Then he headed for the closet where he had left his jacket and briefcase.

"Hatch, wait. Don't you dare walk out of here before we've had a chance to discuss this. Hatch, come back here. I mean it. I swear, if you don't come right back here I'm going to . . . Oh, damn."

He gently closed the door behind him as he went out into the hall.

Hatch was not in the least surprised to find Vincent in his office on Sunday morning. The older man almost always came in on the weekends, just as Hatch did. Benedict looked up, scowling when Hatch stuck his head around the door to announce his presence in the building.

"Where the hell have you been?" Vincent rapped out. "I've been calling you since seven-thirty this morning to find out how things went down in Portland."

"Things went fine down in Portland. Next time you can't reach me at my place, try Jessie's."

Benedict blinked and then started to turn a strange shade of red. "You spent the night with her? You're sleeping with my Jessie?"

"Better get used to the idea, Benedict. I'm going to marry her, remember?"

"You damn well better marry her now or I'll get out my shotgun." Vincent drummed his fingers on the desk and narrowed his gaze. "I suppose this is a sign the courtship is going okay?"

"I like to think of it that way. Before I forget, I'll be gone for a couple of days this week. Jessie and I are going up to the San Juans while she investigates her psychic cult case. You're in charge while I'm out of town. Don't run us into Chapter Eleven, okay?"

"For Christ's sake, Hatch. You're the CEO around here. You can't just take off like this."

"Not much point being the boss if you can't take a couple of days off when you feel like it, is there?" Hatch growled.

"Goddammit, this DEL thing is crazy. Don't waste your time on it."

"No choice. Jessie's decided to waste her time on it, so that means I've got to waste some of mine. You don't want her going into that mess alone, do you?"

"Hell, no. I don't want her going at all."

"She's made up her mind. So I'm going along to ride shotgun."

Vincent glowered at him. "Strikes me she's got you running around in circles. If you can't control her any better than this, I'm not so sure you're the right man for her after all."

Hatch's fingers clamped around the edge of the door. He smiled thinly. "Stay out of this, Benedict. I'm in charge around here, remember?"

"I can cancel your contract anytime, and don't you forget it."

"You won't do that. Not as long as you're getting what you want. And so far, I'm giving you exactly what you want. Oh, yeah, congratulations on Elizabeth's first-place win in the science fair."

"Yeah. Thanks." Vincent nodded proudly. "The kid gets her smarts from my side of the family."

Jessie lounged in the chair next to her mother and watched Lilian methodically try on twelve different pairs of shoes. The saleswoman who had brought out the dozen boxes did not seem in the least dismayed by the prospect of a customer who wanted to try on so many different styles. Lilian Benedict was a regular at the big downtown department store's shoe salon. She never left without buying at least one pair.

"You're serious about this nonsense of going up to the San

Juans to look at some cult headquarters?" Lilian frowned thoughtfully at the pair of patent-leather heels she was considering.

"Afraid so," Jessie said cheerfully. "I don't like those. The spectator pumps look better on you."

The truth was, almost anything Lilian tried on looked good. She had the same innate style that Constance had. Lilian was a few years older than Constance but she kept her dark hair tinted close to its original ebony shade, allowing only a few dramatic traces of silver to show. Her full, womanly figure was still amazingly firm and her fine bone structure ensured that her look of exotic sophistication would hold up beautifully until she was a hundred.

Jessie had frequently wondered about the similarities between Lilian and Constance. They were so much alike, not only in their physical appearance but also in the way they thought and acted. Connie, rather than Glenna, could have been Lilian's sister. Both women found her observation amusing.

"What did you expect?" Lilian had once said to Jessie. "Men are creatures of habit. They're attracted to the same sort of woman over and over again. Second wives often resemble first wives, and they often have a lot in common."

Jessie watched her mother try on the spectator pumps again. "Hatch insists on going up to the island with me."

"That's reassuring. When do you leave?"

"Tomorrow morning. I called the phone number on the invitation card this morning. The person who answered was very helpful. Sounded very professional. We take a ferry to one of the nearby islands. The DEL people will pick us up in a seaplane and fly us to New Dawn Island."

"New Dawn Island?"

"That's what they call it," Jessie said. "Apparently they own it, so I guess they can call it anything they want."

"Sounds completely screwy to me." Lilian shook her head over a pair of red heels the saleswoman was offering.

"We'll be given a tour that lasts a couple of hours and then flown back to the island where we spent the night. That's all there is to it." Jessie shook her head regretfully. "I'm not sure how much I can possibly learn about Susan Attwood's fate or the leader of this DEL thing in just a couple of hours. But at least it's a starting point."

"Well, I suppose there's really nothing to worry about. Hatch should be able to take care of anything that comes up. He's a very competent sort of man, isn't he?"

"Uh, yes. In some ways."

Lilian gave her a sly smile. "I get the impression the big romance is heating up rapidly. Connie says she thinks you and Hatch are already sleeping together."

"That's what I like about this family. Absolutely no privacy."

Lilian chuckled. "You know as well as I do that we're all hoping you and Hatch will work it out."

"I'm not so sure Aunt Glenna feels that way."

"Nonsense. Glenna knows that a marriage between you and Hatch would be the best thing for all concerned. It's the only viable solution to the situation."

Jessie gazed broodingly at the pair of Italian leather sandals her mother had on at that moment. "Doesn't it strike you that it's a bit strange that Hatch is thirty-seven years old and still single?"

Lilian flashed her a look of genuine surprise. "Didn't anyone tell you he was married once?"

Jessie stared at her, dumbfounded. "No. No one mentioned that little fact." Least of all, Hatch. "Divorced?"

"Widowed, I think. Connie told me about it. She said Vince mentioned it in passing a few days ago."

"Widowed. I see." Jessie absorbed that bit of information slowly, examining it from every angle. "I wonder why Hatch never told me about his first wife."

"I gather she died several years ago. Don't fret about it, Jessie. I'm sure he'll tell you all about his first marriage in his own good time."

Jessie rested her elbows on the arms of the chair and laced

her fingers together. She stared sightlessly at a display of glittery evening shoes and contemplated the many similarities she had often observed between Constance and Lilian.

Men are creatures of habit. Second wives often resemble first wives.

Jessie felt a small chill go down her spine. "I hope I don't look like her," she whispered, not realizing she had spoken aloud.

Her mother gave her a sharp glance. "What are you talking about?"

"Hatch's first wife. I hope I don't resemble her. I wouldn't want to be a stand-in for a ghost."

Lilian frowned. "For heaven's sake, Jessie. There's no need to get carried away with the dramatics of the situation."

"Right. This is business, isn't it?"

"You know, I'm amazed you got Hatch to agree to take a couple of days off just to go up to the San Juans with you," Lilian said in an obvious attempt to redirect the conversation.

Jessie stared gloomily at the evening shoes. "No big deal when you think about it. Like I said, it's business.'

CHAPTER EIGHT

Mrs. Valentine, ensconced in an old-fashioned rocking chair in the living room of her sister's Victorian-style house on Monday afternoon was looking appreciably improved. But her expression of welcome turned to one of dismay as Jessie concluded her report.

"You're going to go up there? To the headquarters of these DEL people? Oh, dear, Jessie, I don't think that's a good idea at all. Not at all."

"Don't worry," Jessie said soothingly. "I won't be alone. Hatch will be with me. And we're just going to look the place over. We're not going to try to rescue Susan Attwood or anything. Remember, we're only trying to find some evidence that Bright is a phony."

"Oh, dear," Mrs. Valentine said again. Her fingers toyed nervously with a deck of tarot cards in her lap. "Have you told Mrs. Attwood?"

"Of course." Jessie recalled the conversation with Martha Attwood that had taken place earlier. Mrs. Attwood had been very excited that something concrete was finally going to happen. "She's very anxious for a report. Her main concern is to find out if her daughter is on the island. I'm not sure we'll be able to do that, but we might get lucky. Hatch and I are just going to play it by ear."

"Oh, dear." Mrs. Valentine's gaze sharpened abruptly and her hand stilled on the cards. "Jessie, I'm getting a feeling about this situation. A real feeling. Do you understand?"

"A psychic sort of feeling? Mrs. V, that's wonderful. Maybe you're getting back some of your natural ability."

Mrs. Valentine shook her head in frustration. "It's not that clear. Not like these things were before I fell down the stairs. But I think there's something dangerous in all this. I can sense that much. Jessie, I do not like this. Not one bit. I think it would be better if you don't go to the island."

"But, Mrs. Valentine, all I'm going to do is get a look at what's going on up there at the DEL headquarters. And I've already promised Mrs. Attwood I'll go."

Mrs. Valentine sighed heavily. "Then promise me one thing."

"Of course, Mrs. V. What is it?"

"That you will not do anything rash. Promise me you will stay with Sam Hatchard at all times. He does not strike me as a rash or reckless man. I think we can rely on his good sense." But Mrs. Valentine did not appear completely certain of that analysis.

Jessie's Aunt Glenna phoned to put in her two cents' worth on Monday evening.

"Lilian tells me you've tracked down this DEL outfit and you're going up to take a look at the headquarters tomorrow," Glenna Ringstead said in a disapproving tone. "Do you really think that's a good idea, Jessie?"

"I'm not going alone, Hatch will be with me." Jessie was learning that using Hatch's name was rather like waving a talisman in front of all the people who had serious doubts about the expedition to the island. They all seemed to calm down a little when they found out he was going to be going along.

"I see." There was a distinct pause on the other end of the line. "I assume that the relationship between you and Hatch has taken a more serious turn, then?"

"Uh-huh." Jessie did not know what else to add. She glanced at the clock and saw that it was already after seven. She wondered if Hatch had left the office yet. "But don't get too excited, Aunt Glenna. I admit I'm attracted to the man, but can you honestly see me marrying him? It would never work."

"No," Glenna said quietly. "It wouldn't. As much as everyone would like to have you marry Sam Hatchard, I have to admit it would probably be a disaster for you, emotionally."

Jessie clamped her fingers more tightly around the phone and swallowed heavily. It occurred to her that her aunt's response was not what she had wanted to hear. Had she actually been hoping Aunt Glenna would, like everyone else, blindly reassure her that things could work between herself and Hatch? "Well, I've got to pack. I'll talk to you when I get back, Aunt Glenna. And thanks for recommending all those books on cults. I've learned a lot."

"You're welcome."

The roar of the seaplane's prop engines made conversation virtually impossible. Jessie peered out the window as the pilot eased the craft down into the cove and taxied toward the floating dock. The headquarters of the Dawn's Early Light Foundation did not look at all like the sort of facility she had been expecting to house a group of strong-minded environmentalists.

The pilot, a young man in his early twenties dressed in a spiffy blue-and-white uniform and wearing an engaging grin, chuckled as he shut down the engines. "Not quite what you anticipated, I'll bet. Most visitors are surprised. I guess they expect us to be living in caves and munching on roots and berries."

"Well, I certainly didn't expect anything as plush as this,"

Jessie admitted, surveying the magnificent old mansion that overlooked the cove. "Did you, Hatch?"

Hatch shrugged as he opened the cabin door and stepped out onto the gently bobbing dock. "Who knew what we'd find up here? Bunch of weirdos running around trying to save the world."

Jessie smiled apologetically at the pilot. "Don't pay any attention to him. He's a confirmed skeptic. I'm afraid I'm guilty of more or less dragging him up here today."

"Sure. I understand. A lot of the people I fly in here are skeptical at first. Your guides are on their way. Enjoy your tour." The pilot smiled his charming smile again. He stood with his booted feet braced slightly against the motion of the dock, the breeze ruffling his sandy hair.

He looked extremely dashing in his crisp uniform, Jessie thought. He certainly had the build for it. Jessie eyed the broad shoulders and chest and wondered if he lifted weights as a hobby. With his breezy, all-American good looks and smile, he could have been any corporate pilot working for any private business anywhere. The name engraved on his name tag was Hoffman.

"When does this famous tour begin?" Hatch demanded, glancing at his watch. "Haven't got all day, you know."

Jessie winced in embarrassment and shot another apologetic glance at Hoffman. "Please, dear," she murmured, doing her best to sound like a placating wife, "don't be so impatient. It's a lovely day and I'm sure we're going to enjoy the visit."

"Enjoy myself? Don't be an idiot. If I wanted to enjoy myself, I'd have gone fishing. I wouldn't have agreed to waste my time up here."

"Yes, dear." Jessie hid a quick smile. Hatch was putting on an act, of course. But he was awfully good at it and she suspected he was well and truly into the role. Probably because he really did think this jaunt was a waste of time and effort.

It had been Hatch's idea to adopt the facade of a married

couple. "It'll be sort of like playing good-cop/bad-cop," he'd explained on the drive up from Seattle. "You'll be the gullible, easily influenced, weak-brained little wifey who buys into the whole save-the-world scene."

"Thanks. What part do you get to play?"

"I will be the cynical, jaded, tough-minded husband who has to be convinced."

"You don't think it'll work if we reverse the roles?" Jessie suggested dryly. "I could play the cynical, jaded, tough-minded wife and you could play the gullible, easily influenced, weak-brained husband."

"Are you kidding? You're a natural for your part, already. You're the one who can't say no to anyone, remember? If it hadn't been for me, you'd probably own a couple of hundred shares of a company that makes fat-free cooking oil by now."

"You know something, Hatch? If that company's stock goes up in the next six months, I'm going to hold you personally responsible for reimbursing me for whatever profits I don't make."

He'd smiled faintly. "What happens if the stock goes down?"

"Why, then, I'll be forever grateful, of course."

"I could live with that."

The trip had gone smoothly until this point, Jessie reflected as she watched two figures come down the path toward the cove. It had been almost like setting out on a mini-vacation with Hatch. She'd felt a flash of pure sensual anticipation as she'd watched him load their overnight bags into the trunk of his Mercedes. *She was going off to spend a night with her lover.*

She was having an affair.

"Affair" was the only word she could come up with to describe Hatch's role in her life at the moment. She refused to call their relationship an "engagement" as Hatch insisted on doing and she could not bear to think of it as a one-night stand. That left "affair."

"I'll introduce you to your guides," Hoffman, the pilot, said cheerfully as a man and woman from the mansion stepped onto the bobbing dock. "This is Rick Landis and Sherry Smith. Rick, Sherry, meet Mr. and Mrs. Hatchard."

Jessie nodded politely. "How do you do? We really appreciate your taking the time to tour us around your facility."

"Glad you could make it," Rick Landis said, smiling respectfully at Hatch. He had the same sort of open, easy charm the pilot displayed. His dark hair was trimmed in a short, clean-cut style and he was wearing the same blue slacks and military-style white shirt that comprised the pilot's uniform. He looked to be about the same age as Hoffman, somewhere in his mid-twenties, perhaps. And he appeared to be in the same excellent physical shape.

"Didn't have much choice," Hatch muttered, fleshing out his disgruntled-husband role nicely. "Wife insisted on this little jaunt. Had my way, we'd have gone to Orcas for a couple of days instead."

"Oh, I think you'll find our little island is even more lovely than Orcas Island," Sherry Smith said earnestly. A young woman, no more than nineteen or twenty at the most, she seemed much more intense than either Hoffman or Landis. She was also quite attractive, Jessie could not help but notice. Her hair was long and honey-colored and the blue-and-white outfit she was wearing showed off her narrow waist and flaring hips.

"It's certainly beautiful here," Jessie gushed, as if anxious to make up for her surly husband. She made a show of surveying the scenery, which consisted of the cove, a rocky beach, and the old mansion. A thick forest of green, mostly pine and fir, rose up behind the great house. "Just lovely." She batted her lashes at Hatch. "Isn't it, dear?"

Hatch slanted her a wry glance. "It's okay. Can we get on with this four-hundred-dollar tour? I'd like to get back to our inn in time for dinner."

"By all means," Landis said. "I'm sure that after the tour

you'll feel the four-hundred-dollar donation to the DEL Foundation has gone to a terrific cause. Follow us, please." He turned and led the way back up the path toward the mansion.

"I'll give you some quick background first," Sherry said. "The island was originally owned by a timber baron who made his fortune back in the early nineteen hundreds. He had this beautiful house built as a retreat and as a place to entertain his guests."

"How did DEL get the place?" Hatch asked.

"It was donated to the foundation a few months ago by the last surviving member of the family. Dr. Bright took advantage of the offer to move his headquarters here. The previous owner was a strong supporter of DEL."

"Was?" Hatch glanced at her.

"She was a very old woman," Sherry said sadly. "She died not long after she had put DEL in her will."

"Kind of appropriate, isn't it?" Jessie murmured. "Using a timber baron's old home as the base for an environmentalist operation. Poetic justice."

Landis chuckled. "Not quite. But I'll explain that part later. The general routine is to start with a video presentation of the work of DEL." He opened the front door of the huge house and ushered his visitors into a vast paneled hall. "The show will give you an overview of what we're doing."

"No offense," Hatch muttered as he followed Jessie into a small auditorium, "but I'd have thought a bunch of radical environmentalists would have wanted something a little more environmentally efficient than this old pile of stones. Must cost you a fortune to heat it in the winter."

Sherry shook her head sadly as she handed him a plastic cup of coffee. "I'm afraid that, like most people, you don't really understand what DEL is all about yet. But you will soon."

Jessie eyed the cup of coffee Sherry was offering. "I'll admit I didn't expect to see anyone up here using plastic cups."

Landis nodded, his handsome face turning more serious. "I understand what you must be thinking. Have a seat and let me run the video. That should give you a good idea of what DEL is really doing."

Jessie sat down beside Hatch in one of the plush auditorium seats. She glanced around quickly as the lights were dimmed.

"Know what this reminds me of?" Hatch asked under cover of a rousing musical score that heralded the film.

"What?"

"The kind of expensive presentation prospective clients get when they fall into the clutches of some slick real-estate-investment outfit."

Jessie scowled in the darkness. "Hush. They'll hear you."

Hatch shrugged and sat back as the show began. A deep, concerned, masculine voice filled the room:

Most of the scientific community is well aware that the environment is on the verge of disaster. It will be a disaster every bit as catastrophic as the nuclear winter that would be caused by a third world war. Each day the radioactive waste piles up in our oceans. Acid rain destroys our agricultural lands. The destruction of rain forests threatens the very air we breathe.

The ultimate fate of our planet is no longer a matter of debate. All that can be debated now is the timing of that fate and the method of saving ourselves from it.

"Pretty fancy graphics," Hatch observed softly as the music swelled again. "Someone hired a first-class ad agency to put this show together."

The narrator's voice rose again, this time sounding confident and reassuring:

One man, an expert in computer programming, climatology, and ecology, has studied the problem more intensely than most. His name is Dr. Edwin Bright. And he is the founder of Dawn's Early Light. Meet the one individual who can make it possible for you and me to survive the disaster that is already on its way.

The scene on the film was of the cove in front of the DEL mansion. The camera zoomed in to show a man dressed in well-cut blue trousers and a crisp white shirt standing on the dock. He was gazing past the camera, out toward the horizon, as if he could see something extremely important approaching.

Jessie leaned forward to study the film more closely. Dr. Edwin Bright appeared to be in his late forties and there was no denying the camera loved him. He looked very, very good on film.

He was a striking individual with rugged features, closely cut brown hair, and vivid blue eyes. A pair of steel-framed aviator-style glasses gave him an air of serious intelligence coupled with a bold, decisive, almost military look. When he finally turned toward the camera, his eyes met the lens unflinchingly, as if he could see past it to the audience. The vivid intensity of his gaze was mesmerizing. Jessie remembered what David had reported about the man being extremely charismatic.

"Looks like one of those characters on television who will offer to save your soul if you'll just send him the contents of your bank account," Hatch muttered.

"Shush. I told you, Rick or Sherry will hear you."

Dr. Bright agrees with his fellow scientists on many points. However, he has run his own computer forecasts based on his own calculations. He has simulated climatological events over the next fifty years. There is little doubt that environmental disaster is inevitable. Dr. Bright's estimate of the timing of this disaster differs from many in the scientific community.

According to Bright's carefully constructed programs and calculations, that disaster will overtake us much sooner than most people predict. It will very likely strike within the next ten to fifteen years.

Edwin Bright also disagrees with his associates in the scientific community and with the radical environmentalists on the subject of how to survive this disaster.

Edwin Bright looked straight into the camera and spoke for the first time. His voice was rich, measured and imbued with almost hypnotic intensity:

It is technology that got us into this environmental mess, Bright said grimly, *"and it is technology that will save us. I'm afraid it is far too late to employ conservation measures, in spite of what the liberal extremists tell us. Switching from plastic to paper bags at the supermarket is like trying to plug a leak in a dam with a Band-Aid. In any event, we cannot go back to some primitive time before the invention of electricity or antibiotics. To do so would be to deny the very thing that makes us human, the very thing that can save us, namely our intelligence. Such a retreat into the past is unthinkable. It is, to put it bluntly, too late to return to that world of early death and periodic famine that our ancestors endured. We do not have enough time to reverse our economy or change our life-styles drastically enough to forestall the cataclysm.*

Jessie glanced down at the cup in her hand. "I guess that philosophy explains the plastic. Why bother trying to recycle when the damage has already been done and there's no time left to clean it up anyway?"

"Convenient sort of theory," Hatch murmured. "Bound to appeal to a lot of people. Lets 'em have their cake and eat it too."

But there is hope, Edwin Bright continued in a strong, reassuring voice. *And that hope lies with the work of the Dawn's Early Light Foundation. Here at DEL we are attacking the problem the way real Americans have always attacked their problems: with the power of modern science and technology and with good old American-style know-how. My friends, we are making great progress. With your help, we can continue our important work. But time is short. I urge you to give what you can now, today, to the cause. Without your support, we can do little. With it, we can save the world.*

The narrator took over once more as the camera went high for an aerial shot of the island:

You may be surprised to know that much of the technology

147

needed to save our world already exists. Part of the work of the DEL Foundation is to correlate data on that existing technology and find ways of employing it effectively. We cannot wait for the world governments to do this. They are too bogged down in red tape and bureaucracy. Only private enterprise has the ability to react to this kind of crisis. Farsighted Americans believe in private enterprise and they support it because they know it works. We hope you will help us.

Jessie listened to the rest of the filmed lecture and realized ruefully that she wanted to believe that somehow DEL really could save the world with existing technology. It was reassuring and inspiring to think that the tools were already available and all it took was a master plan to put them into use. She had to remind herself that Dr. Edwin Bright was probably nothing more than a fast-talking salesman.

The music swelled once more as the film came to a stirring conclusion. The lights brightened slowly in the auditorium as the film came to an end.

"I imagine you've both got a lot of questions," Landis said as he got to his feet.

"Right," said Hatch. "For starters I'd like to know how the hell this Edwin Bright came up with his time frame for the total destruction of the environment. Ten to fifteen years is a damn short prediction. Everything else I've read says we'll have longer to solve the problem than that."

"Good question," Landis agreed gravely. "Let's go downstairs to the computer room and I'll show you how we do Bright's calculations."

Sherry Smith fell in behind Jessie as Landis led the way down a darkly paneled hallway. He paused once to open a door briefly.

A hum of voices greeted Jessie as she glanced inside what must have originally been the mansion's formal dining room. Banks of telephones and desks were set up in a long row. They were manned by several men and women who all appeared to be in their early twenties. It was not difficult to figure out what was happening. Jessie focused on the voices of the nearest telephone operators while she scanned the room for anyone who looked like Susan Attwood.

"Yes, sir, Mr. Williamson, we've made enormous progress and we're now dealing with a major corporation on a contract to mass-produce the machine. It will go into production next month and will be available to all of the nation's cities and towns within eighteen months. The profit potential on this is enormous. It is an affordable product and will be mass-produced. You will easily triple your investment in the next eighteen months. Can we count on your donation?"

The operator reminded Jessie of her friend Alison, the stockbroker. She caught Hatch's sardonic eye and realized he was thinking the same thing.

One of the other operators was selling something else.

"As I explained," the vivacious, earnest young woman was saying to the person on the other end of the line, "the Bright Vaporizer totally eliminates all garbage via a chemical process. The end product is pure, clean oxygen. It will eliminate the need for landfills, ocean dumping, and every other kind of garbage facility. All we need is a little more financial help from you. If you can see your way clear to donate a minimum of five thousand dollars, you will be considered a registered investor and thus a potential stockholder. You will share in the profits, which are guaranteed to double every six months for the next five years."

Landis quietly closed the door and went on down the hall to a stone staircase. "The original owner of the mansion had a huge basement built down here," he explained as he started to descend the stairs. "We've turned it into our computer facility. Dr. Bright runs all of his programs on the computers you'll see here. Those programs are being constantly updated with all kinds of information, including the latest climate information and reports of accidental releases of radiation, toxic spills, and such."

"The programs are almost unbelievably complex," Sherry

confided. "We chart the amount of rain forest destroyed each day, the quantity of pollutants being released into the atmosphere from all major manufacturing plants around the world, as well as concentrations of natural gases from such things as volcanic eruptions. Then we do our projections, using the past several thousand years of the earth's climate history."

"And that's just the tip of the iceberg, as they say." Landis smiled as he reached the bottom of the staircase and opened a door in the narrow hall. "A whole different kind of research is done to pull together all the information we can get on existing technology, including the work of small private inventors around the nation and material buried in our country's research labs."

Jessie heard the unmistakable high-pitched whine of computer machinery. She moved to the doorway and stood looking into the windowless room. Hatch came up behind her and studied the scene over the top of her head.

"Hell of an operation," he said, sounding impressed for the first time.

That was an understatement, Jessie decided. A row of computer terminals occupied one long table. Three intent young people, who all reminded her of Alex Robin, crouched in front of the screens. They were so entranced with what they were doing that they did not even glance toward the door.

Fax machines, printers, telephones, and computer modems were sprinkled around the room. The gray concrete walls were almost entirely covered in huge world maps. Charts and bound printouts lay everywhere. In addition to the three people at the computer consoles, there were two other people in the room. They were women who appeared to be about the same age as Susan Attwood. But neither of them looked like Jessie's client's daughter.

"You're welcome to go in and take a closer look," Sherry said encouragingly.

Hatch nodded brusquely and moved on into the room,

followed closely by Jessie. He came to a halt in front of one of the computer screens and studied the display. It showed several rows of numbers.

"What are we looking at?" Hatch asked the man hovering over the keyboard.

"Climate data on northern Europe that goes back two hundred years. I'm using it to run projections for the next fifty years." The young man did not look up. He pushed a button and the numbers on the screen flickered and altered as if by magic. "You can see the warming trend is accelerating rapidly."

Hatch nodded and moved on to the next screen, where the operator explained he was charting seismic activity.

"Dr. Bright believes there will be some major shifts in the tectonic plates due to the recent increased activity of some volcanoes," the man said. "Volcanoes affect the climate in some unusual ways."

Jessie stared at the screen and recalled something Elizabeth had mentioned recently. "What about the destruction of the rain forests?"

"A major problem. But Bright has done a lot of thinking in that area and has come up with some interesting solutions. His main work is in climatology. You know, the ozone layer, global warming tendencies, that kind of thing. In fact he phoned an hour ago and said to double-check some recent projections. He's got some new data that say there might be even less time than we think."

"I see." Jessie began to feel genuinely uneasy. It occurred to her that everything about the DEL operation looked extremely credible. "Where is Edwin Bright?"

"In Texas, I think," the young man said. "He's talking to a scientist there who's come up with a way to seed clouds with a chemical that can neutralize acid rain. Bright wants to help him rush through a patent."

"There is so little time left," Sherry whispered softly.

"Yeah." Hatch tossed his empty coffee cup into the nearest waste can, which was overflowing with discarded computer printouts. "Would someone mind pointing me toward the men's room?"

"Sure. There's one just down the hall." Sherry smiled at him. "I'll show you."

"Appreciate it." Hatch ignored Jessie's annoyed glance as he followed the young woman out the door.

Jessie watched him leave and then turned to Landis with what she hoped was an innocent, curious expression. "I'll have to admit I'm very impressed by all the computers and technology here, but I was under the impression Dr. Bright was more than just a brilliant scientist. The person who gave me the invitation implied he had certain . . ." She hesitated. ". . . certain *abilities.*"

Landis nodded, his eyes meditative. "You're referring to the rumor that Bright has psychic powers, aren't you?"

"Is that all it is? A rumor?"

Landis drew her out of the computer room and shut the door on the high-pitched hum. "I suppose it depends on how you look at it. Dr. Bright is a very brilliant man with an incredible ability to assimilate vast amounts of raw data and come up with forecasts and projections. His brain is virtually a computer. To some people that might make him look like he actually has psychic powers. But he does not encourage anyone to believe that."

"I guess I was misinformed." Jessie remembered that Mrs. Attwood had only assumed Bright was using claims of psychic abilities to influence people such as her daughter.

"And where do you draw the line between natural human ability and real psychic ability, anyway?" Landis asked in a reasonable tone. "Everyone accepts the idea of intuition, and a lot of people pride themselves on the accuracy of their hunches. But if someone has an extraordinary amount of intuitive ability, as Dr. Bright does, people tend to label it a psychic gift."

"Good point. I see what you mean." Jessie wondered if that was what Mrs. Valentine actually had, a keen intuitive ability and nothing more. "You appear to have quite a large staff."

"Only about fifteen people in all. They come to us because they're genuinely concerned with environmental issues and because they believe in our nation's proved ability to find technological solutions to problems. They stay with us because they believe Dr. Bright holds out the best hope for finding answers. We certainly hope you and Mr. Hatchard can see your way clear to assist our work with a donation."

Jessie started to respond to that but closed her mouth when she caught sight of Hatch returning from his foray to the men's room. Sherry Smith was walking down the hall beside him, her pretty face more intent than ever as she talked. Hatch was frowning thoughtfully as he listened. Jessie found herself strangely irritated by the air of intimacy surrounding the two. She turned back to Landis and smiled politely as she took refuge in a traditional wifely excuse.

"About your request for another donation. I always discuss major decisions like that with my husband, Mr. Landis."

"Of course, Mrs. Hatchard." Landis smiled his charming smile and motioned toward the staircase. "Shall we continue our tour?"

CHAPTER NINE

Jessie swirled the liqueur in the balloon glass and ducked her head to inhale the pleasant fragrance. She was feeling cozy and warm and replete. Outside the small restaurant a steady rain was falling. The meal she and Hatch had just concluded had been excellent. There was a fire burning in the hearth of the little dining room and the place was half-full of quietly talking people who were obviously enjoying themselves.

Jessie and Hatch had gone back to the inn after returning from the DEL tour, changed clothes, and walked to the restaurant. It had not been raining then, although the threat had been apparent. Hatch had said little during dinner. He appeared to be lost in thought.

For once Jessie had not felt like baiting him. She had been content, instead, to luxuriate in the unfamiliar sense of companionship. It was gratifying somehow to know they were both mulling over their shared adventure of the afternoon.

The trip had established a new bond between them, she thought. They had something in common now in addition to the undeniable physical attraction, something that had nothing to do with Benedict Fasteners. For the first time she had a glimmer of hope about the future of their relationship.

It was just barely possible that she and Hatch might be able to establish a meaningful communication, she told herself wistfully. The fact that Hatch was obviously concentrating on her investigation tonight was a good sign. He was clearly capable of taking a genuine interest in her work.

Maybe Hatch's devotion to his own career was not quite so single-minded as her father's after all. Maybe he just needed to be lured away from his desk from time to time. Maybe with a bit of coaxing he could learn to develop the playful side of his nature, learn to pause and relax, learn to stop and smell the roses.

Jessie risked a quick assessing glance at her dinner partner as he signed the bill and pocketed his credit card. He was, for Hatch, almost casually dressed this evening. In other words, that meant he was not wearing a business suit. He had on a richly textured charcoal-gray jacket over a white shirt and a pair of black trousers. Instead of his usual discreetly striped silk tie, he was wearing one with little dots all over it. The man had obviously thrown all caution to the winds when he had packed for this trip.

Hatch glanced up and saw her watching him. She smiled warmly and waited expectantly for him to comment on some conclusion he had arrived at concerning DEL, or at least to note what a pleasant evening this had been.

"Damn," Hatch said, frowning slightly, "I wonder if Gresham got his status report in to Vincent this afternoon. If he didn't, I'll hand him his head on a platter when I get back. I've had it with that guy. We're on a critical path with that Portland project. Nobody involved in it can miss even one more deadline."

"Gosh, Hatch, that's about the most romantic thing anyone has ever said to me after a cozy little dinner for two in front of the fire. I could just swoon."

He gave her a blank look for about one and a half seconds.

Then her comment appeared to register. He got to his feet. "If you're not feeling well, we'd better get back to the inn."

"Don't worry. I feel just fine." She wrinkled her nose at him but said nothing more as he steered her toward the door. So much for the assumption that he had been dwelling on her project or her presence. His mind had been on Benedict Fasteners after all.

A few minutes later they stepped out into the misty rain and walked in silence back toward the little waterfront inn where they were staying. Hatch held the black umbrella over both of them and Jessie stayed close to his side.

The street through the center of the small island village was nearly deserted. A single streetlight marked the intersection with the road that led down to the harbor, but other than that there was little illumination. Jessie linked her arm through Hatch's, enjoying the size and strength of him there in the wet darkness. She thought of the bed waiting for them at the inn. Perhaps there was no long-term future for them, but there was the affair.

"Hatch?"

"Yes?"

"Would you mind if I asked you a rather personal question?"

"Depends on the question."

Jessie drew a steadying breath. "Do I look like her?"

"Like who?"

"Your wife?"

The muscles of his arm tightened beneath her fingers. "Hell, no."

"You're sure?"

"Of course I'm sure. What a damn-fool thing to ask. What brought this on? Who told you I'd been married in the first place? Your father?"

"No. I'm sorry, Hatch. I shouldn't have said anything."

"Well, now you've said something, you might as well finish it."

Jessie studied the wet pavement ahead. "I was talking to

my mother. She mentioned that you had been married and that you had lost your wife. That led sort of naturally into a discussion of how men tend to look for the same things in a second wife that they looked for in a first wife. Which led to the observation that she and Connie are very much alike. Mom says men are creatures of habit. Especially when it comes to women. They're attracted to the same types, if you see what I mean, and—"

"I think that's enough, Jessie."

She closed her mouth abruptly, aware that she had begun to ramble. "Sorry."

"You're not anything like her."

"Oh." Jessie experienced a strong sense of relief.

"She had blond hair and blue eyes."

"I see. Pretty, I imagine."

Hatch hesitated. "Yes. Well, in a different way than you are." He was silent for another beat. "She was taller than you."

"Ah."

Hatch shrugged. "That's about it," he said gruffly. "What else did you want to know?"

"Nothing."

"Good." He sounded relieved.

"What was she like?"

"What the hell does that mean?"

"Was she nice?"

"Dammit, Jessie."

"Did you love her very much?" She knew she should quit while she was ahead, but for some reason she could not seem to stop herself. The questions bubbled to the surface, demanding answers.

Hatch came to a halt and pulled Jessie around to face him. In the rain-streaked light that was coming through a nearby cottage window she could see that his face was harder-edged and bleaker than usual. Jessie wished she had kept her mouth shut.

"Jessie . . ."

"I'm sorry, Hatch," she whispered. "Let's just forget it, shall we? It's none of my business. I know that."

He shook his head slowly. "I know you better than that, Jessie. You won't be able to forget it now that you've started thinking about it. You're going to chew on it and fret about it and spin all kinds of questions about it."

She closed her eyes, knowing he was right. "I won't say another word about her. I promise."

"Sure. And if I believe that, you've got a bridge you can sell me, right?" He sighed. "I thought I loved her when I married her. She was everything I needed and wanted in a wife. And she was just as ambitious for me as I was. She was beautiful and understanding and supportive. She was born into the world I was moving into and she knew how to function in that environment. I was on my way up and she was going with me, the perfect corporate wife."

"Hatch, please, don't."

"She worked as hard to help me build my career as I did. She entertained my business associates on short notice. She saw to it we joined the right country club. She never complained when I was called out of town on a business trip. She understood about the demands of my job. She never made a fuss when I was late for dinner or too tired to make love to her."

"Hatch, I really don't want to talk about this any more."

"Neither do I. But you brought it up, so I'll finish it. To make a long story short, we were very happy together for about four years. I had a good position in a fast-moving company. Our future was all mapped out. I thought it was time to talk about having kids. She thought we should wait a little longer. Then a couple of things happened at once."

"What things?"

"The company I was working for was the object of a hostile takeover. When the bloodletting was over, I was out of a job along with most of management. Not unusual in a takeover situation. Olivia took the news badly, though. We were almost back to square one as far as she was concerned."

"And she had a hard time dealing with that?"

"Let's just say she was not particularly interested in starting over from scratch, and I couldn't blame her. I wasn't real thrilled with the idea, myself, but I had confidence that I could do it. I believed in myself, but she didn't. We quarreled a lot. She blamed me for the mess. And then she died in a car accident."

Jessie could feel tears burning in her eyes. "Hatch, I'm so sorry."

"It was rough. I was pretty well out of it for a while after the funeral. Which probably explains why it took me so long to find the note she had left before she got into the car for the last time."

Jessie's insides clenched as she suddenly realized where all this might be leading. "What was in the note?"

"She told me she couldn't tie herself to a loser. She had her future to consider and she was filing for divorce. She planned to marry a friend of mine. Someone I had worked with at the company, someone I had trusted. He had landed on his feet after the takeover. Gone to work as a vice-president for the new owner."

"Oh, Hatch."

"Apparently he and Olivia had been having an affair for six months prior to the accident. The day she was killed, she was leaving to meet him. Olivia said in her note she hoped I understood."

"My God." Jessie had not felt this thoroughly miserable for a long time. "I'm sorry," she said again, unable to think of anything else. "I'm so sorry, Hatch."

"I figured out a lot of things after I read that damned note. I understood at last why she had been so reluctant to talk about babies. She hadn't wanted to get pregnant until she had decided whether or not she would be leaving me."

Jessie could feel his fingers biting into her arms through

the fabric of her jacket. She lifted her hand and touched his cheek. "Please, Hatch. Don't say anything more about it. I should never have asked about her."

His mouth tightened. "You're getting wet. It's damn stupid for us to be standing around out here in the rain."

"Yes."

He took her arm again and started walking. "Anything else you want to know about me? I'd rather get the question-and-answer phase over as fast as possible."

She had a thousand questions but she could not bring herself to ask a single one of them at that moment. "I guess I'm not very good at this sort of thing."

"You might not be good." His mouth quirked wryly. "But something tells me you'll be persistent. Are you sure you don't have any more questions?"

"I'm sure." She reached up to pull the lapels of her jacket closed. "Feels like it's getting colder, doesn't it?"

"Not particularly. You're probably just getting wetter."

"No, it's more than that. It is colder. Or something." A small ripple of awareness went down her spine. Instinctively she glanced behind her. There was nothing to see but the dark, rain-washed street. A car's headlights briefly speared the night behind them and then vanished.

"Something wrong, Jessie?"

"No. For a minute I thought there was someone else around."

Hatch glanced back. "I don't see anyone. Even if there were, it wouldn't be anything to worry about. This isn't exactly downtown Seattle."

"True." She shook off her uneasiness. "What did you think about our tour this afternoon? You haven't even mentioned it since we got back."

"I don't know what to think yet. I want to take a closer look at something I picked up at the mansion first," Hatch said. "Maybe have someone else look at it too."

Jessie glanced up quizzically. "What on earth did you pick up? I didn't see you carrying anything."

"I'll show you when we get back to the room."

"Do you think there's any chance DEL is for real?"

"No," Hatch said flatly. "It's a scam, pure and simple. What we saw today was a first-class boiler-room operation. One constructed with lots of fancy window dressing to impress the suckers."

"I was afraid of that. You know, in a way, I was almost hoping it was for real."

"Jessie, there are no easy fixes for the environmental problems we're facing. Just ask Elizabeth or David."

"I know. Just wishful thinking. You have to admit that all those computer screens full of climate projections and stuff looked awfully convincing. I talked to Landis when you went to the men's room."

"I'll bet he hinted he'd like a sizable donation."

"Well, yes. But more important, I tried to get him to tell me whether or not Bright claims psychic powers. He said some people could interpret the man's combination of intelligence and intuition that way, but he made it clear Bright makes no overt claims to having psychic abilities."

"Smart. Let the sucker think what he wants to think, and play to it. I'm not so sure he'd need to claim psychic gifts anyway. Not to attract the kind of young, hopeful people we saw working at the mansion. They're more than willing to be seduced by the quick-fix promises we heard on that video. And the promise of cashing in on the profits that will be made from all the magic machines supposedly being invented."

"Yes. Bright's pitch is terrific, isn't it? Save the world and make a fortune at the same time. Who could resist?"

"There's a sucker born every minute, Jessie. Just keep in mind how hard it was for you to say no to your stockbroker friend."

"Let's leave Alison out of this. Just how dedicated do you think that staff of Bright's is?"

"Some of them are certainly dedicated enough to offer to

sleep with the prospective sucker in exchange for a sizable donation," Hatch said.

"What? She didn't." Jessie was incensed. "Did she?"

"Ummm."

"What kind of an answer is that? Did that little Sherry Smith try to seduce you or not? Just what were you doing down there in the men's room, anyhow?" Jessie started to demand further explanations, but the odd rippling sensation shot through her nerve endings again. She glanced over her shoulder.

"What's wrong now?" Hatch asked.

"I know this is going to sound crazy, but I don't think we're alone out here."

"We're almost at the inn," he said soothingly. "Just another block."

"Have you ever had the feeling someone was following you?" She quickened her steps, straining to see the lights of the inn through the rain.

"I'm a businessman, remember? Every time I look over my shoulder, someone's gaining on me. Goes with the territory."

"I'm not joking, Hatch. This is making me very nervous. There's somebody back there. I know it."

"Probably a local resident on his way home from the same restaurant."

Hatch sounded as calm as ever, but Jessie felt the new alertness in him. He obligingly quickened his step to match hers.

A moment later they were safely back in the warm, inviting lobby of the small bed-and-breakfast inn where they had booked a room. Two guests who were playing checkers in front of the fire looked up and nodded as Jessie and Hatch went past on their way to the stairs.

Jessie was relieved when she stepped into the bedroom and watched Hatch close and lock the door. She shook the rain off her jacket and hung it up in the tiny closet. "I think that visit to DEL must have made me more nervous than

I realized. Better show me what you picked up on the tour."

"I've got it right here." Hatch pulled a piece of paper out of his inside pocket.

Jessie took it from him as he hung up his jacket and took off his tie. She unfolded it carefully and found herself staring down at one page of a large-size computer printout. It was covered with numbers. "Where did you get this?"

"From the trashcan in the men's room. One of the things about computers is that they tend to produce a hell of a lot of paper. It's tough to control the garbage, even under the tightest security conditions. Someone's always accidentally tossing a few pages into the nearest trashcan." Hatch sat down in the one chair in the room and stretched out his legs.

Jessie sank down onto the bed, stunned. "You went through the trash in the men's room? That's why you asked directions to it? Good grief, Hatch. Whatever made you decide to do that?"

"I wanted a sample of whatever those computer operators were printing out. I was curious to see if it was the same kind of data we were being shown on the screens."

"Is it?" Jessie studied the array of numbers on the printout.

"No. What you're looking at there looks very much like a financial spread sheet, not climate forecasts."

"A spread sheet." Jessie glanced up again. "That would fit with a real scam, wouldn't it?"

"It would fit with a lot of scenarios. That page of data doesn't prove anything, one way or the other. A legitimate foundation would have to track its financial picture just like any other corporation. We need more information before we can get a handle on what's going on at DEL headquarters."

"How do we get more details?"

Hatch contemplated her for a long moment. "For starters, I suggest we have someone who knows computers and computer programs take a look at what's on that piece of paper."

"Why? What will it tell someone else that it won't tell you?"

Hatch appeared to hesitate again before making up his mind to explain further. "If someone who was very good with computers took a look at that page of printout, he might, just might, mind you, be able to use some of the information on it to do a little discreet hacking."

Jessie stared at him uncomprehendingly for a moment, and then realization struck. "Of course. Hatch, that's a wonderful idea. Absolutely brilliant. If we got a hacker to break into the DEL computers, we could see what they're really doing. We could at least find out if their scientific research is for real or just a cover, couldn't we?"

"Possibly. If we got lucky. And if we knew someone we could trust to do the hacking for us."

"But that's just it. We do know someone. Alex Robin would be perfect. He's desperate for work. And he'd be terribly discreet."

Hatch shook his head over her sudden enthusiasm and regarded her with a brooding expression. "Jessie, this is tricky territory. You know that as well as I do."

"If DEL is on the up-and-up, we'll back off immediately. I'll tell Mrs. Attwood that the foundation is legitimate and suggest she try some other approach to getting Susan back. But if DEL is running a scam and we can prove it, then she'll have the kind of information she needs to do something. She can go to the police or the papers and have Bright exposed, just as she wants to do."

"It's a job for a genuine private investigator or an investigative reporter, not an assistant fortune-teller."

"Now, don't be so negative, Hatch. We're not ready to turn this over to someone else yet." Jessie carefully refolded the piece of computer paper and leaned over to drop it into her purse. "We'll try to get more information first. When we have proof, we'll let Mrs. Attwood decide how she wants to handle things. Hatch, I really appreciate this. More than I can say."

"Yeah?"

She nodded seriously. "Definitely. I'll admit I had a few doubts about bringing you along on this trip, but you've certainly proved your usefulness."

"I can't tell you what that means to me."

Jessie scowled at him, wondering, as she frequently did, if he was making a wry joke. She decided once again that he was dead serious. "I couldn't have gotten this far without you, and I truly am grateful. You've given us the first strong lead we've had since I tracked down the invitation that got us into DEL."

"That's something else I've been meaning to talk to you about."

"The invitation? What about it."

Hatch gave her a level look. "Does it strike you that we got hold of that invitation very easily? Maybe too easily?"

"It wasn't easy. I had to work at it. And David helped. It was just my good luck that he attends Butterfield College and was able to find Nadine Willard."

"Jessie, we tough, cynical business types don't like to trust in things like good luck. I'm wondering why DEL went to the effort of laying on that little show for us today with almost no questions asked."

"I don't see what was so strange about it. After all, they're in the business of drumming up big donations."

"Why didn't they arrange to have a whole bunch of potential suckers make the trip at the same time? Why go out of their way to accommodate our schedule? Sending that plane over here to pick us up wasn't cheap."

Jessie paused, struck by those observations. "I see what you mean. You think maybe they're suspicious of us?"

"I don't know what to think yet. But I do know I don't like it. Not one damn bit of it."

"This is getting a tad complicated, isn't it?" Jessie mused.

"A tad."

"But it's kind of exciting in a way too. This is a heck of a lot more interesting than my last job."

"What was your last . . . ? Uh, right. You were working for Benedict Fasteners, weren't you?"

"Don't look so glum, Hatch. Things could be worse. If circumstances had been slightly different, I'd still be working for you."

"I know I should look on the bright side, but somehow it's hard to do that at the moment."

Jessie eyed him cautiously. "Was that supposed to be humorous by any chance?"

"You think I lack a sense of humor, among other fun-loving attributes, don't you?"

"Let's just say the subject is open to question."

"Would it make things simpler if I told you I am extremely serious about taking you to bed tonight?"

Jessie jumped to her feet and in the process accidentally knocked over a small candy dish that was sitting on the table beside the bed. It fell to the floor with a crash.

"Oh, hell," she muttered, bending down to pick it up. At least it hadn't broken. She knew she should be grateful for small favors. Setting the heavy glass dish back down on the table, she stalked to the window.

"Why do I make you nervous, Jessie?"

"I don't know." She took a handful of the curtain and crushed it between her fingers as she studied the rainy darkness outside the window. "Why are you so sure you and I could have some kind of genuinely meaningful long-term committed relationship?"

"I never thought about having a genuinely meaningful long-term committed relationship. I was thinking more along the lines of a marriage."

"See? That's exactly what I mean when I say I can never tell if you're making a joke or if you're serious. It's very disconcerting. Why don't you just answer my question? What makes you think you and I could make a go of it?"

Hatch appeared to turn that question over in his mind for a long moment before he said, "Things feel right with you."

"Right? What do you mean, 'right'?"

He shrugged. "I think it would work out. The two of us, I mean."

She crushed the curtain more tightly in her clenched fist. "But what do you want from a . . . a relationship, Hatch?" She simply could not bring herself to say the word "marriage."

"The usual things. A loyal wife. Kids. I'm thirty-seven years old, Jessie. I want to have children. Put down some roots. I grew up on a ranch, remember? Part of me still wants to feel like I belong to a place. I know I won't have that feeling until I've established a home and family of my own. It's time."

"You sound as if you're listening to some sort of biological clock."

His mouth curved briefly. "Did you think only women had internal clocks?"

"I guess I hadn't thought much about biological clocks at all. Even my own." She sighed. "I would definitely not make you a good, supportive, corporate president's wife. You know that, don't you? I would nag you if you didn't come home on time in the evenings. I would yell at you if you took too many business trips. I would show up at the office and cause a scene if you canceled an outing with one of the children because of a business appointment."

"I know."

She spun around. "Then why in heaven's name do you want to marry me? Are you that eager to get your hands on Benedict Fasteners?"

"No."

"Then give me one good reason," she challenged, feeling oddly desperate. "Why me instead of someone else? Someone who wouldn't give you a hard time about your work?"

Hatch got slowly, deliberately to his feet, his eyes never leaving hers. He moved toward her until he was standing directly in front of her. Then he caught her face between rough palms and brushed his mouth lightly, possessively across hers. "Because I know I can trust you."

Her eyes widened. "Trust me?"

"You might yell at me, nag me, annoy me, infuriate me. But I am almost certain you would never lie to me. And I know I'll have your loyalty because I'll always be tied to Benedict Fasteners and therefore to your family. I'm going to make myself a part of your world, Jessie. You're very loyal to the people in your world, aren't you?"

She stared up at him. "Is loyalty so important to you?"

"I do not think you would have an affair with my best friend. I do not think you would run off with him and leave me a goddamned note telling me you hoped I understood. If you are angry or hurt or feeling neglected, I think you'll complain directly to management, not go behind my back and cry on some other man's shoulder."

"Complain to management." Her lip quivered. "Oh. Hatch. What am I going to do with you?"

"Right now all you have to do is go to bed with me."

CHAPTER TEN

Hatch watched the sweet, wistful longing in Jessie's eyes as he reached out and turned off the light. She wanted him. But then, he had understood that almost from the start. It was the primary reason he had been willing to be patient in his pursuit. A man could afford patience when he knew the end was not in doubt. He would not rush her into marriage.

But after having had a taste of her in bed, he could no longer resign himself to patience in that department. A man had his limits.

Hatch curved his hands around her shoulders, enjoying the delicate, womanly feel of her. She did not pull away. His eyes met hers in the shadows and, as always, he was drawn into the depths of that wide, luminous gaze. He let his hands slide down to the row of buttons below the collar of her silk shirt.

The shirt parted easily as he slowly worked his way down to the waistband of the long, flared skirt. Hatch took a deep breath as he slid his fingers inside the opening and found the warm, scented softness of her skin. His thumb touched the front clasp of her lacy little bra and he unclipped it.

She inhaled sharply and gave a tiny little whimper of desire as he cupped her breasts. Her arms stole softly around his waist and she leaned her head against his shoulder.

"I've decided we might as well try having an affair," she mumbled into his shirt.

He almost laughed out loud at that ridiculous statement. But he managed to control his initial reaction and merely smiled into her hair as he unfastened her skirt. "Do you think we can handle an affair?"

"Well, we're two healthy single people who happen to be very strongly attracted to each other. Neither one of us is the type to get involved in one-night stands." She lifted her head and frowned up at him in the darkness. "Are we?"

"No. I've never been particularly interested in one-night stands," he assured her. "The risk/reward ratio is badly skewed. Frankly, I've never considered them cost-effective."

He heard her swallow a choked little laugh, and her arms tightened around his waist. "Hatch, you are impossible."

"You, on the other hand, are very, very lovely," he breathed as her skirt fell to the floor.

He moved his hands over her, enthralled by the gentle contour of her back and the flare of her hips. He slipped his fingers inside her panties and eased them down until they followed the skirt to her ankles. Then, with a sigh of sheer masculine pleasure he cupped her buttocks and squeezed carefully. She shivered.

The small shudder of unmistakable desire that rippled through her was intoxicating. Hatch did not wait any longer. He leaned over and pulled down the covers of the bed. Then he picked her up in his arms and put her on the sheets.

He undressed impatiently, unable to take his eyes off her as she lay waiting for him. He was fascinated with the dark outline of her nipples, the tiny hollow in her gently curved belly, and the triangular thicket of hair that concealed her deepest feminine secrets.

He was already fully aroused by the time he got out of the

last of his clothes. His body felt taut and strong and powerful. Jessie did this to him, he thought in awe. She made him feel this way. He could not wait to bury himself in her tight, humid sheath.

"I promised myself that this time we'd take it slow." He came down onto the bed beside her and drew her toward him.

"Did you?" Her eyes were shimmering with wonder and sensual excitement. She stroked his arm and touched his hip lightly, fleetingly. Her legs shifted restlessly on the sheet.

"I let you push me too fast last time." He bent his head to kiss the soft, vulnerable hollow of her throat.

Her eyes widened in instant outrage. "Now, just a minute here. I did not push you into making love to me in Mrs. V's office. How dare you blame me for that? You were the one who pushed me into doing it right there on her sofa, of all places."

He slowly combed his fingers through the crisp hair between her legs, aware of the welcoming scent of her. "You might as well face it, sweetheart. You have the power to push me over the edge."

"Hah. I don't believe that for a minute."

"I didn't either. Until I found myself taking you right there on Mrs. Valentine's office sofa." He kissed one tight, firm nipple. "That kind of power is a dangerous thing, Jessie. Be careful how you use it. Who knows where we'll be the next time you push me too far?"

She shivered again as he forced his knee gently between her legs, opening her to his touch. He sucked in his breath, clamping down what was left of his self-control when he realized she was already wet. "Jessie, honey. Jessie, touch me."

She kissed his chest as her fingers floated lightly down to curve around his throbbing shaft. Hatch thought he would explode then and there.

"So much for taking it slow this time," he muttered. He

rolled onto his back and pulled her down on top of him. She knelt astride his hips, her lips parted in sensual wonder. She cradled him in both hands, openly marveling.

"What's so funny?" she demanded in a husky voice as she glanced up suddenly.

Hatch realized he was grinning widely. "Something about the way you're looking at me." It occurred to him that he had never seen such a look of discovery and delight on a woman's face. He had never been wanted in quite this way. It was wildly exhilarating. Pleasure and a very primitive satisfaction rushed through him like a shot of adrenaline.

"Hatch," she whispered, "I truly do not understand any of this."

"Don't worry. You're doing just fine." He tested himself against her, letting her feel the extent of his arousal.

"I don't mean this." She stroked him lightly and smiled in delight when Hatch caught his breath in an undeniable, starkly passionate response. "I mean, why is it you who can do this to me? I know this sounds trite, but the truth is, you really aren't my type at all."

"Why don't you stop trying to analyze it and just put me inside you where we both can feel it?" He reached down between her legs and drew his finger through the slick, wet moisture there. Then he guided himself inside her. He heard her take a deep breath as he pushed himself carefully into the snug passage.

When he was partway inside he clamped his hands around her waist and lowered her slowly down over the full length of him.

"Hatch."

"You fit me so perfectly. So damn good." He could feel her clinging to him, sucking him deeper, holding him prisoner there inside her. Again he had to will himself not to give into the temptation of an early release. It was all he could do to wait while he used his fingers to bring her to her own peak.

She began to move on him, cautiously at first. He watched

her expression through narrowed eyes, enthralled by her responsiveness. He was right. No woman had ever responded to him with such complete and such sensual abandon. She made him feel powerful; the most powerful man on the face of the earth.

He had never reacted to a woman's touch with such violent need.

He let her set the pace as long as possible. But when he felt her start to tighten around him, he lost what was left of his willpower. He had to end this sweet torture or go out of his mind.

Deliberately he tried to insert his finger into her alongside his engorged manhood. There was no room. He had known there would not be, of course. She was already stretched too far, filled too completely with him. But when he added the extra bit of pressure there at the sensitive entrance, she gasped. Her eyes widened briefly and then she shuddered and went over the edge.

"Hatch. Oh, my God, *Hatch*."

He locked his arms around her, swallowing her soft, keening little scream of ecstasy as he thrust himself once more straight to the core of her. "Yes, Jessie. Hold me. *Hold me*."

In that moment he could not have said exactly what it was he wanted from her, but he knew he needed it more than he had ever needed anything in his life. When she collapsed in a soft little heap on top of him he thought he had it.

For a while, at least.

Hatch did not know how long he had been asleep. But he awakened because some sixth sense alerted him to the fact that Jessie had left the bed. He turned over and opened his eyes.

"Jessie?"

She was standing at the window, still nude. He could just barely make out the shape of her gently curving breasts in the pale, watery moonlight. As he watched, she put her face closer to the glass, and he realized she was staring down into the parking lot of the inn.

"Hatch, there's somebody out there."

He yawned. "Probably some guest getting back late from dinner. Come back to bed, honey."

"No, I think he's trying to break into your car."

"The hell he is." Hatch shoved back the covers and came off the bed in one swift movement. A split second later he was at the window, following Jessie's gaze. She was right. A lone figure was hovering near the passenger door of the Mercedes. There was just enough light coming from the weak yellow porch lamp to reveal an object in the man's hand. Even as they watched, the figure raised his arm.

"He's going to smash the window," Jessie said in horror.

"Sonofabitch." Hatch unlatched the bedroom window. He vaulted up onto the sill and stepped out on the ledge.

"No, wait, what are you doing? Hatch, come back here. You're in your shorts, for heaven's sake. Wait until I call the police. For goodness' sake, *Hatch.*"

Hatch swore softly as he saw the figure near the car look up at the sound of Jessie's voice. The man was wearing a stocking mask. "Dammit, Jessie, he heard you. He'll get away."

Hatch stepped down onto the porch roof and in two strides reached the edge. Crouching low, he took a firm grip, swung himself over the side, and lowered himself down onto the porch railing. His bare feet touched the wooden surface and he was grateful there were no splinters.

But he was too late. Light, rapid footsteps sounded on the pavement of the small parking lot. Hatch knew he had lost his quarry even as he leapt from the railing onto the ground. He winced as he felt a pebble dig into his sole. He caught a glimpse of the black-clad figure disappearing around the corner of the inn.

"Shit."

Hatch started after the dark figure but gave up when he realized he was running on sharp gravel. Pursuit was useless.

His bare feet would be torn to shreds. His only chance of getting his hands on the jerk had been the element of surprise, which Jessie had ruined.

Hatch swore again as he limped back to examine the Mercedes. He surveyed the windows anxiously and ran a questing hand along the pristine silver-gray fender. He relaxed a little when he realized that no damage had been done.

The dealer had told him the new state-of-the-art alarm system Hatch had ordered would be available for installation at the end of the month. Hatch decided he'd call when he got back to Seattle and see if he could speed up the delivery date. No place was crime-free these days. It was a damned disgrace when a man could not even park his car out in the open on a quiet little island.

"Hatch. *Hatch.* For heaven's sake, Hatch."

He glanced up to see Jessie leaning out the window. She was clutching his trousers. He opened his mouth to chew her out for having caused the commotion that enabled the man to get away. Then he promptly closed it again as it occurred to him that he was standing around in his briefs in a public parking lot.

"Shit." Hatch grimly held up one hand. Jessie bundled up the trousers and pitched them down to him.

Hatch was adjusting his zipper when a light went on in the room next to the one he and Jessie were using. A plump bald man wearing a T-shirt stuck his head out and glowered down at Hatch.

"What the hell's going on down there? We're trying to sleep up here. You want to get drunk and cause trouble, go somewhere else, you bum."

"I'll do that," Hatch said.

He went up the porch steps, found the front-door key in the pocket of his trousers, and let himself into the darkened lobby.

Jessie was waiting anxiously inside the room. She had put on her robe but her hair was still pleasantly tousled from sleep. Her obvious concern for him was gratifying. Almost gratifying enough to make him forget that she had been the reason the would-be vandal had gotten away.

"Are you all right?" She fussed around him as he lowered himself into the chair.

"Hell, yes."

She frowned as she sank down onto the bed across from him. "Is something wrong?"

"Dammit, Jessie, I nearly had him. If you hadn't started yelling about calling the cops, I would have had him."

"Hatch, it's only a car."

"*Only a car? Only a car?* Do you know what that model costs? Do you know how long I waited for it to be delivered? Maybe you come from the kind of background where beautiful things like that get taken for granted, but I don't."

"Hatch, calm down. Believe me, I appreciate the value of your car. But I value you more than I do your Mercedes. Be reasonable. In this day and age you can't just go around confronting criminals. It's very dangerous. He might have had a gun." She paused. "Or a knife. Like last time."

Hatch went very still. "What are you talking about?"

She hesitated. "I'm not sure if I should say this or not because it will only upset you and if you get too upset, you're liable to start lecturing me again and I don't want you ruining everything, if you see what I mean."

Hatch came up out of the chair, took one step over to the bed, reached down, and hauled her to her feet. "What the hell are you talking about?"

She touched the tip of her tongue to the corner of her mouth. "Well . . ."

"Dammit, Jessie."

"Okay, okay, I'll tell you, but you mustn't get too concerned, because I'm probably wrong."

"Wrong about what?" He tightened his grip on her shoulders.

"About the fact that the guy you just chased off in the parking lot reminded me a bit of the one who broke into

Mrs. V's offices and tried to steal Alex's computer equipment."

Hatch felt himself go cold. "Christ. Are you sure?"

She shook her head quickly. "No, how could I be certain? The man was wearing a stocking mask each time, remember? But there was something about his build. Slight. Wiry. I don't know, Hatch. It was just a feeling. Sort of like the one that made me get out of bed and look out the window in the first place."

"That settles it." Hatch released her and went across the room to check the lock on the door.

"Settles what?"

"You're through playing big-time psychic investigator. This case of yours is developing too many angles and I don't like any of them. I'm declaring it closed, as of now."

Her mouth dropped open in shock. And then outrage kindled in her eyes. "You can't do that. This is my case. I've got a client. And I've got all sorts of new leads to follow. I'm not about to stop my investigation on your orders."

"Look, Jessie, this is no longer a game, understand? I was willing to indulge you for a while because it all seemed relatively safe."

"Indulge me? Is that how you saw it?" She stared at him in gathering fury. "Thanks a lot, Sam Hatchard. I had a hunch that was your attitude but I was willing to give you the benefit of the doubt after you found that computer-printout page for me. You had me almost convinced you were taking my new job seriously, that you were actually interested in my project."

"I am taking it seriously. That's why I'm calling a halt to it."

"You can't stop me from continuing this investigation."

He exhaled heavily and absently rubbed the back of his neck while he tried to think of a better way to deal with her anger. "Be reasonable, Jessie. You know for certain now that you're not dealing with a fake psychic. Edwin Bright is most likely running some kind of scam, from the looks of things.

But he's not seducing his followers by pretending he has psychic abilities. Report that to Mrs. Attwood and you'll have done your job. She needs a real private investigator if she wants to carry this any further."

"At dinner you implied you were willing to help me finish this investigation," Jessie reminded him through clenched teeth.

"Yeah, well, that was when I thought we could play with it a bit longer and keep you happy. But the possibility that some guy is following you around means the fun and games are over."

"Dammit, Hatch, we don't know it was the same man. In all likelihood it wasn't. I knew I shouldn't have said anything."

"Well, you did, so that's that."

"I will not tolerate this condescending attitude toward my new career."

That remark inflamed him further. "I'm not being condescending, I'm being careful. Someone's got to exercise a little common sense around here, and it sure doesn't look like you're going to be the one to do it, does it?"

"If that's the way you're going to be, you're off the case."

He lifted his eyes briefly toward the ceiling in silent supplication. "Case? What case? This isn't a *case*, it's another calculated effort by you to drive some poor innocent employer crazy. Mrs. Valentine has my sincerest sympathy. I know just how she's going to feel when she finds out what's happening."

"Is that right?"

"Damn right. She's going to realize she's got a loose cannon on board, just like every other one of your past employers has eventually been forced to realize. Come to think of it, this proves she's a fraud herself. If she had any real psychic powers she would have known better than to hire you in the first place."

"A loose cannon."

Hatch knew he'd gone too far. She was furious. "Dammit, Jessie, I never meant to say that. I'm sorry. Look, I'm just trying to make a point here."

A violent pounding on the wall that adjoined their room silenced Hatch immediately. He felt himself turning a dull red as the voice of the plump bald man next door boomed through the barrier.

"If you two don't shut the fuck up in there, I'm calling the manager, goddammit. You hear me?"

Jessie glared at Hatch in satisfaction. "Yes, Hatch, why don't you shut up? You're disturbing the neighbors. You're going to get us kicked out of here."

"I don't believe this." He raked a hand through his hair, stunned at his own loss of control. Then he surged to his feet and started to pace the small room. "I am in a hotel room at one o'clock in the morning engaging in a domestic quarrel with a woman who thinks she's some kind of psychic private investigator. I ought to have my head examined."

"I'm sure Aunt Glenna would be glad to do it for you at the usual family discount."

He swung around, his voice very soft as he leveled a finger at her. "I don't want to hear another word about your damned case until morning. Got that?"

Her chin came up and her eyes glittered in anticipation of the next act of rebellion.

"Jessie, I swear if you give me any more grief tonight, I won't give a damn about disturbing the neighbors," he said very quietly.

"Is that a threat?"

"It's a promise. Close your mouth and get back into bed."

"Or else what?" She looked at him expectantly.

"Christ, lady, you don't know when to quit, do you? *Or else* I will put you in that bed myself. And I won't care if you scream the place down while I do it. That should have the idiot next door calling the manager in no time. I'll let you do all the explaining as they kick us out of here."

She flushed. "Honestly, Hatch."

"Yes, honestly, Jessie. *Get back into bed.*"

She got back into bed without a word.

Hatch took off his trousers and got in beside her, not touching her. He was aware of how stiffly she was lying next to him and decided she was probably staring at the ceiling, just as he was. Moments crept past.

"Hatch?"

"Yeah?"

"It would never have worked anyway." She sounded oddly sad rather than angry.

"Your job as a psychic detective? I could have told you that."

"No. I meant us. You and me. A long-term, committed relationship. It would never have worked. You can see that for yourself now, can't you? We'd be at each other's throats all the time."

"It'll work," he muttered, still too angry and frustrated at her obstinacy to risk letting himself get dragged into a detailed discussion of just how it was going to work. In his present precarious mood he was likely to say a lot of things that would only add fuel to the fire. He had his self-control back and he intended to keep it.

"But, Hatch—"

"Go to sleep, Jessie."

She sighed wistfully, turned her back to him, and curled up in a pathetic little ball. A few minutes later Hatch was sure he heard a suspicious sniff. He did not say anything. When he heard another, similar sound he rolled onto his side so that he was facing her back. Then he reached out and pulled her tightly against him, snuggling her into his warmth.

She resisted silently at first and then acquiesced without a murmur. A few minutes later he was sure she was asleep.

Hatch lay awake for a long while, contemplating the fact that he had never allowed a woman to undermine his self-control the way Jessie had. One minute he was making love to her, the next he was involved in an argument that was loud enough to wake the neighbors. That kind of scene would never have happened with Olivia.

Hatch grinned briefly in the darkness and pulled Jessie closer.

The full ramifications of the argument that had taken place in the middle of the night did not sink in until Jessie emerged from the tiny bath the next morning. She came to a halt in the middle of the room, staring at Hatch; who was buckling his belt.

"Oh, my God. This is a bed-and-breakfast place." It was the first time she had spoken to him since she had awakened.

He quirked one brow as he checked for his wallet. "So what?"

She glowered at him. "So we can't possibly go downstairs to breakfast."

"We paid for it. Might as well eat it."

"Hatch, we *can't*. That man from next door and his wife will be in the dining room. And who knows about the people from the room on the other side of us or across the hall? I couldn't possibly face them. Not after that scene we conducted last night."

"We?"

"You were as involved in it as I was. Don't you dare try to wriggle out of this. Hatch, I wouldn't be able to eat a bite, knowing they all heard us last night."

He studied her in silence for a long moment, giving no indication whatsoever about what he was thinking. Then he astonished her with the briefest of rueful grins. "You and me both, babe. Let's get the hell out of here before we run into the neighbors."

Their mutual interest in conducting a hasty exit from the scene of the debacle succeeded in reestablishing communications between them. Jessie realized they were both wary of starting another argument, however, and they did not say a whole lot to each other on the drive back to Seattle. The silence was cautious but not hostile.

Jessie did make one or two efforts to introduce the subject of the investigation of Dawn's Early Light, but did not pursue them when she ran up against a stony response.

It was not until he had carried her overnight case to her front door and seen her safely inside that Hatch finally brought up the topic himself.

"Jessie, I meant it last night when I told you I want you to forget this stupid investigation. Tell Mrs. Attwood you've done all you can. Let her go another route."

He did not wait for her to restart the argument. He simply turned and went back out the door after putting down her bag.

"Hatch, I told you . . ." She broke off to hurry after him as he headed for the stairs. "Wait. Where are you going?"

"To the office. It's only the middle of the afternoon. I've got work to do."

"I should have known," she muttered. She folded her arms under her breasts and leaned against the door frame.

Hatch glanced back once. "See you for dinner. I'll probably be a little late."

"Hold it. I am not altering my life-style to suit your schedule, Mr. Hatchard."

"I recently altered mine to suit yours."

He was gone before she could think of a response. With a muffled groan of disgust Jessie unfolded her arms, closed the door, and stalked over to the phone. She had a duty to call Susan Attwood's mother.

The phone was answered midway through the first ring. Mrs. Attwood's voice sounded very tense.

"Yes?"

"Mrs. Attwood?"

"Yes. Who is this? Is this the lady from Valentine Consultations?"

"Right. Jessie Benedict. I wanted to report back to you on the results of my trip to DEL headquarters."

"Thank God you called. I've been trying to get hold of you."

The shrill edge in the woman's voice alarmed Jessie. "Is something wrong, Mrs. Attwood?"

"No. That is, something has happened. I've changed my mind. Yes, that's it. I've changed my mind. I don't want a silly psychic involved in this. I don't know what got into me, going to you like that. I want you to stop work on this thing right away. Do you hear me?"

"I hear you, Mrs. Attwood, but I don't understand. Don't you want to locate Susan?"

"It's all right. Everything's fine. Just . . . just a misunderstanding on my part. I panicked, that's all. Now, I want you to stop your investigation immediately. I am not going to pay you for any work on my behalf. Is that quite clear?"

"Perfectly clear, Mrs. Attwood." Jessie spoke very gently. "There is the little matter of the four hundred dollars and travel expenses which you did approve the other day, however."

"No. Not one red cent. You should never have gone up there. You're not a real detective."

"But, Mrs. Attwood—"

"Just stay out of this."

Jessie held the phone away from her ear as Mrs. Attwood slammed down the receiver.

CHAPTER ELEVEN

What do you think, Alex? Can you use some of the information on these to get into the DEL computers for me?" Jessie handed him the page of computer printout Hatch had filched from the men's room at DEL headquarters.

"Maybe." Alex studied the printout in the dim light. It was only four in the afternoon but, as usual, he had the shades drawn in his office to create the perpetual twilight he favored. The glow of the computer screen in front of him reflected off the lenses of his glasses.

Alex's working area was a dump site. Candy wrappers, cans of soda, and open bags of potato chips took up every spare inch that was not already occupied by a computer printout or a container of disks.

"Looks like there are a couple of things I could try," Alex mused. "Possible access codes and stuff. You said there was a lot of climatalogical data coming in on his computers. He's probably got an open line into a couple of standard weather data bases. If he has, he's vulnerable. I can probably find him. What do you want to look for?"

"I'm not certain. Financial stuff, I guess. I was hoping Hatch would help me with this. He knows about this kind of thing and could direct us. But he's turned snake mean just because of a minor little incident up in the San Juans."

"How minor?"

"Someone tried to break into his Mercedes. It shook him."

"No shit? That Mercedes he drives? I don't blame him," Alex said with great feeling. "You know what that model goes for these days?"

"It's just a car, Alex."

"That's not just a car. It's one beautiful machine."

"As it happens, the car is just fine. But we'll have to go ahead without Hatch. Now, what I'm trying to find out here is if DEL is a legitimate operation or if it's a scam."

"Why bother?" Alex frowned down at the printout. "If this client of yours took you off the project, why keep working on it?"

Jessie tapped one fingernail lightly on the surface of his cluttered desk. "I'm not sure, to tell you the truth. It's just a feeling I have."

"A feeling about what?"

"About Susan Attwood. I think her mother may have been right. She was sucked into something and she's being used somehow. I have a funny feeling she may be in real trouble."

"Intuition, huh?"

"That's as good a word for it as any."

Alex nodded. "Okay, I'll see what I can do with this."

"You don't mind?"

He grinned, his eyes gleaming with enthusiasm. "Heck, no. This looks like fun."

"I'll pay you."

"How? Your client fired you, remember?"

"We'll work out something. You certainly shouldn't have to do this for free. Mind if I watch?"

"Nope. But this kind of thing can take a while."

Jessie sighed, thinking of Hatch's irritation with her and

how likely he was to spend the entire evening at the office. She did not know if he would even show up at all at her apartment this evening. "I'm not doing anything else tonight."

"Let's see what we've got here." Alex turned toward the computer and went to work.

Hatch flipped absently through a month-old magazine he'd found lying on the table in Dr. Glenna Ringstead's office. He was beginning to regret agreeing to meet Jessie's aunt this afternoon. But when his secretary had informed him that Dr. Ringstead had called earlier in the day and asked to see him, he had decided to be accommodating.

He glanced at his watch for the third time in ten minutes. The secretary seated in the small office frowned reprovingly at him.

"Dr. Ringstead is just finishing up some notes. She'll be with you in a minute."

Hatch nodded, thinking privately that he'd give Glenna five more minutes, max. He had better things to do than hang around a shrink's office. The place made him uneasy.

He tossed aside the magazine and got to his feet. "Mind if I use your phone?"

The secretary shook her head quickly. "No, of course not. Go right ahead."

Hatch pulled the instrument around to face him and punched out Jessie's home number. Still no answer. He tried her office and got the same lack of response. He had been unable to get hold of her since he'd left her at her apartment earlier in the day. He was wondering whether to try Elizabeth's home number to see if she'd gone to visit her, when the inner door of Glenna's office opened.

"Hello, Hatch. Sorry to keep you waiting. I appreciate your taking the time to stop by this afternoon." Glenna stood back, smiling her cool, distant smile. "Come in."

"What's the problem, Glenna?" Hatch walked past her

and examined the softly lit room where she dealt with her patients. He liked it even less than he did the outer office.

"I would have come to see you at your office but, frankly, I didn't want to risk running into Jessie's father. Vincent would be bound to ask what I was doing there, and since this concerns Jessie, I'd rather not get involved in explanations."

"This is about Jessie?" Hatch's sense of uneasiness grew.

"I'm afraid so. Won't you sit down?"

He glanced at the chair. It was situated near a table that held a large box of tissues. He did not like the look of it. "No, thanks. I haven't got much time, Glenna."

"Yes, of course. You're such a busy man. Just like Vincent." She gave him a knowing, superior sort of smile and sat down behind her desk. She folded her hands primly in front of her on the surface of the polished wood. "This is going to be a little difficult to start, Hatch. Please bear with me."

Hatch made a bid for patience. He could see the woman was not having an easy time with this. "Suppose you start with Jessie."

"Yes. Jessie." Glenna paused, looking past him toward a subtle pastel print that hung on the wall. "I am extremely fond of her, Hatch. I have known her since she was born."

"I'm aware of that."

"She has always had a difficult niche to fill in our rather unusual extended family. That has come about primarily because, although she has frequently quarreled with her father, she is the only one who can really deal with him on a consistent basis. He is an extremely difficult man. Do you understand what I'm saying?"

"Sure. She's willing to tackle him when no one else has got the guts to do it. The others have come to depend on her to intercede on their behalf when they want something from Benedict. She does it because she's very loyal to the rest of you and to Vincent. Real simple."

Glenna sighed. "That's putting it a bit crudely, but

essentially you're correct. That's how it works. Vincent Benedict likes to maintain a strong sense of control. He does it in this family by holding all the purse strings."

"The interesting part," Hatch said meaningfully, "is that Jessie never asks Vincent for anything for herself, does she?"

"That's where you're wrong. She got into her present role in the first place precisely because she was seeking something from Vincent. As a young girl she wanted her father's attention and love. God knows, Vincent has never given much of himself emotionally to others. He was a distant, rather remote figure all during Jessie's childhood. So she adopted a role that gave her a way to force him to pay attention to her. In all fairness, it was about the only role available to her."

"So Jessie sets herself up as everyone else's champion in order to get his attention?" Hatch eyed Glenna curiously.

"Yes. She's been doing it so long, it's grown into a pattern of behavior for her. One she does not know how to break."

"The end result is that she's held the whole bunch of you together in some sort of family. What's the point of this little chat, Glenna?"

"I'm trying to explain how and why Jessie got herself trapped in this difficult, anxiety-producing relationship with her father." Glenna hesitated. "And the reason I'm spelling it out is that, as convenient as it would be for everyone concerned, the last thing she needs is another, similar relationship with a husband."

Hatch finally understood. He fought down a surge of raw anger. "You're talking about me, I assume?"

"Yes, I'm afraid so. In all good conscience, I must tell you it would be very unfair to push her into marriage with you. And she's so accustomed to going to bat for the rest of the family that she's liable to let us do just that. In the end she might very well ruin her own life to try to please the family."

"Tell me something, Glenna, just what kind of husband do you think Jessie needs?"

"What she needs and wants is someone who is the exact opposite of her father. A gentle, supportive, nurturing man who is capable of love and friendship. A man who will be family-oriented, not one who will be focused entirely on his work. I am sorry to have to say this, Hatch, but the truth is, you would be very wrong for her. With you she would be repeating the destructive pattern she has established with her father. I'm asking you to think about that before you push Jessie into a permanent relationship. If you care for her at all, you will let her go."

"Let go of Jessie? Don't hold your breath." The cold rage was simmering in his gut now. It was all Hatch could do not to pick up the nearest object and hurl it against the wall. He managed to maintain his outward calm, however, as he started for the door. "I've got news for you, Dr. Ringstead. You may have a Ph.D. but you don't know what the hell you're talking about. I'll make Jessie a damned good husband."

He got out of the office without slamming any doors, but it was a close call.

Let go of Jessie? The woman was crazy. Hatch knew he had never wanted anything as much in his life as he wanted Jessie Benedict.

A few minutes later he was out on the downtown sidewalk in front of Glenna's office. It was five-thirty and the streets were crowded with people heading home or to the nearest bar. He found a phone inside a department store and tried Jessie's home number once more.

Still no answer.

Hatch swore softly as he hung up the phone.

Ringstead was wrong. He was exactly the kind of man Jessie needed and wanted. Hell, she would walk all over one of those sweet, supportive, gentle types. She and her aunt might think that was what she wanted, but Hatch was sure she'd be frustrated within six weeks if she actually got her hands on that kind of husband. Jessie needed someone who was as strong-willed as she was, someone she respected. Someone who could protect her, not only from her own reckless streak but also from the demands of her family.

It did not take a doctorate in psychology to figure out something as basic as that, Hatch decided grimly. It was a quite simple man-woman thing.

Vincent was waiting for him when he got back to his office. He was standing in the hall outside Hatch's door. He scowled and waved a file folder.

"Where the hell have you been? What's going on around here, anyway? Lately you've been away from your desk more than you've been behind it. How the devil do you expect to run this company if you go gallivanting off whenever you get the urge?"

"Back off, Benedict. I am not in a good mood." Hatch pushed past the other man and went on into his office.

Vincent followed, still waving the file folder. "You know what this is? It's a report from the construction firm we hired to build the new warehouse for us. The doors arrived today and the damned things don't fit. Can you believe it? They're all going to have to go back."

"Benedict, that's a problem that someone on a much lower level than you should be handling. I've told you before, you've got to learn to stay out of the details and concentrate on the big picture."

"A whole set of doors that don't fit happens to be a very big picture, goddammit. And there's something else we need to deal with. The Spokane project. We're going to lose out to Yorland and Young if you're not careful."

"No loss." Hatch sat down behind his desk.

"No loss? Dammit, I want that contract. You said you could get it."

"I can and I will if you're dead set on it, but I still think it's not worth the effort. We don't need it. We're moving into much bigger projects now. Leave the penny-ante stuff to companies like Y and Y."

Benedict started to argue further and then halted abruptly. "Jesus. You're really pissed about something, aren't
you?"

"You could say that, yes."

Benedict's eyes narrowed. "You still having problems
with my daughter?"

"Nothing I can't handle."

"Then what's the situation here? Where have you been for
the past hour, anyway?"

"Talking to Glenna Ringstead."

"Jesus." Vincent sat down abruptly and heaved a weary
sigh. "No wonder you're pissed. That woman has a way of
getting a man's back up without half-trying, doesn't she?"

Hatch heard the odd note in Benedict's voice and glanced
up quickly. "I take it you've tangled with her?"

"Once or twice."

"She try to lecture you about Jessie?"

"Sometimes."

Hatch lost what little was left of his patience. "Benedict, I
don't need any obscure remarks. If you've got something to
say, say it."

Vincent massaged his temples and sighed again. "Glenna
and I, we sort of, you know, got involved for a while."

"Involved?" Hatch was startled in spite of himself. "You
and Glenna had an affair? That's hard to believe."

"You're telling me. It was a long time ago. Right after
Lilian and I got divorced. Lloyd Ringstead had taken off for
parts unknown a short while earlier. It was just one of those
things, you know? I was feeling low and so was Glenna. We
got together one night and started commiserating. Drank
too much. Sort of fell into bed. It happened a couple more
times and then we both realized we were acting like fools."

"I'll be damned. Somehow I don't see you and Glenna
together at all."

"Neither did we when we came to our senses. Like I said,
it was just one of those things." Benedict shifted uncomfort-
ably in his chair. "I never mentioned it to Lilian or anyone

else. Neither did Glenna, as far as I know. We were both kind of embarrassed about the whole thing."

"Had she gone back to school to get her doctorate at that point?" Hatch asked.

Benedict shook his head. "No. But she talked to me about it while we were seeing each other. I told her to go ahead, and offered to help pay for it. Hell, David was just a little guy at the time and his old man was gone. Lloyd had worked for me here at Benedict. A damned smart accountant. But I knew Glenna and the kid didn't have any money. And Glenna was Jessie's aunt, for Christ's sake. And I'd slept with her. I dunno. I guess I just felt like I owed her something."

"I'll be damned," Hatch said again.

"I'll tell you one thing. I liked her better before she got that degree in psychology," Vincent confided. "You know, I tried to sort of help David along now and then. But I don't think I did too good a job."

"Hey, he's graduating from college and he hasn't done any jail time. What more can you ask? I've known worse father figures."

Vincent's brows rose. "Yeah? Like who?"

"My own," Hatch said dryly. "A real SOB."

Vincent gave him a thoughtful look. "I'll bet mine could have given yours lessons. That is, if he'd stuck around long enough to bother—walked out when I was eight. Never saw him again."

Hatch nodded. "Sometimes it's better if a kid's father doesn't stick around."

"Yeah. Sometimes. But sometimes I kind of wished I'd had a chance to show the bastard I made something of myself. You know what I mean?"

"I know what you mean," Hatch said.

Hatch did not know whether to be worried or furious when he rang Jessie's buzzer at eight that evening and got no answer. He tried leaning on the button for a while but it was useless. If she was upstairs in her apartment, she was not answering the summons.

He walked back toward his car and stood looking up at the darkened window of her bedroom. On a hunch, he decided to drive to her office.

Ten minutes later he found a parking place on the street in front of Valentine Consultations. One glance told him that the lights were off in the upstairs office.

It occurred to him that she was deliberately avoiding him. He was mentally going through a list of places where she might possibly be at that hour when he remembered Alex Robin. The first step in tracking Jessie down was to ask Robin if he'd seen her that afternoon. Hatch got out of the Mercedes and went to the front door of the office building.

The door was locked but he was close enough to see the faint green glow in the crack of the blinds. He raised his hand and pounded heavily on the outer door.

A moment later Jessie appeared in the doorway. "What in the world? Oh, it's you, Hatch."

He eyed her from head to toe, taking in the tight faded jeans and silver-studded denim work shirt. As he studied her in pointed silence, she nervously combed her hair back behind her ears with her fingers.

"You weren't at home," he said finally.

She stepped back from the door. "Alex and I are busy. If you want to be entertained, you'll have to go somewhere else."

"Damn. I should have known. You gave that printout to Robin, didn't you?" Hatch moved into the hall and strode toward the door of the inner office. Jessie hurried after him.

Alex was hunched over his terminal. He did not bother to look up. "Hey, Hatchard. Sorry about what almost happened to your Mercedes."

"It was a near thing," Hatch admitted gruffly.

"Know how you must have felt. Going to get an alarm?"

"It's on order. For all the good it will do."

Alex nodded. "Ain't that the truth? Anyway, I'm glad you're here. Want to show you something."

"I don't think Hatch is interested in what we've found," Jessie said stiffly.

Hatch threw her a grim glance. "Want to bet?" He turned back to Robin. "Well? What have you got?"

"DEL has two major data bases. One is a financial program and the other is this climate-forecasting thing." Alex stabbed a button on the keyboard. "Take a look."

Hatch watched as rows of numbers moved across the screen. "A spread sheet. You're into the financial data base?"

"One of the programs, at least. There's a lot of information here," Alex said slowly. "Maybe even enough to help us figure out where the money's really going. I could use some professional advice."

"Dammit, I'm not going to help you follow that trail. I told Jessie I want her out of this thing."

Alex's mouth curved ruefully. "So did her client."

"What?" Hatch turned his head to confront her. "You talked to Mrs. Attwood?"

"That's right." Jessie picked up a half-finished carton of takeout potato salad and forked up a bite. "She told me she wanted me to stop the investigation."

Hatch raised his brows. "Interesting. You, naturally, are going full steam ahead."

Jessie shot him a quick glance and then returned her attention to her food. "I think something happened to frighten Mrs. Attwood."

"Then she should go straight to the police," Hatch said flatly.

"Probably. But I don't think she will. She was scared, Hatch. I could feel it. I suspect that someone from DEL warned her off. She said it had all been a misunderstanding. But I don't believe a word of it."

194

"Christ." Hatch shook his head, knowing a losing battle when he saw one. "So what are you two up to here?"

"Just poking around," Alex explained. "Trying to find out what's going on at DEL. Our main goal at the moment is to see if we can find out anything at all about the money. But I'm also curious about this climate program they're running." He punched some more keys.

"Why?"

"I've got a buddy up at the university who's into this kind of thing. I know for a fact his programs aren't projecting any ten-to-fifteen-year disaster scenarios. I'd like to see what he says about these DEL projections. I'm going to download them onto some diskettes and have him take a look."

Jessie spoke up around a mouthful of potato salad. "We want to see if they're genuine scientific projections or some kind of fake theories designed to fool potential investors."

Hatch groaned. "What are you going to do if you do manage to prove the program is a deliberate fraud?"

"Well, I suppose we could go to the authorities with the information," Jessie said slowly, obviously thinking through the situation. "After all, fraud is fraud. We can at least get DEL closed down."

"And how is that going to help Susan Attwood?" Hatch asked quietly. "If she's a part of this fraud, she's guilty of a crime. Do you really want to push things that far?"

Jessie gave him a stubborn look. "I just want to see if she's working with DEL of her own free will or if she's been duped. Please try to understand, Hatch. I can't seem to let this go now. I've gone too far with it. I have this feeling that there's something terribly wrong and that my client's daughter is in some kind of danger."

"You've been playing psychic investigator too long." Hatch turned back to Alex. "Can you do this without alerting anyone on the other end?"

"I think so," Alex said confidently.

"No footprints that would lead anyone back here to you and Jessie?" Hatch clarified, wanting to be absolutely certain on that point.

"Heck, no." Alex pulled his attention away from the screen long enough to squint briefly up at Hatch. "Does this mean you're going to help us?"

"It doesn't look like I've got a whole hell of a lot of choice, does it?"

Something clattered to the floor behind Hatch. He turned his head in time to see Jessie bending down to pick up the plastic fork she had just dropped.

"Want some potato salad?" she asked brightly.

A long time later Jessie stirred amid the tangle of sheets, stretched out one bare foot, and encountered Hatch's leg. "You awake?"

"Yes."

"I've been thinking," she said softly.

"About what?"

"About you. I haven't thanked you yet for staying on the case. I know you're not exactly thrilled with the idea of me pursuing the investigation."

"That's a mild way of putting it."

"Well, thanks anyway," she mumbled.

"Jessie?"

"Uh-huh?"

"Your Aunt Glenna talked to me today."

"Good grief. Why on earth did she do that?"

"She wanted to point out that I'm really not the kind of man you should marry. Even if it would be convenient for all concerned."

Jessie was startled to find herself annoyed. "Aunt Glenna said that?"

"Yes."

"I know Aunt Glenna means well, but sometimes she thinks that because she's got a degree in psychology she knows what's best for the rest of us. It can be irritating."

"But you agree with her, don't you? You told me yourself that I'm not the kind of man you would ever marry."

"Let's not get into that subject, Hatch. It's nearly three in the morning."

He grunted. "Did you know that your aunt and your father once had a brief affair?"

"Really?" Jessie was wide-awake now. "Are you sure?"

"Vincent told me about it this afternoon. He implied that was one of the reasons he helped her pay her way when she went back to college. He felt he owed her something."

"I'm stunned." Jessie sat up against the pillows and wrapped her arms around her updrawn knees. "I can't believe those two would ever get together in a million years."

"Why not?"

"Well, for one thing, she doesn't seem like his type. She's not colorful and sophisticated and outgoing like Constance and Lilian. She's not oriented toward art and design, the way they are. She's so serious all the time. And so clinical, if you know what I mean."

"The affair didn't last long. Your father implied he was at a low point because of the divorce from Lilian and Glenna was getting over being abandoned by her husband. One thing led to another. Then, according to Vincent, they both came to their senses."

Jessie turned that over in her mind. "I can see how it would happen. But it still seems strange, somehow."

"I agree."

"I wonder if Mom knows."

"I doubt it. Vincent said he never told her or anyone else, and he doesn't think Glenna did either. I got the feeling they both regretted the whole thing."

"Strange how you can know the members of your own family for so many years and still not know their secrets," Jessie mused.

Hatch turned toward her, his face unreadable in the deep shadows. "Your aunt talked about you today."

"Is that right?"

"She says you've become the intermediary between your father and the rest of the family because you're the only one willing to tackle him."

Jessie shrugged. "You've said the same thing."

"Yeah. But I don't have a Ph.D. in psychology to back me up. It was interesting hearing my diagnosis confirmed by a professional."

"Oh, for heaven's sake, Hatch. You make me sound like some sort of nut case just because I'm the only one who ever figured out how to deal with Vincent Benedict."

"I didn't mean that. And you're not the only one who can handle him. I can deal with him too."

She slanted him an assessing glance. "That's true. I figured that was because you're so much like him that you understand how his mind works."

"Maybe that applies to you too."

"I'm not anything like him," she protested.

"No? You're just as mule-headed stubborn as he is, for one thing. I can personally testify to that."

Jessie got annoyed. "It's not the same thing at all."

"It's okay, Jessie. I'm mule-headed stubborn too. But that's not my point."

"What is your point?"

"After I talked to Glenna today I got to thinking about us and I want to make sure we have something real clear here. Whatever else happens, I want you to swear to me that you will not let yourself get pushed, urged, bullied, or otherwise forced into marriage with me in order to protect, defend, or placate anyone in your family. Agreed?"

"I've already told you, I have no intention of marrying you."

"I know what you told me, but I happen to think the outcome is going to be a little different. I just want to make certain that when you do marry me, you do it for the right reasons, not because you feel you have to do what's best for the family."

A soft warmth welled up in her. He looked so serious, she thought. "You're the kind of man who usually doesn't worry too much about the means as long as you get the end you want," she noted carefully.

"In this case," he told her as he pulled her into his arms, "I definitely care about both."

"What are you trying to tell me, Hatch?" she whispered, her fingertips braced against his shoulders.

"That I want you to marry me because you damn well can't resist me," he muttered, his mouth moving on her throat. "I want you to marry me because I did such a hell of a good job seducing you and making you fall head over heels in love with me. Got that?"

She caught her breath as she felt his body hardening rapidly under hers. "Yes. Yes, Hatch, I've got it." She waited for him to volunteer the fact that he loved her, but he did not say the words that might have made the difference. And in that fragile moment she was afraid to ask for them.

"Swear?" Hatch prodded.

"I swear. If I ever do agree to marry you, it will be because I love you. But, Hatch?"

"Uh-huh?" He was nibbling at her earlobe now.

"I still have no intention of marrying you."

"I haven't finished this damned courtship yet."

CHAPTER TWELVE

Vincent Benedict was simmering. The initial explosion had dissolved into the customary roiling boil, which in turn was now all the way down to the mild, bubbling simmer.

Jessie was familiar with the pattern. She'd dealt with it all her life. Her father definitely had a problem with money, especially when it came to giving any of it away.

It was not that he was an ungenerous man; quite the opposite. Over the years Vincent had doled out thousands to his clan. But Constance and Lilian were right: he liked to attach strings. He liked to make certain the receivers were properly grateful and that they kept him posted on where every dime went. He felt free to make loud judgments on whether or not the money was being well-spent. He criticized, approved, or grumbled about what the recipient did with the money. And always he wanted everyone to remember where it had originated. Jessie routinely fielded the grumbles and complaints from both sides.

"Jesus H. Christ, those two women are never satisfied," Vincent roared. He slammed a palm down on his desk and regarded Jessie with a baleful gaze. "They're like sponges, always soaking up more of my cash."

"Dad, you know that's not true." Jessie was slouched low in the chair across from her father. She had her legs stretched out in front of her and her thumbs hooked loosely in the pockets of her jeans. She was wearing a snug-fitting, long-sleeved black dance leotard with the jeans, and her hair was caught back behind one ear with a large silver clip.

"The hell it isn't true. What happened to all that cash I gave Connie and Lilian two years ago to open that damn furniture store?"

"It's not exactly a furniture store, Dad, it's more of a showroom they use to give ideas to their clients. Now they want to expand it. Turn it into a design store. They're going to specialize in avant-garde European furniture styles."

"What's wrong with American furniture?" Vincent pointed to the wide mahogany desk in front of him. "Nothing wrong with good, solid American furniture."

"Dad, Connie and Lilian do not have a lot of clients who are into Early American."

"I'll tell you something, Jessie. That European crap is for the birds. I had one of those silly little Italian lamps in here for a few weeks and the damn thing broke."

"Only because you tried to bend it in a direction it was never intended to go." Jessie remembered the lamp. It had been a delicate device. Too delicate for her father's big hands. "And your opinion of Italian furniture has got nothing to do with the issue. The fact is that a lot of people like that style. Connie and Lilian cater to that crowd."

"Probably the same crowd that eats sushi and pays good money to watch films that have subtitles," Vincent grumbled.

"You hit the nail on the head when you said it's a crowd that pays good money for what it wants. Come on, Dad, you're a businessman. You know a business person has to cater to the client's taste. That's all the moms want to do. They've been very successful up to this point, and you know you're proud of them. Why not finance another expansion for them?"

"They treat me like I'm some kind of bank."

"You want them to go to a real bank instead?"

"Hell, no." Vincent turned a dangerous shade of red at that suggestion. "Damned interest rates are sky-high again. Like throwing money down the drain. Can't trust bankers, either. They won't stand by you. First hint of trouble and they call in the loans."

Jessie grinned. "And besides, if the moms went to a bank, you wouldn't have a license to complain, would you? Be honest, Dad. You like controlling the purse strings in this family."

"Somebody has to do it. God knows they all go through money like it was water. No common sense. No appreciation for the hard work involved."

"You know that's not true. The rest of us just aren't as tightfisted about it as you are."

"Yeah, well, maybe that comes from never having had to do without. Men like Hatch and me, we know what it's like to do without." Vincent narrowed his eyes. "How come you never ask me for money?"

Jessie widened her eyes in mocking innocence. "Are you crazy? There would be too many strings attached, and you know it. You'd hound me constantly, asking me what I was doing with it, where I'd invested it, what I was buying with it. You'd probably want weekly and monthly reports. No, thanks."

"You know your problem, Jessie, girl? You're too damn independent. Too blasted stubborn for your own good. When are you going to marry Hatch?"

Jessie blinked. "Don't hold your breath."

"You're sleeping with the man, dammit. He told me so himself. If you can sleep with him, you can damn sure marry him."

"I'll have to talk to him about kissing and telling. Gentlemen aren't supposed to do that."

The door opened behind her and Hatch's voice cut in on the argument. "What's this about gentlemen?"

Jessie looked over her shoulder. "Dad says you've been chatting about my love life. I was telling him that gentlemen don't do that."

"I believe I was making an unrelated point at the time," Hatch said as he came into the room and shut the door behind him. In spite of the calm response, there was a faint tinge of ruddy color high on his cheekbones. "I was telling him not to interfere in our private life, as I recall. Isn't that right, Benedict?"

Vincent scowled at him and then turned back to Jessie. "Forget that. What, exactly, is the status between you two?"

"You'll be the first to know when we've got it settled." Hatch lounged against Vincent's desk, folded his arms, and regarded Jessie with a cool, searching gaze. His eyes skimmed over the tight black leotard that fit her like a glove. He frowned with disapproval. "What are you doing here?"

"Having a little father-daughter chat," she murmured.

Vincent snorted. "She's trying to talk me into giving Lilian and Connie twenty grand to expand their business."

"I see." Hatch did not take his eyes off Jessie. "Have you already made your pitch?"

"Yep," said Jessie. "And since Dad has already changed the subject, I assume he's going to go for it, aren't you, Dad?"

"Hell, I suppose I'll have to. If I don't, those two will end up in the clutches of some smooth-talking banker who'll charge 'em an arm and a leg in interest."

Jessie clamped her hands around the arms of the chair and pushed herself to her feet. "Thanks, Dad. I'll give them the good word. I'm sure they'll be properly grateful and will keep perfect records on how they spend every cent." She gave Hatch a challenging smile. "You'll probably be late getting home tonight as usual, won't you?"

Annoyance sparked in his gaze. "Probably. I've got some figures to go over with your father."

"Hey, don't worry about it," Jessie said airily, starting for the door. "I'll be working late myself. Alex and I are making real headway on our investigation."

Vincent's expression became thunderous again. "Investigation? Are you still fooling around with that cult thing? I thought that nonsense was finished. Hatch said the guy was running some kind of scam, not a cult, and that your so-called client called off the investigation."

"Things have changed," Jessie said.

"What things, dammit?"

"I'll explain it all to you later, Benedict." Hatch straightened away from the desk and went toward Jessie. "I'd like a word with you before you take off, Jessie."

"Sure. 'Bye, Dad."

Jessie winced as Hatch's hand closed firmly around her upper arm. But other than slanting him a reproachful look, she said nothing as he steered her through the outer office and into the hall.

He stopped when he was out of earshot of the secretaries and released Jessie near a potted palm. Coolly, deliberately, he planted one hand on the wall beside her right ear and leaned in close. The pose was deliberately intimidating. It was one of the many things he did well, Jessie reflected. She started to push her hair back and discovered it was already held back by the clip.

"I don't want you doing any more of this," Hatch stated softly.

She groaned. "Hatch, we've been through all the arguments. I've told you, I can't just halt the Attwood case. At least not until I'm satisfied Susan Attwood is all right."

"I am not talking about that damned case," Hatch bit out. "I am referring to what you were doing there inside your father's office. This business of letting the entire family use you to get what they want from Benedict is going to stop.

Whoever wants to ask him for something can damn well ask for it in person. You're no longer the intermediary. Clear?"

She sighed. "Hatch, you don't understand."

"The hell I don't. Just say no, Jessie. Remember?"

"Easy for you to say."

"You'll learn how. All it takes is a little practice. I won't have them using you anymore, Jessie. I mean it. I don't want you doing those kinds of favors for any of them. Not your mother or Connie or David or your Aunt Glenna. Enough is enough."

"But it's easier for me to deal with him, Hatch. Don't you see? I've always done it. I know how to do it."

"The others can damn well learn if it's important enough to them."

She shook her head sadly. "That's just it. It might not be important enough to them."

Hatch stared at her. "What the hell are you talking about?"

Jessie looked up at him, willing him to understand. "I'm afraid they'll all give up on him if they're forced to deal with him directly. After all, Connie and Lilian both gave up on him while they were married to him. David got so resentful and frustrated trying to please him that he finally stopped talking to him. Aunt Glenna says it's a waste of time trying to forge a relationship with Dad. But it's not. Not entirely."

"What you mean is that you've managed to keep some kind of bond established among all of you by doing all the diplomatic work. Jessie, that's wrong."

"Is it?" she demanded softly. "At least this way he's got some kind of family ties and the rest of us have some kind of contact with him. Maybe it hasn't been exactly *Father Knows Best* around here, but at least we've all had a relationship of some sort. It could have been worse, you know. He could have done what David's father did and just disappeared from our lives altogether."

"Christ, what a mess." Hatch's eyes glittered. "Jessie, I

don't want you holding the whole thing together by yourself any longer. With the exception of Elizabeth, they're all adults. They can deal with their own problems."

"I'm supposed to just step out of the picture, is that it?"

"Yeah. That's it."

"This is my family, Hatch. Give me one good reason why I should do what you want," she hissed.

"I thought I'd already explained this part. I want to be damn sure that when you marry me you're not doing it solely for the benefit of the Benedict-Ringstead clan."

"And I've already told you, I have no intention of marrying you." But the protest sounded weak, even to her own ears.

"We'll save that argument for another time. Right now I want to make sure you understand that you're out of the intermediary business. Let the other Benedicts and Ringsteads fend for themselves."

"But I've already promised David I'd ask Dad about financing grad school."

"I'll handle David."

"You'll handle him? Hatch, you barely know him. You haven't been around our family long enough to figure out how to deal with this kind of thing. David's very sensitive."

"So am I," Hatch snarled softly, slapping his other hand against the wall on the other side of her head. "You just haven't bothered to take much notice, what with being too busy worrying about everybody else's sensitive nature. One last time. I want to make damn sure I'm not being married so that David and his mother and the moms and your sister are all being taken care of by you as per usual. Got that?"

"You're about as sensitive as a rhino. And stop talking about marriage. We're having an affair and that's as far as it's going to go." Jessie tried to duck out from under one of his arms and managed to blunder straight into the potted palm. The plant and Jessie both began to topple to the side.

With a muttered oath Hatch caught both palm and woman before they sprawled ignominiously on the floor. He steadied the plant and held Jessie's arm as she spit out a palm leaf.

"I want your word on this, Jessie. I mean it."

"Look, Hatch . . ."

"I said, I want your guarantee not to play go-between for everyone in the family, at least until our relationship has been finalized," he repeated through tightly clenched teeth.

"Finalized?" For a split second, standing there, looking up at him, Jessie felt disoriented. A strange, familiar sense of need hovered just at the edge of her awareness, not her own need, she realized, but something Hatch was experiencing.

"You know what I'm talking about." Once more he put his hand on the wall behind her and leaned in close.

"This is intimidation, Hatch." She was breathless and confused all of a sudden. *Hatch needed her?*

"Damn right. Come on, Jessie, stop wasting my time and your own."

"All right, I promise." The words were out before she had quite realized she was going to say them.

Hatch nodded once, satisfied. "I'll see you at dinner tonight." His fist dropped away from the wall. With one last warning glance he swung around on his heel and stalked back toward Vincent Benedict's office.

Jessie walked toward the elevators on trembling legs. She must have gone crazy there for a minute. She had stood up to him on the matter of the Attwood case. But she'd collapsed completely on this issue. It made no sense.

She sincerely hoped she was not turning into a wimp.

Forty-five minutes later, Jessie parked her car in front of the low, modern building that housed the offices of ExCellent Designs. She opened the car door and got out slowly, not particularly looking forward to the meeting that lay ahead.

Downtown Bellevue was humming with its usual assortment of BMW's and well-dressed suburbanites. Jessie always felt as if she had crossed some sort of international border when she drove over one of the bridges that linked the Eastside with Seattle.

Over here everything always looked clean and trendy and expensive. In Seattle the high-fashion shops and restaurants competed for space with the gritty elements that had characterized real cities since the dawn of time.

Connie glanced up from the design plan she was perusing on her desk when Jessie opened the office door. She smiled. "Hello, Jessie. Is this good news or bad news?"

"A little of both."

Connie made a face. "Better save it until your mother gets here, then. She just went out to get us some coffee. Ah, here she is."

"Hi, Jessie." Lilian Benedict walked into the office carrying two cups of latte. "This is a surprise. I assume you've got some news for us?"

"Dad will give you the money for the expansion," Jessie said, sinking down into one of the exotically shaped black leather-mesh chairs.

"Fabulous. I knew you could talk him into it. Any serious catches this time?" Lilian removed the top from her latte.

"No, but I had a little trouble with Hatch over the arrangement."

"With Hatch?" Constance stared at her in astonishment. "Why is Hatch involved in this?"

"He's not, actually. He just thinks he is. To put it briefly, he got very annoyed that I was doing the asking. I don't think he likes me going to Dad with requests like yours."

"But this is a personal matter between us and Vince." Lilian frowned. "Does he think the money comes directly out of Benedict Fasteners or something?"

"No, it's not that." Jessie shifted slightly in the chair, trying to find a comfortable position. Her father was right. Some of this European design stuff looked better than it felt. "It's me being in the middle that bothers him for some reason. I explained to him that I'm used to dealing with

208

Dad, but Hatch doesn't understand exactly how things work, if you see what I mean."

Lilian and Constance exchanged glances.

"I think we see," Lilian said dryly.

Constance sighed and sat back in her chair. Her long mauve nails traced the rim of the cup she was holding. "He's quite right, you know. We have all tended to let you handle Vincent for us, by and large. You have a knack for it."

"Ummm, true." Lilian studied her daughter. "I wonder why Hatch is interested in that fact."

"I think he believes I'm being used," Jessie said carefully.

Lilian's expression tightened into one of deep concern. "Do you feel used, dear?"

Jessie glanced out the window. "No. I did it of my own free will. It was just the way things were. A pattern, as Aunt Glenna would probably say. I guess I felt that as long as I was running back and forth between everyone else in the family and Dad, we were all still linked, somehow. Still a family."

"Well, it worked, after a fashion," Constance murmured. "We're all living amicably enough in the same region and we're all on speaking terms, except possibly David. Vince has been difficult, but, on the whole, reasonably fair when it comes to money. And if it hadn't been for you, I doubt that Elizabeth would have nearly as much contact with her father as she does have. I think he would have drifted away from her and everyone else if it hadn't been for you, Jessie."

Lilian nodded. "Vincent is like a Missouri mule. You have to keep hitting him over the head with a big stick to get his attention. But when you do have it, he's a decent man."

"I've been the stick," Jessie said.

"For better or worse, I'm afraid so," her mother agreed. "In a very real way, you've been what Glenna likes to call the caretaker in the family, haven't you? The one who holds things together."

"I think Aunt Glenna calls it being the family enabler," Jessie muttered.

Lilian frowned. "I'm not sure I like the fancy new words the psychologists use these days to describe the old nurturing skills. They demean them somehow. And I'm not at all sure 'enabler' is the right word here anyway. But it's obvious Hatch now wants you out of the role, whatever it is."

"He says he doesn't want me marrying him because I'm under pressure to do so," Jessie said slowly.

Constance pounced on that remark. "He's asked you, then?"

"No, not exactly. He's just sort of assumed we'll get married. You know how men like that operate. They're like generals. They set a goal and they just keep driving toward it until they've achieved their objective."

Lilian eyed her curiously. "Does that strange expression on your face mean you're contemplating the same objective Hatch has in mind? Are you finally thinking seriously about marriage?"

"No, dammit, I am not. I seem to be involved in an affair with him, but that's as far as it's going to go."

"But, Jessie, why?" Constance stared at her, perplexed. "If you like him enough to have an affair with him, why not marry him?"

Jessie looked away and suddenly she was crying. "Dammit, I will *not* spend the rest of my life fighting for a man's love. That's one pattern I will not repeat."

"Jessie. Oh, Jessie, honey, don't cry." Lilian leapt to her feet and stepped around her desk to crouch beside Jessie's chair. She put her arms around her and held her close, rocking her gently the way she had when Jessie had been a child and Vincent Benedict had canceled yet another outing on account of business. "It's all right, dear. It's going to be all right."

Jessie groped blindly for a tissue, disgusted with her loss of control and frightened by what it signified about the depth of her feelings for Hatch.

There was silence in the office for a while. Jessie blinked back the tears and blew her nose a couple of times. Then she gave her mother a watery smile. "Sorry. I've been under a lot of pressure lately."

"Being in love can do that," Constance observed gently. "It's quite all right, Jessie. Your mother and I understand. Every woman understands."

"I'm not going to marry him, you know." Jessie wiped her eyes, crushed the tissue, and hurled it into the stylish black cylinder that served as a trashcan. "I am going to enjoy an affair with him for as long as it lasts and then I will walk away. It's highly probable he will walk away first when it finally dawns on him that he's not going to get what he wants."

"You really believe he wants to marry you only because of Benedict Fasteners?" Lilian asked quietly.

"No," Jessie admitted. "It's a hell of a lot more complicated than that. He admires Dad. Wants to please him. And then there's the business angle. We all know that marrying me would be an excellent business move for him. And I admit, there's a physical attraction. I think what it boils down to is that he's satisfied with the package deal."

"Jessie, I think Hatch's feelings run a lot more deeply than that. Whatever else he is, he's simply not a superficial kind of man. Even I know that much about him," Lilian said firmly.

"He doesn't say he loves me," Jessie sniffed sadly. "He says he thinks he can trust me. Says he thinks I'll be loyal. His first wife was running off to meet another man when she was killed, you know. His mother left him and his father when Hatch was only five. Loyalty is very important to Hatch. A lot more important than love, I think. I'm not sure he'll ever trust in love again."

"Frankly, it sounds like the two of you have an excellent basis for a relationship, Jessie," Constance stated.

"Trust and attraction and a couple of good business reasons are apparently enough for Hatch. But they're not enough for me."

Lilian pursed her lips thoughtfully as she got to her feet.

"Are you sure you're not romanticizing this whole thing a bit too much, Jessie? You're twenty-seven, not seventeen. How much can you realistically expect from a man?"

Constance nodded. "Your mother's right, Jessie. You're old enough not to need rose-colored glasses. I hate to break this to you, but having trust and physical attraction between yourself and a man is about as good as it gets. A lot of women never get that much. What are you holding out for?"

"I don't know," Jessie whispered.

The office door opened and Elizabeth ambled into the room. Her brown hair was anchored with two colorful clips and her glasses were slightly askew on her small nose.

"Hi, everybody. What's going on?"

"Hi, Elizabeth." Jessie blinked back the remaining moisture in her eyes. "I'm just sitting here sobbing my heart out for no good reason."

"PMS, huh?"

Constance groaned. "This is what comes of sex education in the schools."

"I didn't hear about that at school. I heard about it from you," Elizabeth informed her mother. She sauntered over to Jessie. "I bet you're crying on account of Hatch, aren't you?"

"Afraid so," Jessie said.

"Why don't you just punch him out instead?"

"That would probably be a much more satisfying approach to the problem," Jessie said. "But he happens to be a lot bigger than I am."

"I don't think he'd hit you back," Elizabeth said, thoughtful. "At least, not very hard."

"Of course he wouldn't hit me back. Which is exactly why I can't start pounding on him," Jessie explained patiently. "It wouldn't be fair, you see. He couldn't retaliate in the same way."

"So what does that leave?" Elizabeth asked.

"I don't know," Jessie said. "I'm still trying to figure that out."

"What it leaves," Lilian said deliberately, "is common sense."

Constance smiled. "We know you'll do the right thing, dear. You always have."

Somewhere halfway across the bridge it came to Jessie that what she wanted from Sam Hatchard was proof that he could love her enough to choose her over Benedict Fasteners or anything else on the face of the planet if it ever came to that.

But Constance and Lilian were right. It was totally unrealistic to even contemplate such a scenario. What could she do? Tell him she would marry him if he walked away from the business arrangement he'd made with her father? That would be blackmail. Even if he did it, he would be disgusted with her for demanding such a sacrifice when there was no legitimate need for it. And she would be disgusted with herself for doing it.

As she had told Elizabeth, a woman had to fight fair.

A small, distinct sense of dread washed over her. There was a dark gray fog lying just beyond the edge of her awareness, as if the future held some bleak danger.

If this was what it was like to have premonitions or intuition or some other psychic ability, Jessie decided, she did not care for the sensation.

Hatch let himself warily into Jessie's apartment at eight o'clock that evening. He was not certain what kind of welcome to expect after the scene that had taken place in the hall outside Vincent's office door that afternoon.

He got a strong hint about what was in store when Jessie barely glanced up from the couch where she lay reading a book.

"Hi," she said without looking up from her book.

"Hello." Hatch closed the door and set down his briefcase. He noticed the lights were off in the kitchen. "Did you want to go out to get a bite to eat?"

"I already ate an hour ago. I told you, I don't serve dinner this late."

"I see." Hatch realized he was starving. "Any leftovers?"

"It was ravioli again. You weren't here, so I ate the whole package. You can't expect me to hold dinner for you, Hatch. Not when you don't even bother to call and let me know you'll be late."

Hatch felt a wave of chagrin. "I don't think of eight o'clock as being real late."

"I do."

"It's been a long time since I had to call home to tell someone I'd be late for dinner. Guess I'm out of the habit."

"Uh-huh. Well, don't let it worry you." Jessie turned the page in her book. "You don't have to account for all your time to me. We're just sleeping together. It's not like we're married or anything."

"You're really pissed about this, aren't you?"

"No, just realistic."

He winced inwardly and walked over to the couch to stand looking down at her. "Would it help if I said it won't happen again?"

She slanted him an uncertain look out of the corner of her eye. She was obviously taken aback by the offer. "Is that a promise?"

He hunkered down beside her, not touching her. "It's a promise, Jessie."

She sat there gnawing on her lower lip for a while and Hatch knew she was recalling all the similar promises her father had given her over the years. Casual, meaningless promises that nine times out of ten wound up being broken.

"I guess I could make you a peanut-butter sandwich or something," she said, tossing aside her book. She got to her feet and headed for the kitchen.

Hatch heaved a silent sigh of relief and followed. He knew he had come very close to disaster that time. And all because he had been a little late for dinner.

"Jessie, one more time for the record. I am not a carbon copy of your father. I don't break my promises."

She glanced up, her eyes meeting his over the refrigerator door. "I know."

Hatch realized they had just passed a major milestone. He was grinning like an idiot. "Say that again."

"Say what again? I know?" She opened the peanut-butter jar and reached for a knife.

"The whole thing. Say you know I am not a carbon copy of your father and that you know I don't break my promises."

She swirled the knife inside the jar of peanut butter. "I know you are not a carbon copy of my father and I know you don't break your promises."

"Damn right," Hatch said. "I'm glad we got that much straightened out. You got any bread for that peanut butter or do I have to eat it off the knife?"

CHAPTER THIRTEEN

The phone rang that evening just as Jessie was reaching for her nightgown.

"Hello?"

"Jessie, it's me, Alex." Robin's voice was bubbling with excitement. "Listen, you're never going to believe this, but I think I've found Susan Attwood."

"You *what?*" Jessie sat down abruptly on the edge of the bed, clutching the nightgown. Hatch came out of the bathroom and eyed her questioningly.

"It's true, Jessie," Alex said quickly. "I've been watching to see what kind of passwords and access codes are being used to enter the different files. One of the codes is matched with the name Attwood. She's updating the climate program right now. Plugging in some new temperature numbers. And that reminds me, I've got something else to tell you. My friend at the university got back to me a half-hour ago."

"And?"

"First, he knew something about Edwin Bright. Said the guy is one of those characters in the scientific community who always operate way out in left field. He hadn't heard much about him in recent years. Bright's theories and calculations are not accepted by any reputable people."

"Ah hah."

"Second, he said that it was clear that some of the important numbers in this climate-projection program are phony. Says Bright must be making them up. He also implied it wouldn't be the first time."

"Do you think Susan is helping him produce misleading data?"

"No." Alex sounded defensive suddenly. "I think it's more likely she's just inputting numbers that he's given her."

Hatch came over to the bed, his expression intent. "Is that Robin?"

"Just a second, Alex." Jessie looked up at Hatch. "He thinks he's found Susan. She's on the computer right now, running a climate program."

"Ask him if he can communicate with her through the computer."

"I heard what Hatch just asked," Alex said. "Tell him I can do that. Want me to get her attention now?"

Jessie gripped the phone. "He says he can do it. Hatch, this is so exciting. I'm going to have him try to contact her right now."

Hatch shook his head. "No. Tell him to wait until you and I can get over to the office. I want to think this through for a few minutes."

Alex spoke in Jessie's ear. "I heard him. See you two in a bit."

Jessie heard the phone go dead on the other end of the line. "I can't believe this." She leapt off the bed, hurling the nightgown into a corner. She grabbed her jeans. "What a break. We can talk to her in person. Come on, Hatch, let's go."

"I hope Robin laid in his usual supply of junk food. That peanut-butter sandwich didn't go far."

Twenty minutes later Jessie and the two men were

crowded around the computer screen. Somehow Hatch seemed to have taken command of the situation, much to her annoyance. Jessie was not quite certain how it had happened. She suspected it had to do with his natural leadership talents and with the fact that Alex, being a man, was automatically inclined to take orders from another male. It was extremely irritating, but there did not seem to be much she could do about it at the moment. The important thing was to make contact with Susan Attwood.

"Don't give her any idea of who you are or where you are," Hatch told Alex. "Just let her think that you're a concerned environmentalist who's also a hacker. Maybe someone who's involved in climate-projection programs and who's heard about Bright's calculations and wants to review them. And for Christ's sake, don't give her anything that can be traced back here. Understand?"

"Sure, Hatch." Alex eagerly started punching keys on the board. "I'll start by questioning the data she's trying to input. She won't be alarmed, just confused at first. She'll think it's the computer querying the information she's feeding it. When she starts responding, I'll ease into letting her know there's a real person asking."

Alex's initial query trickled out across the bottom of the screen. Jessie read it over his shoulder:

New temperature ranges for arctic quadrant do not match projections. Please explain source.

"What if the query pops up on someone else's screen?" Jessie asked.

"There's no one else on-line right now. It's the middle of the night, don't forget. She's working the late shift alone." Alex studied the response he had gotten from Susan.

Source is Bright calculation. The words appeared above Alex's on the top half of the screen.

Calculation not correct, Alex typed.

Please explain.

"She's confused, and no wonder," Alex said. "The program she's working with is not written to be interactive on this level. Up until now it's just accepted whatever numbers it gets and crunched them."

"Okay," Hatch said slowly. "Let her know you're here."

Am concerned about projections produced by this program. They don't match my own, Alex typed.

Who are you?

Alex hesitated and then typed, *Green.*

Are you with DEL?

No. Concerned about same subject. Wrong data extremely dangerous, Alex typed.

Show me the differences between your calculations and ours.

"We're in luck," Alex said confidently. "She's the naturally curious type, like most computer junkies. She wants to solve the puzzle before she does anything else. Attagirl, Susan. I'd do exactly the same thing, especially in the middle of the night when there's nothing better to do. I think you and I are two of a kind." He hunched over the keyboard and started typing furiously.

Jessie glanced at Hatch and smiled wryly. Hatch shrugged and reached for the bag of potato chips that was lying on the desk next to the computer. They both sat there munching while Alex lured Susan Attwood into an extended conversation about data errors and bad projections.

Have recently been concerned about this myself, Susan finally admitted several minutes later.

Hatch put down the bag of potato chips. "Bingo," he said softly.

"Told you she was bright." Alex looked proud, as if Susan were his protégée. "Smart enough to know something was wrong."

"Ask her if she's ever worked with the financial program," Hatch ordered.

"If I do that, she'll know we're interested in the money as well as the climate stuff," Alex warned.

219

Jessie finally took a hand. "Tell her you stumbled over the other program while looking for this one and that you were curious about the projects the foundation is financing."

"And tell her," Hatch added swiftly, "that the money doesn't look like it's going into normal research-and-development costs. See if she's had any concerns about those transactions."

Jessie whipped around in her chair to stare at Hatch in astonishment. "You never said anything about the R-and-D stuff looking strange."

He shrugged again. "I'm not sure what is happening. I just know it isn't a normal R-and-D spread sheet."

"You could have said something."

"I'd already told you the whole thing was probably some sort of scam. This is nothing new. I'm just fine-tuning my theories now."

Alex broke in quickly. "If you two would stop squabbling, we might get some more answers from Susan. Okay, Hatch, you want me to ask directly about offshore accounts?"

"Something tells me we should be a little more subtle than that," Jessie muttered, still annoyed.

"Jessie's right. Just ask her why the financial-management program doesn't look right and see what she says."

Alex obediently typed in the question. There was a long pause before the answer came back on the top half of **the** screen:

Who are you, Green? Please tell me.

"She's getting nervous," Jessie said. "I think it's time to tell her the whole truth."

"I agree," Alex said.

"You're liable to scare her off completely if you do," Hatch warned.

Jessie shook her head, staring intently at the screen. Her intuition was guiding her now. "No. She's already scared. And not because of us. Let's find out what's really going on here. Alex, ask her if she feels safe working for DEL."

"Just like that?"

"Yes. Hurry." Jessie was feeling a sense of urgency. She leaned forward to peer over Alex's shoulder.

"All right, go ahead," Hatch said slowly, after giving Jessie a speculative glance. "Start the question with her first name."

Susan, are you safe where you are?

Jessie held her breath and realized that Alex was doing the same thing as they waited for a response. Only Hatch still looked calm.

I'm not sure. I'm getting scared, Green. Please tell me who you are.

"Tell her," Jessie said, "that we've been looking for her and if she wants to leave DEL, we'll help her. Tell her that her mother is very worried."

"Tell her that her mother is also scared," Hatch put in thoughtfully. "That should do it."

Jessie nodded. "Good idea. Susan may not know that Mrs. Attwood has been threatened."

"Has she?" Alex asked, surprised.

Jessie nodded grimly. "Yes, I'm sure of it."

The response from Susan came immediately. *Is my mother all right? Have been told I may not contact her until after my training period is finished.*

"Tell her that Mrs. Attwood will not talk to me about the problem. Tell her I'm very worried about her," Jessie said.

Alex started to type in the words, but before he could get halfway through the sentence, Susan started typing something of her own.

Clear screen. Someone coming.

In a stroke Alex wiped everything off his own screen and sat back in his chair with a low groan of frustration. "She's in trouble."

"Looks like it," Hatch agreed quietly. "But we don't have any idea of how much trouble. She might just be getting nervous. Wants to come home. Afraid to admit she's made a mistake."

"I think," Jessie said slowly, "that it's more serious than that. I think she's in real danger."

Hatch and Alex looked at her.

"How do you know that?" Hatch finally asked.

Jessie shook her head, helpless to explain the sense of urgency that was growing stronger by the minute. "Just a feeling I've got." She jumped to her feet. "I'm going to go see Mrs. Valentine. With any luck, she'll have recovered some of her ability. Maybe she can tell me if I'm right in thinking Susan's in trouble."

"Jessie, it's midnight," Hatch pointed out.

"Mrs. V will understand. Do you want to come with me, Hatch?"

"I don't think I've got much choice," he muttered, standing up reluctantly.

"I'll keep an eye on things here," Alex said. "I won't attempt to contact Susan. I'll just monitor the screen in case she decides to try to find me again. If she puts out a query, I'll respond."

Jessie glanced back once from the door. Alex was sitting in front of his screen, gazing into the green glow with worried eyes.

There was another screen glowing in the living room of Mrs. Valentine's sister. A television screen.

Mrs. Valentine, wearing an old robe and slippers, answered the doorbell on the first chime. "Oh, there you are, Jessie, dear. Come in. I've been expecting you. Hello, Mr. Hatchard. So nice to see you again."

"Hello, Mrs. Valentine," Hatch said. "Sorry about the late-night visit."

"Don't worry about it. As I said, I was expecting you."

Jessie threw her arms around her boss and hugged her tightly. "You were expecting us? Mrs. V, does that mean you've recovered your psychic abilities?"

"What little ability I had seems to have begun returning," Mrs. Valentine said modestly. "Won't you sit down? My sister has already gone to bed. I was just watching TV until you arrived."

"This is wonderful, Mrs. V." Jessie sat down on the old sofa. "Isn't it, Hatch?"

"It's interesting," Hatch said coolly.

"Don't mind him, Mrs. V. He's a born skeptic. Now, let me tell you why I'm here at this hour."

"Something to do with Susan Attwood, I imagine." Mrs. Valentine looked resigned.

"Mrs. V, you *are* getting back your powers. This is wonderful."

"Simple deduction, I'm afraid." Mrs. Valentine smiled. "I couldn't imagine anything else that would have you so agitated. Better tell me everything."

"Right."

Jessie plunged into a full account, including the fact that Alex Robin had managed to contact Susan. Hatch added a few desultory comments on the probability of a scam being run by the Dawn's Early Light Foundation.

"We're starting to get very concerned about Susan's safety, Mrs. V," Jessie concluded a few minutes later. "I wanted to consult with you before we did anything else."

Mrs. V gazed at the television screen for a long while. Then she turned her head to meet Jessie's anxious eyes. "I think, my dear, that you are right to be concerned about poor Susan."

"I was afraid of that. We've got to do something."

"Perhaps you should call the police," Mrs. Valentine suggested. "This sort of thing should be turned over to them, don't you think?"

"Good idea," Hatch agreed.

"I'm not so sure," Jessie said slowly. "For one thing, we don't have any real evidence that she's in danger. Susan hasn't exactly asked for rescue. I think we should ask her what she wants us to do." She stood up abruptly. "Come on, Hatch. Let's go. No point keeping Mrs. V up any later. She's confirmed my worst fears."

"I do wish you would turn this over to the proper authorities, dear." Mrs. Valentine looked anxious.

"That's just it, Mrs. V, there are no proper authorities. Not yet, at any rate. We don't have any proof of a crime or even any evidence of danger to Susan. Don't worry, we can handle this," Jessie assured her.

"Oh, my goodness." Mrs. Valentine trailed after them to the door. She frowned as Jessie walked out onto the old-fashioned porch. "Jessie, dear . . ."

"Yes, Mrs. V?"

"You will be careful, whatever you do, won't you?"

"Of course. But it's Susan Attwood who's in danger, not me."

"I'm not so sure about that." Mrs. Valentine glanced at Hatch. "You'll take care of her, won't you." It was more of a statement than a question.

"Yes," Hatch said quietly. "I'll take care of her."

Mrs. Valentine looked somewhat relieved. "Oh, well, then, perhaps it will all be okay. But I'm really not certain I like this new aspect of our business. Not certain at all."

"I don't blame you, Mrs. Valentine," Hatch said. "Any way you slice it, there's no doubt but that Valentine Consultations is headed in new directions."

"Oh, dear," said Mrs. Valentine.

Jessie dialed Alex's number just before she climbed into bed. It was answered on the first ring.

"Heard anything more from her, Alex?"

"No. I think she's lying low."

"When's her next shift on the computer?"

"Tomorrow night. If she maintains her present schedule."

"Maybe she'll talk to us then," Jessie said.

"Unless they've gotten so suspicious they've removed her from the job," Alex said glumly.

Jessie put down the phone and turned to look at Hatch, who was lying back against the pillows, his hands behind his head. He was naked to the waist and the covers were bunched around his hips, exposing the broad, smoothly muscled expanse of his chest.

"I'm really worried, Hatch."

"I know you are." He gave her a small wry smile. "Come to bed and get some sleep. There's nothing more you can do tonight."

Jessie went over to the bed and crawled in beside him. The heat of his body enveloped her as he pulled her close.

"Hatch?"

"Uh-huh?"

"I'm glad you're helping me out on this case. I get the feeling I'm in a little over my head."

"You think you're in over your head now? Just wait until this is all over and I bill you for my services."

"Hatch, are you serious?"

"I'm always serious."

At one o'clock the next afternoon, Hatch grabbed his jacket and started for the door of his office.

"I'll be out for the next couple of hours," he said to his secretary as he went past her desk.

"Yes, Mr. Hatchard."

Twenty-five minutes later Hatch was waiting outside a classroom at Butterfield College. David Ringstead sauntered out of the room behind fifteen other students. He looked startled to see Hatch.

"What are you doing here?" David demanded. Then he frowned in sudden alarm. "Is anything wrong? Is Mom all right?"

"Nothing's wrong. I wanted to talk to you and I figured this would be the easiest way to do it. Can we go someplace where we can get a cup of coffee?"

"Why?"

"I told you. I want to talk to you."

David shrugged. "All right. There's an espresso bar across the street."

"Fine."

"Mind telling me what this is all about?"

"It's about money," Hatch said easily.

"Shit." David shoved his hands into the back pockets of his jeans. "You're here to tell me the old bastard won't finance grad school, right? Why you? Why didn't Jessie come?"

"That's a lot of conclusions to jump to without knowing any facts. But I guess that's what philosophers are trained to do, isn't it? No wonder they have a hard time finding jobs outside the academic world."

"Shit."

Hatch sighed as he pushed open the door of the espresso bar. "Look on the bright side. I'm buying."

A pale, lanky-haired young woman behind the counter smiled wanly at David.

"Hi, David. How's it going?" she asked.

"Fine. You?"

"Okay, I guess. What will you have?"

"Latte," said David.

She turned in mute question to Hatch.

"Coffee," Hatch said. "Plain coffee."

They stood in silence while the young woman went to work at the gleaming espresso machine. When she handed them their cups, Hatch led the way to a corner table in the nearly empty café.

"Friend of yours?" Hatch asked idly, nodding faintly toward the wiry woman who was now busy cleaning up around the machine. Her washed-out blond hair swung forward, shielding her bad complexion.

"Not exactly. Met her when I was asking around for information on DEL."

Hatch slid the young woman a second glance. "That's Nadine Willard?"

"Yeah." David sipped the foam off his latte. "Now, suppose you stop messing with my head and just tell me what all this is about."

"No problem. It's real simple, David. I don't want you

SWEET FORTUNE

pressuring Jessie to go to her father for money for grad school. Got that?"

David scowled. "What is it with you, anyway? What do you care about something that's just between Jessie and me?"

"I want Jessie out of the loop."

"The loop?"

"Right. The loop. From now on, anyone who wants something from Vincent Benedict can go and ask for it himself, directly. You don't use Jessie anymore."

David's expression tightened into a sullen frown. He sat back and stuck his legs out under the small table. "Jessie's never minded handling the old bastard for the rest of us."

"I mind."

"No offense, but who the fuck cares if you mind?"

Hatch took a taste of his coffee. "Put it this way, David. If you try to use Jessie to run interference for you, I will personally squelch any possibility you might have of getting money out of Vincent Benedict. Believe me, I can do it. Benedict and I think alike. I know just how to convince him that you shouldn't be given one more dime for your education."

"You're a real son of a bitch, aren't you?"

"I can be," Hatch agreed.

"Mom said she was afraid something like this would happen."

"Something like what?" Hatch eyed him curiously.

David lifted one shoulder in resignation. "That things would change. She said the old bastard was going to try to create a son for himself by getting one to marry into the family. She said if he succeeded, we'd all lose in the end. Looks like this is the start of it."

"You seem to be missing the point here, David. I did not say you couldn't try to talk Benedict into anything you want. Just don't use Jessie to do it for you."

"She's the only one who can deal with him. Everybody knows that."

"Have you ever tried dealing with him yourself?"

"Shit, yes." David slammed his half-finished cup down on the table. He turned fierce eyes on Hatch. "You think I haven't tried to please the old man? Hell, I spent most of my life trying to be the son everyone said he wanted. Ever since I was a little kid, I tried to be a macho, hard-charging type for his sake."

"Is that right?"

"Yeah, it is damn sure right." David leaned forward. His hands circled his cup in a crushing grip. "I went out for football because of him. Spent eight weeks in a cast when I broke a leg because some idiot linebacker fell on top of me. I got a job on a fishing boat one summer because Benedict said I was a wimp and needed to toughen up. I hated it. The smell was awful. And the endless piles of dead and dying fish made me sick to my stomach. I still can't bring myself to eat fish."

"David—"

"I've studied karate for years, trying to prove to Uncle Vincent I was made of the right stuff. Mom and the old bastard decided I should get to know the family business, so I tried working construction one summer." David shook his head at the bitter memory. "Should have seen my coworkers. Their idea of a good time was getting off work and heading straight for the nearest tavern. Their idea of intellectual conversation was a detailed discussion of the tits on the latest Playmate of the month."

"I know the type," Hatch said dryly, thinking back to his own younger days.

"Then, in sheer desperation, Mom convinced Uncle Vincent to let me try working in the head office."

"I take it that didn't work either."

"Hell, no. I couldn't do anything right. The old bastard was always yelling at me. Said I lacked the instincts for running a company like Benedict Fasteners. I started taking business-administration classes so I could develop the instincts, and he just laughed. He said no fancy college classes would ever give me what I needed. He said I just wasn't tough enough to follow in his shoes. And you know something? He was right."

"Benedict can be a little rough on people," Hatch admitted. No wonder Jessie had wound up running interference between David and her father. With her soft heart, she must have felt sick about the failure of that relationship.

"Yeah, well, as far as I was concerned, that last bit was the end. I walked away from Benedict Fasteners without a backward glance. Told Mom to forget trying to make me into a chip off the old Benedict block. Hell, I didn't even have any Benedict blood in me. I was a Ringstead. Why should I go out of my way to please the old man? Jessie was right."

"About what?"

"She told me I wasn't meant for the business world. She said I should go off and do what I wanted to do, not what someone else wanted me to do. I'll never forget the night she sat me down and said that to me. It was like she'd set me free somehow, you know? Everything was a lot clearer after that."

"So you switched your major from business administration to philosophy?"

"You got it." David swallowed the last of his latte.

"You're no longer interested in trying to please Benedict," Hatch observed slowly. "But you're more than willing to take money from him to finance your education?"

"Damned right. Bastard owes it to me."

"How do you figure that?"

David looked at him in disgust. "Don't you know? My father helped him build Benedict Fasteners."

"What the hell are you talking about?"

"My father used to work for Benedict back in the old days. He was an accountant. He pretty much set up the business, got it on its feet. He virtually created the little empire Uncle Vincent owns today." There was a hint of pride in David's voice now. "If it hadn't been for my father,

Mom said, Benedict would have gone under back at the beginning. The old bastard didn't know anything about business in those days. All he knew was construction."

"He knows a hell of a lot about business now," Hatch observed.

"So he learned. Mostly from my father, the way I see it. Took advantage of my dad. And when he didn't need Dad anymore, he fired him."

"Fired him? Are you sure?"

David gave him a disgusted look. "Of course I'm sure. Mom told me all about it. Benedict used Dad up and got rid of him rather than make him an equal partner in the business, the way he should have. My father wasn't like Benedict. He was an intellectual type, you know? Not a shark. Getting fired was hard on him. He just split."

"You remember all this? You couldn't have been more than a small boy."

"Of course I don't remember all of it. I've figured most of it out from little things Mom and Benedict and Connie and Lilian have let slip over the years. The bottom line is, Uncle Vincent owes me, just like Mom says."

"Christ," Hatch muttered. "Nothing like airing a few family secrets." He sat in silence for a while, thinking.

"You finished with this little man-to-man chat?" David asked. "If so, I've got another class in fifteen minutes."

"Just one more thing, David."

"Yeah?"

"I happen to think you're a lot tougher than your father was. The fact that you put up with all the hassle from Benedict over the years and then chucked the whole scene to find your own path tells me that."

"So?"

"So I think you've got what it takes to go to Benedict yourself and ask for the loan for grad school." Hatch swallowed the last of his coffee and got to his feet. "You want to make the old bastard pay for what he did to your father? Go ahead. Make him pay through the nose. Take every last dime you can pry out of him and spend it on a degree in philosophy. You couldn't ask for a better revenge, believe me."

"Yeah, that did occur to me. He really can't stand the idea of me getting a degree in philosophy," David agreed with grim satisfaction.

"Just make sure you take your revenge all by yourself," Hatch concluded quietly. "Don't involve Jessie in it."

David looked up swiftly. "Mom always said it was easier for Jessie to get the money from Benedict."

"Not anymore. I'm in the way now. Besides. Take it from me, David, vengeance is a lot sweeter when you take it in person. That's my little bit of philosophical wisdom for the day. Based on a lot of real-life experience. Think about it."

Hatch went out the door and walked to where he had parked the Mercedes.

CHAPTER FOURTEEN

I hope you did the right thing. I'm not so sure about this, Hatch. I just don't know." Jessie twiddled her fork in her penne pasta and sun-dried tomatoes and gazed uncertainly at Hatch.

"Stop worrying about it. It's done and that's the end of it." Hatch tore off a slice of bread from the loaf in the basket and sank his teeth into it.

The noise from the evening dinner crowd sharing the cozy restaurant with Jessie and Hatch was a contented hum. The food being served at the tables was typical Northwest-style cuisine, which meant intriguing and innovative combinations of fresh fish, pasta, and vegetables.

"I don't know." Jessie gazed moodily down into her pasta as if it were a particularly cloudy crystal ball. "Maybe you shouldn't have been so hard on him. I've told you David's very sensitive."

"I don't give a damn about his sensitivity," Hatch muttered. "I just want to make sure that from now on he does his own dirty work."

"He and Dad don't get along very well. I've told you that. They barely even speak to each other."

"You of all people should know it's not necessary to get along well with Vincent in order to deal with him. You've just got to have some staying power. It's up to David now. If he wants the cash for grad school, he can ask for it himself. You're out of it. No more rescue operations on behalf of the family."

"You're making up new rules for me and the others based on the way you like to do things. That's not fair, Hatch. The rest of us don't work the same way."

"I don't care how the rest of the clan works. I just want you out of the loop. At least for a while."

"What gives you the right to interfere in my life this way?"

"I don't see it as interference. I see it as cutting through a few of the knots in which you've got yourself tangled."

Jessie was speechless for an instant. "You have an incredible audacity, Hatch. Cutting through the knots, my foot. As if you knew what you were doing. You're not some kind of professional family counselor."

"Damn right I'm not. But I learned a long time ago that it's usually easier to cut through a knot than it is to unravel it."

"Stop talking about knots," she snapped.

"All right. What would you like to talk about? Our forthcoming engagement?"

She tensed instantly, the way she always did when he mentioned marriage. "We don't have any concrete plans for an engagement."

"Maybe we'd better make some," he mused. "I'm beginning to think we've been fooling around long enough."

Jessie felt goaded. "Maybe I like fooling around. Maybe I'd be content to fool around forever. Did you ever consider that possibility? The situation isn't bad the way it stands now. Not for me, at any rate. I'm getting the best of both worlds. All the advantages of an affair and none of the disadvantages of marriage."

"So you're just using me, is that it?" He gave her a thoughtful look. "Should I start withholding sex in order to prod you into marriage?"

Jessie flushed warmly. She glanced quickly to the right and then to the left, trying to ascertain if anyone at a neighboring table had overheard the remark. Then she glowered at Hatch. "Is that supposed to be a joke?"

"No. I have no sense of humor, remember?"

Jessie stopped fiddling with her fork and picked up the knife instead. She began tracing small agitated triangles on the tablecloth. "I'm not so sure about that."

"Is that right?" Hatch munched on a clam. "What changed your mind?"

"I haven't changed my mind. Not yet, at any rate." She raised her chin. "But I am reconsidering the issue."

"How about doing something a little more productive?"

"Such as?" she asked.

"Such as setting a date for a wedding."

"So you can get it on your calendar?" she retorted. "Get the big day properly scheduled into your busy life? Are you sure you can make time for a honeymoon? We're talking two whole weeks here, Hatch. That's the traditional length of time, I believe. Are you sure you can stay away from the office that long?"

"It's amazing how much work you can get done in a hotel room if you bring along the right equipment," he said seriously. "What with fax machines and modems and laptop computers, a man can take his office with him these days."

"There isn't going to be any wedding." The knife Jessie had been using to draw little patterns in the tablecloth suddenly jumped out of her fingers and teetered on the edge of the table. She watched in dismay as it toppled over the edge. It landed on the carpet in merciful silence. When she glanced up to meet Hatch's gaze she thought she saw a cool satisfaction in his eyes.

"It's not funny," she muttered.

"I know."

She was incensed. "I'll bet you do think it's funny, don't you?"

"No. How could I, with my nonexistent or, at best, extremely limited sense of humor?" he asked reasonably. "Forget the knife, Jessie. The waiter will bring you another one. Tell me something."

"What?"

"Do you still think I'm incapable of giving our marriage the amount of attention it would need?"

"After that crack about bringing along a fax machine and a modem on your honeymoon, what else am I supposed to think?"

"I give you my word of honor they won't get in the way," he said earnestly. "I work very efficiently."

Jessie stared at him. He *was* teasing her. She was almost certain of it. And she was rising to the bait like a well-trained little fish. She forced herself to relax before she dropped anything else on the floor.

"Come on, Jessie. Tell me the truth. I'm not nearly as much like your father as you thought back at the beginning. Right?"

"Okay, I admit it. You're turning out to be a very different sort of man, even though you've got a lot of the same workaholic tendencies. My father would never have helped me figure out what's happening to Susan Attwood." *Or gone out of his way to keep Elizabeth from being disappointed at the science fair. Or worried very much about my motives for marrying you,* she added silently. *Not that I am going to marry you,* she corrected herself immediately.

"So I'm not such a bad guy, after all? I think we're making some progress here."

"Maybe we are. I have to tell you something, Hatch. I'm not sure you're right to try to yank me out of the family loop, as you call it, but I will say that no one has ever tried to rescue me from anything before. It's kind of a novel experience."

Hatch started to smile slowly, but before he could say anything else a bird-faced woman with frizzy gray hair and tiny half-glasses perched on her beak of a nose stopped beside the table.

"*Jessie*. Jessie Benedict, it is you. I thought it was when I saw you from over there." She nodded toward a booth on the other side of the crowded restaurant. "Haven't seen you in ages. How is everything going? Did you find another job?"

Jessie looked up, recognizing the woman at once. It was hard to forget someone who had once fired you. "Hello, Mavis. Nice to see you again. Mavis, this is Sam Hatchard. Call him Hatch. Hatch, meet Mavis Fairley. You and Mavis have a lot in common, Hatch."

"We do?" Hatch was already on his feet, acknowledging the introduction with grave politeness.

"Do we, indeed?" Mavis echoed brightly, waving him graciously back into his seat. "And what would that be, I wonder? Are you by any chance in the health-food business?"

"No. I'm in nuts and bolts."

"Hatch is the new CEO at Benedict Fasteners," Jessie explained. "And what you both have in common," she added with a benign smile, "is that you've each had occasion to fire me."

"Oh, dear." Mavis looked instantly concerned. "Not another unfortunate job situation, Jessie?"

"Afraid so."

"She was wreaking havoc in her father's company," Hatch said matter-of-factly. "What kind of damage did she do to your firm?"

"To be perfectly blunt, she was driving off customers right and left. She managed my downtown store for a while. I'm in health foods, as I said, and sales began plummeting almost immediately after she took over. She was being a bit too straightforward with the customers, if you take my meaning."

"I think I get the point." Hatch's brow rose. "A little too honest, Jessie?"

"I simply told them the truth about the products they were buying and sent a few of them who looked particularly ill to a doctor. That's all," Jessie stated.

"It was enough to butcher my bottom line within a month," Mavis confided to Hatch. "She was so nice, and such an enthusiastic person, though. I really hated to let her go, but business is business."

Hatch nodded in complete understanding. "Believe me, I know the feeling, Mavis. Business is business."

For some reason that struck Jessie as funny. She started laughing and could not stop. Hatch smiled in quiet satisfaction.

The next morning Jessie walked into the small building housing Valentine Consultations with a sense of impending disaster weighing on her. As soon as she opened the front door of the building she saw the green glow seeping out from the cracked doorway of Alex's office. She pushed open the door and glanced inside.

The place was in its usual state of disarray. Alex, his head cradled on his folded arms, was fast asleep amid the clutter of empty soda cans and pizza cartons. He stirred as Jessie stepped into the room.

"Did you spend the whole night here, Alex?"

"Hi." He yawned, rubbed his eyes, and reached for his glasses. "Yeah. I was here all night. Started talking to Susan. After she went off-line, I fell asleep."

"You contacted Susan again? Is she all right?"

"She's starting to sound real scared, Jessie. Said she thinks she's being watched. I told her that I'd get her off that island anytime she wants."

"No kidding?" Jessie sat down in the chair next to his. "What did she say to that?"

"She panicked. Said absolutely no police."

"Hmmm." Jessie glanced at the screen and saw the words that had appeared on the top half. "Is that her last message?"

Alex frowned. "No, I cleared the screen after her last one. Holy shit." He leaned closer, alarmed. "That's a new one. She must have sent it to me while I was asleep."

Jessie leaned forward to read. It was the longest message she had yet seen from Susan Attwood.

I'm really getting scared, Green. I want out of here. I think I saw data I shouldn't have seen. Please come and get me. The cove on the eastern side of the island. There's a buoy marking it. Please be there in a boat at midnight tonight. Green? Green, are you still there? I hope you get this last message. I've got to get out of here. Good-bye, Green. Please, no cops. I'm so afraid. I just want to get away from here. I hope you're still there, Green.

"Holy shit," Alex said again. He surged up out of the chair. "We've got to rescue her."

"Of course we do." Jessie glanced at her watch. "We'll have to get moving. It'll take time to get to the islands and arrange to rent a boat. Do you know how to operate one?"

"No. Damn." Alex swung around, his eyes frantic. "We've got to find someone who knows how to pilot a boat. Someone who can keep his mouth shut."

Jessie thought for a moment. "My cousin, David, spent a few months on a fishing boat up in Alaska. He knows about boats."

"Think he'd help us?"

"I think so. I'll call him." Jessie reached for the phone.

"After you get hold of him, you'd better call Hatch," Alex said.

Jessie winced. "He's going to explode when he hears what we're planning to do."

* * *

She was right. Hatch exploded.

"I don't know how I let you three talk me into this. I must be going crazy." Hatch stood at the helm of the small cruiser as David let it drift silently toward the buoy that marked the small cove. The heavily forested island rose like a great black blot against the starry sky.

It was close to midnight and there was a moon. The night air was crisp and there was no fog. When they had gotten near the island David had shut off the running lights, eased back the throttle, and used the lights from the mansion as a guide. The buoy had been right where Susan Attwood had said it would be. A good twenty-minute walk from the house. Maybe longer, given the rough terrain.

Hatch had been uneasy since Jessie had phoned him that morning. If he had not known better, he'd have thought he'd developed a few psychic abilities himself lately. But it was nothing that fancy or complicated. Just his common sense trying frantically to reassert itself.

"We couldn't call the cops in on this," Alex said from the back of the boat, where he sat beside Jessie. "I promised Susan."

"He's right, Hatch. She seemed to think she would be in even more danger if we called in the authorities," Jessie said. "She just wants off that island."

"What can go wrong?" David asked in reasonable tones, his attention on the entrance to the cove. "We just go in, pick her up, and leave. Piece of cake."

Hatch heard the thread of excitement in David's voice and groaned. "Haven't you three learned yet that anything that can go wrong *will* go wrong?"

"Come on, Hatch," Jessie said in bracing tones. "Don't be such a spoilsport. David's right. We just get in and get out. No problem."

"I'll remember that." Hatch looked at her. All four of them were wearing dark clothes, on his instructions. But the attire definitely did the most for Jessie. She looked like a sexy little cat burglar in her tight black pullover sweater and black jeans. He suddenly wished she were anywhere but here, somewhere *safe*.

"Ready?" asked David. "Here we go."

"No." Hatch gazed at the cove, straining to see something, anything, in the thick darkness ahead of him. The sense of wrongness was heavier than ever. "Not here. It's just a little too damn obvious. Let's put in somewhere else along the shore."

"But this is the spot, I'm sure of it," David said.

Hatch nodded. "I know it is. But let's see if there's another place we can go in. We can hike back overland to the cove and see if she's waiting where she's supposed to be waiting."

Alex left his seat and rushed forward. "We're wasting time. Susan will be scared and cold. We've got to get her out of there."

"If she's there, we'll find her," Hatch assured him. "Sit down, Robin. Let's go, David."

David shrugged and fed the engines a bit more power. The boat churned quietly through the cold black water. A few minutes later they were out of sight of the cove.

"What about here?" David asked, indicating another small indentation in the shoreline that was just barely visible in the moonlight. "We can tie up to those rocks and walk back to the cove."

Hatch studied the natural jetty formed by a rocky outcropping. "All right. Let's try it."

David eased the craft slowly and carefully toward the rocks. He called out soft directions to Alex and Jessie, who scurried to obey.

A few minutes later the boat was bobbing gently next to the jetty. Alex jumped out to secure it with a line.

David turned to Hatch. "Okay, boss. We're all set."

Hatch set his jaw. Now came the hard part. He turned to Jessie. "Alex, David, and I will go ashore and find Susan. Jessie, you will stay here with the boat."

The mutiny was immediate and expected.

"No way," Jessie snapped. "I'm coming with the rest of you."

"I want you to stay here," Hatch said in his most reasonable tones. "That way, if something happens, you can go for help."

"Nothing's going to happen. We're just going to get Susan and leave."

"Leaving you behind is what's known as Plan B," Hatch said.

"I'm the one who organized Plan A. I have a right to be a part of it." Jessie looked at the other two men. "I'm going with you."

David glanced swiftly at Hatch and then shook his head at Jessie. "He's right, Jess. Somebody should stay here."

"Yeah," said Alex, nodding in agreement. "Makes sense."

"Then one of you stay here," she retorted. "You're trying to leave me behind because I'm the only female in the crowd, and I won't have it."

Hatch got out of the boat. "We're wasting time. You're staying here, Jessie. If we're not back in fifteen minutes, you radio for help."

"I don't know how to use the radio."

"Show her how to call for help, David."

David nodded and began giving concise instructions. Jessie listened but she looked distinctly annoyed. When she finally muttered reluctantly that she understood, David leapt out of the boat to join Alex and Hatch. They all stood there gazing down at her, a united masculine front.

Jessie scowled up at them, her hands on her hips. "This is my big case and you three are taking over. It's not fair."

Hatch felt a pang of guilt that lasted no more than two seconds. "They also serve who only sit and wait," he reminded her.

"Get out of here before I fire the lot of you."

"Right. We're on our way." Hatch started off immediately, followed by the other two.

The night breeze rustled overhead in the boughs of the

trees. Water slapped softly at the rocky shoreline. The soft sounds muffled their footsteps. Hatch glanced back once or twice, making certain Jessie had obeyed orders. She and the boat were soon out of sight as the three men moved into the thickly wooded landscape.

It did not take long to reach the cove. Hatch put out a hand, silently halting the others as they reached the point where the trees thinned out. Not caring for the sparse cover in that region, he motioned Alex and David toward a jumble of tree-shrouded boulders. There they crouched, concealed amidst the drooping branches and disordered rocks, and scanned the beach.

A tiny, blond figure dressed in jeans and a sweater huddled near the water's edge. She carried a computer-printout-size folder under her arm. Her back was to them as she anxiously searched the dark horizon.

"There she is," Alex said triumphantly. *"Susan.* Over here."

"Shut up," Hatch snarled softly, making a grab for Alex's arm. But Alex eluded him. He broke out of the trees and raced toward the figure.

The blond whirled around. She was wearing glasses. Definitely Susan Attwood.

"Green? Is that you?"

"Yeah, it's me. Green. I mean, Alex."

"Dammit, Robin, come back here, you ass," Hatch muttered under his breath, knowing that it was too late to stop the younger man.

"I think he's in love," David murmured. "Kind of touching, isn't it?"

"Kind of stupid, is what it is." Hatch watched as the pair on the beach dashed toward each other, arms outstretched. "Looks like something out of a television commercial. All we can do now is hope Susan is here alone."

"Hey, you don't think this is some sort of setup, do you?" David asked.

"How should I know? I'm in the nuts-and-bolts business. This isn't exactly my field of expertise." But he'd seen enough street fighting, both in and out of the corporate world, to know that it always paid to keep an ace in the hole.

The couple on the beach were embracing now. Hatch could not hear what was being said but he was relieved when Alex turned Susan toward the trees and started forward.

"Here they come," David observed, drawing back deeper into the shadows. "We'll be out of here in a couple more minutes."

But at that instant a dark figure stepped out of the trees on the far side of the cove. He had his arm extended and there was no mistaking the object in his fist. The gun glinted in the moonlight.

"That's far enough, you two," Rick Landis announced. "Hold it right there."

"Damn," Hatch whispered. He felt David freeze beside him.

"Christ, who's that?" David asked in the softest of voices.

"One of Bright's people. A guy named Landis. I had a feeling he was more than a tour guide." Hatch watched intently as Landis moved closer to his captives. "I knew this was not a good idea. Why in hell did I let Jessie talk me into this?"

"Don't feel too bad about it," David said consolingly. "Jessie can be very persuasive."

"Yeah, I know. Come on."

"What are we going to do? Go for help?" David followed as Hatch faded back into the forest.

"I have a nasty feeling that by the time we got the authorities here, Susan and Robin would have disappeared."

"So what do we do?"

Hatch made an executive decision. "Something simple and straightforward, I think. This is the shortest route back toward the mansion. We wait until they go past us and then one of us jumps down on top of Landis and bashes his head in."

David considered that. "Who does the bashing?"

Hatch shot his companion a sidelong glance and made another executive decision. "You're the one who studied karate."

"Damn." David sounded both thrilled and appalled. "I sure as hell never tried to use it on anybody."

"Did you learn enough to drop that guy?"

"Well, yeah. Maybe. Theoretically. Under the right circumstances. Like I said, I've never been in a real fight."

"This won't be a real fight. If we do this right, Landis won't know you're on top of him until it's all over."

"What are you going to do?" David asked softly.

"What I do best: supervise. And keep an eye out for a guy named Hoffman."

"Who's he?"

"Someone who reminded me a lot of Landis. Quiet."

"Come on, you two," Landis was saying in a loud voice. "Let's move. We haven't got all night."

Susan's response was soft and tearful on the night air. "Please let us go. I won't tell anyone a thing. I promise. I just want to get away from here."

"Too late for that now, you stupid little bitch. You should have stuck to inputting the data and not gone snooping."

"Stop threatening her," Alex said fiercely, placing himself squarely in front of Susan.

"You must be the famous Green, huh? We figured you had to be a hacker. Nobody else could have gotten into that data base. Bright was worried for a while that you might be someone dangerous. But when Susan here started making arrangements for the dramatic rescue at midnight, we knew we weren't dealing with the cops. Just an amateur."

Hatch prayed Alex would have the sense not to mention the fact that he had not come here alone tonight.

"What are you going to do with us?" Alex demanded.

"The boss has a few questions to ask you. After that, I think it's safe to say we won't need either of you around anymore."

"Don't you dare hurt Alex," Susan wailed. "He was just trying to help me."

"It's all right, Susan," Alex said soothingly. "He won't hurt either of us."

"Give me a break," Landis said. "You're both dead meat. You think Bright can afford to let you live after what you found out, Susie, baby?"

"I told you I wouldn't tell anyone. Please, Landis. Let us go."

"Shut the fuck up and move. Back to the house."

Hatch glanced back at David, silently telling him to be ready as the other three started toward the pile of boulders. Landis was making his captives keep as close to the shoreline as possible, Hatch noted with relief. That route would bring them past the jumble of boulders where he and David were hiding.

With one last reassuring nod at David, Hatch faded back into the trees. *An ace in the hole.*

Hatch sensed David's nervousness as the younger man flattened himself against a boulder, but he also sensed the determination in him. David was going to do his part, come hell or high water. Jessie's cousin was no wimp.

David waited until Alex and Susan had gone past. Then Landis was below him, cursing as he pushed aside a swaying branch.

David did not hesitate. He came down off the boulder feetfirst.

The gun Landis had been holding went off. The shot roared through the woods, louder than thunder on the night air. It was followed by a heavy thudding sound and a stifled shout that faded out quickly.

Silence descended.

The hair on the back of Hatch's neck stirred. He glanced

to his right and saw a lone figure slither out from a heavy veil of tree limbs. Moonlight glinted on the gun in his hand.

Hoffman.

The pilot was being cautious, waiting to assess the situation before he moved in.

"Hey, Hatch," David called, his voice infused with the euphoria of the victorious male. "I got him. It's okay. Come on out. *I got him.*"

The figure Hatch was watching froze, the gun still aimed in the general direction of the activity. But it was obvious the second armed man now realized there was another presence in the woods. He started to turn, nervously searching the undergrowth.

Hatch knew it was the only chance he was going to get. Hoffman had started his scan from the wrong direction.

Hatch launched himself forward. He struck solid flesh and threw a short, savage punch. The gunman choked on a groan, dropped the gun, and reeled forward. Hatch went in low and hit him a second time. Hoffman collapsed on the damp ground.

"Hatch?" David burst forth from a small stand of trees. "You okay? What's going on here?" He halted abruptly when he saw the man on the ground.

"His name is Hoffman," Hatch said. "He's a buddy of the one you just took out. These two must have comprised Bright's security force."

"What are we going to do with them?" David asked, glancing back over his shoulder.

"Leave them here. I don't want to drag them all the way back to the boat, that's for sure." Hatch scooped up the gun Hoffman had dropped. "Everything go all right back there?"

"Yeah." David's voice filled with excitement once again. "Landis is out cold. Shit. I never thought that karate stuff would really work." He was obviously awed at his own success.

Hatch gave him a faint grin as they moved back through the trees. "Nice job. You can cover my back anytime."

"Thanks." David's grin spread from ear to ear. "All right. Hey, it's a deal. Anytime."

"You guys okay?" Alex demanded as Hatch and David reached them. He had a protective arm wrapped around Susan's shoulders. Susan was whimpering softly.

"We're fine." Hatch shoved Hoffman's gun into his belt and handed Landis' to Alex, who did the same. "Now we all get back to the boat. Fast."

"You didn't tell me you had anyone else with you, Alex," Susan murmured to Robin.

"There wasn't time to explain. That bastard with the gun appeared out of nowhere," Alex said.

"I should have known you'd have it all planned out," Susan said admiringly. "You're so brilliant, Alex."

"Kind of a rough plan, but it was the best I could do on the spur of the moment," Alex said modestly.

David slid Hatch a knowing look. "I told you the man's in love," he muttered.

"You pegged it. Let's get moving here." Hatch realized that the sense of urgency he was experiencing had not diminished. If anything, it had grown stronger in the past few minutes.

This was absolutely the last time he was going to let Jessie talk him into one of her crazy schemes, he vowed silently. The woman was a menace to herself and others. She needed to be kept on a tight leash, and from here on out, Hatch intended to do exactly that.

He kept that glowing promise before him like a talisman as he followed the others through the trees back to the little cove where Jessie and the boat were waiting.

Less than five minutes later, just as they were moving out of the trees and onto the rocky beach, a familiar voice split the night air.

"Don't come any closer," Jessie yelled. "He's got a gun."

But it was too late. Alex, Susan, and David had already moved out into the open. Hatch alone was still shielded by the thick foliage as he took in the scene on the shore.

Jessie was standing helplessly in the gently bobbing boat. Edwin Bright had one arm around her throat. In his other hand he held a gun to her head.

"By all means, let's have your friends come a little closer, my dear," Edwin Bright said loudly.

CHAPTER FIFTEEN

What happened to Landis and Hoffman?" Bright called from the boat.

"We left them back there in the woods," David answered with astonishing calm.

"Who are you?" Bright demanded impatiently.

"A friend of Jessie's."

"The one they call Hatchard?"

David was silent.

"Answer me," Bright roared, "or I'll put a bullet through her head."

"No," David finally said, offering no further explanation.

"Dammit, where's Hatchard?" Bright yelled. "I know he's the one behind all this, the one who screwed this thing up. Where the hell is he?"

"Dead," David said, improvising with laudable speed. "Landis got him. Didn't you hear the gunshot?"

"*Dead?*" Jessie's shriek pierced the air. "*No*, he can't be dead. I'd know if he were dead." She jerked backward and forward in a frantic, violent motion that, added to the swaying action of the boat, was more than enough to take both her and Bright off-balance.

"Watch it, you bitch, we're going over," Bright shouted, scrambling to retain his balance. It was too late. He released Jessie in an effort to save himself from toppling over the edge of the bobbing boat.

But Jessie's momentum was too strong. She lost her footing and fell backward, flailing wildly. Bright tried to dodge her arm and could not. It caught him across the throat and she carried him with her as she went into the water.

Jessie screamed again just as she hit the cold water. Bright plunged in beside her, swearing furiously.

Hatch raced out of the trees and ran past the others, who were staring at the scene in stunned amazement. He dashed along the rocky jetty, leapt into the boat, and peered over the side.

"Jessie."

Jessie was bobbing in the water, her dark hair plastered to her scalp. She pushed wet tendrils out of her eyes and looked up at him with a glowing smile. "I knew you were alive."

Hatch ignored Bright, who was sputtering and gasping next to her. He leaned down, caught Jessie's raised hands, and hauled her straight up out of the black water and into the boat.

"That water's damn cold," Alex said as he stepped into the boat. "It'll kill a person in less than thirty minutes. Better get her into one of the blankets."

"He's right." David jumped into the boat and opened a locker. He dragged out a blanket. "Jessie, get your clothes off and get into this. You'll be okay. You were in the water only a couple of minutes."

Jessie nodded, already beginning to shiver violently. "My God, I'm cold." She grabbed the blanket, pulled it around her, and started to strip off her jeans underneath it.

"Hey, goddammit, help me," Bright shouted from the water. When no one responded, he struck out for shore.

The splashing caught Hatch's attention. "David, untie the

boat. Keep it between Bright and the shore. I want to talk to him."

David's brows rose but he said nothing. He and Alex quickly untied the boat and let it drift gently between Bright and the shoreline, blocking escape from the bone-chilling water.

"Goddammit, you can't do this," Bright yelled, floundering desperately. "Get me out of here. I'll freeze."

Hatch planted both hands on the hull and looked down at Bright. "Actually, that's not a bad idea."

"Are you crazy? You'll be killing me. People die of hypothermia out here all the time," Bright screamed.

"He's right," Jessie observed. "It's amazing how fast hypothermia sets in. A few minutes in this water followed by a few minutes standing around in the cold air and it's all over. He's been in that water several minutes already."

Hatch glanced at Alex. "Think he could make it safely back to the house on his own?"

Alex frowned consideringly. "Doubt it. Ambient temperature is in the forties now, and it's a good twenty-, twenty-five-minute hike. He's been in that water long enough to start the hypothermic process. Yeah, I'd say getting back to the house on his own is starting to look real iffy."

"You can't do this," Bright wailed in panic and despair.

"Swim to shore," Hatch told Bright. "I'll meet you there with a blanket. You tell me a few things I want to know and I'll let you have the blanket. Refuse to talk and I'll take my blanket and go home."

The threat was a virtual death sentence and everyone knew it, including Bright. He struck out for shore.

Hatch took one of the blankets and vaulted out of the boat onto the rocks. "Wait here," he said to the others.

He did not hurry to the rescue. When he reached the shoreline, Bright was already out of the water, hugging himself as shudder after shudder went through him. He had lost his glasses in the fall overboard and he peered at Hatch with slitted eyes.

"Give me that blanket," Bright hissed.

Hatch stopped a few feet away. "First you tell me a little bit about the operation."

Bright's eyes widened slightly. "What are you, some kind of pro? What happened to Hoffman and Landis, anyway?"

"They're both out of the picture. Talk, Bright. You'll never make it back to the mansion alive without this blanket."

"Fuck off."

"Suit yourself." Hatch turned and started back toward the boat.

"Wait, you bastard," Bright said through chattering teeth. "You can't leave me like this."

Hatch glanced back over his shoulder. "I don't see why not."

"Shit. I could die out here."

"That's not my problem, is it?"

Bright stared at him. "Dammit, what's going on? I know you're a pro. You must be. The girl's mother hire you?"

"I'm just a businessman, Bright."

"Businessman, hell. Who are you, goddammit? Who hired you?"

"You know that woman you were holding the gun on a few minutes ago?"

"What about her?" Bright snarled.

"You might say I did it for her. She's the lady I'm going to marry."

"Shit."

"Now you probably have a clearer understanding of why I don't have any real ethical problem with the idea of you freezing to death out here." Hatch turned and started once more toward the boat.

"Stop, goddammit, I'm coming with you." Bright staggered forward. "You've got to take me with you. I don't think I can make it back to the house. I'm freezing."

Hatch paused, thoughtful. Then he shook his head. "No, I don't think it's worth taking you with us. If I thought you might talk to the authorities, I'd say yes, but something tells me you won't say a word."

"I said wait, you bastard. I'll talk." Bright was clearly desperate now.

Hatch dangled the blanket in front of him. "Prove it. Tell me something real interesting."

"Like what?"

"Like which offshore bank you're using. Tell me where the money goes. Explain how you divert it. Little things like that. Convince me. And then show me something that looks like proof."

Edwin Bright glowered sullenly at him in the moonlight. And then another racking shudder went through him. Without a word he reached into his pocket and pulled out a dripping wallet. He held it out to Hatch.

"There's a list of accounts in there," Bright muttered through chattering lips. "And a key to a safe at the mansion."

"That sounds promising." Hatch handed over the blanket while he started going through Edwin Bright's wallet.

Bright clutched at the blanket and started to strip off his clothes. "I was right, wasn't I? You are a pro. Government or private?"

"Private. Very private." Hatch found several interesting items in Edwin Bright's wallet, including the list and the key. "Tell me something else now. Was that one of your people who broke into Valentine Consultations?"

Bright stepped out of his pants. "Yeah. We knew Attwood's mother had just hired that damned fortune-teller to find her daughter. We needed to know how much Valentine knew."

"How about after we took our scenic tour of the facilities? Was that one of your people who tried to break into my car?"

"We couldn't figure out how you were involved. We were trying to get a fix on you. The idea was to search the car. Look, this was just a good scam. Nobody was supposed to get hurt."

"Is that right?"

"Hell, yes. I didn't want trouble. But I've got a major investment in this operation. I've run it twice already back East and made a fortune. The idea is to get in and get out. Find a place to set up shop, recruit a few kids from the local college campus to man the phones and computers and put on the show. Then we make the pitch and wait for the money to roll in. I don't hang around. Two or three months is plenty of time to get set up and rake the cream off the top."

"Why try it here?"

"Hell, everybody knows the Northwest is hot for the environment. Everyone around here wants to save it. Besides, an old lady back East who had already forked over a hundred grand died and left the foundation this island. It was too good an opportunity to pass up. But I figured to sell the place in a few weeks, dump the kids, and head for the next location."

Hatch nodded. "Well, I think that about does it. Thanks for wrapping up a few of the loose ends for me." He started toward the boat again.

"Wait, goddammit. You've got to take me with you. I won't make it if I have to walk back to the mansion alone. I'm too damn cold, even with this blanket. I need warm liquids."

"All right. If you can make it to the boat, you can come with us. But don't get any bright ideas like trying to intimidate Susan, or I'll throw you overboard. I doubt the fish will even notice one more load of toxic waste in the Sound."

"Is that supposed to be funny?" Bright asked through clenched teeth.

"No. I don't have a sense of humor. Just ask anyone."

"Shit. I knew you were a pro."

Jessie was euphoric. The adventure had ended on a note of shining success and she could not wait to tell Mrs. Valentine every detail.

The police had taken statements and dispatched a boat to New Dawn Island to see what was going on there. Bright was in the local hospital under guard. He was being treated for the early stages of hypothermia. He was already demanding a lawyer.

The computer printout Susan Attwood had brought with her, as well as the list and key from Bright's wallet, was in safekeeping in the hands of the police. Susan had phoned her mother from the police station and Mrs. Attwood had broken down in tears of relief. She had explained that a man who fitted Hoffman's description had told her that her daughter would disappear forever if she did not call off the investigation.

Jessie was already mentally preparing her report to Mrs. Valentine. She knew her boss was going to be thrilled with the results of the case. Business would be flowing into Valentine Consultations as soon as the story hit the newspapers.

But now was the time for celebration.

Jessie sat tailor-fashion in the middle of the bed and gazed happily around at her little group of intrepid adventurers. They were gathered together in a room at the same inn where she and Hatch had stayed on the occasion of their first visit to Edwin Bright's island. Several cans of soda recently purchased from the inn's vending machine had been opened and were bubbling freely. Bags of potato chips were being passed around. It was a festive sight.

"I want to thank you all for what you did tonight," Jessie said. "Valentine Consultations is deeply grateful for your assistance on this case." She raised her glass of cola toward

Alex. "First, to Alex, for cracking the computer and making contact with Susan."

"To Alex," David said grandly.

"To Alex." Susan Attwood blushed rosily and looked at Alex as if he were the reincarnation of Albert Einstein.

Hatch, sprawled in the chair near the window, took a swallow of cola and nodded at Alex. "Hell of a job, Robin."

"Thanks. It was nothing." Alex was flushed with pride and embarrassment. His eyes kept straying to Susan's admiring gaze. "Anytime you need help on a case, Jessie, just let me know."

"Why, thank you, Alex." Jessie beamed fondly at him. Then she raised her glass in David's direction. "To David, who has shown he is that rarest of all beings, a philosopher who is also a man of action. A true Renaissance man."

"I wouldn't go that far," David muttered, turning almost as red as Alex. But he was grinning hugely.

"To David," Alex intoned. "I owe you one, friend, for what you did to that jerk who was holding a gun on Susan."

"Yes," Susan said shyly. "Thank you, David. You were wonderful. Almost as wonderful as Alex."

Hatch took another swallow of cola. "I told you that you didn't need anyone running interference for you, Ringstead. You can do your own dirty work just fine."

David met his eyes. "So you did."

"To Susan," Jessie continued, hoisting her glass again. "Who bravely got out of the mansion with the proof of Edwin Bright's fraud."

"To Susan." Alex gazed at her with pride and longing in his eyes.

"To Susan." David held up his glass.

Hatch munched and nodded at Susan. "Bringing that printout showing Bright's financial setup was a stroke of genius, Susan. The authorities are going to have a field day."

"It was nothing." Susan blushed again. "I just wish I hadn't been such a gullible idiot in the first place."

Alex touched her hand. "Don't blame yourself, Susan. You had only the best intentions."

"The others I worked with there at the mansion were innocent too, for the most part." Susan glanced anxiously around the room. "The people who manned the telephones, as well as the computer operators and programmers. We all believed in Edwin Bright. We thought he was a true genius who was being deliberately ignored by the establishment because his predictions were so alarming. And you know how the government is about bad news."

"Nobody likes to hear talk of disaster," David agreed. "It's easier to kill the messenger than deal with the real problem."

Susan nodded sadly. "Those of us who went to work for Bright thought we were dealing with the real problem. We believed the climate forecasts were accurate and we thought the money was needed desperately for Bright's technology-development plan. I'd started having some doubts, but it wasn't until Alex contacted me and pointed out the anomalies in the forecast data that I really questioned what was going on. Then I stumbled over a record of Bright's scam back East and knew for sure something was wrong."

"I wouldn't worry about the others," Hatch said. "The authorities will probably only go after Bright."

"Fortunately, the people who got conned into working for Bright are all basically data-oriented," Alex said. "Show them where the data are wrong and they'll buy into the truth. They're not the type to follow Bright blindly, as if he were some guru. Not when they've seen the facts."

Susan nodded soberly. "I think that's true. Edwin Bright is a charismatic man, but without solid data to back up his claims, no one I know is going to follow him."

"Not everyone who worked for Bright got conned," Hatch said thoughtfully. "A few of them were in it for the money. Landis and Hoffman, for example. Not exactly your average wide-eyed innocents."

David gave him a sharp glance. "You think there might be more hired muscle like Landis and Hoffman running around?"

Hatch shrugged. "How would I know? I'm a businessman, not a detective. But there was a lot of money involved. It just seems remotely possible that if Bright had those two on the payroll, he might have had others."

Susan frowned. "If he did, I never saw them on the island."

"That's reassuring." Hatch took another swallow of cola.

"I'm sure the authorities will pick up everyone involved very quickly," Jessie declared crisply, although she couldn't meet Hatch's eyes. "Now, then, your attention, please." She tapped the edge of her glass with her fingernail. "I have one more toast to make before we conclude this celebration. To Hatch. Without whose unflagging zeal and noble leadership this mission would never have been accomplished."

A cheer went up around the room.

"Don't forget to mention my gold card," Hatch said. "You used it to get the guy down at the marina to rent you a boat in the middle of the night, remember?"

"To Hatch's gold card," Jessie repeated dutifully. It was a joke. She was sure of it. In fact, she was almost positive. It *had* to be a joke.

"To Hatch's gold card."

"To Hatch's gold card."

Hatch met Jessie's laughing eyes and smiled coolly. "One more toast," he said softly. "To Jessie. Who is going to marry me. Soon. Aren't you, Jessie?"

A sudden silence descended on the room. Jessie froze, her glass halfway to her lips. Her gaze collided with Hatch's and she was unable to look away. She loved him. And just look what he had gone through for her sake. Surely no man would go through all that unless he cared at least a little. She took a deep breath.

"Yes," Jessie said.

This time the cheer that went up shook the paintings on the walls and rattled the glassware on the end table. Hatch gazed at Jessie with deep satisfaction as Alex and David whooped in approval.

"About time," Hatch said softly.

A loud pounding began on the other side of the adjoining wall. A man's voice yelled from the next room.

"For Christ's sake, will you hold it down in there? We're trying to get some sleep."

Hatch groaned, shut his eyes, and sank deeper into his chair.

Jessie grinned. "This makes the second time poor Hatch has nearly been kicked out of here," she explained to the others. "Guess we better not come here on our honeymoon, huh, Hatch? A little too embarrassing for you."

"I never even considered this inn for our honeymoon," Hatch muttered without opening his eyes. "No telephones in the rooms. That means no business calls, no modem hookup, and no way to run a fax machine. How could I function?"

Jessie hurled a pillow at him while the others dissolved into laughter.

A long while later Jessie emerged from the bathroom to find that Hatch was already in bed. He had turned out the light. She could see him waiting for her in the shadows, his broad shoulders dark against the snowy pillows. His eyes glittered with a masculine anticipation that sent a delightful chill down her spine.

A wave of shyness threatened to overwhelm her as she went slowly toward him. This was the first time she had been truly alone with Hatch since the others had retired to their own rooms a short while ago. It was the first time she had been alone with him since agreeing to marry him.

"What's the matter, Jessie?" His voice was deep and dark. "Nervous now that everyone else has gone?"

"No, of course not. Why should I be nervous?" At that moment Jessie stubbed her toe against the leg of the chair, tripped, and sprawled across the bed. Mortified, she buried her face in the blanket. "Good grief, how can I marry a man who turns me into a walking disaster?"

"The same way I can marry a woman who gets me into situations where I wind up running around in the woods in the middle of the night playing hide-and-seek with people who carry guns," Hatch said. "Very carefully."

Jessie tried to stifle a laugh and failed. "That was a joke. I know it was."

"You're wrong. I meant every word. In fact, I have never been more serious in my life." Hatch pulled her up so that she lay beside him on the pillows. His expression was very intent as he speared his fingers through her hair and gripped the back of her head. "We're engaged now, Jessie. It's official."

"Yes." She knew her lower lip was quivering. She could feel it. A sense of desperation tore through her. "Hatch, I love you."

"I'm glad." He covered her mouth with his own and rolled her onto her back, crushing her into the bedclothes. "I want you to love me, Jessie. I want it very, very much," he muttered against her lips. Then he deepened the kiss. His tongue invaded her mouth.

Jessie felt herself plunging into deep water for the second time that night. But this time the water was warm, not icy. Her arms went around Hatch's shoulders as the weight of him bore her downward. For long moments she was caught up in the spell of his lovemaking, unable to think of the future or the past, longing only to please and be pleased, to satisfy and be satisfied.

She slitted her eyes briefly when she became aware of Hatch's hand gliding down the length of her, lifting the hem of her nightgown. Then his fingers were on the insides of her thighs and she sucked in her breath.

He parted her, moistening his fingers in the sweet, liquid warmth he had drawn forth. His lips found her nipples through the fabric of the gown as he touched her intimately. When she lifted herself against his hand and cried out softly, he groaned.

"Touch me," he muttered. "Yes. There. Hold me. God, Jessie. *Yes*."

He was naked beneath the sheets, his body heavy with arousal. She curled her fingers around him and felt the drop of moisture at the broad, blunt tip of his manhood.

"Hang on." He took a deep breath and pulled away from her, groping for something on the nightstand. "Give me a second. I've got it here, somewhere."

She opened her eyes again and saw the stark need on his face. Lightly, wonderingly, she touched his cheek. "You said you wanted children."

"Yes. Damn. *Yes*. Jessie, are you sure?"

"I'm sure. I think, with a little practice, you would make a very good father, Hatch."

He stopped groping for the condom and pushed her flat on her back once more. His mouth captured hers in a kiss of searing need as he surged heavily into her warmth.

Hatch lay awake for a long while after Jessie fell asleep in his arms. One hand crooked behind his head, he watched the patterns on the ceiling and thought about the future.

He was not in the clear yet and he knew it, even if Jessie did think everything was tied up with a neat pink bow. Hatch understood that the potential for disaster still loomed. It was his way to calculate the odds and to take risks when the time was right. He had learned the hard way to do it in his personal life just as he did it in business.

He knew he had done a good job of cementing his future with Jessie by deliberately linking himself to Benedict Fasteners and the entire Benedict clan. He had been as thorough as possible about the task. Jessie was devoted to her family and he was rapidly becoming a part of the family. Everything was under control so long as nothing forced Jessie to have to choose between him and the rest of the clan.

The last thing Hatch wanted was for Jessie to ever have to make such a choice.

Hatch did not kid himself on that score. He knew that if Jessie were ever placed in a position where she had to choose between him and her family, the odds were not going to be in his favor. For Jessie, family would always come first.

And the family was bound by Benedict Fasteners.

The control of the company was the key.

Hatch turned the problem over in his mind a few more times. He did not like uncertainties. This was not the first time he had contemplated a method of getting Jessie out from under the responsibility she faced. He was definitely vulnerable as long as she had the long-term duty of looking after the firm for the rest of the family.

Hatch examined the plan he had been working on for the past few days. It was almost time to implement it. There was some risk involved, but he was fairly certain it was minimal now. With every day that passed he was more in control of the company and of his relationship with Jessie. With every passing day he was more certain that Vincent Benedict trusted him.

Hatch knew it was time to make the final move in this high-stakes game he was playing with his own future.

It was nearly dawn when Jessie stirred in the depths of the tangled bedding. She brought her elbow, which had somehow gotten caught in an awkward position above her head, down by her side. She collided with something solid.

"Oooph." Hatch winced.

"Sorry." Jessie propped herself up to look down at him in concern. "Did I hurt you?"

"That's supposed to be my line." He touched his side with tentative fingers. "But since you ask, I think I'm going to survive. Damn. Is it morning already?"

"Afraid so. I wouldn't worry about it. We've got a while yet before everyone heads downstairs for breakfast."

"Good. I need some more sleep. I've had a very hard night."

She chuckled. "Yes, I know."

He looked offended. "I was speaking in the literal sense."

"So was I."

Hatch sighed. "For the record, I would just like to point out that the worst hours I have ever worked in my life were the ones I just put in for Valentine Consultations. Remember that the next time you complain that I'm a little late getting home in the evening."

"Now, wait just one minute here—"

"Forget it. I don't feel like pursuing this conversation. Let's change the topic."

"To what?"

"To our engagement."

"What about it?" Jessie asked.

"You seem to have thrown yourself somewhat wholeheartedly into the thing," he pointed out carefully. "It was your idea to forget the protection last night, wasn't it?"

"Yes. Are you sorry?"

"Good God, no." He reached out and pulled her down across his chest. "Jessie, I know you've had your doubts about marrying me, but I promise you I'll do my best to make certain you don't regret this."

"I'll see that you do. Your best, that is."

Hatch smiled ruefully. "Yeah, you probably will. Nag, nag, nag."

"You got it." She squirmed into a more comfortable position. "Hatch?"

"Hmmm?" His fingers toyed with her hair, pushing it back behind her ears.

"I've been thinking about David."

"What about him?"

"He's different somehow. I can feel it."

Hatch smiled fleetingly. "Your famous intuition?"

263

"I think so," she said quite seriously. "It's because of you, isn't it?"

"Me?"

"You made him an important part of the rescue operation."

"I didn't *make* him an important part. He was an important part."

"He wasn't the only one in the crowd who knew how to fight," Jessie said gently.

Hatch shrugged. "David needed to know he could handle himself in a fight if he had to. He's been trying to prove himself to Vincent since he was a kid. But a man doesn't start growing up until he realizes that the only one he has to prove himself to is himself. I offered him a way to do that. Lucky I did, or we'd never have known about Hoffman being in those woods until it was too late."

"Very profound, Hatch."

"You like that, huh? Well, I've got something else even more profound to say to you."

Jessie tipped her head to one side at the new note in his voice. "And that is?"

"I think it might be best if you quit Valentine Consultations."

"Quit my job?" Jessie jerked herself upward and off the bed and stood glaring down at him. "Are you out of your mind? This is the best job I've ever had."

"I don't want you involved in any more rescue operations like the one last night." Hatch sat up slowly and put both feet flat on the floor. "And I'm afraid that when the news hits the papers, people who've lost kids to cults will be flocking to Valentine Consultations. You'll want to rescue each and every one of them. It's too dangerous. I won't have it."

"Hatch, it won't be like that. This was a fluke case."

"You can say that again. But the longer you live, the more you realize there are a lot of flukish things in this world. Jessie, I don't want to argue about this."

"Good. Because I don't want to argue about it either." She turned and stomped into the bathroom, slamming the door behind her.

Half an hour later they joined the others downstairs in the breakfast room. The dining area smelled strongly of freshly brewed coffee, pancakes, eggs, and frying bacon. Alex, Susan, and David were already occupying one of the large tables. They looked up expectantly as Jessie and Hatch entered the room.

"Uh-oh," David murmured, his eyes on Jessie's set face. "Do I detect trouble in upper management already?"

"Jessie has always had a problem fitting into the corporate hierarchy," Hatch said as he sat down and picked up the menu.

"He means I don't take orders well." Jessie slanted Hatch a fulminating glance.

"She'll learn," Hatch said easily.

CHAPTER SIXTEEN

So do you love him or what?" Elizabeth leaned over the railing and peered down into the murky green depths of Elliott Bay. Sea gulls bobbed on the water, searching out french fries and other discarded edibles from an assortment of plastic cups, paper, and litter that floated on the surface.

The Seattle waterfront with its shops, restaurants, and aquarium was only sparsely crowded this afternoon. A few tourists were strolling along on the sidewalk behind Elizabeth and Jessie and there were some joggers heading toward the park at the far end of the promenade.

"Of course I love him. Why else would I agree to marry him?" Jessie frowned down at the trash that marred the beautiful bay.

"Because everyone in the family wants you to?"

"I'd do a lot for this family, Elizabeth, but I would not marry someone just to keep everyone happy."

"Aunt Glenna says sometimes people do weird stuff just to please relatives."

"I wouldn't do anything that weird," Jessie assured her.

"Don't worry about me, kid. I'm not doing this for you or David or the moms. I'm doing it for me."

The sun sparkled on the lenses of Elizabeth's glasses as she looked up. Her small face was screwed into an expression of serious concern. "You're sure?"

"I'm sure."

"What changed your mind about Hatch? You told me you couldn't ever marry him."

"That was before I got to know him better."

Elizabeth nodded. "You mean you've decided he's not like Dad after all?"

Jessie smiled to herself. "No. Whatever else he is, he is definitely not like any other man I've ever met."

"Well, if you're sure you know what you're doing, I guess it's okay." Elizabeth stepped back from the railing. "You want to go through the aquarium now?"

"Sure."

"You ever miss your old job there?"

Jessie made a face. "Not in the least. Something about cutting up plain ordinary fish to feed to fancy exotic fish just didn't appeal to me. Seemed a little unfair, somehow."

Elizabeth grinned. "They let you go because you kept wanting to rescue the plain ordinary fish, didn't they?"

"Aquarium work was obviously not a good career path for me."

"You think working for Mrs. Valentine is a good career for you? The moms say they hope you'll settle down and find a real job after you marry Hatch."

Jessie recalled the argument she and Hatch had had on that subject. Not another word had been spoken concerning her career at Valentine Consultations since they had all returned from the San Juans yesterday afternoon. But she knew Hatch better than to think he was going to let the matter drop.

"I don't know why everyone's complaining about my working for Mrs. V," Jessie muttered. "It's obvious I'm at last in an upwardly mobile position. Business is going to boom in a few days when word gets out about the Attwood case."

"Have you finished your report for Mrs. Valentine?"

"Not yet. I'm still working on it. I want it to be really impressive. This case is going to totally revitalize Valentine Consultations and I want to be sure she appreciates the brilliance of the way I handled it as well as the new marketing potential of the firm."

Elizabeth giggled and then was silent for a moment as she glanced down over the railing once more. "You know, I wonder what Elliott Bay was like before people started throwing garbage into it."

"Spectacular." Jessie looked out toward the majestic Olympics. When one viewed it from a distance, the sound was as beautiful as it must have been two or three hundred years ago. "It still is spectacular. It just needs to be cleaned up, and that's going to take some hard work and a lot of money. There aren't any easy answers and there's still so much we don't know about ecology and the environment."

"I can sort of see why people got excited about what Edwin Bright was selling."

"So can I," Jessie said. "Too bad it wasn't for real."

Later that afternoon Jessie bounded up the sidewalk and into the downstairs hall of her office building. As usual there was a green glow emanating from Alex's office. She poked her head inside and smiled at the sight of Susan Attwood and Alex huddled together in front of the computer.

"What are you two working on?" Jessie asked.

"Hi, Jessie." Susan smiled shyly.

Alex glanced over his shoulder, squinting against the glare from the hall. "Oh, hi, Jessie. Susan and I are going through some more of the DEL files for the authorities. You've got a visitor upstairs."

"Wow. A new client? Already? Word travels fast."

"Don't get excited. It's your Aunt Glenna."

Jessie wrinkled her nose. "Come to ask me if I really understand the full ramifications of what I'm doing by getting myself engaged to Hatch. I suppose I'd better reassure her. At least she didn't summon me to her office to interrogate me this time."

Alex shrugged and turned back to the computer screen. "Let Hatch handle her if she gives you a hard time. He's good at handling things."

Susan nodded soberly. "Yes. Why don't you do that?"

"I can handle my own family, thank you very much." Jessie made a face at the back of Alex's head and closed the door.

It struck her as she stalked up the stairs that everyone appeared to have forgotten she was the one who had organized the rescue of Susan Attwood. She should have thought twice about letting Hatch go along on the mission. That was the problem with a natural leader. He gave orders naturally and people naturally tended to follow them. Afterward he got all the credit. Naturally. Nobody recalled who the real brains of the operations had been.

Aunt Glenna was standing at the window gazing down at the sidewalk below when Jessie pushed open the door and walked into the office. She was dressed in a crisp, sober gray suit with a pale blue blouse and low businesslike pumps. When she turned her head Jessie could see that her eyes looked even more serious than usual behind the lenses of her black-framed glasses.

"There you are, Jessie. Your friend downstairs let me in." Glenna glanced at her watch. "I can't stay long."

"Have a seat, Aunt Glenna." Jessie dropped into the chair behind the rolltop desk and decided to take the offensive. "I expect you're here to congratulate me on my engagement."

Glenna did not move from her position near the window. "There's no need to be facetious, Jessie," she said gently.

"Sorry."

"I am naturally concerned that you know what you are doing. There has been a great deal of pressure on you from the rest of the family to go through with this marriage."

Jessie smiled and leaned back in the squeaky chair. She picked up a pencil and began tapping the point on the desk. "It's all right, Aunt Glenna. I promise you, I've come to this decision all by myself. I know what I'm doing and I'm not doing it to please the family. I appreciate your concern, though."

Glenna nodded slowly. "I was afraid of that. You're doing it for yourself, aren't you?"

"Yes."

"I had begun to suspect that."

Jessie scowled. "Suspect it?"

"It's strange, really. But I never thought you were the type to become obsessed with your role as Vincent's heir. I always believed it had been thrust upon you and was basically unwelcome. I assumed, based on the patterns of early childhood, that your tendency to be an enabler had motivated you to accept the role, but I never actually thought you wanted it. I never thought the money and the power meant that much to you."

"Money and power? What are you talking about?"

"I always saw you as trapped. I actually felt sorry for you, you know. I wanted to help you set yourself free. But now it's obvious that you're in this position willingly."

Jessie sat forward abruptly, shocked. "Aunt Glenna, what is this all about? I'm not marrying Hatch in order to get control of the company. The last thing I want is control of Benedict Fasteners."

"Are you certain of that, Jessie? Have you looked deep within and asked yourself why you really want to marry Sam Hatchard? Isn't it just possible that you've grown to like your position in the family? That what started out as a way of forcing Vincent to bond with his family has now become a means of exercising power?"

Jessie's eyes widened. "You're crazy, Aunt Glenna." She realized what she had just said and flushed in embarrassment. "I'm sorry, I didn't mean that literally."

"Jessie, ask yourself if the real reason you're marrying Hatchard isn't that you think you'll be able to control the company through him. You can have it all this way, can't you? The power that goes with being Vincent's heir and none of the responsibility for actually managing Benedict Fasteners."

"For heaven's sake." Jessie tossed the pencil down on the desk. "Even if I was marrying to secure my position as Dad's heir, I'd be a fool to think I could control the company through Hatch. Nobody controls Hatch."

"That's probably true. But you may have deluded yourself into thinking you can control him. You may think you can manipulate him the way you've learned to manipulate your father."

"I don't manipulate Dad."

"Of course you do. You're the only one who can, and everyone in the family knows it. That's why you've become the intermediary for everyone else." Glenna's voice was still remote and detached. The psychological authoritarian of the Benedict clan was pronouncing judgment.

"On the rare occasions when he listens," Jessie concluded crisply, "I can sometimes get Dad to pay attention and do the right thing. But that's only because I'm willing to dig in and go toe to toe with him. You know as well as I do that sometimes even that's not enough."

"It's worked for the most part, though, hasn't it, Jessie? You have the real power in this family. He's made you his sole heir. We all go through you when we want something from Vincent. To keep and consolidate that power, all you have to do is marry the consort Vincent has handpicked for you. I should have realized all along that you were maneuvering toward your own goal." Glenna started for the door.

"Aunt Glenna, wait. I don't understand what this is all

about. Why are you so upset about my marrying Hatch? This way the company stays in the family and has a chance to go big, just as you and the moms have always wanted."

"Don't be ridiculous. I am not upset."

"Yes, you are. I can feel it." Jessie jumped to her feet behind the desk.

"I simply want you to analyze your own motives in this."

"I am marrying Hatch because I love him."

"Nonsense. Don't be so bloody trite, Jessie. No one marries for love. That's just a label we slap on other, more fundamental drives: power, money, control, security, sex, family pressure. Those are the real reasons people marry. Do yourself a favor and decide which of them are the reasons you're engaged to Sam Hatchard."

"*I love him.*"

"Really?" Glenna was amused in a distant sort of way. "And does he love you?"

Jessie went still. "I think so. Yes. Of course he does."

"Has he told you he loves you?"

Jessie lifted her chin. "That's a very personal question, Aunt Glenna. I don't have to answer it."

"No, you don't. Not to me, at any rate. A word of advice, Jessie. Be very cautious if Sam Hatchard ever does tell you he loves you because a man like that will do whatever he has to do, say whatever he has to say, crush whomever he has to crush, in order to get what he wants. And he wants Benedict Fasteners. Even if he has to use you to get it."

"Dammit, that's not true."

"Unfortunately for all of us, Vincent has made it true. No one can stop you from marrying Sam Hatchard, Jessie. But I wonder how long you can spin out your fantasies. How long will you be able to convince yourself that Hatchard would have married you if Benedict Fasteners hadn't been your dowry?"

"Aunt Glenna, that's unfair."

"I'm sorry, Jessie. I'm a doctor, not a fortune-teller who

looks into a crystal ball and tells people what they want to hear the way your Mrs. Valentine does. I'm trained to understand and assess people's motives, even if they choose to lie to themselves or others about them."

Glenna went out the door and closed it very gently behind her.

"Hold it right there, Aunt Glenna." Jessie darted around the end of the desk and threw open the door. She flew to the staircase railing and leaned over to call after her aunt. "What's your motive in all this? Why are you so damned angry at the way things are turning out?"

"I never wanted things to turn out this way." Glenna did not look up as she descended the stairs.

"Why not? You wanted Benedict Fasteners to stay in the family. You've said so."

Glenna stopped on the bottom stair and swung around. For the first time her face lost its controlled, aloof expression. Anger blazed for an instant in her eyes and her mouth was pinched with rage. "Yes, I want Benedict Fasteners to stay in the family. Of course I do. The future potential of the firm is enormous. *But it should have gone to the rightful heir, not to you.*"

"The rightful heir?" Jessie instinctively stepped back from the rail, appalled by the fury in her normally self-contained aunt. "Whom are you talking about?"

"I'm talking about David, damn you. David should have inherited Benedict Fasteners. *Vincent owed me that much.*"

Glenna whirled and strode quickly out the downstairs door. The glass in it trembled as she slammed it shut behind her.

Jessie finally tracked her mother down in a stylish waterfront condominium where Lilian was supervising a bevy of craftspeople.

"No, no, I do not want the track lighting extended into the sitting area. The small room is supposed to be a library."

Lilian frowned intently over a set of blueprints while the electrician waited patiently. "Did you bring the fixtures for the kitchen?"

"They're downstairs in the truck," the man said. "I'll bring them up after I get this damned fancy Erector set installed in the ceiling."

"Fine. Remember, I want to approve the kitchen fixtures before they go in."

"Right."

Lilian stepped back to join Jessie. She kept her eyes on the electrician as he began setting out his tools. The smell of fresh paint emanated from a bedroom. "You've got to watch these people like a hawk. Turn your back for one second and they've put in the wrong fixtures or painted a wall white when you've distinctly ordered taupe. Then they try to convince you to accept the mistake."

"Mom, I've got to talk to you."

"I didn't think you were here because you've decided to pursue a career in interior design. What's the problem? Worrying about wedding plans already? I told you Connie and I would handle it for you. We're thinking of coral and cream for the colors. What do you think?"

"I think it sounds fine as long as you don't try to stuff Hatch into a coral tux. Listen, Mom, this is serious. I had a weird visit from Aunt Glenna this afternoon."

"Is that right?" Lilian frowned at the electrician. "Please don't start any work until you put down drop cloths. This wooden flooring was just put in a few weeks ago and it cost my client a fortune. I don't want it nicked."

The electrician obediently started to put down drop cloths. Lilian glanced at Jessie.

"What were you saying about Glenna?"

"She was very upset. Came to see me at my office."

"That is a little unusual for Glenna, isn't it? What did she want?"

"I got the feeling she wanted me to call off the wedding," Jessie said bluntly.

That got Lilian's attention. "Is she out of her mind?"

"I kind of wondered about that myself. But I think she was just plain angry."

"About what? Everyone in the family wants this marriage."

"Aunt Glenna said she thought Dad should have left the company to David."

There was a prolonged silence from Lilian. She kept her gaze on the electrician, but it was obvious she was thinking about something besides track lighting. "Interesting. David has absolutely no talent whatsoever for managing a large business like Benedict."

"Neither do I."

"That's not entirely true, dear. You had the absolutely brilliant ability to attract Sam Hatchard, who is fully capable of running it."

"Thanks, Mom. You really know how to make a daughter feel special. Why not just come right out and say Dad is using me to buy himself the son he always wanted. One who can take Benedict and expand it into a 'giant in the industry'?"

"Don't be silly, dear."

"Does it bother you to think that Hatch might be marrying me in order to get control of the company?"

"No, not in the least. The company is forever tied to you, and you are tied to the family. By marrying you, he is actually marrying into both the company and the family. We're assimilating him, if you see what I mean. It's going to work out just fine. In any event, I like Hatch. And it's about time you married someone. Why not him?"

Jessie decided not to pursue that useless line of discussion. "Mom, why does Aunt Glenna feel so strongly about David having a right to Benedict?"

Lilian sighed. "I suppose it all goes back to when Lloyd Ringstead disappeared. Glenna and your father had a brief affair."

"You know about that?"

"Of course. I'm not an idiot. It didn't last long, for obvious reasons. Anyone could see they weren't suited to each other. I never said anything because there was no point. Vincent and I had just gotten our divorce and Glenna was trying to deal with the trauma of Lloyd's having vanished into thin air. I suppose Vince and Glenna comforted each other for a time."

"Is it possible David is, well, more than my cousin?" Jessie asked hesitantly.

Lilian blinked in astonishment. "Are you asking me if David could possibly be Vincent's son?"

"I guess so. Aunt Glenna seems to feel very strongly about Dad owing her something."

"The answer about David is no," Lilian said firmly. Then she frowned thoughtfully. "At least, I think the answer is no. If he were your half-brother that would mean there were actually two affairs between Glenna and Vince, one a few years before Lloyd vanished. David was four when his father left, remember."

"True. But it's not an impossible scenario. If Glenna and Dad got it on once, they might have gotten it on twice."

"Frankly, if Glenna thought she could press a paternity suit, she would have done so by now. And it wouldn't have been necessary in the first place."

"Because Dad would have been more than willing to claim David if he thought he was his son?"

"Exactly. Vince has always wanted a son."

"I think you're right," Jessie said slowly. "So why does Aunt Glenna think she has such a big claim on Dad?"

Lilian shrugged. "Must have been that brief affair they shared all those years ago. Some women don't know how to let go."

Jessie awakened in the middle of the night, aware that something was wrong. It took her a minute or two to realize that Hatch had left the bed. She lay without opening her eyes, listening for noises from the bathroom. When there were none, she listened for noises from the kitchen.

When the ominous stillness became oppressive, she finally lifted her lashes. The first thing she noticed was the faint glow of light coming from the living room. She glanced at the bedside clock and saw that it was nearly two in the morning.

Pushing back the covers, she got out of bed, pulled on a robe, and traipsed toward the door. A niggling suspicion was gnawing at her. She paused in the hallway when she saw Hatch sitting at the kitchen counter. He had put on his trousers, but no shirt. His bare feet were hooked over the bottom rung of the stool. His briefcase was open on the floor at his feet. Papers and computer printouts were scattered across the top of the counter. He was punching numbers into a small calculator.

Jessie leaned against the wall, arms folded beneath her breasts. "Couldn't sleep?"

He glanced up, eyes hooded and watchful. "I didn't know you were awake."

"Obviously." She straightened away from the wall and ambled slowly over to the counter. "It's all right, you know. You could have just told me earlier this evening you had to work on some papers after dinner. I'm not a total fanatic about your schedule."

"Yes, you are."

She scowled at him as she opened the refrigerator door and started rummaging around inside. "Not true. I accept the fact that there will be the odd occasion when your work requires some overtime. I can tolerate a reasonable amount. After all, as you pointed out, look what my job requires in the way of unusual hours. There I was having to run around at midnight up in the San Juans." She closed the refrigerator door and carried a plate of cream cheese over to the counter.

"Let's not start making comparisons between my job and yours." Hatch eyed the cream cheese. "What are you doing?"

"Fixing a little midnight snack. As long as I'm up, I might as well eat. Want a bagel?" She hovered near the toaster oven, bagel in hand.

"All right."

Jessie smiled benignly and popped the bagels beneath the broiler. "Now, then, suppose you tell me what was so terribly important you had to sneak around in the middle of the night to work on it?"

"First tell me how mad you are."

She looked at him innocently. "Not mad at all."

He looked unconvinced. "Okay. I had an idea on a new approach to use on this bid your father wants to make to undercut Yorland and Young. Thought I'd crunch the numbers and see how it looked."

"Dad really wants to get that Spokane contract, doesn't he?"

"Yes."

"It's personal, you know."

"No, I didn't know," Hatch said, looking at her with new interest. "But I was beginning to wonder. This thing just isn't big enough to bother with unless there are extenuating circumstances."

Jessie checked the bagels and decided they were ready. She opened the toaster-oven door. "Yorland and Young pulled a fast one on Benedict Fasteners a couple of years ago. Walked off with an important contract that Dad felt should have been his. He just wants revenge, that's all."

Hatch nodded thoughtfully. "I can understand that."

"I rather thought you would." Jessie plunked the hot bagels down on a plate and carried them over to the counter. She sat down across from Hatch. "I'll try not to get cream cheese on your important stuff."

"Appreciate that." Hatch watched her slather cream cheese on a bagel.

"So how did you get to be such a big authority on revenge? Who taught you to understand my father's point of view?"

"It's not important," Hatch said softly. "It was all over a long time ago."

"Oh, yeah?" She eyed him with interest. "So what company did you squash or beat out or otherwise get even with?"

"A company called Patterson-Finley. It was an engineering firm."

Jessie stared at him, remembering the day of the science fair when her father had bragged about how Hatch had crushed the company in a hostile takeover bid. "That takeover was a personal act of vengeance on your part? What did you have against Patterson-Finley? What had it ever done to you?"

Hatch looked at her. "I'm not sure now is a good time to go into this."

"I've got news for you. You're not going to get a better time. I want to know the whole story and I want to know it now."

Hatch leaned his elbows on the counter. "You're really going to make a demanding sort of wife, aren't you?"

She chuckled. "Better get used to it. So, what was the deal with Patterson-Finley?"

Hatch was silent for a long moment. Then he shrugged. "The man my wife was going to meet on the day she was killed?"

"Yes?"

"His name was Roy Patterson."

Jessie nearly choked on her bagel. "The same Patterson as the one in Patterson-Finley?"

"Right. Now, if that's the end of your questions, I'll finish off these numbers and get back to bed."

Jessie watched as he returned to the calculator. "Was it worth it?" she asked.

"Tearing apart Patterson-Finley? Yes." He did not look up.

"He was your best friend, wasn't he?" she whispered. "And he was running off with your wife. You must have loved her very much to exact that kind of vengeance."

"Whatever I once felt for her died when I found her note saying she was leaving me because I was a loser and she needed to be with a winner."

Jessie considered that. "Nobody goes after revenge the way you did unless he feels very intensely about a woman."

"You don't understand revenge, Jessie. It's best cold, like the old saying has it, not hot. At least for me it is. It's not an act of passion."

"Just a business thing, is that it?"

Hatch nodded slowly. "You could say that. Yes. A business thing."

"Bull." She got to her feet and started back toward the hall that led to the bedroom. "You loved her and when you lost her it tore your heart out. You went after your vengeance with everything that was left in you." She paused in the doorway. "Tell me something, Hatch. Will you ever take that kind of risk again? Will you ever let yourself love again? Or is a long-term, committed relationship called marriage all I'm ever going to get from you?"

"Jessie." His voice was a dark growl of warning.

"What?" She'd turned back toward her room.

"You know there's more to it than that."

"No," she said. "I don't know that. Sometimes I delude myself into thinking there's more to it than that. But other times I wake up alone in the middle of the night and I panic. Because I don't know for certain, you see. I love you. But I don't know if you love me."

"Dammit, Jessie."

"Good night, Hatch."

She went back into the bedroom and crawled into bed, curling into herself.

"Jessie."

She turned her head just far enough to see him filling the doorway. Wordlessly she watched him walk toward the bed. His fingers were busy at the fastening of his trousers.

"You know there's more to it than that," Hatch said again as he got into bed beside her. He was already fully aroused.

"No."

"Yes." He pulled her into his arms, his mouth rough and heavy on hers. "Yes, dammit. There's a hell of a lot more to it than that."

"Yes," she whispered. There had to be a lot more to it than that. She was banking her entire future on the possibility that he could one day tell her he loved her.

CHAPTER SEVENTEEN

There was nothing quite like the sense of pride, satisfaction, and accomplishment one got from a job well done, Jessie decided. She gazed down at the neatly typed five-page report that lay on top of the desk. It was truly a thing of beauty. Mrs. Valentine was going to be extremely impressed.

Alex had let Jessie use the word-processing program on his computer to assure a crisp, polished finish to the report. Both right and left margins were justified, the spelling was letter-perfect, and the prose was in a businesslike style.

Jessie had stopped at an office-supply store on the way to work to buy a handsome report binder in order to add a further touch of professionalism.

No doubt about it, Valentine Consultations was never going to be the same. A new era had arrived for the psychic-consulting business. The morning papers had broken the news of the DEL case and Jessie knew the phone was going to start ringing off the hook at any minute.

She looked up expectantly when she heard a familiar tread on the stairs. A moment later the office door opened and Mrs. Valentine walked in wearing her professional attire. She had on a dark green turban, a wide-sleeved green paisley blouse, and a long green skirt that fell to her ankles. The usual assortment of beads and chains covered her bosom, tinkling merrily as she came through the door. She had a newspaper tucked under one arm.

"Mrs. V, you look great. How are you feeling?"

"Fine, dear. Just fine. I can see again, if you know what I mean. Such a relief."

Jessie smiled happily. "I'm so glad, Mrs. V. Go on into your office. The tea is almost ready. I'll bring it right in."

"Thank you, dear. I could use a cup of tea." Mrs. Valentine unfolded the newspaper as she headed for the inner office.

Jessie hurried over to the tea tray and spooned tea into the pot. She hummed cheerfully as she reached for the kettle of boiling water. When all was ready, she arranged the pot and two delicate cups on the tray, added a tiny bowl of sugar cubes and a spoon, and picked up the tray.

On the way past the rolltop desk she paused long enough to place the neatly bound Attwood report on the tray. Then she entered Mrs. Valentine's private office.

Mrs. Valentine had the newspaper spread out on top of her consulting table. Her reading glasses were perched on her nose and she was deep into the front-page story.

Jessie glanced at the headlines as she set down the tea tray. She grinned with satisfaction. "Local Psychic Exposes Multimillion Scam."

"Oh, my." Mrs. Valentine read carefully to the end of the last paragraph and then turned to the next page to continue. "Oh, my goodness."

Jessie could hardly contain her excitement. She hovered on the other side of the desk with eager impatience until Mrs. Valentine had finally finished the article. When her employer eventually closed the newspaper and sat back in her chair, looking somewhat stunned, Jessie could not wait any longer.

"Well, Mrs. V? What do you think? Valentine Consultations is going to be famous. People will be beating down our door. We'll be scheduling appointments weeks in advance. This is going to be the most important psychic-consultation agency in the city, maybe in the whole state."

"Jessie, dear . . ."

"I've been doing some planning. We'll probably have to take on additional staff to deal with the paperwork, but that's okay. I've had some experience in personnel work. I'll handle that end of it."

"Jessie . . ."

"But I'm wondering if we shouldn't get another psychic to work with you." Jessie frowned in thought and began to pace the office. "We're going to be awfully busy and I don't think we can depend too much on my abilities. The truth is, much as I hate to admit it, I don't think I have any real psychic talent. I'm much more suited for management."

"Jessie, there is something we must discuss, dear."

"I'm going to speak to Mom and Connie about coming up with some sketches for a redo of the interior design of the office too."

"Something important, Jessie, dear . . ."

"We want the place to look businesslike, yet charming and a bit otherworldly. Successful, yet unconcerned with success, if you know what I mean."

"Jessie . . ."

"We may eventually have to look for larger office space. But we can wait for that, don't you think?"

"Jessie, I'm afraid I'm going to have to let you go, dear."

"Also, I was thinking it might be a good idea to . . . What did you say?" Jessie came to an abrupt halt and stood staring down at Mrs. Valentine. "Mrs. V, you can't mean that."

Mrs. Valentine heaved a massive sigh. "I am so sorry, dear. You know I'm extremely fond of you. You're a delight to have around the place. But I'm afraid Valentine Consultations is, uh, too small an operation to warrant an assistant."

Jessie gripped the edge of the desk with both hands. "But

that's just it, Mrs. V. It won't be a small operation once these headlines hit the streets. The phone will be ringing off the hook. We're going to go *big*."

"That's precisely what I'm afraid of, dear. I never meant Valentine Consultations to go big. I liked it the way it was. Just a small, pleasant little business I could run by myself. I had doubts the day I hired you, but I liked you so much, I overcame my premonitions of trouble. You'd think I, of all people, should have known better. Now look what's happened. You've ruined everything. I may have to close entirely until the excitement dies down."

"Mrs. V, are you firing me?"

Mrs. Valentine sighed again. "I'm afraid so, dear. Don't worry, I shall be happy to give you a good reference."

The telephone on the rolltop desk started to ring.

Hatch paused briefly at Grace's desk before going on into Vincent Benedict's office. "Hold all his calls until I come out, will you, Grace? No interruptions."

"Yes, Mr. Hatchard." Grace smiled. "By the way, I saw the full story of your adventure with Jessie in the morning papers. It sounds as if it was all terribly exciting."

"That's one way of describing it." Hatch went on past the desk and into the inner sanctum.

Benedict looked up, frowning in disapproval at the unannounced visit. "I'm in the middle of something, Hatch. Is this important?"

"Very." Hatch put down the file he had brought with him and went over to the coffeepot to pour himself a cup. He carried the coffee back across the room and leaned against the edge of Vincent's massive desk. "Seen the morning papers?"

"Goddamn right, I saw the morning papers." Vincent tossed down his pen and leaned back in his chair. "When you told me what had happened up there in the San Juans, you left out a few minor details, didn't you?"

Hatch shrugged. "A few."

"I'm damn glad that nonsense is over."

"So am I."

Vincent paused and slanted Hatch a speculative glance. "David really clobber that guy?"

"Knocked him cold with a karate punch. Saved the day. We probably wouldn't have gotten out of that mess alive without him."

"I'll be damned." Vincent nodded, quietly pleased. "Maybe he'll be okay. Maybe he's going to turn out different than Lloyd, after all."

"Maybe it's time you gave him credit for being his own man."

"Yeah. Maybe." Vincent picked up his pen. "Like I said, I'm glad the whole thing is finished. But I'm holding you personally responsible to see to it that Jessie doesn't get herself into any more scrapes like that one."

"I'll do my best."

Vincent eyed him. "Speaking of Jessie, you two set a date yet?"

"No. But we're going to make the formal announcement of our engagement on Friday evening. Jessie said she was going to book a table at her favorite restaurant, the one down in the Market. Everyone in the family is invited. Even you."

Vincent grinned. "Reckon I can make that." He pulled his calendar across the desk and jotted a note on Friday's date. Then he leaned back in his chair again. "You in here to talk business or just pass the time of day?"

"Business." Hatch sipped coffee meditatively. "There are a few things that need to be cleared up before Friday."

"You're talking about buying into Benedict Fasteners, aren't you? Don't blame you for wanting to get the deal done. You've waited long enough."

"It's a little more complicated than my share of the deal, Vincent. There are a few other people involved."

Vincent scowled. "What the hell are you talking about now?"

"I'll lay it out in plain, simple terms. We can go over the details later. I want you to agree to divide the company into four equal parts, Benedict. One-fourth goes to David, one-fourth to Elizabeth, and one-fourth to Jessie. I'll buy the last quarter and I'll run the business."

Vincent's mouth dropped open. For an instant he was obviously speechless. When his voice returned, it came out in a full-throated roar. *"Are you out of your head?* Break up Benedict Fasteners? After all the sweat I've put into this company?"

"I'm not talking about breaking it up. I'm talking about keeping it in the family, just like you've always intended. But this way all the involved parties own a piece of it. That gives them a vested interest."

Vincent slammed his fist down on a stack of papers. "None of them knows a goddamn thing about running a company like Benedict Fasteners."

"That's what you've got me on board for, remember?"

"Jesus, man, you don't know what you're saying. Give David a chunk of this company and there's no telling what kind of trouble he'll start. He's always blamed me for Lloyd running off. And the boy has no common sense. He's going to study philosophy, for crying out loud. The kid's a flaming liberal with radical notions about the environment and things like that. He'd make all kinds of trouble for me if he owned a quarter of the business."

"I can handle David." Hatch took another swallow of coffee. He was fully prepared to weather the storm. He had expected nothing less when he had walked into Vincent's office. When it was all over, Benedict would calm down and agree to his plans.

"You think you can handle David, huh? Well, what about his mother? Glenna's an iron maiden, pal. She's bitter and she's weird. There's no telling what she would do if she got her hands on David's shares."

"David's not a kid any longer. The very fact that he's opted for grad school is proof that he's willing to take a stand against his mother. She wanted him to stay here at Benedict."

"You're wrong. Giving a piece of Benedict to that side of the family would be inviting disaster. And what about Elizabeth? She's just a kid. Twelve years old, for Christ's sake. You can't go turning over a quarter of this company to a twelve-year-old kid. What if Connie remarries? The new guy might try to get involved in the company and he could use Elizabeth's shares to do it."

"You're her father, remember? You can retain control of her quarter until she comes of age. Or you can make Jessie the trustee until then."

"And then what? That's less than ten years away," Benedict raged. "With the plans you've got, the firm will be three times the size it is now. Maybe bigger. Elizabeth will be dissecting rats' brains or something for a living. You want some ivory-tower research scientist trying to make business decisions for one-fourth of this outfit? She won't know what the hell she's doing."

"I have a hunch Elizabeth will be content to let Jessie guide her when it comes to making decisions for Benedict."

"Jessie? That's a joke. Jessie doesn't know beans about running this show either."

Hatch smiled faintly. "But Jessie will be married to me, remember? She'll let me make all the decisions for Benedict Fasteners. I'll be running the show, just like you planned all along."

"Except that half of the ownership will be in other hands. No, I won't have this company torn into little pieces, dammit."

"Not little pieces. Big pieces. Pieces which I will control either directly or indirectly."

"You can't be certain of retaining control of things if you've got three other owners involved. They could outvote you if they got together and decided to go in a different direction."

"There's a risk, I'll admit it. But I know your family, Vincent. The risk is a small one. I can deal with it."

"You don't know that, goddammit." Benedict pounded the table once more and shot to his feet. "There's no way to be certain you can stay in command if you've got the company divided up into quarters."

"I'm willing to chance it."

"Well, I'm not," Vincent shouted. "I've seen plenty of family-owned companies torn to shreds this way. It won't happen here."

Hatch looked down into his coffee. "You don't have a choice, Benedict."

"What the frigging hell does that mean? Of course I've got a choice. I say we don't split things up and that's final."

"Not if you want me to marry Jessie and run your company, it isn't."

Suddenly the office was silent. For a minute Vincent stared at Hatch, mouth agape. Then he sat down, clearly stunned.

"Are you telling me you won't marry Jessie unless I agree to cut up Benedict Fasteners?" Vincent asked, as if trying to make certain he had understood.

"I didn't say that. I'll marry her, all right. But I won't buy into Benedict and I won't stick around here to run it for you. I'll take Jessie and leave the state. We'll start over somewhere else. Oregon, maybe."

"Bullshit. I'll cut Jessie off without one red cent."

Hatch nodded. "Just as well. Because if you did go ahead and leave the company to her, I'd make sure she divided it up when she took possession."

"The hell you would," Benedict said softly, too softly, his eyes shrewd and angry. "You're bluffing."

"Have I ever lied to you, Benedict? Either agree to portion the company out among David, Elizabeth, Jessie, and me or forget the whole deal. I'll take Jessie and leave town."

"She won't go with you, you sonofabitch."

This was the tricky part, Hatch knew. Now he was bluffing for all he was worth. Everything was riding on his poker-playing skills. His fingers tightened on the coffee cup. "She will, you know. She loves me."

"You make her nervous. She told me so herself."

"She'll still come with me, Benedict."

"Bullshit. Not if she knows you're walking away from Benedict Fasteners," Vincent snarled. "That woman may be featherbrained about some things, but she knows her duty to her family. She won't walk away from her own people. Everyone depends on her, and she knows it."

"Everyone had better stop depending on her, then, because things are going to be different around here."

"They sure as hell are." Vincent's eyes narrowed shrewdly. "I'm canceling your contract, Hatchard. Effective right now. You're *fired*, you sonofabitch. Get out of here. You've got one hour to clean out your desk."

For an instant Hatch thought he had not heard correctly. This was not the result he had calculated. Dazed, he covered his shock by getting to his feet and slowly putting the empty coffee cup down on the desk. Without a word he headed toward the door.

"Goddammit, Hatchard, you ever change your mind and get your common sense back, you know where to find me," Vincent yelled after him.

"I won't change my mind. By the way, that file I left on your desk is the final breakdown on the Spokane job. You can undercut Yorland and Young with that bid and Benedict can still make a small profit. But my professional advice is to forget it. It's not worth it."

"Goddammit, Hatch . . ."

Hatch went out the door and closed it quietly. He stood still for a minute, adjusting to the one-hundred-and-eighty-degree turn his life had just taken.

"Mr. Hatchard?" Grace's voice was laced with concern. "Are you all right?"

Hatch forced himself to focus on her. "Call my secretary, will you, Grace?"

"Certainly, sir. What should I tell her?"

"Tell her to pack up my desk. Have everything sent to my apartment. I won't be coming back to the office."

Grace stared at him in astonishment. "You're leaving us, Mr. Hatchard?"

"It looks that way." He gave her a rueful smile as he walked to the elevators. "I've just been fired."

"Mr. Hatchard . . ." The telephone in Grace's hand dropped onto the desk with a loud crash.

Hatch stood at the window of his high-rise apartment and stared out at Elliott Bay. It was a terrific view and he wondered why he had not spent more time in the front room admiring it.

The answer to that was simple. Jessie's place had always seemed so much cozier and more inviting, more like home.

He tore his gaze away from the view and glanced around the place he had rented shortly after moving to Seattle. It was in pristine order, of course. Everything was in its proper place. There was not a speck of dust anywhere. The cleaning service he'd hired saw to that. Damned place looked as though no one actually lived in it.

He had not even unpacked a lot of his things, he reflected. There had not been time. From the moment he'd arrived he had been immersed in work and in the roller-coaster business of courting Jessie. His apartment looked more like a hotel room than a private residence.

Fired.

It was hard to believe it was all over. Hard to believe everything he had been working toward had just gone up in smoke. Hard to believe that Vincent Benedict had called his bluff.

Impossible to believe he was going to lose Jessie.

Hatch had been so certain he could force the older man

into splitting up the company, so confident of his own ability to deal with Vincent Benedict. He should have known right from the start that Benedict was too tough and too wily and too damn stubborn to get maneuvered into doing anything he did not want to do.

Hatch had played poker with an old pro and he had lost. He had risked everything on a bluff.

And threatening to take Jessie away had been nothing more than a bluff. Hatch told himself he should have known Benedict would be too savvy to fall for it. It was crazy to think Jessie would actually walk away from her family and her self-imposed responsibilities to go off with a man who made her nervous. Her first loyalty was to the clan. He had known that from the beginning. Hell, he'd used that knowledge to maneuver her into a relationship with him.

It was crazy to believe she would run off with a man she had agreed to marry in the first place only because everyone around her was urging her to do so. A man whose main attribute was that he was Vincent Benedict's handpicked candidate to take over the operation of Benedict Fasteners.

Hatch did not delude himself. He had been in this position once before and he knew how the chips would fall. Jessie was not Olivia. He was fairly certain she genuinely cared for him. But the fact that she had convinced herself she was in love with him would hardly be enough to make her run off with him when everything else in the relationship went sour.

Hatch told himself he had to be realistic about the situation. He had to see it from a woman's point of view.

Running off with him would mean leaving everything Jessie held dear. It would mean leaving Elizabeth. It would mean leaving Seattle. It would mean abdicating her loving responsibility to her family and her duty to Benedict Fasteners.

It would mean casting her fate with a man who would be essentially starting over. Women, Hatch knew from experience, rarely did dumb things like that in real life.

He glanced at the liquor cabinet and thought about pouring himself a drink. He needed one badly.

He decided to wait until he had seen Jessie. He would need one even more after that.

Outside the lobby door of Jessie's apartment house, Hatch leaned on the buzzer. He had the key Jessie had given him, but for some reason he did not want to use it. He was not coming home from work this time. He was paying a last visit.

"Yes?" Jessie's voice sounded odd through the speaker.

"It's me."

She did not say anything more, but a second later a hissing noise told him the lock had been released. Hatch pushed open the door, walked inside, and started up the stairs.

He glanced around and realized how familiar it all seemed. He had gotten accustomed to coming here at the end of each day. He had gotten to like the idea of knowing Jessie would be waiting for him with a glass of wine and that there would be mouth-watering smells coming from the kitchen.

It was easy to see why there was a strong instinct in men to keep women in the home. They had a way of making things much more comfortable for a man.

Not that any man would ever be successful in keeping Jessie barefoot and pregnant, he thought wryly.

Pregnant.

The possibility of getting Jessie pregnant hung tantalizingly in the air. If she were pregnant, she might feel compelled to marry him, after all.

But he did not want her to be forced into that kind of decision, he told himself, trying to be noble.

On the other hand, it just might work. Jessie felt so strongly about the importance of fatherhood. She had spent most of her life building bonds between Vincent and his family. The last thing she would want to do was deny her own child its father.

But the odds of getting her pregnant before she found out what had happened this afternoon were staggeringly against him. They had, after all, been making love without protection for only two days. If he kept his mouth shut tonight, he might get one more shot at it, but the odds were still bad. And his luck had not been running well lately.

Jessie opened the door for him on the second level. She had her hair slicked back behind her ears and she was dressed in a black jumpsuit. He saw the anxiety leap into her eyes the instant she got a good look at him.

"Hatch, is something wrong?"

She did not know anything yet. Now was the time to keep his mouth shut. Give himself one more chance in bed with her. Maybe stack the odds a little more in his favor. But, hell, she had always been honest with him. He owed her honesty in return.

"Your father fired me today." He was surprised at how calm the simple words sounded. Hatch stood there in the doorway waiting for the devastating reaction and wondered what he would do without this woman in his life. He could not seem to think that far ahead. All he could do was wait for the blow.

"He fired you?" Jessie finally got her mouth closed. "Dad canceled your contract with Benedict?"

"Yes."

"You're unemployed?"

Hatch nodded, propping one shoulder against the door-jamb. He shoved his hands into his pockets. "Looks that way."

"You won't be running Benedict Fasteners?"

"No." He drew a breath. "I'll be leaving Seattle soon. I'll be starting over somewhere else. Oregon, maybe. Or Arizona. I just stopped by to tell you."

"Hatch, this is incredible. I can't believe it." She blinked and then her green eyes filled with mirth. She started to giggle, and the giggle turned into full-blown laughter. "Oh, my God. We've finally got something in common."

Hatch frowned, at a loss to understand what was happening. "Jessie?"

"I got fired today too."

Hatch looked at her. "What?"

"You heard me," Jessie got out between gasps for air. "Mrs. V fired me. Said she didn't like the direction I was taking Valentine Consultations. Said she would give me nice references. Oh, my God, this is so funny. You and me both fired on the same day. I can't believe it."

"Somehow I hadn't seen it in a funny light."

Jessie blinked away the moisture the laughter had brought to her eyes and gulped in air. "No, of course not. You poor thing. I'll bet you've never been through this before, have you?"

"There was one other time," he reminded her deliberately.

She nodded, reaching out to yank him through the door. "That's right. I'd almost forgotten. Back when you were married to Olivia and your company got taken over." She closed the door behind him and threw the dead bolt. "Still, that was years ago. You haven't had my vast experience with the situation. Come on in and I'll show you how it's done."

Hatch felt as if he had just fallen down the rabbit hole. Nothing seemed to be going according to the script. "How what's done?"

"How you celebrate getting fired, of course. Since you've had such limited experience, I'll guide you through it. First, you sit down." She pushed him onto a stool in front of the counter.

"What happens next?"

"Why, next you open a bottle of champagne, of course. As soon as I left the office this morning, I bought one. I stuck it in the refrigerator hours ago." She opened the refrigerator door and grabbed the bottle sitting on the top shelf. "This is the real thing, you know. From France, not California. I splurged. I always do when I get fired."

"I see."

"Personally," she said as she peeled back the wire that held the cork in place, "I vote for Oregon. I've been to Arizona, though, and it's very nice. We can go there if you think we should. But it would be easier for Elizabeth to visit if we went to Oregon. On the other hand, I guess we really can't be too picky, can we? I mean, both of us being unemployed and all."

The cork came out of the bottle with a bang, striking the ceiling. Champagne started to billow forth, threatening to cascade all over the kitchen floor.

Hatch reached out, took the bottle from Jessie's hands, and quickly poured the sparkling liquid into the glasses.

Then he grabbed Jessie and pulled her into his arms. She went into them willingly, laughter and love gleaming in her eyes.

CHAPTER EIGHTEEN

D oes this mean," Hatch asked carefully a few minutes later as he slowly released her, "that you still view us as being engaged?"

Jessie picked up her champagne glass and shot him a startled glance over the rim. "Are you trying to wriggle out of the engagement?"

"Hell, no."

"Aunt Glenna said you might."

"Might what?"

"Might lose interest in me if I didn't bring Benedict Fasteners along as my dowry."

Hatch was annoyed. "What a coincidence. I was wondering if you'd lose interest in me if marrying me meant losing Benedict Fasteners. Your father says he's going to cut you off without a cent, by the way. I don't think I mentioned that, did I?"

"That's Dad for you. He's so engrossed with the bottom line that he just naturally assumes it's everyone else's first consideration too. How did it happen, Hatch?"

"Me getting myself fired? I gambled. Tried to bluff an old poker player, and he called. I should have known better." He thought about that. "Hell, I did know better. I realized there was a risk. But I had to take it."

"Why?"

"I wanted to cut a few more of the knots that keep you tap-dancing between your father and the rest of the family. I thought that if I could arrange for Elizabeth and David to each get a quarter of the company, you'd be out of the loop permanently."

"Out of the loop?"

"That was Plan A. Split up the company among the logical heirs and let me buy a quarter of it. That would put everyone on a more or less equal footing. No one would be dependent on you to make certain they got their fair share of the inheritance. The moms would stop pressuring you, and maybe a chunk of the company for David would appease Glenna. You would no longer feel like you had to hold the whole thing together all by yourself."

Jessie's mouth fell open in amazement. "You tried to make Dad give us all an equal portion of Benedict Fasteners?"

"Yeah. Like I said, that was Plan A. Seemed like a good idea at the time."

"Dad has never been willing to even listen to that idea. I told you that. Lord knows I tried it out on him a few times in the past. He's been absolutely nonnegotiable on the subject. Seems to think it might tear the company apart."

"I told him to trust me to hold things together. Obviously he didn't."

Jessie propped her elbow on the counter and balanced her chin on the heel of her palm. "What made you decide to push him so hard if you knew you might lose everything in the process?"

Hatch met her eyes. "I told you, I was just trying to get some of the family pressure off you."

She started to smile. "There's more to it than that, isn't there? You wanted to prove to yourself I'd marry you even if I didn't have to. Hatch, that's so sweet."

"*Sweet?* Christ, lady, it is anything but sweet. It's a full-scale financial disaster. Talk about shooting myself in the foot."

She bit her lip. "Are you really upset about losing Benedict Fasteners?"

"No, dammit. I can live without Benedict. But I don't think it's sunk in yet that you've lost it too, if you marry me."

"Big deal."

"Cutting you off from your inheritance," he continued evenly, "also effectively cuts you off from your primary role in the family."

"I'm no longer the intermediary, as you called it," Jessie said slowly, nodding in comprehension. "It's going to feel a little strange at first."

"Better be prepared to feel more than just a little strange," he growled. "You don't seem to understand that everyone is going to be madder than hell. They're all going to feel threatened now. Marry me, and everyone's share of the big pie they were all counting on is at risk."

"Why? What do you think Dad will do now?"

"Who knows? Vincent will either sell the company outright or he'll continue to run it as he has been running it. Either way, the family can kiss off the idea of taking Benedict Fasteners into the fast lane."

"Dad loves that company. I can't see him selling out."

"I can. He doesn't like being pushed around any more than I do. He's fully capable of selling it just to prove he can't be manipulated. He's into revenge, in case you haven't noticed. Look what I've gone through to beat out Yorland and Young for him, just because the company once undercut him on a contract."

"True. And you, of all people, understand vengeance, don't you?"

Hatch sighed. "Yes. I do. And even if he doesn't sell, he won't be able to turn Benedict Fasteners into what everyone wants it to become. The firm is thirty years out-of-date and so is Vincent's management style. He won't be able to revitalize the company unless he gets someone like me on board. He knows that. I doubt he'll bring himself to trust anyone like me again."

"Which means that Benedict Fasteners will stay a small-time regional business. I don't think that's such a bad fate."

"Everyone else sure as hell will, including your father. They've had the carrot dangled in front of them now and they won't forget what was once within reach. They're going to blame you for depriving them of it. I'm sorry, Jessie."

"I'm not." She was quiet for a minute. "Tell me, just out of curiosity, did Dad leave you a way back?"

Hatch smiled wryly. "Sure. All I have to do is come to my senses, crawl back, and tell him we'll do things his way."

Jessie looked surprised. "He said that? He ought to know you'd never go back on those terms."

Hatch lifted one shoulder in dismissal. "It was probably all he could think of on the spur of the moment. When he recovers from the shock, he'll turn the pressure on you. So will everyone else."

"Let 'em. I've already made my decision."

He still did not completely understand what was happening here. "Why?" he asked bluntly.

"Because I love you, of course. I told you that."

"Yeah, I know you said that, but—"

She silenced him by putting her fingertips over his mouth. "Do you love me?"

He allowed himself to think about it for the first time. "Hell, I guess so. I wouldn't have gone through all this otherwise."

She wrinkled her nose. "Be still, my beating heart. Let's try this from another angle. Would you have given up your chunk of Benedict Fasteners and the future you've got planned for it and for yourself for the sake of any other woman of your acquaintance?"

"Of course not." He swallowed champagne and hid a slow grin.

"Then say it, damn you."

He smiled into her eyes, finally beginning to relax for the first time that day. "Jessie, I love you."

Her own smile widened happily. "Was it worth it? Losing everything for love?"

A great weight seemed to be lifting from his shoulders. "Is that what I just did?"

"Uh-huh."

"You tell me if it was worth it," he said softly.

"Yes. Most definitely yes."

"Yes," he repeated. "Most definitely yes." He took the wineglass from her hand and set it down on the counter next to his own. Then he got to his feet and scooped her off the stool and into his arms.

"Lord," she whispered, eyes filling with passion as he carried her toward the bedroom. "I just wish I had a staircase. This would be so much more romantic if you carried me up a staircase, don't you think?"

"No. At my age a man has to consider his lower back," Hatch said seriously.

She punched his shoulder. "That was a joke. Darn it, this time I know that was meant to be funny. Wasn't it?"

Hatch started to chuckle. The next minute he was laughing out loud, a deep, full-throated roar of a laugh that came from far down in his chest. And as his own triumphant mirth echoed in the white bedroom, he realized he could not remember the last time he had allowed himself to surrender to sheer, unadulterated happiness.

Hatch woke from a pleasant, dozing sleep and felt the soft warmth of Jessie's body curled into his own. Her sweetly curved derriere was nestled against his thighs, and his hand cupped one rounded breast. A nipple thrust into his palm. Hatch squeezed gently.

Jessie shifted against him. "You rang?"

He chuckled and kissed her shoulder. "Just wanted to see if you were still awake."

"Ummm. Actually, I've been thinking. I know how much you counted on getting your paws on Benedict Fasteners."

"I'd rather have my paws on you."

She smiled and turned her head on the pillow to look at him. "That's nice and it certainly represents a drastic reordering of your personal priorities, for which I am extremely grateful. However, I also feel a little guilty about all this."

Some of Hatch's good mood started to slip. "Don't say that, Jessie. You've got nothing to feel guilty about. If anyone should be feeling guilty, it's me. In one fell swoop I've just changed your whole life."

"You mustn't say that." She touched his cheek gently. "As far as I'm concerned, that one fell swoop proved for certain that you loved me and I shall treasure the memory forever."

"Then what are you thinking about so seriously?"

"I could try talking to Dad for you," she said. "See if I can get him to climb down off his high horse. I know neither one of you is the type to back down. You're both so stubborn. But maybe if I sort of mediated things, I could find a compromise for both of you."

"Try it and I'll paddle your butt so hard you won't sit down for a week."

She blinked. "I beg your pardon?"

"You heard me. Jessie, this is between your father and me. You are not involved. Got that?"

"But I am involved."

"No. You said yourself, you've already made your decision. You're going to marry me, right?"

"Yes, of course, but—"

"Then you've made your choice. Your first loyalty is to me now, not your family."

"Yes."

"You aren't going to play go-between this time, honey. I won't let you. You're on my side of the fence and you're not going to try to straddle it. I don't need you to rescue me. All I need or want is you. Got that?"

She smiled mistily, her fingers splayed on his bare chest. "Got it. You know, I think that's about the nicest thing anyone has ever said to me."

He grinned. "You mean threatening to paddle your backside?"

She yanked on a handful of chest hair and looked satisfied when he winced. "No, I meant the part about needing and wanting me. Just me. Not me because I can act as an intermediary or because I can get something for you from Dad or because I can smooth things over and hold it all together. But me, just because I'm me."

"Remember that, okay?" He slid his hand down over her thigh.

"Okay."

"Jessie?" His fingers were tangled in the nest of hair between her legs now.

"Uh-huh?"

"You're sure about wanting to have my baby?"

"I'm sure. I think you'll make a good father, Hatch."

"Thank you for trusting me that much. I know what that decision means to you." He kissed her throat and pushed his leg between hers. The womanly scent of her body filled his head. He was already hard. "No one has ever trusted me as much as you do. Walking away with me will mean starting over, you know."

"I know. I don't have a lot of money saved, but I've got some. We can sell one of the cars. I hate to say this, but it should probably be the Mercedes."

"Damn."

She patted his arm sympathetically. "On the plus side, I'm very good at finding jobs."

He moved on top of her, cradled her head between his

hands, and smiled down at her. "It's not going to be too bad. I've got the stake I was planning to use to buy into Benedict Fasteners. I'll use it to start up another management-consulting business. I've done it once. I can do it again."

"I know."

"Most of the money will have to go into the new business, though. There won't be a lot left over. Not for a while."

"Don't worry about it." Jessie stroked his shoulders. "I'm not. I know you can make it work, Hatch."

He looked down at her glowing face and was filled with a deep sense of wonder and awe. "Where have you been all my life?"

"Waiting for you." She drew him down to her, wrapping her legs around his waist and her arms around his neck.

Hatch entered her with a slow, aching tenderness, letting her pull him deep within her body. He watched the desire grow in her eyes and knew a sense of completeness that he had never felt before in his life.

Nothing else really mattered, he decided. Not the uncertainties that lay ahead, not the loss of the bright, successful future he had been planning at Benedict Fasteners.

Nothing mattered except Jessie and the baby they were going to make together.

"I'm going to be one hell of a father for our kid, Jessie." It was a vow as binding as any oath he would ever take.

"Yes. I know."

"But I'll be an even better husband."

"I know." She smiled brilliantly up at him. "And don't worry. Maybe we can find a way to keep the Mercedes."

"Damn right we will."

Elizabeth finished paying for the book on famous women scientists, picked up the paper sack, and turned from the counter to join Jessie.

"I'm ready. You want to go look at clothes now?" Elizabeth glanced up inquiringly as they left the bookstore and ambled out into the crowded shopping mall.

"Nope. I don't want to be tempted," Jessie said, feeling extremely noble and virtuous and terribly thrifty. "Hatch and I will have to watch every penny for a while until he can get his new business established."

"Does this mean the big wedding production is off?"

"Afraid so. Don't worry, you'll still get to be my attendant. We'll just be cutting back on some of the extras. Like serving a large buffet to three hundred wedding guests, the way the moms had planned."

"I'm still going to get to wear the dress Mom picked out for me? And the little hat?"

"Definitely. Hatch and I will probably just wear jeans, naturally, but you can wear the fancy bridesmaid's dress. No problem."

Elizabeth slanted her a speculative glance to see if Jessie was teasing her. "Thanks. I can hardly wait. What about the engagement party?"

"Oh, it's still on for Friday night. Hatch refused to let me cancel it. Said we weren't so hard-up that we couldn't celebrate the engagement. It won't cost all that much, anyway, if only you and David show up. Do me a favor and don't order the lobster, okay?"

"It's going to seem strange, just David and me there."

"I know," Jessie said quietly. "But we'll all have a good time."

Elizabeth looked away, apparently studying a window display. "I'm going to miss you, Jessie."

Jessie put her arm around her shoulders and hugged her. "I'm going to miss you too. But you'll be able to come and visit us as often as you want."

"Hatch won't mind?"

"No. He won't mind."

"Do you think you'll go all the way to Arizona?"

"Hatch isn't sure yet. A lot depends on where he thinks the best prospects are for his new business."

"I hope you just go to Portland. I could get down to Portland on the train as often as I wanted."

Jessie took a deep breath and blinked back the moisture in her eyes. "I sort of hope we go to Portland too. But either way, it will be all right, kid. I promise you."

"Everything's going to change, isn't it?"

"I'm afraid so."

"I hope you're going to be real happy with Hatch." Elizabeth turned her face upward again, revealing the tears behind her glasses. "I want you to be happy, Jessie."

The tears in Jessie's own eyes spilled over. "Thank you, Elizabeth. Thank you very much." Jessie pulled her into her arms and the two of them stood in the middle of the mall and cried until a security guard finally stopped and asked if anything was wrong.

Jessie and Elizabeth shook their heads and walked outside to where Jessie's car was parked in the garage.

Lilian and Constance were both waiting in the office of ExCellent Designs when Jessie drove up with Elizabeth. Elizabeth grimaced when she opened the office door. She glanced back over her shoulder. "Watch out, Jessie. They're both going to let you have it."

Constance frowned at her daughter. "Why don't you run outside and amuse yourself, Elizabeth? Lilian and I want to talk to Jessie."

"Sure, Mom." Elizabeth gave Jessie a sympathetic glance on her way back out the door. A brief silence followed as it closed behind her.

"Well, Jessie." Lilian regarded her daughter with a straightforward, serious expression from the other side of her desk. "Why don't you tell us what this is all about?"

Jessie shrugged and sat down in one of the uncomfortable Italian chairs. "There's not much to tell. The engagement party's still on for Friday. Hatch and I haven't set the wedding date yet, but it will be soon. We'll probably be moving to either Portland or Phoenix. That's about all the information I have at the moment. Stay tuned. Film at eleven."

"This is hardly a joking matter." Constance leaned forward and folded her arms on her desk. "Is the deal between Hatch and Vincent really off?"

"Yes. Hatch made it a condition that the company had to be equally divided among him, David, Elizabeth, and me. Dad wouldn't go for it."

"For God's sake, we all know he wouldn't go for that kind of arrangement. We've been trying to get him to do it for years." Constance slapped the desk. "Damn that man."

"Who? Vincent or Hatch?" Lilian asked dryly.

"Both of them," Constance muttered.

"The question," Lilian murmured, "is what are we going to do now?"

"Nothing," Jessie stated.

Lilian shook her head. "Jessie, you've got to be realistic about this. There is simply too much at stake. You can't just opt out of this mess now."

"I'm not exactly opting out. I've made a choice."

"The wrong one," Constance snapped. She sighed. "Jessie, be reasonable. You've said yourself that your feelings for Hatch are uncertain."

"I never said that. They're very certain now. I've made my decision, Connie. I'm sorry if it's not the one you think I should have made, but it's the one I want to make."

"There are a lot of futures at stake here," Connie shot back. "My daughter's income from Benedict Fasteners is in jeopardy. So is yours and David's. You can't just walk out."

"Yes, I can." Jessie smiled gently. "I'll tell you something. It's really not as hard as I thought it would be. Besides, let's get real here. Nobody's going to starve. You may not get as rich as you once thought you would when you assumed Benedict was going to become a giant in the industry, but things won't be all that bad."

"Are you kidding?" Constance looked appalled. "Without you around to handle Vincent, there's no telling how bad things will get."

Lilian nodded. "She's right, Jessie. Things could get very

nasty. Vincent will make us beg for every penny. You know what he's like."

"So don't ask for a cent. That'll drive him crazy in no time," Jessie suggested dryly. "He likes the sense of control he gets from holding the purse strings. My advice is to cut the strings."

"Easier said than done," Lilian said quietly. "When I think of what Benedict Fasteners could have become . . ." She let the words trail off.

"You're talking about cutting off the strings of my daughter's potential inheritance which could be huge if Benedict goes big," Constance pointed out.

"Elizabeth will do all right. It was never Dad's money she needed. It was Dad's love and attention."

"Well, she'll get even less of that now that you're going to be leaving, won't she?" Constance pointed out.

"There's your own inheritance to be considered too, Jessie." Lilian gave her a chiding glance. "It's easy enough now to say you're going to chuck it all for love, but how will you feel five years from now when you've got children of your own?"

"I would like my children to know their grandfather," Jessie said. "But they won't need his money. And neither will I." She stood up and slung her shoulder bag over her arm.

"Jessie," Lilian said quickly, "think about this. You've been unsure of your feelings for Hatch all along. Don't rush into anything now. Give yourself time. Consider all the ramifications. You don't know what Hatch's motives are in all this. He might think he can use you against Vincent somehow."

"No. He's not going to use me. He loves me." Jessie smiled. "For myself, not because I'm useful. If anything, I've probably caused Hatch more trouble than anyone he's ever run into before in his entire life."

"What are you talking about?" Lilian demanded.

"Look at it from his point of view, Mom. I dragged him into a crazy adventure. He nearly got killed because of me. He's lost his chance to make Benedict Fasteners the cornerstone of the empire he'd planned to build when he decided to rescue me from my role in the family. And now he's going to be more or less starting over financially because of me."

"You're looking at this from a skewed perspective."

"I'm not so sure about that." Jessie went to the door and paused, her hand on the knob. "When you think about it, he's really given me one heck of a courtship, hasn't he? Obviously the man is in love."

"Jessie, we're just asking you to be reasonable about this," Lilian cut in swiftly. "What if Vincent is mad enough to sell out? Even if he doesn't, we all know the company needs to be modernized if it's to stay competitive, and Vincent can't do it. The chance to turn Benedict Fasteners into a corporate giant is too important to let slip away."

"You'd need Hatch to do it, and Dad fired Hatch," Jessie reminded her.

"But you could fix it, dammit." Constance threw up her hands in exasperation. "You can deal with Vincent. Get him to see reason. Get Hatch to see reason."

"Dad would make Hatch crawl."

"It's called compromise, dammit," Constance shouted.

"It's called pride," Jessie said. "If Dad and Hatch are ever going to find a way to work together, one of them will have to back down. And I can tell you right now, it won't be Hatch."

"You know it won't be Vincent," Lilian warned.

Jessie nodded. She knew her father as well as anyone. "I know. Oh, by the way, you're both invited to the engagement party on Friday evening."

"You can't really expect us to help you celebrate this fiasco of an engagement, Jessie," Constance muttered.

Lilian frowned at her daughter. "Go home and think it over, Jessie. Think it over very carefully. You don't want to abandon your family for a man who is so unreasonable he'll walk out on a multimillion-dollar future."

Things felt a little eerie, Jessie thought later as she parked her car in front of her apartment building and got out. She had the oddest sensation of impending disaster again, rather like the feeling she'd had about the Attwood case.

It was probably caused by the array of changes she was confronting in her life. After all, a great deal had happened at once. She had been fired from a job she had really thought was going to work out. She had gotten engaged to be married. She had become the cause of a lot of serious tension in the family, when normally she was the one who smoothed things over for everyone.

Her life was undergoing a tremendous upheaval, she reminded herself. It was probably normal to feel vaguely uneasy and perhaps even threatened. She reached into the backseat for the two sacks of groceries she had just bought at the supermarket. Grasping one in each arm, she backed out of the car.

Jessie heard the roar of the suddenly accelerating engine just as she closed the car door. Automatically she glanced to the right to look down the normally quiet street.

The dark brown car was no more than a few yards away, still accelerating rapidly. It was coming straight toward her.

Jessie screamed and dropped the two sacks of groceries. In a split-second calculation she realized she could never make it across the street in time.

She did the only thing she could do. She pressed herself flat against the side of her own car, praying the driver would at least see and try to avoid the vehicle, even if he had not seen her.

The brown car whooshed past so close that Jessie's purse caught on the fender. The bag sailed into the air and landed yards away. She felt a rush of wind sucking at her, got a glimpse of windows tinted so dark it was impossible to see the driver, and then it was all over.

All over and she was still in one piece. Barely.

Jessie nearly collapsed as she peeled herself away from her car. The vehicle that had almost run her down was already squealing around the corner, vanishing from sight.

"Damn drunk drivers," an old woman on the sidewalk yelled in sympathy. "They oughta get 'em all off the road once and for all. Take away their cars, I say."

Jessie just looked at her.

She was still staring blankly at the groceries scattered across the street when Hatch's Mercedes pulled into the empty parking space behind her car a few minutes later.

Seeing the scattered groceries, he was out of the car in a flash, racing toward her.

"Jessie?"

She almost fell into his arms. Nothing had ever felt so strong and reassuringly secure as Hatch did in that moment.

CHAPTER NINETEEN

Y ou're sure you're okay?" Hatch asked for what must have been the fiftieth time.

"I'm okay. Honest. Just a little shaken up." Jessie sat at the kitchen counter gripping the cup of hot tea he had just made for her. "Calm down, Hatch. It was just one of those things. I should have been more careful getting out of the car."

"Damn right, you should have been more careful."

Jessie cocked a brow at him. "Do I detect a lessening in the degree of sympathy you feel? Is this where you start lecturing?"

"Now that the shock is over, I'm entitled to start lecturing." Hatch leaned back against the sink, his arms folded, eyes hooded. "Christ. Next time you get out of a car, look behind you. Got that?"

"Believe me, I'm not likely to forget it."

"I just wish that old lady on the sidewalk had gotten a license plate."

"There wasn't time, Hatch. I'm telling you, it was all over in a matter of seconds. Everything happened so fast."

"And you didn't get a look at the driver?"

Jessie shook her head. "I told you, tinted windows. Not that I would have had time to take notes anyway. I was too busy trying to meld myself to the metal of my car. There's nothing to report to the police except that a brown car nearly hit me. Unfortunately, that sort of thing happens to innocent people all the time. All a person can do is be careful."

"Remember that." Hatch fell silent. His gaze turned brooding.

"Hatch?"

"Yeah?"

"What are you thinking?"

"About a few things."

"That certainly clarifies the issue," Jessie muttered. "Let's have it. What's going on in that convoluted brain of yours?"

"I was just thinking that the police haven't picked up the DEL guy who broke into your office and tried to get into my car. They're investigating Edwin Bright and they've got Landis and Hoffman, but what if there was another one running around?"

Jessie's eyes widened. "You don't think he'd be after me, do you?"

"Probably not," Hatch said a little too quickly. "If he exists, and if he's got any sense, he's skipped town. And even if he was dumb enough to still be around, he'd be more likely to go after Susan Attwood. She's the one who's supplying most of the hard evidence against Bright."

"True. Do you think we ought to call Susan and Alex?"

Hatch chewed on that. "The thing is, it really doesn't make any sense for that jerk to still be in the picture. Assuming there is a jerk, he was just hired muscle. If he was smart enough to escape the police net, he should be smart enough to be long gone. But it can't hurt to call Robin. I'll tell him to keep an eye on Susan and to lock his doors and stay out of dark alleys for the next few days."

"What are you going to do?"

Hatch smiled grimly. "Keep an eye on you and make sure you lock the doors and stay out of dark alleys for a while."

Jessie was not particularly surprised to get the summons from her father the next morning on her answering machine. The message was gruff and betrayed no hint of any emotion except anger.

"I want to talk to you ASAP. Not at the office. I'm going home early. Come by the house around five."

At five that afternoon Jessie dutifully went up the steps of the big white house in which she had been raised. The Queen Anne neighborhood was one of the nicest in Seattle, the homes large, expensive, and well-maintained. The house to which Vincent Benedict had brought two brides was an old one with a graceful garden. A professional took care of the flowers. Jessie's father had no interest in gardening.

Vincent answered the doorbell with a glass of whiskey in his hand. He glowered at his daughter.

"About time you got here." His gaze went past her to where Hatch's Mercedes was parked at the curb. Hatch was leaning against the fender, idly studying the tree-lined street. He did not glance at the doorway. "What the hell's that bastard doing here?"

"Keeping an eye on me."

Vincent's face turned red. "What in damnation for? Is he afraid I'll make you see sense?"

"Not exactly." Jessie walked on into the hall and headed for the living room.

Vincent closed the door and followed her. "Wait just a blasted minute. Did Hatch send you in here to argue his side of this thing?"

"I'm here because you asked me to stop by, remember? It's only five o'clock, Dad. Hours before your usual quitting time. I assume we are about to discuss something on a par with World War III?" Jessie examined the garden outside the bay windows. It was as pristine and perfect as the rest of the house. Nothing was out of place. It was a house in which nobody really lived. Her father came here only to sleep and change his clothes. He *lived* at Benedict Fasteners. He always had.

"You know damn well what we're going to discuss. Jessie, things have blown up in our faces."

"Not my face. I'm strictly on the sidelines this time." She sat down on the arm of one of the cream-colored chairs Constance had bought while she was in residence. The furniture in the room was about equally divided between Lilian's selections and Constance's. Everything meshed beautifully, which spoke volumes about the relationship between Vincent's two ex-wives.

"Don't give me that crap about being on the sidelines. In this family, you're never on the sidelines. You're always right square in the middle. You want something to drink?"

"No, thanks. I promised Hatch I wouldn't stay long."

"Hatch. That sonofabitch. I just wish to God I'd known what a viper I was bringing into my nest when I hired him."

Jessie raised her chin. "Watch it, Dad. You're talking about the man I'm going to marry. The future father of your grandchildren."

"Jesus. You can't marry him, Jessie. That's just it. At least not until he comes to his senses and backs off. He's gone crazy, wanting me to split up the company. This whole thing has gone far enough, and you're the only one who can end it."

"What do you want me to do?"

"Do what you usually do, dammit." Vincent waved the hand that held the whiskey glass. "Fix it. Make everybody calm down and do the reasonable thing."

"In this case the reasonable thing means make everybody do what you want, right?"

"It so happens that what I want is the best thing for the company and therefore the best thing for the family," Vincent growled.

"Hatch doesn't think so."

"Who gives a damn what that man thinks?"

"I do." Jessie smiled. "And I'm sorry, Dad, but this time I can't fix things. I can't even try."

"Why the hell not?"

"Well, for starters, Hatch has threatened to paddle me if I try to mediate between the two of you."

"Threatened you?" Vincent's head came around swiftly, eyes glittering with rage. "That sonofabitch has threatened to beat my little girl? I'll tear him apart, by God. I'll rip him to shreds."

"Relax. You know as well as I do that Hatch would never hurt me," Jessie said.

"No, I damn well do not know that. I don't know what to expect from Sam Hatchard now. I thought I knew that man, but I was obviously wrong. He's turned on me, Jessie. Like the shark he is."

Jessie raised her eyes heavenward. "Give me a break, Dad. That's a gross exaggeration and you know it."

"So fix it, dammit. Do something. You can't go running off with him."

"Why not?"

"Because the company needs him and the family needs you, that's why not."

"I'm sorry, Dad. But this is something you're going to have to fix on your own." Jessie got to her feet and walked over to him. She stood on tiptoe and brushed her lips against his cheek.

"What about the family?" Vincent rasped as she turned to leave.

"I love all of you, but you're forcing me to make a choice. I've made it."

"Jessie, wait, goddammit. Come back here." Vincent's voice was ragged. "Don't you see? If you leave, I'll lose all of 'em. Elizabeth, David, Connie, and Lilian. You're the only thing that keeps them tied to me. You and Benedict Fasteners."

"I'm sorry, Dad, but I don't want to go on doing the job alone anymore. You're going to have to help."

"I won't let Hatch tear apart everything I've worked to build," Vincent bellowed. "Do you hear me? I won't let him do it, Jessie. I can't."

"Dad, if you want it all—me, the family, and the bright future you see for the company—you're going to have to trust Hatch as if he really were your son." Jessie walked down the hall toward the front door. She paused before opening it. "By the way, you're invited to our engagement party. Seven-thirty tomorrow evening. I gave Grace the name of the restaurant, just in case."

"Don't be expecting me, goddammit. I won't sanction this . . . this damn engagement."

"I only invited family," Jessie said gently. "So I'm not expecting a big turnout at all."

Out on the street Hatch watched with interest as a light green Buick pulled in to the curb and Glenna Ringstead got out. She had her hair in its familiar tight coil and she was wearing her usual formal gray suit and black pumps. She did not immediately see Hatch lounging against the Mercedes fender. It was obvious she was concentrating on her mission to Vincent Benedict's house.

Hatch wondered how she had known that Vincent was home at this time of day.

"Hello, Glenna."

Glenna whipped around, startled amazement registering on her handsome features. "Hatchard. What are you doing here?"

"Jessie's inside talking to her father. She'll be out soon. I don't think they've got a lot to say to each other."

Glenna's eyes narrowed. "It's true, then? You and Vincent have quarreled and Jessie's running off with you?"

"Somehow when the bride is twenty-seven and the groom is staring forty in the face, 'running off' doesn't seem like quite the right description. That sounds more like two high-school kids eloping."

Glenna looked impatient. "But you are going to marry her?"

"Yes. I'm going to marry her."

"And Vincent did fire you?"

"I was told to clean out my desk and be out of the building within an hour. Didn't even get two weeks' notice, which Jessie tells me is standard. She ought to know."

Glenna's eyes brightened with rare satisfaction. "I knew it wouldn't work. I told Vincent all along that he was making a mistake bringing you into the company. He didn't need you to take Benedict Fasteners to the top. All he had to do was train David to follow in his footsteps. Now maybe he'll see reason."

Hatch shrugged. "Something tells me David is never going to want the job."

"He will. He just needed a little time to grow up and mature. Now that you're out of the picture, it's only logical for Vincent to give my son another chance. He owes David that much, and he knows it. I'm going to tell him so."

"I wouldn't count on it, Glenna. David's not cut out for the corporate world. Jessie's right. He'll be much happier in an academic environment."

"Jessie doesn't know what she's talking about. How could she? She's had no training in psychology, no advanced degrees of any kind. She can't even hold on to a job, for God's sake. Yet she thinks she knows what's best for everyone. It's about time she got out of the way. Without her around we're all going to be a great deal better off."

Hatch raised his brows. "Think so?"

"I know so." Glenna turned and strode up the walk.

The door opened and Jessie emerged from the house just as her aunt started up the steps. Her eyes flickered with surprise.

"Hi, Aunt Glenna. What are you doing here?"

"I've come to see your father."

"Right. Well, I hope you can make it to the engagement party tomorrow night. Seven-thirty."

Glenna nodded stiffly. "I'll be there."

"Good."

Hatch straightened away from the fender as Jessie came down the steps. He opened the car door for her. "You okay?"

"Yes."

"You sure?"

"Yes, I'm sure." She smiled wearily up at him as she slid into the front seat. "It's strange how people box themselves into little corners and won't come out, even though it's in their own best interests to do so, isn't it?"

"People get into patterns, like you said. Patterns are hard to break."

"Aunt Glenna was the one who first pointed out the patterns in people's lives to me."

"Speaking of Glenna . . ." Hatch glanced back toward the house. The front door was just closing. Hatch shut the car door and went around to get behind the wheel.

"What about Aunt Glenna?" Jessie asked as he turned the key in the ignition.

"She seems to think she's finally gotten what she's apparently wanted all along."

"Me out of the picture?" Jessie asked shrewdly. "Yes, I know." She gazed back at the closed door of the big white house as the Mercedes pulled away from the curb. "I hope she's happy now."

"Something tells me that woman is never going to be happy for long," Hatch observed. "But I'll give you odds she'll come to the engagement party to celebrate this turn of events."

The waiter took in the five faces seated at the table that had been set for eight. He cleared his throat as he handed out menus. "Are we still waiting for the other members of the party, sir?" he said to Hatch.

Jessie bit her lip and Hatch glanced at his watch. In

addition to herself and Hatch, only Aunt Glenna, David, and Elizabeth had arrived at the restaurant for the engagement party.

"I don't think there's much point waiting any longer," Hatch said. "It looks like they won't be joining us, after all. Bring out the champagne and that bottle of sparkling water."

"Yes, sir. I'll be right back." The waiter moved off through the crowded dining room.

Elizabeth stared at Hatch, her eyes wide with curiosity. "I can't believe you both got fired on the same day."

"Must have been fate," Hatch murmured.

David grinned. "Sounds more like bad luck to me."

"Same thing." The corner of Hatch's mouth kicked up as he traded a look with the younger man.

Glenna gave Jessie a cool, remote, oddly satisfied smile. "I'm sure it's all for the best."

David glanced toward the door. "Looks like the old bastard is going to stand you up, Jessie. You know, somehow I thought he'd at least put in an appearance."

"He's not real happy with me right now," Jessie said quietly.

"It's the moms I don't understand," Elizabeth said. "I told them they should come, even if they were mad at you. But they said you were making the biggest mistake of your life and that you were going to cause everyone a whole lot of trouble and be real sorry later. They said they couldn't be a part of it."

"Maybe in time they'll understand that I had to do it," Jessie said, her eyes going to Hatch. He smiled at her and grasped her hand under the table.

"So, where are you two going to wind up living?" David asked quickly, obviously determined to turn the conversation into less troubling channels.

"Portland, probably," Hatch said.

Elizabeth brightened. "Good. That's not far away at all."

Hatch grinned. "That's why I decided to take Jessie there

instead of Phoenix. We wanted to be someplace where you could come and visit easily."

"Thanks." Elizabeth looked at her sister. "Like I said, I can come down on the train."

"It's going to work out just fine," Jessie said firmly.

The waiter returned with the champagne and the sparkling water. Everyone watched attentively as he went through the ritual of opening the wine and pouring it. When he had left the table, Hatch picked up his glass.

"We're here tonight to make my engagement to Jessie official. I'd like to thank everyone—"

"Hold it," David broke in, his eyes on the door of the restaurant. "We've got more guests."

Jessie and the others turned to look toward the entrance. Lilian and Constance stood there, handing their coats to the hostess.

"It's the moms," Elizabeth announced gleefully. "They came after all!"

Jessie realized she was suddenly feeling a little more relaxed and happy. She smiled at her mother as Lilian moved toward the table. Lilian smiled back ruefully.

"Hello, Mother, Connie," Jessie said softly. "I'm glad you could make it after all."

"You're just in time to join us in a toast." Hatch got to his feet and held out a chair.

"So I see," Lilian murmured, her eyes on her daughter.

Elizabeth grinned up at Constance as David rose to seat her. "Hi, Mom. I'm sure glad you two decided to come. We missed you guys."

"Well, it was fairly obvious you were going to go ahead without us," Constance said in her usual pragmatic fashion. "Didn't seem much point in ignoring the whole thing. If Hatch is determined to carry Jessie off, I suppose we're all going to have to learn to adjust to the situation."

"We are, of course, overwhelmed by your gracious acceptance of the situation, Mrs. Benedict," Hatch said.

"We're here, aren't we?" Lilian retorted.

"Yes, you are, Mrs. Benedict," Hatch allowed. "And we appreciate it. I think. Have some champagne."

Glenna gave Constance and Lilian a distant but approving glance. "On the whole, I think it was a good idea for the two of you to put in an appearance. Failure to be supportive at times like this can cause irreparable damage to the parent-child relationship later on."

"I don't think they need your approval, Mom," David said in an undertone. "They're here because they care about Jessie just as much as everyone else does. Even if they do think she's making a mistake."

"How true," Constance drawled. Then she smiled at Hatch. "I do hope you find a job soon. Lord knows Jessie isn't a reliable means of support. She can't hold a position longer than six months."

Jessie grinned. "Hey, I resent that. I may not be able to hold a job, but I can sure find them. I've found more jobs than you can count."

Lilian groaned. "That's the truth." She turned to Hatch. "Well? Have you got anything lined up yet?"

"I'm still figuring out how to collect unemployment," Hatch murmured. "It's rather complicated. I had no idea there was so much paperwork involved. But if I don't get it sorted out fairly soon, there's always welfare."

"Unemployment? Welfare? You mean you haven't even started looking for another job? And you're going to marry my daughter?" Lilian stared at him, clearly aghast.

"Relax, Mom." Jessie chuckled. "That was a joke. Hatch has a little trouble with jokes. Or maybe I should say people have a problem with Hatch's sense of humor."

Lilian rolled her eyes and looked at Constance for backup. "Just what I need. A son-in-law with a warped sense of humor."

"Better than one with no sense of humor at all," Constance pointed out.

"Come on, you guys," Elizabeth interrupted. She seized her glass of orange sparkling water. "We were just about to drink a toast to Hatch and Jessie. I've never gotten to drink a toast before."

Hatch picked up his glass. "Let's try this again. We are here tonight to officially announce the fact that Jessie and I plan to marry as soon as possible. I thank you all for being here to celebrate this momentous event with us. I know it isn't easy for some among you to accept this situation, but who the hell cares? This is the way it's going to be. First, to my lovely, loyal, beloved Jessie."

Jessie blushed warmly under Hatch's searing gaze. There was so much love and possessiveness in his eyes that she trembled under the onslaught. A deep certainty welled up within her. There was no doubt about it. She was doing the right thing.

Everyone at the table was in the process of hoisting his or her glass when David halted the toast for a second time. Once again his eyes were on the restaurant entrance. "Wait," he said softly. "We've got one more late arrival."

"Who on earth?" Frowning, Glenna turned her head to glance toward the door.

"Well, for heaven's sake. Who would have guessed?" Lilian shook her head in silent wonder.

"I'll be damned," Constance stated, her eyes warm.

"I always knew he was as stubborn as a rogue elephant," Hatch said with cool satisfaction. "But I never said he was stupid."

Jessie was already on her feet, Elizabeth right behind her. They both raced toward the big man standing near the hostess's desk.

"Dad." Jessie reached Vincent first and wrapped her arms around his waist, laughing joyously. "I'm so glad you came."

"What the hell else could I do, Jessie? You're my daughter. And if you insist on marrying that stubborn sonofabitch, then I guess he and I had better find a way to get along."

Elizabeth clung to Vincent's arm and grinned up at her

father as he bent to kiss her cheek. "I knew you'd come, Dad. Just like I knew you'd come to watch me when I won first prize at the science fair."

Vincent smiled benevolently down at his offspring and then looked at the curious hostess. "My daughters," he explained proudly. "The elder one's getting engaged tonight."

"Yes, sir." The hostess smiled. "Congratulations. I believe everyone at the table is waiting for you."

Jessie led the way back to the big table and took her seat beside Hatch as Elizabeth plunked herself down in her own chair. Hatch got to his feet and eyed Vincent.

"Glad you could make it, Benedict."

"Always said you were a damned marauding shark." Vincent sat down between Lilian and Constance, who each leaned over to give him an affectionate peck on the cheek. "Should have known once you made up your mind to have my daughter, nothing short of the crack of doom could have stopped you."

"You were right." Hatch sat down again.

An odd, charged silence descended on the table. Jessie was acutely aware of the strange tension flowing around her. It was as if everyone was waiting for the other shoe to drop.

Hatch and Vincent continued to eye each other across the width of the table, reminding Jessie of two gunslingers outside a saloon at high noon.

"The thing you got to remember about sharks," Vincent said slowly, "is that they bite."

"That's why we have teeth," Hatch explained.

"And God knows, if Benedict Fasteners is ever going to have a shot at moving into the big time," Vincent continued "it'll need a shark with a lot of teeth in charge. I'm reinstating your contract, as of now, Hatch."

An audible collective gasp could be heard from almost everyone at the table.

"It's not quite that simple," Hatch reminded him gently.

"There's the little matter of splitting up the company among Jessie, Elizabeth, David, and me."

"Hell, I know that." Vincent scowled at him. "I wouldn't be here tonight if I wasn't agreeing to that part of the deal."

Jessie sat back in her chair, limp with relief as cheers of delight went up around the table. These were followed by an exuberant whooping shout from David. Heads turned in the restaurant.

"Well," Constance said with deep satisfaction as the clamor died down, "I'm pleased you've decided to be reasonable about this after all, Vince. Didn't think you had it in you."

Lilian smiled at her ex-husband and patted his hand. "Congratulations, Vince. You're doing the right thing."

"Way to go, Dad." Elizabeth was grinning from ear to ear. "Now Jessie can stay here in Seattle."

"Hatch was right." David looked at Vincent. "You might be stubborn as all hell, but you're not entirely stupid."

"Thank you, David." Vincent slanted him a wry glance.

"What if," Hatch said coolly, his expression unreadable, "I decide I don't want to go back to work for you?"

Another audible gasp was heard. This time everyone turned to stare at Hatch, who did not appear to notice that he was now the focus of attention.

Vincent smiled grimly, looking very sharklike himself. He picked up the bottle of champagne and poured himself a glass. "Why, then, I'll just have to sue you for breach of contract, won't I?"

Hatch allowed himself a slow grin. "You'd do it, too, wouldn't you, you sonofabitch."

"In about two seconds," Vincent agreed equably.

"Then it looks like I'll be going back to work at Benedict Fasteners," Hatch said. Under the table his hand closed fiercely around Jessie's. "And the company will have some new owners."

She turned her head to look at him, realization dawning

slowly as she saw the cool triumph in his gaze. Then she started to laugh. Everyone stared at her in astonishment.

"Honest to God, Hatch, if you tell me you planned it this way, I swear I'll dump the rest of this champagne over your head," Jessie managed to get out between giggles.

Hatch smiled and pulled her close long enough to cover her mouth in a quick, hard kiss. "Sometimes a man just gets lucky."

The scraping of a chair on the far side of the table broke through Jessie's euphoria. She turned to see Glenna rising to her feet in a quick, jerky movement. Her aunt's face was twisted with rage.

"No," Glenna said forcefully. "No, this isn't right. It's not right, I tell you."

The shocking sight of Glenna Ringstead looking nearly out of control held everyone at the table spellbound.

"It should have been David," Glenna hissed through set teeth. "It should have been my son you put in charge, Vincent. The company should go to him. *All of it.* Not just a quarter, but all of it. He deserved it after what you did to his father. Damn you. Damn you to hell. *It's not right.*"

Before anyone could respond, Glenna whirled around, still moving in a stiff, unnatural manner, and fled toward the door.

It was David who broke the stunned silence that followed. He looked at Vincent. "Don't you think it's time you told me just what you did do to my father?"

Vincent's sigh was one of deep resignation. "Maybe it is. I think you can handle it, David. I didn't always think that way, but now . . ." He flicked a glance at Hatch. "Now I have a feeling you can."

CHAPTER TWENTY

You want the God's honest truth, David?" Vincent asked.

"Yes."

"Your father was one of the smartest men I've ever met. Your mother was right: back at the beginning, I depended on him. Without his abilities I would never have gotten Benedict Fasteners off the ground. I knew construction and I thought I knew the industry, but I didn't know much about running a business."

"And my father did?"

"He sure did. Like I said, he was real smart that way. But two years after we finally started turning a decent profit, Lloyd nearly stole the company blind."

David stared at him. "He *what?*"

"He embezzled over three hundred thousand dollars before I realized what was going on. That was a lot of money back then. Hell, still is. Benedict Fasteners nearly went under."

David shook his head, looking stunned. *"No.* I don't believe it."

"You asked for the truth and I'm giving it to you. Straight. Man-to-man. No more chocolate-candy coating to make it palatable, like your mother always wanted me to do."

David's expression was nearly blank. "But Mom always said he was brilliant."

"He was. Your father was a brilliant, lying, cheating thief. And when I found out what he was doing, I fired his ass. Gave him a choice between clearing out and going to jail. He cleared out. Glenna decided not to go with him. Couldn't blame her. What kind of future would the two of you have had with a man like that?"

"Mother always said you owed us," David said in a dazed voice.

"When your dad left I told her I'd see to it that you and she never suffered. Told her I felt I owed her that much because of what Lloyd had contributed to the company in the early days. And because she was Lilian's sister and . . . well, there were other reasons." Vincent glanced uneasily at his two ex-wives, who were watching him with rapt attention. "Like I said, I felt I owed her."

"Why didn't anyone ever tell me the full truth?" David demanded tightly.

Vincent shrugged. "In the beginning it was because you were too young to understand. And because Glenna wanted the truth kept from everyone in the family. I went along with it. But I think that over the years she sort of chose to forget what really happened."

"She just focused on how much her husband had done for the company back at the beginning and on the fact that you owed her," Lilian said. "That explains a lot about her possessiveness toward you and the firm."

"And why she always felt David should have inherited," Constance added thoughtfully.

"I can't believe you never told me the truth." David shook his head in bewilderment. "I can't believe you kept that kind of secret for so long."

"A boy doesn't need to hear that kind of thing about his father," Hatch said quietly.

"Yeah," said Vincent. "Doesn't do a kid any good to know his old man was a complete bastard. Sort of makes things harder than they are already. Just ask Hatch. Or me."

"Why am I getting the full truth now?" David looked straight at Vincent. "Because I asked for it?"

"Nah." Vincent picked up his champagne glass. "I've been sitting on that secret for years. Could have taken it to my grave. I'm telling you the facts now because I think you can handle 'em, in spite of what your mother says about you being so goddamned sensitive."

"What makes you think that?"

"Hatch here told me you pulled your own weight when you went along on that stupid trip to rescue the Attwood girl. And you didn't send Jessie to ask me for money for grad school, like I was expecting you to do. All things considered, I figure you've turned into a man. You don't need protecting anymore."

Hatch shrugged into his jacket and picked up his briefcase. He gave Jessie a very serious look as he paused to kiss her good-bye at the door of her apartment. "Try to stay out of trouble while I'm gone."

"You betcha." She smiled beatifically up at him and batted her eyelashes.

Hatch groaned. "Why do I even bother to ask?" He kissed her soundly. "I should be back by ten tonight unless the flight is late."

"Sure you don't want to stay over in Spokane and come back in the morning?"

"No, I do not want to spend the night in a hotel room in Spokane when I can spend it here in your bed." Hatch scowled and glanced at his watch. "I just want to get this damn contract signed, sealed, and delivered before the wedding so I can enjoy my honeymoon."

"This is that dippy little contract that Dad's so proud of stealing out from under Yorland and Young?"

"Right. And if I don't get it out of the way, your father will be calling me every day we're away, asking me when I'm going to come back and handle it."

"Knowing Dad, that's probably true. Don't worry about me. I'll just be sitting here patiently waiting by the hearth with your pipe and slippers."

"The hell you will. You're going to cook yourself an entire pound of ravioli and eat it all."

"Look at it this way: after an entire pound of ravioli, I'm not likely to get into any kind of trouble." She laced her arms around his neck. "I love you, Hatch—wing tips, boring tie, and all."

His smile was slow and sexy. "Is that right?"

"Uh-huh."

"Must be because I'm so damn good in bed."

"Must be."

"Just as well. Because I love you too, even if you can't hold a job." He kissed her nose and then he kissed her mouth, hard.

And then he was gone.

It was much later that day, right after she'd eaten the pound of ravioli for dinner, in fact, that Jessie started to feel restless and uneasy. The sense of wrongness was so acute she could hardly stand it. She glanced at the clock. Hatch was not due home for another three hours.

"I wish you were here, Hatch."

Jessie tried to read, but all she could think about was how badly she wanted Hatch to be home.

The phone rang shortly after eight. Jessie pounced on it, although she could not have said why.

"Hello?"

"Jessie, dear, is that you?"

Jessie exhaled a sigh of relief. "Oh, hello, Mrs. V. Yes, it's me. How are you?"

"Fine, dear. I was just sitting here watching television and I had a sudden urge to call and see if you were . . . well, all right."

"I'm just fine, Mrs. V."

"Good. I'm afraid I just had one of my little spells of uneasiness and it seemed to have something to do with you. Dear me, I do hope that blow on the head hasn't made my inner vision unreliable."

"I appreciate your concern, Mrs. V. Is, uh, everything going all right at the office?"

"I've had to close it until things die down. I plan to reopen in a few weeks when everyone's forgotten the Attwood case. Do you know, though, I'm going to miss you. Have you found a new job?"

"Not yet, Mrs. V. But I'm sure something will turn up. It always does."

The phone rang again at nine o'clock, just as the long, slow twilight of late spring was fading into night. Jessie grabbed the instrument a second time.

The voice was that of a woman and it sounded disturbingly familiar. But it was impossible to identify because she was apparently speaking through a cloth. The message was short and to the point.

"If you ever want to see your precious Elizabeth alive again, you will come to the new Benedict warehouse now. If you tell anyone or bring anyone with you, the child dies. You have thirty minutes."

Nausea welled up out of nowhere. Jessie's knees went out from under her and she nearly collapsed on the sofa. Frantically she tried to remember Elizabeth's schedule for Monday evenings. Was there a soccer game tonight? She could not recall. Blindly she dialed Connie's number. There was no answer. She tried the office of ExCellent Designs. Again no answer. Then she glanced at the clock.

Twenty-eight minutes left of the thirty she had been given. There was no time to see if Elizabeth was safe, no time to determine if the call was a cruel hoax. No time to do anything but get to the new warehouse in the south end of town.

Jessie grabbed her car keys and rushed to the door.

She nearly fell down the stairs in her haste to reach the car. Outside on the street she fumbled desperately with the keys. She had just gotten the door open when she felt herself pinned by a pair of blinding headlights.

Memories of nearly being run down a few days earlier brought another wave of panic to Jessie's throat. But even as she turned to run she realized the car was pulling in to the curb behind her Toyota, and then she saw that it was Hatch's Mercedes. Jessie ran toward it.

"Hatch. She's got Elizabeth. I have thirty minutes to get there. No, about twenty-five now. Oh, God."

Hatch was out of the car, moving swiftly toward her. "Who's got her? What are you talking about?"

"I don't know," Jessie sobbed. "A woman, I think. Maybe someone I know. But her voice was disguised. She just called. She's taken Elizabeth to the new Benedict warehouse. Told me if I didn't come alone, she'd kill her."

"We'll take your car because she'll be expecting it. Get in. I'll drive."

"She says I have to go alone. Hatch, I'm so scared."

"Just get into the car. We'll figure this out on the way."

He was already pushing her into her car, getting in beside her, and starting the engine. Jessie tried to collect her wild thoughts. Something struck her suddenly.

"What are you doing home an hour early?"

"I caught an early flight."

"But why?"

"Damned if I know," Hatch said. "A couple of hours ago I just had a feeling I wanted to get home sooner than I'd planned. I made some excuses to the people I was dealing with, phoned the airport, and got on an earlier flight."

"Thank God. Hatch, I'm so afraid."

"You said it was a woman's voice?"

"Yes. I'm sure of it. Muffled, but it sounded vaguely familiar. Do you think . . . ?" Jessie could not bring herself to finish the question.

"That it was Glenna who called? I don't know, Jessie. But we have to face the fact that it's a possibility."

"I can't believe it. Why would she do such a thing?"

"You know why." His mouth tightened as he guided the Toyota onto the freeway that sliced the city in half. "A part of her still thinks that everything should have gone to David. I wonder if she's finally flipped completely and decided that the best method of ensuring that David inherits everything is to get you and Elizabeth out of the way."

"No. She wouldn't kill Elizabeth. She would not do such a thing."

"We don't really know what she'd do, Jessie. There's a lot of old anger buried in her. A lot of bitterness. What happened at the engagement party the other night might have been too much for her. Took away her last hope. Might have pushed her over the edge."

Jessie shook her head, unwilling to believe such a possibility. "I've known her all my life. I just can't believe Aunt Glenna would go this far. I won't believe it until I see it for myself. Hatch, what are we going to do?"

"Give me a minute to think about the layout of the new warehouse. I took a look at the plans last week. Thanks to your father's outdated management style, the doors were rehung last week and we started moving inventory into the place. There should be a lot of cover inside the building by now, what with equipment and product stored in there." Hatch fell silent beside her, his face set in forbidding lines.

A few minutes later he turned off the freeway and drove into a dark, silent warehouse district in the south end of the city. Buildings loomed, their windows unlit for the most part. Huge trucks were parked for the night near loading docks. The streets were empty.

"Hatch? We're almost there."

"I know." He glanced at his watch. "I'll get out at the next corner and cut through those two buildings over there. That will bring me into the back of the warehouse."

"How will you get inside?"

"I know the security-system code. Your father and I chose it together so we could both memorize it."

"How would Aunt Glenna get it?"

"Hell, she's family, isn't she? And she's smart."

"That's true. You want me to drive straight up to the front entrance?"

"Right. But stay in the car. Let her know you're there but don't make it easy for her. She'll have to think about her next move, and that should give me some time to act. Glenna's not a professional kidnapper and she's got a very rigid personality. My guess is she won't know what to do if things don't go exactly according to plan. Still, we don't want to push her too far. She's obviously unstable."

"We're assuming it is Aunt Glenna."

"I'm afraid she's the logical candidate. But that's in our favor. It won't be easy for her to kill Elizabeth. We'll have some negotiating time." Hatch stopped the car a moment later and got out. He closed the door and leaned down to speak through the open window as Jessie slid into the driver's seat.

"Remember. Stay in the car. Keep the engine running. If she calls to you, pretend you can't hear her."

"All right." Jessie's fingers trembled on the steering wheel. She watched as Hatch vanished down an alley between two darkened buildings. His dark gray suit blended perfectly into the shadows. Then she turned the corner and drove toward the warehouse.

There was no sign of life around the entrance of the building. But one of the front doors was open, revealing a gaping darkness inside. Jessie brought the car to a halt, leaving the engine running as Hatch had instructed. She waited.

Long moments passed in terrifying silence. Jessie began to

wonder if Glenna or whoever it was inside had realized she was there. The thirty minutes were up.

Fearing that the kidnapper might think she had not followed orders and would do something violent, Jessie cracked open the car door. She had to get out and see what was happening.

At that moment a familiar voice shouted at her from the gloom of the open doorway.

"Jessie." Elizabeth's small figure came pelting out of the building. "Jessie, watch out."

"Elizabeth." Jessie was out of the car without even pausing to think. She ran toward Elizabeth, instinctively grabbing her arm and jerking her off to one side of the entrance. Something told her to get her sister out of the direct line of sight.

An instant later a shot crackled through the darkness. It shattered the awful stillness that cloaked the warehouse.

"Jessie, she pushed me out here to get you out of the car. She's got a gun."

"I can't believe she'd actually shoot us. I just can't believe it." Jessie dragged Elizabeth farther away from the main entrance, deep into the shadows around the corner of the building.

Elizabeth clung to her hand. "What are we going to do?"

"Hush." Jessie pressed herself back against the wall of the building, trying to listen. She held her sister close to her side. "Hatch is here," she whispered in Elizabeth's ear.

"Geez. That's a relief."

"You think I couldn't have handled this on my own?" Jessie muttered.

"Nothing personal, but something tells me Hatch is better at this kind of thing."

"Something tells me you're right."

Another shot echoed through the night, and then a vast silence descended on the warehouse. Jessie and Elizabeth held their breaths.

A moment later Jessie heard footsteps coming around the

corner of the building. It was the familiar, solid-sounding tread of a pair of wing tips.

"Jessie? Elizabeth? It's all over."

"Hatch."

Both sisters ran to him and Hatch opened his arms to catch them both close for a moment.

"I think," Hatch said after a while, "that you'd better come and take a look at the kidnapper, Jessie."

Jessie closed her eyes, steeling herself. "Yes, I guess I'd better. What am I going to tell Mom? And David?"

"Not too much, if I were you." Hatch's voice was wry as he led the way back into the warehouse and turned on a workman's light.

Jessie stared down at the familiar wiry figure lying unconscious on the floor. A stocking mask lay crumpled beside her pale face.

"Nadine Willard."

"You know her?" Elizabeth asked curiously. "She tried to tell me you did when she grabbed me in the rest room at the mall, but I didn't believe her. Then she pulled that gun out of her purse and made me go with her. She even knew how to deactivate the security system. She cut some wire and did some things with a pair of pliers."

"Yes, I know her," Jessie said, meeting Hatch's eyes with a sense of chagrin. "I vote we don't ever tell anyone about our earlier suspicions."

"I agree," Hatch said dryly. "Dr. Ringstead would no doubt diagnose us both as severely paranoid."

"She was working for Edwin Bright all along," Jessie explained to Lilian, Constance, and Elizabeth two days later in the offices of ExCellent Designs. "A real dedicated type. The kind Aunt Glenna told me got lured into cults. She idolized Bright. Thought he was some kind of savior."

"And he used her," Constance said.

Jessie nodded. "She had a strange background. Grew up in a rough neighborhood and got into gangs and drugs at an early age. Had some trouble with the law when she was caught breaking into houses. But she seemed to have straightened out. She got her GED, got into Butterfield, and was holding down a job."

"And then she got involved with Bright?" Lilian asked.

"The police say he used her as sort of an inside person to screen the people he was recruiting. She was the one who broke into Mrs. Valentine's office and later tried to get into Hatch's car. She was trying to find out how far our investigation had gone and whether or not we were a genuine threat to DEL."

"And when she realized it was all over for Bright, she decided to try to get rid of the people who could testify against him. Starting with you." Lilian shuddered.

"Her first try was the night she nearly ran me down. She was fanatically devoted to Bright. She was going to try to kill all of us involved in the case. She started with me because she blamed me for having carried on the investigation in the first place." Jessie paused. "She had actually tried to stop things right at the beginning."

Constance looked at her. "What do you mean?"

"Mrs. Valentine called to say she recognized her picture in this morning's paper. Nadine is the one who pushed her down that flight of stairs."

Lilian shuddered. "She'd found out that Mrs. Attwood had gone to her?"

Jessie nodded. "Nadine apparently believed in Mrs. V's powers and was afraid that a true psychic might be able to hurt Edwin Bright's cause. Nobody worried about me for a while, until it became apparent I was determined to pursue the case. Then things got complicated. Bright told her to let Hatch and me come on out to the island so that Landis and Hoffman could assess the situation."

"But they still weren't overly concerned until they found out Susan had been contacted," Constance concluded.

"Right."

Constance laced her fingers together on top of her desk

and looked at Elizabeth. "I hope you understand that you are never again going to go to the mall with your friends. From now on out, one of us goes with you or you don't go."

"Ah, Mom," Elizabeth muttered.

Jessie patted her hand consolingly. "Don't worry, Elizabeth. I'll go with you whenever you want. The way I figure it, I owe you about a hundred trips to the mall."

"Fat lot of good that will do," Elizabeth complained. "Hatch won't let you out alone now either."

Jessie grinned. "He's a little overanxious these days, but I expect he'll relax after the wedding."

"Who's overanxious?" Hatch asked as he came through the door with several cups of coffee. He glanced around at the smiling faces of the four women. Then he shrugged. "You finish telling them the story, Jessie?"

"I told them everything."

"Good. Then we can get out of here." He glanced at his watch. "I've got a lot of work to do before we leave on our honeymoon."

A month later Jessie awoke in the pink-and-white bridal suite of the luxurious beachfront hotel. Outside the lanai window, sunlight danced on the incredibly blue tropical sea. She stirred, aware of Hatch's strong, solid warmth beside her. His arm lay across her breasts, his face buried in the pillow beside her.

For a long moment Jessie reveled silently in the perfection of the Hawaiian morning and the promise of the future that stretched out before her.

The wedding had been hastily planned but had gone off without a hitch, thanks to Lilian and Constance. Elizabeth had been adorable in her bridesmaid attire. Nobody had tried to stuff Hatch into a coral tuxedo. He had waited for her at the altar in austere black and white and it had suited him perfectly. Her father had walked Jessie down the aisle and handed her over, with an expression of deep satisfaction, to the man he had personally chosen for her.

Vincent had danced with his ex-wives at the reception, clearly enjoying himself in a way that surprised everyone who knew him. He did not excuse himself to make a single phone call to check in at the office.

Nor did Hatch.

"What's so funny?" Hatch shifted slightly, opening his eyes. The sexy, hungry memories of the night were reflected in his gaze.

Jessie turned in his arms. "I was just thinking that you haven't made one phone call or sent a single fax since we got here."

"We've only been here a day. Give me time."

"I'm going to slap your wrists if I see you reach for the phone." Jessie propped herself up on one elbow. "Happy, Mr. Hatchard?"

"Yes. Definitely yes." He ducked his head to kiss the tip of one rosy breast.

"It went well, didn't it?"

"The wedding?" He kissed the other nipple. "It went fine. If you overlook the way your father was bragging to everyone about how he had found your husband for you."

Jessie laughed and then sighed as Hatch slid his leg between her thighs. "I'm willing to give him some credit."

"What about giving me the credit? I took one look at you and knew I was the right man for you."

"True. You know, I'm going to be embarrassed every time I look Aunt Glenna in the face. Thank heaven she doesn't know what we thought on the way to rescuing Elizabeth. I was afraid she wouldn't come to the wedding."

"David had a long talk with her. Told her he knew everything and that he was satisfied and she should be too." Hatch's hand closed over her thigh, clenching gently.

"David certainly seems to be getting along much better with Dad these days." Jessie's legs shifted restlessly on the sheet.

"Ummm." Hatch was kissing her throat now.

"Did I tell you what Dad said to me at the reception?"

"No."

"He said it was time I stopped fooling around working for other people." Jessie inhaled sharply as Hatch's fingers moved to her inner thigh. "He said I was never going to be happy unless I was my own boss. Said I was a lot like him in that respect."

"Yeah?"

"Hatch, you're not listening. It's my future I'm trying to discuss here. I've been doing some thinking, and I've got an idea for starting up my own business."

"I'm your future," Hatch informed her, unabashed at his own arrogance. He lowered himself along the length of her, eyes gleaming in the morning light. "And you're mine. Any further discussion on the subject is hereby tabled until later. There is another matter on the agenda that needs to be taken care of first. Priorities, Mrs. Hatchard. Always remember, one must stick to priorities."

She looked up at him through her lashes and wrapped her arms around his neck. "God, I love it when you play chief executive officer."

Three months later Hatch looked up from a financial summary as Vincent Benedict stormed into his office and tossed a file onto the desk.

"Have you seen those contract terms? Personnel just sent them up for review. They're outrageous. Absolutely outrageous. Dammit, Hatch, what the hell are you going to do about her? She's gone berserk."

"I assume we are discussing Jessie?" Hatch opened the file and glanced at the proposed contract from a temporary employment agency called Intuitive Services. The owner and sole proprietor of the firm was one Jessie Benedict Hatchard. The company slogan was spelled out on the letterhead: "We Anticipate Your Short-Term Personnel Requirements."

"Damn right we're discussing Jessie."

Hatch glanced at the terms of the contract and scowled.

Jessie was asking for a year-long contract to supply software design services to Benedict Fasteners. She was featuring two exceptionally talented programmers and designers named Alex Robin and Susan Attwood. "You're right. She's asking too much. Tell personnel to keep negotiating."

"Won't do any good," Vincent said, looking glum. "They tell me this is her final offer."

"Then tell them to call off the deal."

Vincent looked shocked. "But this is Jessie's first big contract. I want her to have it."

"If she's going to run her own business, she's going to have to learn to be more competitive when she goes after a contract."

"Dammit, man, this is *Jessie*. Your wife. My daughter. Don't you want her to make this temporary-employment-agency thing work? It's ideal for her. The first decent career move she's ever made. Hell, no one knows more about short-term employment than Jessie."

"I agree." Hatch leaned back in his chair and eyed Vincent with amusement. "And I don't doubt for one minute that she'll make the business fly. She's got a lot of you in her."

"Don't you think we ought to give her the contract? We need a couple of good computer jockeys on board to design those new financial programs. You said so yourself."

"I know. But if we let her lock us into these terms, we'll never be able to get out of them. Tell personnel to try again, and if they can't get her to lower the cost, tell them to kill the deal. She'll learn fast."

Vincent heaved a sigh. "You're probably right."

Hatch grinned. "You know I'm right. Hey, this was all your idea, remember? Don't worry. It'll work out."

"I hope so. I want to see her make a go of this agency of hers." Vincent narrowed his eyes shrewdly. "Don't suppose you could, uh, sort of talk to her tonight?"

Hatch laughed and shook his head. "Impossible. Jessie has this strict rule, you see. No business after I get home from work." He glanced at the clock. "And speaking of home, it looks like it's about time to call it a day."

Vincent frowned. "It's only five-thirty."

"I know." Hatch stood up and put on the jacket of his conservative pin-striped suit. "I've got to get moving. Jessie and I are involved in a major project and I don't want to be late."

"What major project?"

"Planning the baby's bedroom." Hatch stroked the scarlet petals of a brilliant lily in the bouquet on his desk. Jessie had sent the flowers to the office that morning in honor of the third month of their marriage. "Your grandkid will be here in another five months, Benedict. See you in the morning. Oh, and don't forget dinner at our place on Saturday night. Elizabeth will be there. And be on time. Jessie has another rule. If you're late, you don't eat."

Hatch went out of the office and headed home to where Jessie and the really important part of his life were waiting.

ENJOY ALL THE ROMANTIC ADVENTURES OF

JAYNE ANN KRENTZ

THE GOLDEN CHANCE	67623-7/$6.99
SILVER LININGS	01962-7/$6.99
SWEET FORTUNE	72854-7/$6.99
PERFECT PARTNERS	72855-5/$6.99
FAMILY MAN	01963-5/$6.99
WILDEST HEARTS	72857-1/$6.99
GRAND PASSION	01961-9/$6.99
HIDDEN TALENTS	01965-1/$6.99
TRUST ME	51692-2/$6.99
ABSOLUTELY, POSITIVELY	77873-0/$6.50
AMARYLLIS (WRITING AS JAYNE CASTLE)	
	56903-1/$6.50
ZINNIA (WRITING AS JAYNE CASTLE)	
	56901-5/$6.50
DEEP WATERS	52420-8/$6.99
SHARP EDGES (HC)	52310-4/$24.00

New York Times bestselling author

JAYNE ANN KRENTZ

DEEP WATERS

"There is no finer exponent of
contemporary romance than the
immensely poplar Jayne Ann Krentz."
—*Romantic Times*

Available from Pocket Books

POCKET
B O O K S

1266-02

Jayne Ann Krentz *writing as*
Jayne Castle

Amaryllis Lark is undeniable beautiful. She's also one of the best psychic detectives on St. Helen's, the earth colony recently cut off from the mother planet, yet not so very different from home—a place where love still defies the most incredible odds. Lucas Trent, the rugged head of Lodestar Exploration, isn't keen on the prim and proper type, and Amaryllis is *excruciatingly* proper.

Amaryllis

Amaryllis may have psychic powers, but she can't read minds—least of all her own. When a wild murder investigation leads to a red-hot love affair, Amaryllis is shocked, Lucas is delighted—and no power on heaven, earth, or St. Helen's can keep them apart!

Available from Pocket Books

POCKET
B O O K S

1238-01